A
SIMPLE SINGING

Books by Leslie Gould

THE COURTSHIPS OF LANCASTER COUNTY

Courting Cate
Adoring Addie
Minding Molly
Becoming Bea

NEIGHBORS OF LANCASTER COUNTY

Amish Promises
Amish Sweethearts
Amish Weddings

THE SISTERS OF LANCASTER COUNTY

A Plain Leaving
A Simple Singing

THE SISTERS *of* LANCASTER COUNTY / BOOK TWO

A
SIMPLE SINGING

LESLIE GOULD

BETHANYHOUSE
a division of Baker Publishing Group
Minneapolis, Minnesota

© 2018 by Leslie Gould

Published by Bethany House Publishers
11400 Hampshire Avenue South
Bloomington, Minnesota 55438
www.bethanyhouse.com

Bethany House Publishers is a division of
Baker Publishing Group, Grand Rapids, Michigan

Printed in the United States of America

Library of Congress Cataloging-in-Publication Data
Names: Gould, Leslie, author.
Title: A simple singing / Leslie Gould.
Description: Minneapolis, Minnesota : Bethany House, [2018] | Series: The sisters of Lancaster county ; Book 2
Identifiers: LCCN 2018002379| ISBN 9780764219702 (trade paper) | ISBN 9781493414765 (e-book) | ISBN 9780764232053 (cloth)
Subjects: LCSH: Amish—Fiction. | Lancaster County (Pa.)—Fiction. | GSAFD: Christian fiction.
Classification: LCC PS3607.O89 S56 2018 | DDC 813/.6—dc23
LC record available at https://lccn.loc.gov/2018002379

Scripture quotations are from the King James Version of the Bible.

Cover design by LOOK Design Studio
Cover photography by Aimee Christenson

Author is represented by MacGregor Literary, Inc.

18   19   20   21   22   23   24   7   6   5   4   3   2   1

To my husband, Peter,
soldier and healer.

Therefore to him that knoweth to do good,
and doeth it not, to him it is sin.

James 4:17

–1–

Marie Bachmann

DECEMBER 2013

I wish I could say I was overcome with happiness as my sister Jessica pledged her life to her beloved. But I wasn't. She looked so lovely in her blue dress that I'd helped her hem the night before. She was never known for her domestic abilities, including when it came to orchestrating her *Hochtzich*. She'd spent her childhood helping our *Dat* farm, while I'd been properly trained by our *Mamm* to run a home and all that it entailed.

But regardless of what Jessica lacked, she and Silas were very much in love. Their misty eyes shone as they smiled from ear to ear at each other. However, my eyes were completely dry as I perched on the wedding party bench.

I'd lost so much in the last year. My father had died. My best friend, Gail, had moved to Ohio after Jessica returned to Lancaster County. And my youngest sister, Leisel, had left home for a new life in Pittsburgh, where she attended nursing school.

Someone opened the back door of our shed where the service was being held, and an icy blast of wind tore through the building. It was the first Thursday in December, and the weather was as cold as my heart.

I glanced toward the door, expecting our brother Amos and his daughter, Becca, but it was our *Aenti* Suz slipping into the service. Amos lived in Colorado and had hoped to attend and bring Becca, whom we'd never met. But they hadn't shown up yet. I guessed that their flight had been delayed by the weather.

Bishop Jacobs took Jessica's hand and Silas's hand in both of his and said, "I bless this couple and their marriage in the name of the Father, the Son, and the Holy Spirit."

He looked out over the congregation and asked, "Will you pledge to pray for and support this couple throughout their life together?"

Of course everyone agreed. Except for me. I stayed silent as I shifted on the hard bench. I glanced first at my Mamm in the front row. She sat straight as a rod, nodding her head in agreement. And then over to the other side where my brother Arden sat with a smile on his bearded face. Nine months ago, neither wanted Jessica to come home again. Now she was the prodigal daughter who'd been welcomed with open arms.

Thankfully, after another scripture reading and prayer, the service was over.

As everyone followed Jessica and Silas out of the shed and toward the house, even though I knew it was expected that I would help my family greet our guests, I set my sights on the barn instead, wrapping my cape tightly around my body to try to ward off the icy chill. Aenti Suz stopped me, grabbing my arm as I tried to hurry by her.

"Where are you going?" she asked.

I pulled my cape even tighter. "I just need to get some fresh air."

She laughed. The music in her voice told me she saw right through me, but if there was one thing I knew, it was that Aenti Suz would love me no matter what.

"Just give me a minute." I pulled away from her. "Then I'll come straight into the house, I promise."

Without looking back, I marched toward the barn, the cold wind stinging my eyes. *Winder* had arrived with a vengeance.

For years, Psalm 37:4 had been the verse I'd held on to. *Delight thyself also in the Lord: and he shall give thee the desires of thine heart.* I *had* delighted in the Lord since I was a child. I followed the *Ordnung*, down to hem lengths, hat widths, and *Kapp* ties, making sure everyone in our family adhered to our church's unwritten rules. I honored my mother and my father, even when I didn't agree with all the traveling and other things he did when he was alive. I respected Bishop Jacobs. I never missed church. I made pies and quilts for auctions to raise money for good causes. I took care of the sick—not like Leisel did, but as best I could.

I helped in other ways too. Just over a month ago, in late October, I'd volunteered to have the district singing at our place because another family couldn't. True, I loved the *Youngie* singings. They were my favorite of all our community gatherings. And it had been a perfect autumn day with the leaves changing on the trees in the woods and the last of the fall flowers blooming. But the point was, I'd put the needs of the district first.

Jessica had always been so capable and strong, and Leisel so smart and caring, but I'd been the most grounded in our faith. The one who knew just the right scripture for the right situation. The one who could be counted on to pray. The one who supported the bishop and ministers of our district, no matter what.

But now I wondered if I would ever realize the desires of my heart. All I wanted was to marry a *Bavvah* in our district, one who owned his own farm. Was that too much to ask?

Apparently so, because it seemed there wasn't a single one who was eligible right now, and instead of it being my wedding day, it was Jessica's. My sister who had joined the Amish and then left. Who was shunned and then returned. Why had she been rewarded instead of me?

I was twenty-one. Certainly not an old maid, but without any viable prospects, it could be years before I married.

I pulled in a raggedy, icy breath as I marched along. *Jah*, I knew how ridiculous my thoughts were. That was why I wouldn't share them with anyone. I wouldn't complain. Or whine. Or lower myself to voice my shameful response to my sister's happiness. Not at all. We were called to love one another.

And I did love Jessica. I just needed to rant, if only in my head, for a few minutes.

I pushed open the barn door and fell over the threshold, inhaling the scent of hay and grain. Jah, it was cold inside the barn but nothing like the frigid outdoors.

I heard him singing before I saw him. I guessed it was a Mennonite *Leet* or perhaps an *Englisch* song because I didn't recognize it.

I shut the door quietly behind me and stepped farther into the barn. For a moment the beautiful melody warmed me—at least my heart, if not my body.

I'd expected Gordon to still be in the shed or helping in the house, not in the barn.

I wouldn't admit it to anyone—because I was the faithful

sister, the one who never questioned what was done or what our community stood for—but the music of the Englischers and even the Mennonites did appeal to me. A wave of peace washed over me when I sang. It wasn't something I'd felt much of lately.

Gordon's baritone voice grew louder as he sang, "Come into His presence singing Alleluia! Alleluia! Alleluia!" as he hurried around the corner of the stalls. Catching sight of me, he froze and stopped singing.

"Marie," he said. "What are you doing here?"

"I just needed a moment, that's all." I sighed, leaning up against the whitewashed wall. I had been looking forward to the next verse. "I didn't expect you to be in here."

"A cow's in labor and having a hard time." His deep brown eyes were full of concern. That was Gordon—concerned for everyone and everything, person or animal, plant or tree. "I was checking on her before going to help in the house. I think she'll be a while though." On our dairy farm, there always seemed to be a cow in labor. It wasn't like in the old days when they all birthed their calves in the spring.

When I didn't respond, Gordon asked, "Could I walk you to the house?"

"Jah." I stepped back to the door and pushed it open, bracing myself for the cold.

"Is everything all right?" Gordon asked as he stepped to my side.

"It's fine," I answered.

"Want to talk?"

"No." That was the last thing I wanted, even though Gordon was always willing to listen.

"What is it?" he asked.

I hesitated. "I'm just feeling out of sorts." I was sure he could see right through me too, and that he'd know I was feeling sorry for myself. I quickly tried to make it sound as if that wasn't the case. "My sisters are both so strong and determined and directed. I'm feeling uncertain about my own future."

His voice filled with kindness. "You're one of the strongest people I know. Earnest. Disciplined. Confident." He abruptly stopped talking and then blushed, as if he'd said too much. He was such an endearing young man.

"Oh, you're just trying to make me feel better." I quickened my step and he matched it. "But thank you." I meant it. His affirming words comforted me, a little anyway. Maybe my future wasn't as helpless as I feared.

The wind gusted, and Gordon stepped closer to me as if to shield me from the force of it. "No," he said. "I'm not trying to make you feel better. I truly believe that."

Embarrassed, I tried to smile even though my face stung from the cold. But then I ducked my head and forged ahead, concentrating on the path through the snow instead of talking.

When we reached the house, we climbed the steps to the enclosed back porch that was part of the original cabin my ancestors built back in 1752, in the Leacock Township of Lancaster County. I hooked my cape on a peg and Gordon hung his work coat and took off his hat, revealing his wavy dark hair.

As we stepped into the kitchen, the tangy scent of the meatballs in tomato sauce greeted us, but before I could fully appreciate it, Mamm gave me a funny look. "Where have you been?"

I smiled without answering. "What would you like me to do?"

Beyond us, men were setting up the tables for the first sitting of the meal, and Silas and Jessica had gathered around the *Hochtzicht* table with everyone in the wedding party but me.

Mamm nodded toward Bishop Jacobs, standing by Dat's study, which Mamm had converted into a sewing room. It took me a moment to recognize who stood next to the bishop.

"Look who's home," Mamm said. "All the way from Florida."

Elijah Jacobs turned toward me. He had an impish grin on his tanned face.

"Marie," he said, brushing his sundrenched hair from his forehead. "How have you been?"

"Great." I grinned back at him. Elijah had always been a bad boy, and I'd always been a Goody-Two-Shoes. However, even though I'd never admitted it to anyone, I'd always had a crush on him, ever since we were young. I was happy to see him.

Gordon, always the gentleman, stepped forward and extended his hand. "Elijah," he said. "I'm Gordon Martin. I work here on the Bachmann farm."

"Nice to meet you." Elijah shook his hand back with vigor. He appeared so grown up. My heart swelled.

Once Gordon pulled away, he shook Bishop Jacobs's hand while Elijah grinned at me again. I couldn't help but note that his smile seemed even more endearing than it had when we were scholars. My heart contracted as I smiled back, hoping to convey just how happy I was to see him.

<hr />

The house was crowded for the wedding meal, but we'd decided that running food to the shed in the cold would be more difficult than making do inside. We'd moved all of the furniture except for our long oak table out of the main floor of the house—putting some pieces upstairs, some into the backroom of the shed, and some into a storage room in the barn. Now the men and boys continued to set up tables and benches for the meal, while the potato cooks finished up and the servers congregated to receive their instructions. Even though the furnishings were gone, our home still felt warm and cozy, as it always did. Our house had served Bachmanns for over two hundred years, something I thought of nearly every day.

Soon the wedding party, including me, was seated at the head table, and then Arden led us all in a silent prayer. The servers began distributing the meatballs, mashed potatoes, green beans, sweet corn, chow chow, pickled beets, and rolls. I barely tasted the food as I watched Jessica and Silas and tried to make out what they were saying over the clatter of forks and knives against the dinner plates. They seemed incredibly happy. I hated to admit it, but they were a much better match than Silas and Gail, who had courted before Jessica's return. Silas had been kind and attentive to my friend, but it was obvious he was meant for my sister. They had an easiness about them that was usually seen in older couples.

I spotted Mamm in the crowd, eating with Aenti Suz. I imagined she especially missed our Dat today. I know I did. And I was sure both Jessica and Silas did too, although from the joyful expressions on their faces it was hard to tell.

Once I finished my food, I headed to the kitchen with my plate, even though some members of the clean-up crew were already wandering around collecting things. Another crew was distributing pieces of pie from table to table.

Once in the kitchen, I decided to help and dished up bowls of mashed potatoes for the second serving. Gordon slipped back outside, to the laboring cow, I assumed.

We had an army of helpers, and others on the clean-up crew were already hard at work tackling the first round of dishes. I'd heard that Englischers hired caterers and servers at their weddings, but that was something we never needed to do in our community. We all pitched in to help each other—especially when people joined in marriage, when someone died, or when there was an illness or accident in the family. That's what it meant to live in community.

From the island in the kitchen, I had a view of the front door. So did Jessica, apparently, because when it opened and Amos stepped through with an Englisch girl wearing a skirt and boots, my sister practically flew into his arms in a very non-Amish demonstration of affection. Regardless, I choked up for a moment as he wrapped his arms around her, burying Jessica in his big winter coat. When he let her go, he quickly introduced her to his daughter.

Tears stung my eyes. The girl looked like Jessica and me. Dark eyes. Long brown hair, although mine was lighter. Of course hers wasn't pulled back in a bun—it fell loose around her shoulders in waves. She smiled sweetly and shook Jessica's hand but appeared a little overwhelmed by the scene around her. Jessica glanced around the room and finally spotted me.

"Marie." She motioned to me as Silas reached Amos and shook his hand.

I dropped the metal spoon back into the potatoes and made my way around the tables, wiping my hands on my apron. Mamm and Aenti Suz had seen Amos and Becca too and beat me to greeting them. Something had changed in my Mamm in the last six months. When Amos came for Dat's funeral, she was as cold as today's December ice storm. But then something shifted. When Jessica disclosed she'd invited Amos to her wedding, Mamm had simply said she was glad of it.

I, on the other hand, still felt frustrated with my brother, who was Arden's twin. Amos had left us all those years ago. Did he really think he could return, again and again, as if nothing had happened?

Mamm wasn't Arden and Amos's biological mother. Theirs had died when they were ten. I sometimes forgot she wasn't Arden's—but never Amos's. The twins were as different as could be.

But now she greeted him in front of our entire district. And then she took Becca's hand and pulled her close. I'd expect such a thing from Aenti Suz, but such warmth from my Mamm was shocking.

As I reached the crowd, Mamm was telling Becca how delighted she was to meet her. "You are always welcome in our home," she said.

After Aenti Suz greeted the girl, it was my turn. "I'm Marie. *Wilcom.*"

She didn't extend her hand to me as she had the others. "Daddy told me about you." From the expression on her face, I guessed what he'd said hadn't been good.

I turned away from her to greet Amos, wondering what his response would be to me, but he had stepped away to shake Arden's hand.

An elbow bumped my arm and I turned, thinking Becca had nudged me or perhaps Jessica, but it was Elijah, a grin on his face. He whispered in my ear, "Families can be complicated, jah?"

I didn't answer. What did Elijah know about family conflict? All of his siblings had joined the church and settled down. And he would too, after spending his running-around years in Florida. At least I hoped he'd come home to stay—and soon.

"Want to sneak out for some air?" he asked, his voice still low.

Now, that was something that actually appealed me. "Sure," I said. "Let's go out the back." No one would notice we'd left, I was sure.

⋙⋘

After we'd bundled up on the back porch, Elijah suggested we go to the barn.

I shook my head, not wanting to bump into Gordon again. But I didn't tell Elijah that. "Let's go to the shop. We can see if anything still needs to be cleaned up in there."

I wasn't sure if Elijah would want to help with that sort of thing, but he responded with a positive, "Good idea."

We couldn't speak as we trudged outside. I could barely keep my balance and manage to keep breathing. On the other side of the fence, out in the pasture, the old oak tree's snow-covered branches swayed in the icy wind. The sight made me shiver all the more.

It wasn't until we reached the shop and Elijah had flung the door open, and then forced it shut against another gust, that he sputtered, "You can't imagine how thankful I'll be to get back to Florida."

"I bet," I answered. "When do you leave?"

"After Christmas."

"So you won't stay for the Epiphany?"

He shook his head. "January starts our busy season. I need to be back before the crowds arrive."

I knew of people who spent weeks and sometimes even months in Pinecraft, Florida, each winter, but no one from our family had ever gone. The truth was, I didn't like to travel far from home, and going to Florida always seemed excessive. I especially balked at the saying, "What happens in Pinecraft, stays in Pinecraft." It sounded so fallacious. But I had to admit, the warmer weather was appealing, especially during weather like we'd been having.

The temperature in the shop had definitely fallen since the service, but it was still bearable. The propane heaters had been turned off and all of the benches had been moved out, but there were still some folding chairs that had been put into use that we usually stored in the back room. We moved those, even though furniture from the house was stored there too, and then grabbed two brooms and began to sweep.

As we worked, Elijah asked me about Amos. I told him about my brother leaving sixteen years ago and then returning last March for Dat's funeral. "This is the first time any of us have met his daughter. We didn't even know she existed until last spring."

"None of you knew?"

"Well, Dat did," I said. "And he told Mamm at some point." It sounded as odd as it was. I would have never guessed that Dat would be one to keep secrets.

I didn't want Elijah to ask why Becca had been cold to me, so I changed the subject and asked him about Florida.

"Well," he said, "it's as warm as you've heard. Of course it's downright hot in the summer, but very comfortable in the winter. And it's always a lot of fun. Plain folks come from around here, of course, but also from Ohio and even Indiana, plus there are a lot of great Englischer tourists and residents too. I've met lots of fascinating people."

I was afraid I wouldn't fit that category.

"I work in a bakery, both in the kitchen and at the front counter. I live in a house with a group of other Youngie." He grinned. "All guys. We have a revolving door. Some workers come for a few months—others for a long amount of time. Some of us are there all year round."

Hoping he'd keep talking about Florida, I said, "Remind me how long you've been down there."

"Off and on for the last three years."

We'd been eighteen when he left.

"How long do you plan to stay?" I reached the far wall of the shed and shook out my broom.

He shrugged. "I'm not sure," he answered. "Probably not for long." He grinned again. "I'm not getting any younger."

"What does that mean?" I teased.

He laughed. "Well, my parents are pressuring me to come home and settle down."

"But perhaps you'll find a girl from Ohio or Indiana and leave Lancaster County altogether."

"Perhaps."

I expected him to grin again, but instead, with a serious expression on his face, he said, "I plan to come home by summer—maybe even late spring—and help my Dat farm. My parents have offered me the land, and that's hard to pass up."

I didn't say anything, afraid I might come across as too enthusiastic. Instead, I thought of my rant on the way to the barn just a couple of hours earlier. Was Elijah who the Lord had in mind for me all along? He was going to farm, in our district. And I'd been enamored with him since I was a girl. I breathed a prayer asking for forgiveness for my earlier negativity. Then again, it hadn't been all rant. Not really. It had been part prayer. Was God answering it already?

Elijah added, "I didn't like farming much before, but I know I can't work in a bakery for half the day and play on the beach for the other for the rest of my life."

I kept sweeping, thinking about the Jacobses' old farmhouse. It was in tip-top shape and wouldn't need any updating. And it was only a few miles from our farm. Perhaps God had heard the desires of my heart. I could be marrying Elijah on our farm by next fall . . . but in late October or early November, when the weather wouldn't be icy cold.

I was enjoying hiding out in the shed with Elijah. He'd run with a wild group after he turned sixteen, while I didn't run at all because I'd already committed to living a life I'd never regret. By the time I was eighteen, I'd joined the church, as I always knew I would, and never looked back. Hanging out with Elijah now felt daring, for me, but oddly comfortable too. Mamm often said that opposites attract, pointing out that she was a homebody while Dat loved adventures. Plus, she was a rule follower like me, while Dat had been more open to other ideas—not in the same way as Elijah though. The point was, being different had worked out just fine for them. At least it seemed so to me.

As Elijah pivoted upon completing another row of sweeping, the shed door swung open and Gordon stepped inside, clapping his gloved hands together. "There you are," he said to me. "Your Mamm sent me to find you." He motioned toward the broom. "I'll finish the sweeping."

"Oh, it can wait," I said. "We were just taking a break from the crowd."

"No," Gordon said. "There's nothing else I need to do."

"Should I stay and help?" Elijah asked.

Gordon shook his head. "Go back to the house. It won't take me long." He smiled kindly at both of us.

But as I handed my broom to Gordon, I detected a bit of sadness in his eyes as his hand brushed against mine.

"*Denki*," I said. "You're always so thoughtful."

He smiled, but then turned toward Elijah.

"So you've been living in Florida."

Elijah nodded. "Jah, in Sarasota."

"Not Pinecraft?"

Elijah shook his head. "I hang out there a lot, but I'm closer to the beach."

"I've been going to Sarasota in January for the last three years with a group from my church to work in a shelter. We'll be going again next month."

"I've had a few groups like that come into the bakery where I work. They usually stay at that Mennonite church a little north of the shelter."

"That's the one."

"That's not really my thing, but I appreciate you pitching in," Elijah said. "I'll see you around then." He grinned. "Here and down there, maybe."

Gordon held up his hand in a wave, and Elijah opened the door. I pulled my cape tight and stepped back into the wind. We didn't speak until we reached the back porch.

"Is Gordon one of those do-gooders? One of those over-zealous people who just don't know when to quit?" Elijah held the door for me.

"I do know that he does a lot of volunteer work," I answered, thankful to be out of the wind. "He seems to care a lot about others." When Elijah didn't answer, I asked, "Why?"

"Oh, we just see a lot of church groups who are looking for an experience. As if claiming to work in a shelter or a soup kitchen is an excuse to go on a trip when they should just book a vacation instead." He laughed a little as he wiggled out of his coat.

"Oh," I said, but then felt compelled to add, "I don't think that's how it is with Gordon. He seems to genuinely care about others."

Elijah nodded. "He definitely seems like a decent guy—even if he is Mennonite."

"Says the guy who hasn't joined his church yet," I teased, hanging up my cape.

"Hey." Elijah hung his coat on the peg next to my cape. "I will soon. I promise."

– 2 –

Elijah stayed for the evening meal, even though his parents had left long before. When I asked how he was getting home, he patted the pocket of the down vest he'd worn in the house all day and said, "Billy."

"Pardon?"

"Billy Lapp," he whispered. "Do you know him?"

I shook my head.

"He's my buddy from Florida. We're roommates down there." He took out his phone. It wasn't a flip phone, but a fancy one with the Internet and all that.

"Oh." I guessed he planned to call his friend—or probably text him.

Because I'd joined the church at eighteen and hadn't been one to run around anyway, I didn't know much about cell phones. I guessed that might make me seem awfully quaint to Elijah, who appeared to be quite familiar with the ways of the world.

We were standing at the opposite end of a table from Amos and Arden, while Becca sat with Aenti Suz, Mamm, and my sister-in-law, Vi, at another table.

"Come join us," Mamm called out to me, patting the seat beside her.

Elijah nudged me. "I'll catch you later," he said. "Before I leave."

I sat down with the other women in my family. Soon Elijah joined Arden and Amos. They were soon laughing, although I couldn't tell at what.

Vi asked Becca all sorts of questions about school. What did she study? *Everything she possibly could.* How were her grades? *She had a four point GPA.* Were her classmates wild? *No.* Did she date? *No, she was only fourteen.* Did she drive a car? *Only on her grandparents' ranch—but she'd get her license as soon as she turned sixteen.* Did she go to church? *Of course.* Even though she was only a freshman in high school, she already planned to go on to college to study animal medicine. She answered each question with confidence, although she wasn't arrogant. She turned to me and asked if I went to college.

"Oh no," I answered. "My education ended with the eighth grade."

A confused expression fell over Becca's face. "What do you mean?"

"Your Dat didn't tell you?"

"Tell me what?"

Aenti Suz took over, probably afraid I might shame the poor girl. "Our schools go through the eighth grade. After that, scholars might take up a trade, apprentice with someone in the community, or do correspondence courses. Our philosophy is that education never ends, even though school does. We learn the basics and then specialize in what we need after that."

"Oh." Becca stayed silent for a moment and then asked, "But what about your third sister? Why can she become a nurse?"

"Because she didn't join the church," I answered, a little annoyed at Amos's failure to educate his daughter about our ways.

She still seemed confused, and not because she wasn't smart. She obviously was. Were we really that odd to her?

"How about a piece of apple pie?" Aenti Suz asked Becca. She nodded. "Yes, please."

Aenti Suz turned her attention to me. "How about you?" I nodded.

As she stood and left the table, Becca asked Vi about her cousins—Milton, Leroy, Luke, Brenda, and Pam.

"They already went back to our house," Vi said.

Becca's face fell. "I was hoping to get better acquainted with them."

"Perhaps tomorrow," Vi said, but I couldn't help but wonder if she and Arden wanted to keep their kids away from Becca. I knew they'd been leery of Jessica's influence on their family, until she returned to the Amish. Brenda was four years younger than Becca, and I imagined she found her cousin fascinating.

As Aenti Suz returned with the pie, Gordon came through the kitchen with his coat and boots still on, a concerned expression on his face. He searched the crowd for a moment, spotted me, and mouthed, "Where's Arden?"

I pointed behind me.

"Thanks." He hurried around our table.

"Who's that?" Becca asked.

"Our farmhand, Gordon."

"Did he only go through the eighth grade too?"

"Actually, he graduated high school," I answered, cutting into the pie and inhaling the sweetness, along with the hint of cinnamon and nutmeg. "He's Mennonite." Conservative Mennonite, to be exact, which meant he could drive a plain black car, have a high school education, and play a guitar.

"Oh." Becca smiled as she lifted a bite of pie from her plate toward her mouth. "He's cute."

She was right. He was handsome with his dark hair and intense brown eyes.

She swallowed. "And he has a normal haircut."

Gordon's hair was thick and wavy, so it fell nicely around his head, and his cut didn't look as Plain as the Amish style. I hadn't noticed before.

She scooped up another bite of pie. "So could you marry him?"

"What?" I sputtered.

"You know, if you two were dating." She slipped her fork into her mouth.

I shook my head. "First of all, the Amish court—we don't date."

She raised her eyebrows.

"And, no, a member of the Amish church can't marry a Mennonite. We can only marry another person who has been baptized in our church and is in good standing. Allowing mixed marriages would destabilize our communities."

She wrinkled her nose. "Weird."

I took a deep breath, reminding myself it wasn't Becca's fault she didn't understand our ways.

She turned in her seat, her fork still in her hand, most likely to examine Gordon a little more closely, but instead her eyes fell on Elijah. "He's cute too. Is he Amish?"

"Born and raised," I said. "But he hasn't joined the church yet. Plus, he lives in Florida."

"Really?" Becca turned back around. "That's surprising."

Vi started to explain about Plain people vacationing in Pine-craft and some of the Youngie going down there to work. I didn't listen though. I was trying to hear what Gordon was saying to Arden, but both of my brothers stood and started to follow Gordon without my catching a word of what was going on. But then Amos stopped at our table and told Becca a cow was having a hard delivery. "Want to come watch?"

She immediately pushed back the bench and abandoned her half-eaten piece of pie. "Of course!" Her enthusiasm reminded me of Jessica. In fact, it was a good thing Jessica was in the living room or she probably would have wanted to go out with the others too.

"Come on," Amos said to Becca and then glanced down at me. "Is there a work coat we can borrow?"

"Sure." I slid my fork under my last bit of pie. "Jessica's old coat is on the back porch—it's the rattiest one out there."

Singing started in the living room and Mamm said to me, "Go join the other Youngie. I know how much you enjoy the music."

I nodded. I did. It would have been fun for Gordon with his rich baritone voice to join us, but I knew he was needed in the barn. I quickly finished my last bite and then picked up my plate and Becca's too.

As I stood, I realized that Elijah hadn't joined the others. He still sat on the bench, finishing his pie.

"Aren't you going with the men?" I asked him.

He grinned. "I'm no help when it comes to cows."

I shook my head. "What are you talking about? You're going to take over your family farm."

He shrugged. "I'll figure it out when the time comes."

I nodded toward the living room. "Want to join in on the singing?"

He wrinkled his nose and then yawned. "Actually, I think I'll head home."

He followed me toward the kitchen. As he caught up with me, he whispered, "Do you ever get tired of singings and volleyball games? Hay rides? And frolics?" I could feel his breath on my neck.

I turned around slowly, facing him. "Actually, I don't," I whispered back and then smiled.

He laughed and spoke normally. "You always were a rule follower." He paused for a moment. "But, speaking of singings, will you go to the one on Sunday with me?"

I stepped backward, nearly tripping over my own feet. Finally, I managed to stutter, "You want to go to the singing?" He hadn't gone to singings even before he left for Florida.

"Jah, it's at my folks' place," he replied, clearly enjoying my surprise. "We'll have a lot of fun. You'll see."

Two hours later, all of the festivities of the wedding day were over and the dishes were all washed and the food put away. We wouldn't return the benches to the church wagon until the next morning though, when it was light outside. Silas and Jessica were spending their wedding night upstairs in what used to be Mamm's sewing room. There was no reason for them to venture to their new home on the Stoltz farm, where Silas worked, and then return the next day to help with cleaning up after the wedding and moving the furniture back.

I was just heading up the stairs when Becca returned to the house with the men. I kept going.

"Wait," Mamm called out to me.

I pivoted slowly and returned to the living room, yawning.

I'd been up since four in the morning and was more than ready to go to bed.

"Becca's going to sleep in your room."

"Oh."

"Hold on," Mamm said and then offered Gordon a piece of pie and cup of coffee before he went home. I didn't think he'd take Mamm up on her offer, but he did. He drove a car, a very plain one, so it wasn't like he'd be freezing in a buggy and need a cup of coffee before he left.

"I'll have another piece too," Becca said.

Mamm turned toward me. "Would you serve our guests? And then take Becca up with you once she's done? She can sleep in Jessica's bed. The sheets are fresh."

Resigned, I stepped toward the kitchen island where the pies were. I understood from Mamm that I was to chaperone the two also. There would be no leaving Becca with a young man—not even one as trustworthy as Gordon. Mamm lived by the Ordnung, even more so than I. We were always to be beyond reproach. That was one fault she found in Dat—that he cared little for what others thought of him or our family in general.

It seemed Gordon and Becca took forever to finish their pie. They talked about what happened in the barn, replaying each scene of the calf's birth. It had been a breech, and Gordon and Amos had ended up having to pull the calf. Together, Gordon and Becca had worked on the creature until it started breathing. Clearly, she and Gordon shared a love of farming, just as Jessica and Silas did. I, on the other hand, much preferred sewing and cooking and cleaning over anything that had to do with the land or animals.

As the two slowly ate their pie, Jessica and Silas told the last of their friends farewell and then started up the stairs. Everyone else headed for home, except for Gordon.

Finally, he took the last drink of his coffee and declared it was past time for him to be on his way. I quickly scooped up the empty mugs and plates, and washed them. Gordon finally readied himself to go. Having my hands submerged in the hot water was my consolation prize for still being up instead of in my warm bed.

As he stepped through the kitchen toward the back porch, Gordon told me farewell. "See you tomorrow," he said.

I waved as I placed a plate in the dish rack.

Becca yawned, and I motioned toward the stairs. "You can go on up," I said.

"No, that's all right. I'll wait for you."

After I'd finished, I grabbed a flashlight and escorted Becca up to my room, fearing she might bump her leg in the dark.

All my life, I shared a bedroom with Jessica and Leisel, then just with Leisel, and then with Jessica when she returned and Leisel left. I thought, starting tonight, I would have a room of my own for the first time in my life. But it would have to wait a few more days. As we climbed the stairs, Becca asked how old Gordon was.

"Twenty-two," I said. "I think." I knew he was close to my age.

"That old?"

I nodded.

"I thought he was younger."

"No," I answered, a bit alarmed by her questions.

She laughed. "I was just teasing. I'm way too young to be interested in anyone. And even if I were a decade older, I wouldn't be interested in an Amish guy."

"Mennonite," I said.

She shrugged as we reached the landing. "You said that before, but it seems the same."

I didn't bother to explain there was actually a big difference. Besides driving a car, he played a guitar and flew on airplanes. Jah, he had far more freedom than we did, which was fine with me. I had no regrets about what I wasn't allowed to do.

"Ouch!" Her voice was much louder than it needed to be.

I stopped. She bumped into me.

"What happened?" I shone the flashlight toward her.

She held up her hand. "I whacked it against the wall. How do you get around in the dark?"

I didn't bother answering. I could navigate our home blindfolded.

As soon as we reached the bedroom, I turned on the battery-operated lamp. "That's a little better, but it's still so dim," Becca said. "How can you see?"

"You get used to it," I replied.

"And so cold." Rebecca wrapped her arms around herself for just a moment. But she then reached into her bag and pulled out a pair of shorts and a T-shirt.

"Are those your pajamas?"

She nodded.

"You'll freeze in those." I grabbed a flannel nightgown from the bureau and tossed it toward her.

I then grabbed my own nightgown and headed down the hall to change and brush my teeth. When I returned, Becca was under the covers, her teeth rattling. "I have an electric blanket at home," she chattered. "Plus we have central heat. I didn't know anyone in the United States lived this way."

It was my turn to laugh. At least she had the flannel nightgown on, and I guessed her skimpy pajamas on underneath it. She wouldn't freeze. I climbed under my layers of quilts and told my niece good-night as I turned off the lamp. I thought I'd fall asleep right away, but instead I stayed awake, aware of Becca shivering. Finally, I got up and pulled another quilt from the closet and spread it over the top of her.

She thanked me, and a few minutes later we both fell asleep.

I rose early the next morning, showered, dressed, and tiptoed down the stairs to start the coffee before anyone else in the house was up. But as I stood at the kitchen window, humming "Wherever He Leads, I'll Go," I could see the lanterns in the barn were lit and guessed that Gordon had already arrived to do the milking. It had snowed more during the night, and the path needed to be shoveled between the house and barn—and to Aenti Suz's *Dawdi Haus* too.

I continued humming as I worked. At church, we sang songs in German from our *Ausbund* hymnal, first printed over four hundred years ago. But we mostly sang Englisch hymns at the Youngie singings. Those were my favorite. And the songs I overheard Gordon sing while he worked.

Without realizing it, I sang the words out loud. "'Take up thy cross and follow me,' I heard my Master say . . .'"

"*Guder Mariye.*"

I jumped, relieved that it was Jessica. Years ago, Mamm had limited me to humming in the house because she feared I was becoming prideful about my singing. It was an order I did my best to obey, although sometimes I broke into song without realizing it.

I turned toward my sister. "Good morning to you too."

Silas tended the fire in the woodstove in the living room and then headed out to help Gordon with the milking, which he didn't need to do. Arden and the boys would be out to help soon. But that was the kind of person Silas was.

Frankly, I was surprised Jessica didn't join him, but I was grateful that she stayed inside to help me because neither Mamm nor Aenti Suz were up yet. I guessed the wedding day had worn them out.

As Jessica and I worked, she asked me what I thought of Becca.

"I'm not sure what Amos told her about our life." I grabbed a mixing bowl to start the biscuits. "But she was surprised that we didn't have central heat." I chuckled.

Jessica simply said, "Poor thing." She greased a baking pan and then began mixing an egg casserole.

I'd never lived with heat in a house, besides from our wood-stove. Jessica had lived in an apartment for three years, and I guessed it had heat—although I'd never asked her.

Jessica whisked the egg whites. "Isn't it a blessing to finally meet her? To think, if Amos hadn't come home for Dat's funeral, we wouldn't even know she exists."

I nodded, but honestly I didn't care as much about our Eng-lisch relatives as Jessica seemed to. It wasn't as if we'd ever see her after this. When I married, I wouldn't invite Becca and Amos. *When?* I smiled, thinking of Elijah. I slipped the biscuits into the oven and then pulled the leftover ham from the refrigerator as Amos shuffled into the kitchen and straight for the coffee. After pouring himself a cup and taking a big swig, he said he was heading out to the barn.

Surprisingly, Becca came down soon after. She wore jeans, a bulky sweatshirt, and the boots she'd had on the day before. She yawned as she practically stumbled into the kitchen. She shook her head when she saw Jessica. "What are you doing here?"

Jessica smiled, a puzzled look on her face. "What do you mean?"

"You just got married. Shouldn't you be in a hotel or something?"

Jessica laughed. "Jah, it's a little hard to explain, but it's the way we do things. Silas and I will help finish the cleanup today and then go on to our new home."

Becca wrinkled her nose. Clearly we didn't make sense to her. She sniffed. "Do I smell coffee?"

"Jah." Jessica pointed toward the pot. "The mugs are to the left of the stove."

"Is everyone out doing the milking?"

"We're not," I said. "You're welcome to help us in here."

She shook her head. "I don't do so well with cooking. I'll go see if I can help outside." After she'd drained her cup, she left us too.

Jessica slipped the casserole into the oven. "I really like her."

No doubt she did. Becca definitely reminded me of Jessica at that age.

When Mamm came downstairs, she pulled the little table in the corner over near the big table, leaving just an inch of space. I pursed my lips but didn't say anything. When Amos came for Dat's funeral, he and Jessica sat in the corner at the shunning table. I'd heard of other families placing two tables just an inch apart, but Mamm had never done it before. Perhaps she didn't want to alarm Becca.

After breakfast, which included Vi and Arden's family, we spent the day moving furniture and cleaning up. Amos and Becca pitched in to help and seemed to enjoy themselves, and I overheard Becca call Mamm *Grandma*, even though the Amish term was *Mammi*.

I snuck a look at Mamm to see if she minded, but she had a smile on her face and appeared pleased.

Vi and Arden must have been all right with their children being around Becca, because they all came over in the afternoon for a snack. Brenda and Milton then gave Becca a grand tour of the farm, including the woods.

I pulled out leftovers for our supper. Again, the shunning table was only an inch away. Becca gushed over the farm, commenting on how different it was from her Colorado grandparents' ranch, saying she "really loved the Bachmann land."

I wondered if Amos told her that her Amish ancestors had lived on this property since 1752—long before her Englisch ancestors ever headed west.

After supper, Jessica said she and Silas were going to head on over to the Stoltz farm. Mamm asked her to tell John and Mildred hello. It seemed that Mildred wasn't well enough to come to the wedding because of her cancer, which was a shame. I hadn't met them, but from everything Jessica said, they were good people.

After Silas had hitched his horse to his buggy, we all told them good-bye. Then Amos gave Jessica a big hug, and so did Becca. I understood the two wouldn't see Jessica for a long time, but it wasn't really our way to be so affectionate. However, Jessica hugged them back tightly. She whispered something in Becca's ear, although I couldn't tell what. Living as an Englischer had made Jessica more emotional, I was sure. She'd never been sugary before, but now she was like maple syrup in November. Thick and sweet and all over everything.

I didn't step outside to watch Jessica and Silas go. I'd see them at church, unless the weather turned worse. Even if it did, I hoped the singing wouldn't be canceled, and I'd still be able to see Elijah.

Amos walked Jessica and Silas out to their buggy, and when he stepped back inside he had his cell phone in his hand. He glanced up at Becca, who stood with one hand leaning against the table.

"We'd better get going tonight too. There's another storm coming in, and I'm not sure we'll be able to make it to the airport in the morning."

Becca frowned, but then Amos said, "You have your PSAT test Monday, remember? You can't miss that."

I had no idea what Amos was referring to, but Becca agreed. "I'll go grab my bag."

Within fifteen minutes, they were on their way too. Then Aenti Suz went out to her Dawdi Haus. I asked Mamm if she wanted to play a game of Scrabble, but she yawned and said she was going to bed. "Make sure and turn the lamp off when you turn in."

I assured her I would. With nothing to do, I wiped down the kitchen counters again even though I just had an hour before. The house felt so strange without Jessica. I thought I was fine with her leaving—but the truth was, I'd never felt so alone in my entire life. I missed both of my sisters horribly.

My thoughts fell to Elijah, eager for the next verse of my life to start. Jah, I'd always adored Elijah even though I knew he wasn't *Mann* material. Yet. But perhaps he would make a good husband. And soon.

That's what I wanted. A husband from our community. Someone who could someday be chosen to be a minister in our district, or even a bishop. I'd be fine with "like father like son."

I wanted a man I could stand by, and elevate and influence. A man who would appreciate my gifts and contributions. A man I could truly submit to.

And, jah, I wanted a big old farmhouse I could clean and decorate, and I wanted to fill it with children. I wanted a garden. I wanted to can and cook and sew and quilt.

I could only hope God was finally answering my prayers for all of those wishes through Elijah Jacobs. I could imagine telling our future children years from now that God truly did work in mysterious ways, while Elijah stood beside me, a look of adoration on his face.

— 3 —

Amos was right about the storm. So much *Shnay* fell that church was canceled the next morning, something that I couldn't remember happening for years. But by late afternoon, it had stopped. Our farm sparkled as the sun came out.

Mamm, Aenti Suz, and I all sat at the table and were playing a game of Scrabble when Milton stopped by the house to tell me that Elijah had left a message on the barn phone that he would pick me up for the singing in his Dat's sleigh.

"Goodness," Aenti Suz said. "That sounds like fun."

Mamm's eyes shone. "Marie . . ."

When she didn't say anything more, I asked, "What is it, Mamm?"

She shook her head but kept smiling.

"*Ach*, he's going back to Florida. . . ." My voice trailed off as I wondered for the first time if he had a whole string of girlfriends down there.

Mamm pulled her tiles closer. "I doubt he'll be gone for long."

Aenti Suz placed the word *partner* on the board and then laughed a little.

"What is it?" I asked.

"Oh, nothing."

"It's something," I countered.

Aenti Suz smiled. "It's just that you and Elijah are about as different as can be."

"But opposites attract." Mamm picked up a tile.

I nodded. Plus, there was the fact that I'd been attracted to him for years, which I wouldn't admit. Not now. Someday it would become part of our story. Perhaps he'd been attracted to me all along as well.

As Mamm added an *s* to *partner*, Aenti Suz said, "Time will tell."

I agreed.

I dressed warmly and waited at the living room window for Elijah to pick me up. Soon it was dark, and the light of the nearly full moon bounced off the white landscape. The entire evening was enchanting, except, minute by minute, I feared Elijah had stood me up.

As if she could read my mind, Mamm said, "Don't worry, he'll be here."

When I was about ready to give up hope, a sleigh came up our drive. I quickly told Mamm good-bye as I slipped on my cape and stepped to the door. As I opened it, I could hear bells as Elijah pulled the sleigh to a stop. I hurried down the steps.

Elijah waved, jumped down, and then helped me into the sleigh. As I glanced back at the house, I spied Mamm looking out the window. She waved, and I waved back, not caring if Elijah knew how pleased Mamm was that we were going out.

"I doubt many will show up for the singing," he said. "If no one else comes, we can have a snack with my Mamm and Dat. Would that be all right?"

"Of course," I answered.

As it turned out, I was the only one who showed up, and I wondered if Elijah had planned it that way all along. When I asked him, he said he thought there was the possibility that some other Youngie would make it through the snow. "A slight one," he added with a grin.

I was disappointed not to be able to sing, but his parents were welcoming, as always. We all sat at the table, sipping hot chocolate and eating pecan pie. I'd always gotten along well with Bishop Jacobs, unlike Jessica, and now with Dat gone he'd become like a second father to me.

Elijah's mother, Laura, was reserved but still a kind person. I wasn't sure who Elijah got his personality from—but it wasn't from either of his parents. They were both so serious and conscientious.

We talked about the weather, then Jessica and Silas and their new home on the Stoltz farm. Finally, Laura asked about Amos and Becca and if I expected them back anytime soon.

I shook my head, not knowing what else to say. I didn't see any reason for them to return.

"How is Arden and Jessica's arrangement of managing the farm working out?" Bishop Jacobs looped his thumbs through his suspenders.

I wrinkled my nose. Our father had set up an odd arrangement with his lawyer before he died that required Jessica and Arden to make all decisions about the land together, which prevented Arden from selling rights to a fracking company or selling off a chunk of land for development. I simply shrugged my shoulders and said, "You'd have to ask them." It wasn't that I was avoiding gossip—the truth was, I didn't know. I wasn't interested in our land. The house was my domain.

After a while, Elijah said he'd take me home. Once I thanked his parents, we were back out in the sleigh.

"Sorry," he said.

"About what?"

"My parents. They're a little boring."

I laughed a little. "Most are."

He shook his head. "Your Dat wasn't."

That was true. "Your parents are wonderful. I enjoyed spending time with them." *And you.*

"Denki." He turned toward me, his eyes shiny. "That means a lot." He chuckled. "Even though I find them"—he grinned—"as I said, unexciting."

"Well, then I'll appreciate them doubly for both of us."

He didn't respond for a long moment and then in a breathy voice said, "I'd like to see you more while I'm home, if possible."

My heart raced. "I'd like that too," I said.

We rode along in silence, the moon lighting our way. When I snuck a glance at Elijah, he was smiling, and I realized I was too.

※

More snow fell in the next week, more than we'd had in years, and I didn't see or hear from Elijah, not even two weeks later at church. His Mamm said he was ill.

We hoped Leisel would come home for Christmas, but she left a message saying she wouldn't make it. Between working in a nursing home and the bad roads, she didn't have enough time for a trip that would take even longer than usual. Jessica, Silas, and his mother, Edith, joined Mamm, Aenti Suz, and me, along with Arden and Vi and their children. It was a happy day, although my thoughts continually turned to Elijah.

I did see him the day after Christmas, on second Christmas,

at his parents, when Mamm and I stopped by to deliver the homemade gifts we'd made for them—a quilted table runner and a jar of apricot jam.

Elijah was attentive, apologizing for not coming by. "I came down with the flu," he said, "and spent a week in bed. I'm just now feeling better."

We chatted for a few minutes and then he said he'd be heading down to Florida in a few days. "I'll stop by and see you before then, I promise."

I said I'd like that. Jah, I was disappointed we hadn't had more time together, but we would once he moved home.

I hoped Elijah would come by the next day, perhaps to take me for a ride in the sleigh again, or to join us for dinner or even for just a piece of pie in the afternoon. I spent the morning cleaning and then baking, humming one song after another as I worked.

Sadly, by late afternoon it was clear Elijah wouldn't be stopping by, and I could feel my mood grow darker.

Toward supper time, Arden dragged Gordon into the house as I mashed potatoes to go with meatloaf while Mamm set the table and Aenti Suz filled a pitcher with water.

"Gordon needs some dinner," Arden said.

"I really don't." Gordon grasped a backpack in both hands. "I can get something on the way."

"He's going straight into town." Arden stood at the kitchen doorway, tugging on his gray beard. "He's going to volunteer at a homeless shelter after working all day in the cold. He needs a hot meal first."

"Of course we'll feed him." Mamm smiled at Arden. "We have plenty."

My mood brightened a little at the sight of Gordon. He wasn't Elijah, but after a quiet day I welcomed company. I finished the potatoes and grabbed another plate from the cupboard. "Go wash up," I said to him. "We'll be ready to eat in a couple of minutes."

In no time, Arden had left and then Gordon joined us, dressed in a clean set of clothes. He placed his backpack on the porch and then sat down at the table with us. After a silent prayer, we passed the food around, and Aenti Suz started grilling Gordon about the shelter.

"It's overflowing with clients right now because of the cold weather," he said. "We collected blankets at church, and I'm going to deliver them tonight."

"Who's going with you?" Aenti Suz passed me the meatloaf.

"Just me," Gordon answered.

"Why don't you take Marie along?"

Gordon gave me a shy smile and then said, "She'd be better off here, safe and warm."

"The roads are all plowed." Aenti Suz took the potatoes from Mamm. "There's no danger involved. And your car is warmer than a buggy."

He laughed a little. "Actually, it's not."

"What do you think?" Aenti Suz turned to Mamm. "Wouldn't it be good for Marie to see what a shelter is like?"

Mamm shrugged.

The truth was, I had no interest in visiting a homeless shelter, but I'd had such a boring day that going anywhere seemed appealing. I turned toward Mamm. "I'd like to go," I said.

"Great." Aenti Suz beamed. "I'll do the dishes so you can leave as soon as you're done eating."

Gordon gave me an odd smile. Perhaps he didn't want me to tag along. Or perhaps he thought I didn't want to even though I'd just said I did. I wasn't sure how to interpret his response.

Twenty minutes later, I climbed into Gordon's car. It was all black, including the bumper, which I was pretty sure he'd spray-painted. And he hadn't lied about the heater—the car was actually colder than a buggy, mostly because we didn't have wool blankets over our legs.

"Sorry," he said, as he wiped the inside of the windshield with an old towel. "Along with the heater not working, the defroster is having problems too." He smiled at me. "They seem to be connected."

We didn't talk much as he turned on the New Holland Pike and headed toward the city, but after a while, he asked if I minded if he sang.

"Of course not." I wrapped my arms around my middle, hoping to generate some warmth.

"Do you know 'It Is Well with My Soul?'" he asked.

I shook my head. We sang a lot of Englisch hymns at singings, but I didn't recognize that one.

He began it. It was a pretty melody, and the words were haunting. "'When peace like a river attendeth my way, When sorrows like sea billows roll, Whatever my lot, Thou has taught me to say, It is well, it is well, with my soul.'"

Whatever my lot. I thought of the exciting lives my sisters were living while I waited for what was next for me. Three weeks ago, I felt sure it was Elijah. But he'd pretty much ignored me since then.

I sighed. I needed things to be well with my soul.

Gordon sang the last note of the song as we neared the city, and then said, "I often lead singing at the shelter. The songs are snippets of God's truths. Many of the clients won't listen to us talk about the Lord, but they love to sing."

"Oh?"

"Jah. For people with a lot of worries, the music grabs their attention right away. They're more likely to remember the words of a song than the words of a sermon."

That made sense. My very first memory was of singing at church, long before I could understand the sermons.

Gordon stopped at a traffic light. "The shelter is downtown," he said. "We don't have much farther to go."

"Are there a lot of homeless people in Lancaster County?" My head was turned toward a bank of snow at the edge of a street. A few lonely souls walked along the sidewalk.

"I've read there's between three hundred and four hundred on any given day," he said. "The third most of any city in the state."

That surprised me. "Are all the homeless men?"

Gordon shook his head. "There are plenty of women and children too. We do our best to refer to clients at the shelter as 'unhoused' rather than homeless."

"Why?"

"Well, 'home' doesn't always refer to a building. A tent can be a home. Or a car. Or a shelter. Many of these people have a sense of home and community. What they need is a house or apartment. A safe, warm, permanent place to live."

I nodded, not being able to truly comprehend needing a house—or a home. I turned toward the window, gazing at the row of houses. Some had lights on inside. Others were completely dark. A young boy without gloves on his hands ran up the steps to one at the end of a block.

Soon we were in the heart of downtown with tall buildings and lots of people dressed in warm coats and hats and gloves rushing down the sidewalks. Gordon parked the car and pointed to a brick building across the street. "That's the shelter."

Gordon climbed out of the car and then hurried around to

my door and opened it. He gave me his hand, saying, "It might be slick."

Once I was out of the car, he opened up the trunk, which was stuffed with blankets, including several handmade quilts. We grabbed as many as we could—about half—and crossed the street at the light. There were a few people smoking outside of the building. Gordon, over the top of the stack of blankets, greeted one of the men by name. The man hurried up the steps and held the door for us. As we passed through, Gordon introduced the man—Walter—to me.

The man greeted me warmly, saying any friend of Gordon's was a friend of his.

Once we were inside, a tall, middle-aged man with a bit of a belly stepped out of an office. "Thank you, God," he boomed and then slapped Gordon on the back. "This is exactly what we needed tonight."

Gordon quickly introduced me to Tony, and then said, "We have more blankets in the car. And I brought my guitar too."

"Perfect," Tony said. "We're just finishing supper. We'll sing in the dining hall." He took the stack of blankets from Gordon. "Take Walter with you to get the rest and put those in the men's hall."

Tony indicated I should follow him, I guessed to where the women slept. We headed up a staircase with the load of blankets, and then stepped into a room where workers were spreading out sleeping pads.

"Look what just arrived!" Tony held his stack of blankets high.

The workers turned toward him. One of them shouted out, "Hallelujah!"

"All freshly laundered," Tony said, "and ready to use."

I thought of the Mennonite women who had washed each blanket and quilt, making sure the donated items were clean and ready to bless someone in need.

Two of the workers approached us and took our stacks. As we turned to go, they were already placing the blankets on the pads.

"Does each person only get one blanket?" I asked.

"It'll depend on how many people and how many blankets," Tony said. "But our numbers the last two weeks have been the highest ever. The last few nights some of our clients only had a coat to wrap up in."

I followed Tony back down the stairs to the foyer as Gordon and Walter came back into the building. Gordon carried another stack of blankets in one hand and his guitar in the other.

"Take those on downstairs," Tony said. I guessed that was where the men slept.

"Marie," Gordon said. "Would you grab my guitar?"

I took it from him and then stepped against the wall to wait, balancing the weight of the instrument. It felt good in my hands.

"Come on into the dining hall," Tony said to me. "Gordon will find us soon enough."

I followed Tony toward the clatter of dishes. Rows of tables were filled with men, women, and children. Most wore their coats. All shoveled food into their mouths. Some sort of noodles with chicken. And peas, green salad, a roll, and a cookie. Some drank red punch while others had coffee.

Tony clapped his hands and then spoke loudly. "Gordon just arrived with his guitar."

A man at the table closest to the door laughed and pointed at me.

"Ah well," Tony said. "You're right, this isn't Gordon. This is Marie. Gordon will be joining us shortly. As soon as the meal is over, we'll spend some time singing."

Several people smiled at me as I stepped back against the wall, trying to hide my discomfort. Even from where I stood, there was an unwashed odor in the room. Several of the people, both women and men, had dirty fingernails. Didn't they know to wash their hands before they ate? I'd always been taught that cleanliness was next to godliness. Perhaps they hadn't.

One of the women's coats was open, showing an immodest top. Another woman's hair was a ratty mess. Surely she could comb it out and at least braid it.

I took a shallow breath, impressed that Gordon volunteered on a regular basis. A few minutes later, he slipped into the room and took his guitar from me.

As the clients finished up, they took their trays to the back of the room where there was a kitchen and several workers who scraped and rinsed plates.

I asked Tony if the kitchen workers were part of the staff.

"Oh no," he said, "they're all volunteers. This is our regular Monday night crew, but we also have groups—scouts, different churches, sports teams, and students looking for volunteer hours who all come in on a regular basis."

Gordon pulled an empty chair from the table and placed it in the front of the room. I sat down at the first table next to a woman with a little boy with curly hair. I asked him his name and he answered, "Rory." He appeared to be five or six.

"Do you go to school?" I asked.

He glanced at his mother and then muttered, "Sometimes." Then he scrunched up his nose and asked, "Why are you dressed that way?"

His mother nudged him and said, "Don't be rude."

"No, it's all right." I smiled at him. "I'm Plain. We believe in dressing modestly. That's why I wear this dress and cape." I patted my head. "And a covering on my head."

"It's kind of cool." He smiled back, his eyes twinkling. "I guess."

Gordon began strumming his guitar.

The woman leaned toward me. "How do you know Gordon?"

"He works on my family's farm."

"So, you're Mennonite too?" She didn't appear to be too much older than I was.

"No. Amish."

"Well, thank you," she said. "For coming here tonight. We all appreciate everything Gordon does for us."

I was about to ask what all he did, when he began singing a song I didn't recognize, but the clients did. They sang with him.

I hummed along to the songs I didn't know, picking up the words and tunes, and then belted out the songs I recognized: "Amazing Grace," "The Old Rugged Cross," and "How Great Thou Art." The Amish never sang with instruments, but I found my voice quickly matching the music from Gordon's guitar. All of it lifted my soul, as a sense of joy filled me that I hadn't felt since before Dat had died. Soon I realized I was tapping my foot—and then I noticed Gordon was too. One time, he caught my eye and smiled.

I felt a freedom I hadn't since I was a girl, from back before Mamm warned me about being prideful about my voice. No one would tell how loudly I was singing. Certainly not Gordon, nor anyone else in the room.

Tony closed his eyes and held his hands up as Gordon started another song. "Lord of all . . ."

I had to consciously hold my arms down. I wanted so badly

to raise them. To sway to the music. To allow my body to express the harmony I felt inside. The love of Christ, and the joy in the Lord that music created.

Of course I didn't raise my arms or sway to the music. I stayed put, in my place.

Gordon's voice increased in volume. I didn't want the singing to end. The only consolation was the ride home with Gordon, when hopefully we could sing some more.

My chest grew tight as a memory flooded through me. Dat, playing a harmonica in the barn. Me, singing along—a song, perhaps a hymn, although I couldn't remember now which one. Jessica was shoveling grain into a trough while Leisel cradled a kitten. All the while, Dat and I were making music together and it was filling me up in a way I never thought possible. But by the look on his face, I knew he'd experienced the feeling before.

Gordon held on to the last note of the last word—"Hallelujah!"

The music and word reverberated through my being and I held on to the note as long as I absolutely could.

Once it ended, Tony walked up to the front and stood next to Gordon. "Hold on to these words, to this music," he said. "Know that God wants to lead you, that He wants to provide for you, that He wants you to trust Him." He smiled at the group, making eye contact as he scanned the room. A shiver shot down my back. I sensed a genuine love in both Gordon and Tony for the people they served. "Let's bow in prayer," Tony said. As he prayed, I shivered again, especially when he asked a blessing on everyone who was in the room and those who might still be out in the cold on such a bitter night.

After he said "amen," Rory ran up to Gordon while his mother slowly stood. When she did, her coat opened and I could tell she was pregnant and probably due soon. She took a step and then let out a gasp.

Coming out of my reverie, I reached for her arm. "Are you all right?"

She groaned and swooned. I held on to her as best I could as she slid to the ground. I couldn't keep her up, but I did prevent her from hitting her head. "Gordon!" I yelled as I knelt beside the woman.

Thankfully he heard me and rushed toward us. "Chrissie," he said. "What is it?"

But she didn't answer. Her eyes had rolled back in her head.

Gordon shouted for Tony. "Call 9-1-1." Then he said to me, "Take Rory to the kitchen. Stay there until we know what's going on."

— 4 —

We sat in the emergency department waiting room with Rory until Tony, who had been out in the hall making phone calls, told Gordon to take me home. "I'll give you a call in the morning," he said, "and let you know how Chrissie is."

I stood. "What about Rory?" He couldn't spend the night at the hospital.

"His grandmother is on her way." Tony reached down and patted the boy's shoulder as he spoke. "She'll take him home for the night."

I had a million questions but didn't want to ask them in front of Rory.

"Thank you, both of you," Tony said. "I don't know what I would have done without you tonight."

Gordon shook the man's hand. "Call me if you need to. I can come back in, no problem."

Tony nodded and then embraced Gordon. They slapped each other on the back and then let go. Then Tony shook my hand, and Gordon and I both told Rory good-bye. I knelt down beside him. "Remember the last song we sang tonight? The one about how the Lord holds us close, always?"

He nodded.

"God, who created the entire universe, is here with you to-night. He loves you, and He loves your mom."

"And the baby?"

"Jah," I said. "He loves all of you."

Rory nodded, and I patted his shoulder and then stood. Gordon and I slipped out of the waiting room and then on down the hall, through the doors of the warm hospital and into the freezing night.

We didn't speak until we were in the parking garage and inside Gordon's car, but then I couldn't help but ask, "If Rory's grandmother is coming to get him, why aren't he and Chrissie living with her?"

Gordon started the engine and then turned his head toward me. "It's hard to understand, but often these situations are more complicated than they seem."

I was dumbfounded. I didn't know anyone who would leave their daughter and grandchild on the streets. "What did Chrissie do?" I asked. "To deserve that? Drugs? Something worse?"

"Marie . . ." Gordon's voice trailed off.

"What?"

He sighed. "I don't speculate about the clients. About what they did or do or don't do. About why they're living on the street. There are rules they have to follow to spend the night in the shelter, but their lifestyles are between them and—"

"But she has a child! A sweet, innocent little boy. Why would she do that? Why would she put him at risk? And now another baby too?"

Gordon shook his head. "There could be all sorts of reasons." He backed out of the parking space. "I just want to get you home. Your mother is probably frantic."

It was ten o'clock. She wouldn't be panicking if I were out with Elijah.

I tried to keep my teeth from chattering, but the interior of Gordon's car was freezing.

"I'm sorry," he said. "I really need to get this heater fixed, or more likely get a new car."

As we drove along, I remembered my earlier longing to sing with him on the way home and talk about music. All of that was gone. Partly from exhaustion. But I sensed my questioning about Chrissie and her situation added to it. Gordon was always so kind and caring, but now I wondered what he really thought of me.

The truth was, I'd enjoyed the singing tonight. *Enjoyed* was actually an understatement. I'd experienced a bit of heaven, but that didn't mean I was cut out for volunteering at a homeless shelter. Jah, a homeless shelter. Honestly, I couldn't even comprehend Gordon's explanation to call the clients *unhoused* instead of *homeless*. Obviously, he and I were from two very different worlds and mindsets. Perhaps I lacked compassion, but I couldn't imagine returning to volunteer again. Not that I'd actually volunteered. I'd simply sang—something that came quite naturally to me.

"How is Leisel doing?" Gordon asked as we left the city. I wasn't sure if he really cared or if he was just making conversation. "Will she be able to come home soon?"

"Hopefully," I said. "But I know that between nursing school and work, she's really busy."

"Have I told you my sister is in college?"

"No." I leaned back in my seat. I didn't think Gordon had told me anything about a sister or anyone else in his family, for that matter. Jessica said once that his father had left the family when Gordon was young and then had died a few years later, but that was all I knew.

"She—April—is at the university in Philly. She's a junior."

"Oh. Is she a year younger than you?"

He nodded.

"I didn't realize Conservative Mennonites could go to college."

"Most don't," he said. "But my mom is a teacher, and my dad was too, and she really wanted us to get an education."

"But you haven't? Not beyond high school, right?"

"That's right," he said. "I wasn't sure what I wanted to study. Plus, this way I can help April get through school." Even in the darkness I could tell he was blushing. He probably thought he sounded prideful to reveal he was helping her, but I didn't think so. I thought it was a sweet brotherly gesture.

He added, "She's studying political science."

"Wow," I said.

We rode in silence for a while. I thought about Gordon's mother working as a teacher and wanting him to get an education. I wondered if she was disappointed that he worked as a farmhand. "So why did you get a job on our land?"

"My grandfather was a farmer. I have fond memories of visiting them in Ohio—that's where both of my parents grew up. I wanted to see how I liked it."

"And?" I asked.

He shrugged and smiled. "I really enjoy it. . . ."

"But not enough to do it the rest of your life?"

"Something like that," he said. "Which is actually a blessing, right? It's not like I'd ever be able to afford a farm."

He was right about that.

"What happened to your grandfather's farm?"

"He sold it a few years ago. Some of the money went toward helping my father."

"What happened?" I asked, my voice low.

"He was mentally ill. It turned out he had bipolar disorder, but it wasn't diagnosed for a quite a while. He ended up on the streets in Cincinnati until my mom and his parents found him. He was okay if he'd take his meds, but he wouldn't for long. He ended up being hit by a truck when he tried to run across a busy highway."

"Oh," I said. "I'm so sorry."

"Thanks," he answered. "I was pretty angry with him when I was younger. Once I understood mental illness better, I became more empathetic. He's the one who taught me how to play the guitar. After he left, I stopped playing. But I started again in high school, which helped me heal from losing him. Honestly, volunteering at the homeless shelter helps too."

We both had lost our fathers, but under very different circumstances. I was more impressed than ever at Gordon's steadiness, at his faithfulness. He'd suffered but turned his grief into helping others.

After a few minutes of silence, he said, "I know I'm not supposed to compliment you or anything, but I could hear you singing tonight. I suspected you were a soprano—and I was right. But I didn't expect your voice to be as beautiful as it is."

My face grew warm, even in the freezing cold. Because I didn't know how to respond, I didn't.

"I'm sorry," he said. "I didn't mean to embarrass you."

"It's all right." I paused for half a second and then asked, "Is your mother okay with you playing the guitar and all of that?"

He nodded. "She's a music teacher at the Mennonite school I attended. Choir. Piano lessons. Plus, she leads a handbell choir at our church."

Surprised, I asked, "What's that?"

"Bells?"

I nodded.

"Just what it sounds like, but each bell is tuned to a different note. They're played by a group of people."

"I see," I said even though I didn't, at least not entirely. I faced the passenger window and concentrated on the snowy landscape, thinking about Gordon's mother. She was a single mother and earned money to raise her children by teaching music. Gordon's family was Plain, but very different from mine, even more than I'd realized.

But then I thought of when Dat played his harmonica. Arden would go home after the milking was done, and Jessica, Leisel, and I would stay out in the barn with Dat. Maybe for fifteen minutes or so, he would play and I would sing. And then he would let me play it sometimes. Jessica and Leisel would try to, but they couldn't get it to work the way I could.

When Gordon turned onto Oak Road, he said, "Thank you so much for coming." A minute later, he parked in his usual spot, turned off his car, and then opened his door. Before I could manage to find the handle, he ran around and opened my door for me.

I climbed out. "You don't need to walk me to the door."

"No, I do," he insisted. "I need to explain what happened to your mother."

Gordon and I walked side by side up to the front door, and then I led the way inside.

Mamm's voice greeted me before Gordon even shut the door. "Marie, is that you?"

"Jah, Mamm," I answered.

"I'm sorry," Gordon said as we stepped into the living room. "There was an emergency at the shelter. . . ."

Mamm was perched on the edge of her rocking chair. On the couch, in the dim light, I could see Elijah with his hands on his knees. He stood, and Gordon quickly stepped toward him, shaking his hand.

"What are you doing here?" I stuttered at Elijah.

"Keeping your Mamm company." He nodded toward the woodstove. "And tending the fire."

"I didn't see your buggy."

"I put my horse in the barn. The buggy's out back."

"Oh," I said.

"What in the world kept you so long?" Mamm asked.

Gordon quickly explained about Chrissie having a seizure and being transported by ambulance to the hospital. "We followed in my car, with her little boy."

Mamm's voice was sympathetic. "What an ordeal."

Gordon nodded. "The director of the shelter drove his car to the hospital too. We left the boy with him."

I added that his grandmother was on her way to pick him up.

Gordon added, "Hopefully I'll hear in the morning how Chrissie and her baby are doing."

Mamm's hand went to her throat. "Baby? You didn't say anything about a baby."

"She's pregnant," Gordon explained. "Close to nine months, I think."

"Oh dear," Mamm said. "Why was she volunteering at the shelter?"

"She wasn't," I said. "She's homeless—I mean unhoused."

"What?" Mamm pivoted toward me. "Why would she be, when she has a mother?"

I shrugged, not saying I'd had the exact same question.

Mamm's voice wavered as she spoke. "I can't imagine all of

the bad choices, all the consequences that lead to that sort of thing. Thank goodness the boy is with his grandmother now."

Gordon looked as if he wanted to say more on the topic, but he didn't. Instead he said, "I'm sorry I got Marie home so late." He turned to Elijah. "And my apologies to you as well."

Elijah shrugged.

"See you tomorrow." Gordon glanced at me and then at Mamm as he headed to the front door.

I called out, "*Gut'n Owed*" after him and Mamm did too, although in a quieter voice.

"Goodness," she said as the front door closed. "I shouldn't have let you go with him."

I took off my cape. "It wasn't that bad." Although I hadn't known what to do when Chrissie had the seizure, I was glad I'd been there for Rory.

And the music, the songs, had awakened something I hadn't felt in years.

Mamm stood. "I'll go on to bed and leave you two alone." She turned toward me. "I don't want to get in a long discussion tonight, but in the morning I need to speak with you."

"All right." My face grew warm again, wondering if there was something I'd done besides staying out later than she expected. I always did my best to honor her, to obey her. That had been my biggest desire since I was a girl.

As she started up the stairs, I sat down in her rocking chair.

"Wait a minute," Elijah teased. "I braved a freezing night like this to come visit you, and you're going to sit all the way over there?" He patted the couch beside him. "Come on over here."

I gave him a sassy smile.

"I don't bite," he said. "And I promise not to try to kiss you or anything like that."

"All right," I said, although I honestly wouldn't have minded if he tried to kiss me. Having him stop by was reviving my hopes. I stepped over to the couch and sat beside him.

"You're going to love your Mamm's idea." He put his arm around me. "You can't believe how hard it is for me not to tell you."

"You know?"

He nodded.

"Come on," I begged. "Give me a hint."

"It involves your Aenti Suz."

I leaned away from him and peered into his eyes. I couldn't think of anything Mamm would plan for me that would involve Aenti Suz, except maybe a quilting bee.

He grabbed my hand and pulled me closer. "You're going to be as thrilled as I am. I promise."

Elijah stayed until midnight, mostly teasing me. When he finally got ready to go, he said he was leaving for Florida the next day.

I groaned. "So soon?"

"Jah," he said. "But don't worry about it, really." His eyes danced.

He'd promised he wouldn't kiss me, but he did give me a sweet peck on the cheek. I walked him to the back door and then watched from the enclosed porch as he made his way to the barn to harness his horse.

So much for courting Elijah Jacobs while he was home. We'd have to pick back up when he returned to Lancaster for good.

The next morning, I stumbled down the stairs, bleary-eyed, to make breakfast for Mamm and Aenti Suz. I was surprised to find my mother sitting at the table with her hands wrapped around a mug of coffee. The fire was already stoked, and she appeared to be in a good mood. Perhaps she wasn't mad at me after all.

I stopped at the woodstove, attempting to warm up.

"Did you have a good time with Elijah last night?" Mamm asked.

"Jah." I rubbed my hands together. "But he's leaving today for Florida. I hoped he'd be here a few more days at least." I turned toward Mamm. "He said you have a surprise for me?" I didn't remember ever receiving an unexpected gift from Mamm. Even my birthday and Christmas presents were never unexpected— they were always something I needed. A new coat. A pair of boots. A hope chest.

Mamm had a sly expression on her face.

"You really do have a surprise for me?"

"I'm going to tell you at breakfast. When Suz is here."

"Well then." I stepped away from the stove. "I'd better get started."

I cooked scrambled eggs and sausage, and then toasted the bread I'd made the day before. I buttered it on top of the island in the middle of the kitchen, and then spread the apricot jam I'd made last summer on each piece. I didn't sing, of course, nor even hum. There were times that even my humming got on Mamm's nerves.

Just as I finished, Aenti Suz came through the back door with a platter of sticky buns. Together we carried the food to the table and then we all settled in our chairs. Mamm led us in a silent prayer and then we began to eat. Neither my mother nor my aunt said anything. I hoped I didn't appear as excited as I felt. The truth was, with Leisel living in Pittsburgh, Jessica married, and Elijah pretty much a no-show, my life had been pretty boring. I welcomed a surprise.

Aenti Suz asked me about the evening before, and I told her about what happened at the shelter.

"I'm so glad you were there to help," she said.

I nodded. "And then when I came home Elijah was here."

"Oh really?" Aenti Suz raised her eyebrows.

"Jah. He's going back to Florida today, but he said Mamm had a surprise for me, and you're involved."

Aenti Suz leaned forward. "Bethel. Does Elijah work and live where I think he does?"

Mamm nodded.

"Jah. Pinecraft," I said. "Or right next to it anyway."

Aenti Suz ignored me and addressed Mamm. "Don't you think that would have been good information to pass on to me?"

Mamm kept her eyes on her plate as she said, "I thought you knew. Don't you remember that Bishop Jacobs said he thought it was a perfect idea?"

I tried to keep my voice calm. "What are you talking about? What does Bishop Jacobs have to do with this?"

My aunt leaned back against her chair, sighed, and then said, "It seems I should have known. Or at least guessed." She turned her head toward me but spoke to Mamm, saying, "You should tell her."

Mamm raised her head, made eye contact with me, and then paused for a moment before saying, "I'm sending you to Florida for four weeks with Suz."

I dropped my fork on the table and then it bounced to the floor.

As I scrambled to pick it up, Mamm said, "We already have a cottage. Your Dat rented it before he got sick, hoping I'd go with him. You'll leave the day after the Epiphany."

"Why don't you go with Aenti Suz?" I sputtered.

Mamm's face fell. "You don't want to?"

"No, I didn't say that. But why me? You should go."

Mamm wrinkled her nose. "You know I don't like to travel. I'd told your Dat, but he hoped I'd go anyway. But since he's passed, I want this for you."

Did she feel sorry for me? Because I'd never had any adventures in my life? But the truth was, I was more like her. Not one to travel.

I wasn't going to turn it down though. Not when Elijah would be in Florida—not when he was obviously excited to have me visit. And not when Bishop Jacobs had given his blessing.

"Denki, Mamm," I said. "It's a wonderful surprise."

She beamed. "You're welcome."

I turned to Aenti Suz. "Have you been to Florida before?"

"Years ago," she answered. "You'll need to take your flip-flops. And only a sweater, although we'll need our warm coats and boots on the bus. Your lightest dresses . . ."

The back door opened as she spoke. Arden stepped into the kitchen, followed by Gordon.

"Join us," Aenti Suz said. "We have plenty of food."

Arden shook his head. "I'm going on home to give the kids a ride to school." Unlike the Englisch schools, our scholars didn't take off the week between Christmas and New Year's Day. "I was just showing Gordon in." He grinned. "I'll meet you in the barn when I get back."

Gordon nodded and then said, with his hat in his hand, that he'd heard from Tony. He turned to Aenti Suz. "He's the director of the shelter."

"I see," she said. "Marie told me what happened last night."

"Oh good." Gordon looked at me. "Chrissie had a seizure due to high blood pressure. It turned out she had a condition called eclampsia. They ended up doing a C-section and delivered a baby girl. Five pounds four ounces. Eighteen inches long. Tony said both mother and daughter are doing well."

"Wonderful!" Aenti Suz clapped her hands together.

"What good news," I said to Gordon. "Denki for letting me know."

He nodded and then turned to leave.

"Have a sticky bun first," Aenti Suz said.

"I need to get back to work."

Aenti Suz cleared her throat. "Marie, get Gordon a cup of coffee and a plate. Gordon, sit."

We both obeyed.

"Now," Aenti Suz said. "Bethel and I just surprised Marie with a trip to Pinecraft. She and I are leaving in a week. I know you're going to be down there soon. Tell us when. And where."

My face grew warm as I placed the coffee and plate in front of Gordon. Here I'd thought Mamm and Bishop Jacobs were scheming to allow me to spend more time with Elijah. But now I couldn't help but wonder what Aenti Suz was up to—and why it would involve Gordon Martin.

⁂

The day after New Year's, Aenti Suz hired a driver to take us into Lancaster to do some shopping. Sunscreen and lotion were on the top of our list. Or her list, anyway. I couldn't see myself spending a lot of time on the beach. On our way home, she asked the driver to swing by Silas and Jessica's place. The Stoltz farm was off Highway 30 on Garden Lane.

"I think it would be nice to say hello." Aenti Suz smiled at me as she spoke. We'd seen Jessica and Silas at Christmas, but I agreed it would be nice to see their home.

John and Mildred Stoltz had built a Dawdi Haus on their property and moved into it right before Jessica and Silas's wedding. Jessica begged them to stay in their farmhouse, but Mildred had stage-four breast cancer, and she and John felt the Dawdi Haus would be easier for them to manage. That gave Jessica and Silas the big farmhouse to live in and furnish. Thanks to the collection of stuff Dat and Mamm had accumulated—and what had been passed down through two centuries in our house—they had what they needed, and we still had a collection of leftovers out in a storage room in the barn.

When the driver pulled up by the house, Jessica stepped out onto the back porch. I was surprised she wasn't out working on the farm with Silas. She wore an apron and a heavy sweater. She waved, obviously happy to see us.

"We won't be longer than fifteen minutes," Aenti Suz said to our driver.

"Take your time," the man said. "I'll keep the heater going and take a little nap."

Aenti Suz chuckled. "All right, make it a half hour then."

"Come on in," Jessica called out.

We hurried up the back steps. An icy wind blew again and the sky threatened a new snowstorm.

Jessica's kitchen was fairly warm. She had two peach cobblers sitting on the counter, and I guessed one was for John and Mildred. The kitchen was dated—old cupboards, counters, and linoleum—but everything was clean and freshly painted.

She pointed to the table in the corner. "Do you have time to sit down and have some coffee?"

"Just that much time," Aenti Suz said. "We just wanted to pop in and say hello."

We chatted while Jessica started the coffee. I stepped toward the table and put my purse on it, noticing an envelope with Leisel's name on the return address. I felt a twinge of jealousy and felt one of my judgmental looks, one that my sisters sometimes pointed out, creep across my face. I hadn't received a letter from Leisel. Then again, I hadn't written to her either.

I couldn't deny that Jessica and Leisel were closer than I was with either one of them. At one time Jessica and I had been best friends, or at least she thought we were, but I'd actually been jealous of her for years. She was strong and coordinated and preferred being outside farming with Dat. They'd developed a close relationship while I stayed inside, working with Mamm. Early on, I picked up that Mamm didn't approve of Jessica's helping with the farm and, I'm embarrassed to admit, I capitalized on that—criticizing Jessica to Mamm and doing my best to stay on Mamm's good side.

As Jessica glanced at me, I tried to put the letter from Leisel out of my mind. I was an adult now, and I needed to avoid any sort of jealousy, along with everything else that might entangle me.

The back door swung open and Silas entered with a load of wood in his arms. He greeted us, deposited the wood in the box by the stove, and then brushed his hands together.

"How about a cup of coffee?" Jessica asked. "And a piece of cobbler? Aenti Suz and Marie have a driver waiting, so we need to be quick."

Silas agreed. He followed Jessica to the counter as Aenti Suz poured the coffee. He bent toward Jessica and whispered something. Perhaps I imagined it, but by reading his lips it seemed he said, "Are you feeling better?"

Jessica smiled up at him and simply nodded.

The expressions on their faces forced me to look away. It was as if I'd seen something I shouldn't. Concern on his. Some sort of hope on hers, mixed with the hint of something more. But above all, their faces expressed their love. The commitment between two people who were, besides husband and wife, best friends. I couldn't imagine what it was like. Not at all. I'd never experienced anything close to it. But hopefully it was something that would soon grow between Elijah and me. Anticipation swelled inside of me.

As we all settled at the table with our coffee and cobbler, Jessica shared that Leisel had written and said she was sorry not to make it home for Christmas. I smiled sweetly, hiding my hurt.

Then Jessica said, "Oh! Mamm told me about you going to Florida. I'm so happy for you!" There wasn't even a hint of jealousy in her words. "She also reminded me that Elijah Jacobs lives down there." Jessica lifted her eyebrows as she smiled.

"Jah," Aenti Suz said before I could answer. "He does live down there." She took a sip of coffee. "And Gordon is going to be down there on a mission trip during our second week there."

"Goodness." Jessica wrapped her hands around her mug, her eyes sparkling. "Sounds like it's going to be a great time."

I simply nodded, not wanting to encourage her to tease me. She and Silas had started courting before they'd even turned sixteen, although covertly. Then, after she left, she dated an Englischer in Harrisburg. I was the one who'd never courted at all.

I concentrated on eating the peach cobbler, which was delicious, while Aenti Suz asked about Mildred Stoltz. It seemed the two had known each other years ago. Our aunt asked Jessica to tell both John and Mildred hello.

Jessica was so happy we stopped by, but she understood we couldn't stay long. Anyway, she'd see us on the Epiphany, just four days away. In no time, we were telling them good-bye and then we were on our way home, looking forward to seeing Jessica and Silas soon.

But, as it turned out, they didn't come over for the Epiphany, or Old Christmas as we often called it. Gordon knocked on the back door as Aenti Suz and I cleaned up after breakfast, saying that Silas had left a message. Jessica wasn't feeling well.

Aenti Suz thanked Gordon and then invited him in for a cup of coffee. He hesitated, but then, probably remembering how insistent she was the last time, accepted her offer.

As the three of us sat at the table, Aenti Suz asked what his plans were for the day.

"I'm going back to the shelter," he said. "Tony is shorthanded, and I'm going to help prepare supper."

"Good for you," Aenti Suz said. "But won't your mother miss you?"

He smiled. "She's going with me. So is my sister—she doesn't return to school until day after tomorrow."

"How lovely," Mamm said.

The Mennonites, or at least the Martin family, definitely did things differently than we did.

He turned to me then and said he hoped we'd have a good trip. Then he added, "I mentioned before that I'll be down in Florida in two weeks."

I nodded. Jah, he had. So had Aenti Suz.

"There's a group of unhoused youth that travels from this area to Florida each winter. We'll be reaching out to some of them, in hopes that we'll be able to reconnect with them in the spring and summer when they come back here."

"Fascinating," Aenti Suz said.

"Of course, we'll be helping others in the shelter too, regardless of where they spend their springs and summers."

I couldn't imagine such a life, and I wondered if providing services actually changed things for any of the youth in the long run. "I can't help but think of Chrissie and Rory," I said. "If they didn't have the shelter to help them, do you think they'd stay with her mother? Where they belong?"

Gordon gave me a patient smile. "You're not alone in thinking that way. And for some of our clients, the best place for them would be with their parents. But not for all of them. For some, home is an abusive place. Or there are drugs in the house. Others don't have parents who can help them."

"Why not?" I asked.

"Some of their parents are deceased. Others are incarcerated or ill or too impoverished."

"Oh." My father was dead, but I had my mother. If my mother died, I'd have Arden and my sisters, not to mention Aenti Suz. And Amos, who I knew would help me, even at a distance. "And they don't have other family who can help?"

"Some of them do, but not all," Gordon explained. "The goal is to get them reunited with their families, if it's a healthy situation."

"Are there some who simply prefer to be on the streets?" I asked.

He nodded. "A few, but most would like to be with family or have a home of their own. Everyone should have shelter and food."

I wrinkled my nose, figuring I wasn't cut out for that sort of work. I loved the music the evening I was at the shelter with Gordon, but I didn't see that I had much to contribute as far as helping Englischers with their problems.

"Anyway, it would be great to see you when we're down there," he said. "If that would be possible."

71

Before I could answer, Aenti Suz said, "That's a wonderful idea. We'd love to find out more about the work you're doing there." She reached into her apron pocket and pulled out a slip of paper. "Here's the phone number where you can reach us."

I shook my head at her, but neither noticed. It was obvious she'd written the number down ahead of time, hoping for a chance to give it to him.

Aenti Suz clearly thought the world of Gordon. Then again, she was my father's sister. He'd been a lot like Gordon, always eager to help others. I admired that in my father, although his service to others often took him away from Mamm and us girls.

Gordon finished his coffee and then said he'd be on his way. "I won't be back to help with the milking this afternoon," he said. "Arden said he and the boys would do it." He turned toward me. "Have a great trip, and hopefully I'll see you soon."

I smiled. "That would be nice." But I wasn't sure that I meant it. I had no desire to see his volunteer work in Florida. I'd seen enough in Lancaster. And besides, I hoped to spend as much time as I could with Elijah.

Mamm and I had a quiet day with just Aenti Suz because Arden and Vi and their children went to her parents' farm for the day. It was actually too quiet, and for the first time I wondered how Mamm would do with me gone.

When I asked her, she answered, "I'll be fine. I have a lot of quilting to do, Jessica promised she'd come over to check on me, and Vi invited me over to their house for suppers." She seemed sincere. Our family had changed so much in the last year, but Mamm seemed to be accepting it.

Of course I'd packed for our trip the day before, throwing in some kitchen towels to embroider and add to my hope chest, but Aenti Suz wasn't ready at all. When Mamm went upstairs to take a nap, Aenti Suz invited me over for a cup of tea in her Dawdi Haus and to keep her company while she packed. With nothing better to do, I accepted her invitation.

She had a big suitcase open on her small table, and stacks of clothes and books were piled on the dining room chairs. I sat down on her small but very comfortable sofa.

As she brewed the tea, she said how pleased she was that Mamm wanted me to accompany her to Florida.

Honestly, I was surprised too. Mamm didn't like any of us going far from home. I guessed it was her desire for me to marry Elijah that won her over, but I said, "Maybe she's getting over her fears."

Aenti Suz held a summer dress in her hand. "When your mother was young she wasn't fearful, but that changed when your sister Rebecca died. I think she was so afraid of losing you three girls, of Jessica and then you and Leisel, that she became rigid. She was so determined to follow all of the rules, as if that would protect all of you, that she found herself confessing to the bishop for the littlest thing, including if she feared she'd gossiped about someone or even had a bad thought. She hated that your father lived with such freedom in his friendships, travels, and thoughts. She was sure God would punish him—and her—by taking another child."

"Wow," I said. "That's awful." I did remember, as Mamm and I cleaned and cooked together over the years, her fretting over all sorts of things. That was probably where I got my propensity to measure dress hems and hat brims.

"Forgive me." Aenti Suz put her dress in the suitcase. "I've probably said too much." She sighed and then asked me more about the night I helped Gordon at the shelter.

I told her it had opened my eyes to the situations of others, and although I appreciated Gordon's desire to serve, it was obvious I didn't share his gifting.

"Well," Aenti Suz said, "Gifting helps, but service can be learned." She turned toward me as she poured the tea. "Could I tell you a story? About one of your great-great-great-aunts?"

"Sure," I said. Anything would be better than being lectured about my lack of desire to serve.

"Her name was Annie Bachmann," Aenti Suz said. "And she lived here, on this farm, in your house, with her sister, Sophia, her brother Josiah, and their parents. This was just over one hundred fifty years ago, during the Civil War."

—5—

Annie Bachmann

JUNE 1863

Annie stepped out of the coop, swatting dust and grain from her apron with one hand as she clutched the basket of eggs in the other. Just as she headed toward the back door of the house, her brother Josiah started yelling, "The Rebs are coming!"

He bolted over the split-rail fence from the field and rushed past her, his hazel eyes wild. He continued on toward their whitewashed house, shouting his message over and over.

Annie followed after him, half walking and half running. It wouldn't do to crack any of the eggs before they could eat them for breakfast. When she reached the back porch, recently screened in by Dat, Josiah was talking a mile a minute to their parents and sister, Sophia.

"Hiram Fisher said so." Josiah gasped for air. "The Rebs are on the Pennsylvania and Maryland border, headed this way."

Dat tugged on his long, gray beard. "That doesn't mean they'll come here to Leacock."

Josiah swiped at his brow. "But they could."

Sophia, whose bed was on the back porch in hopes the fresh air would help her health, sat up. "Is there to be a battle nearby?"

"No," Dat said. "We need more information before jumping to any conclusions."

"Go ask Hiram," Josiah said. "He just told me. He said to let you know right away." The Fishers were Mennonite, and Sophia was sweet on their son, Richert, who to the dismay of all had joined the Union Army a year ago, along with another Plain boy in the area, Cecil Troyer.

"I won't ask now," Dat said. "An hour or two won't make a difference."

Mamm wrinkled her brow. She'd aged drastically in the last two years, since the war had started and Sophia had fallen ill. "But what about George and Harriet?" Along with being Annie's sister-in-law, Harriet was also Cecil Troyer's sister. The Bachmanns had two soldiers to worry about.

Mamm continued. "Perhaps we should send a message to them to come here."

Dat shook his head. "We'll do no such thing. There's no reason to be alarmed."

Mamm sighed and took the basket of eggs from Annie. "I'll finish up breakfast."

Dat turned to Josiah. "Are the chores all done?"

"Almost." He retreated back down the stairs and Dat followed.

Annie sat down next to Sophia and took her hand. "Try not to worry about Richert."

"Annie!" Mamm's voice carried from the kitchen. "I need you to run over to the Fishers for me."

"I'll be back." Annie squeezed Sophia's hand and headed to the kitchen.

Mamm met her at the door. "Go see if Eva has some valerian for Sophia—she didn't sleep much last night." Mamm dropped her voice to a whisper. "Ask Eva what she knows about the Rebs, in case Hiram didn't tell Josiah everything. I don't want to wait until your Dat feels inclined to inquire about it. I'll save breakfast for you."

Soon after Richert had joined the Union Army, Sophia had been diagnosed with consumption. Annie and Mamm had been caring for her ever since.

"Run along," Mamm said. "Tell Eva I'll get over to see her sometime soon."

Annie did as she was told and walked out to the lane and turned to the left. The leaves of the old oak danced in the breeze, over the emerald green field. The lush grass was nearly tall enough to mow.

It was early June and already muggy. Hopefully rain would fall by evening and settle the dust on the lane. Cows and horses grazed in the pasture, and the herd of goats—seven to be exact—bleated in their corral next to the barn as Josiah milked the nanny.

A flock of swallows swooped this way and that, and then flew back toward the barn as Annie neared the woods. She stepped to the side of the lane and walked under the branches of the trees. A thistle snagged the skirt of her dress, and she freed it carefully so as not to tear it. She didn't have time to catch up on the mending as it was, let alone add to it.

Sophia, who was twenty, three years older than Annie, had always done the mending, until she fell ill. She'd also done most of the sewing and tended to anyone who was ill, besides helping Mamm with the baking, the garden, and the cooking and canning.

Annie did her best to keep up with all the chores now, but she feared she could never match Sophia's competency. Nor her sister's sweet spirit.

They all knew Sophia's diagnosis meant she'd likely be gone within a few years, if not sooner. But still, they prayed for a miracle. Annie couldn't bear to think of it. Sophia was her sister and her dearest friend.

So much had happened in the last few years. Their oldest brother, George, had married Harriet and moved to southern Lancaster County, to Peach Bottom on the Susquehanna River, closer to the Maryland border. Their little boy, Noah, who was now two, had been born there soon after Abraham Lincoln had been inaugurated. Even though Annie's father thought highly of the new president, they all knew having him as the new leader meant trouble for the country.

Soon the southern states seceded, one by one, and the war began. Some Plain folk had fled to Canada to protect their sons while others, such as Richert and Cecil, joined the Union Army. And then, a few months ago, Congress had passed the Federal Conscription Act for those twenty and older. However, thanks to their own representative, Thaddeus Stevens, nonresistant folks were allowed to pay three hundred dollars for someone to fight for them.

That's what others in their community planned to do, even though it was nearly an impossible amount of money for most. She guessed her father would come up with it for Josiah, who, at eighteen, would be of the age to serve in a couple of years. But surely the dreaded war would be over by then. Most thought it would only last three months at the beginning, and no one guessed it would go on the two years that it had, with no end in sight. She knew it would be difficult for her parents to come up with the money, but it would be impossible for Josiah to go against his beliefs and kill another human being.

She passed the woods and stepped back onto the dusty lane, striking up a tune as she walked. She sang "Abide with Me," a hymn Sophia had taught her when they used to sing as they did their chores. As Annie marched along, a wagon came over the crest of the hill. She shaded her eyes against the morning sun. Her heart raced. It was Samuel Yoder, the young man who had been courting her for the last few months. His family lived closer to Lancaster City, and his father was a cheese maker. Most likely Samuel was making a delivery. Annie had met him at an auction the summer before, when she'd accompanied Dat and Josiah.

Annie waved, and after a moment Samuel realized it was her and waved back. She increased her pace, and when they met, Samuel stopped the wagon in the middle of the road.

He would turn twenty in a few months, so he would soon need to pay the three hundred dollars too, should the country still be at war then.

They greeted each other warmly, and then Samuel took off his hat and ran his hand through his dark hair. Annie asked where he was headed.

"I have a delivery at the inn out on the highway, but I had a message to deliver to Hiram Fisher first," he answered.

"Oh? What about?" she asked, wishing he could stop by the house and sit for a while.

"Business." He wiped his chin with the back of his hand.

She couldn't imagine what business he had with Hiram Fisher. She doubted it had anything to do with cheese. Sometimes he made deliveries for other businessmen though, so perhaps it had something to do with one of them.

"What do you know about the Rebels coming? Josiah said Hiram told him they're at the border."

Samuel nodded. "That's right. They've been tearing through Maryland and are heading this way."

"To Lancaster?"

He placed his hat back on his head. "No one knows for sure. Well, no one save Robert E. Lee."

"What do you think is going on?" she asked.

He rubbed the side of his face and grinned. "The only thing I know for sure is that I need to be going. I'm stopping by your place—I have a newspaper for your Dat that I said I'd drop off when I was out this way. I hoped you'd have a few minutes to see me." He tipped his hat. "Where are you headed?"

"Over to the Fishers to see about an herb for Sophia." Annie smiled up at him and stepped closer. Samuel was a good man, a hard worker, and a leader among the Amish community in the area. He'd never run off to war, thrusting her into the turmoil Richert had put Sophia through. Jah, Samuel Yoder was a man Annie could trust, the one she hoped to marry someday.

He reached down and took her hand for a brief moment. Then he let go of it and tipped his hat, saying, "I'll see you soon. I promise."

She smiled again at Samuel, the sun behind his head. "I look forward to that time."

He nodded again, a grin on his face, and then snapped the reins. She stepped back and watched as the wagon rolled down the lane. Then she hurried on toward the Fishers' farm.

There were so many things she appreciated about Samuel, besides his trustworthiness. Because he lived much closer to

Lancaster and made deliveries to taverns, shops, and homes, he was always a wealth of information. He even delivered to Thaddeus Stevens's tavern and sometimes ran errands for the representative. Jah, Samuel knew as much as anyone as far as what was going on in Lancaster County.

She doubted the Fishers could tell her anything more than Samuel could. In fact, they'd probably gotten their information from him.

No one was in the garden or the barnyard as Annie stepped onto their property.

She slipped up the back steps and toward the closed door. Instead of knocking, she opened it as she called out, "Eva! Hallo!"

Eva wasn't in the kitchen, but a man was. A man she'd never seen before. A man with dark skin and wild eyes.

❧☙

She froze in the doorway and then finally found her manners. "Forgive me for barging in." Her voice wavered as she spoke. "I'm Annie Bachman."

The man nodded at her but didn't say a word. He wore a raggedy shirt and torn pants, and a jagged scar ran across his face.

"I'm a neighbor," she explained. She'd seen freed blacks at the market in town a time or two.

Then, just as she was about to ask where Eva was, she heard footsteps on the staircase behind her, coming from their second floor. "Annie?"

She turned.

Eva stood at the bottom of the stairs.

"Hello," she said. "I just met . . ." Her voice trailed off.

"Archer." Eva's voice sounded odd. "He's helping Hiram, since we're shorthanded with Richert gone."

81

Annie knew it was hard to find farmhands with so many men having left for the war.

"How is Sophia today?" Eva quickly asked.

"About the same, but she hasn't been sleeping well—that's why I'm here. Mamm hopes you have some valerian."

"I do," she said. "Out in the herb garden. I'll go out with you."

Eva told Archer that Hiram would be back shortly and then led the way toward the garden, stopping by the little shed for a spade.

As they walked, Annie asked what Eva knew about the Rebels coming.

"Oh, I don't know much," Eva said. "Hiram heard they were in northern Maryland, near the border."

Annie guessed Samuel had told him that.

Eva stopped at her herbs and dug up a valerian plant by the root. "You can use the root today and dry the leaves for later."

Annie took the plant from her and asked if there were any other remedies that might help Sophia.

"St. John's wort," she said. "I have some drying in the shed."

Annie waited as Eva returned with the herb. "Brew it into a tea, and have her drink it before bed."

"Any other advice?"

Eva's eyes watered, and she swiped at them. "Keep her comfortable. I'll come over and check on her in a day or two." The woman was known as a healer in their community, attending to women in labor and to the ill and injured. A doctor had seen Sophia too, but he confirmed that there was nothing to be done that would cure her.

"Tell your Mamm and Sophia hello—and that I'll see them soon." Eva was usually chattier, but it seemed she wanted Annie to be on her way.

Annie thanked Eva and headed toward the road as Hiram stuck his head out of the barn. Annie waved, and he tipped his hat. That's when she noticed his horses harnessed and hitched to his wagon. Had he just arrived home? Or was he planning to leave?

Three years ago, the Bachmanns feared Sophia would marry Richert and join the Mennonites. Now Richert was off fighting and Sophia was dying. Life could take all sorts of unexpected turns. None of them knew what the future held.

As Annie hurried home, swinging the valerian in one hand and holding the St. John's wort carefully in the other, she thought of Eva's knowledge. If Sophia hadn't fallen ill, Annie was sure she would have trained under Eva to become the next healer in their community. Sophia had always been the one to nurse whoever was ill in the family.

When Annie arrived, Samuel had already gone on his way with his deliveries. She hurried up the back steps onto the enclosed porch. Sophia reclined on her bed, but when she heard Annie she sat up and mentioned the newspaper Samuel had left. "Would you get it and read it to me?"

Sophia had grown paler in the last half hour, which made her eyes appear even larger than they were. Annie knew her sister worried about Richert and hoped for some news of his unit. Last they knew, he was fighting in Virginia.

"Samuel also brought a letter," Sophia said. "For Mamm."

Mamm often received letters from her mother and sister, who lived together in Chester County. Annie guessed this latest was one from them, although every once in a while George's wife, Harriet, wrote with their news.

Annie took the bundle of valerian and St. John's wort into the house and left them on the table next to the newspaper and a plate of food, obviously for her. Annie ate quickly as Mamm and Dat's voices drifted through the house. It took Annie a moment to realize they were on the front porch. Perhaps they'd gone out to speak in private when she'd come in through the back door.

When she'd finished eating, Annie stepped to the front door. "Dat," she said. "Sophia's hoping that I'll read her the newspaper. Would that be all right?"

"Jah," he said. "That's fine."

She hesitated for a moment.

"Go on," Mamm said. She held a piece of paper in her hand. Most likely the letter Sophia had mentioned.

Annie grabbed the newspaper and headed to the porch. The day was heating up, but a breeze still blew through the screened windows. The porch had, in 1752, been the original Bachmann cabin. The river rock fireplace still remained on the far side, and the walls, up to the screened windows, were logs, stacked on top of one another and chinked with mortar. They were now all whitewashed. Dat, and all the Bachmann men before him, cared for the old section of the house, preserving it, along with the land too. None of them took their home or land for granted. God had provided—and they were grateful.

Sophia, propped up by pillows now, smiled at the sight of the paper. Annie doubted there was much news about the Union Army—if there had been, Dat probably wouldn't have let Annie read it to Sophia.

Annie brushed the dust from her apron and climbed up onto the end of the bed. She scooted up against the wall until her back was against it and opened up the newspaper.

"Where shall I start?" she asked.

"At the beginning," Sophia answered.

"And read the entire thing?"

"Of course," she answered.

Annie dropped the newspaper in her lap. "First, tell me what you overheard Samuel say to Dat."

"They were only in the kitchen for a minute. And their voices were so low I couldn't make out a thing."

Disappointed, Annie began reading the newspaper, starting with the first article on the front page. Union General U. S. Grant defeated Confederate General J. E. Johnston in Jackson, Mississippi.

"That's good," Sophia said.

Annie didn't agree or disagree with her. It was good if it meant the war might end sooner rather than later, but she didn't want to think of the lives lost because of the battle. War made no sense to her.

She read the next article, this one about a new millinery shop that was opening in Lancaster. "All the ladies of Lancaster County will soon be visiting for a new hat that will usher them into the summer season."

Sophia laughed. "Did you make that up?"

"No." Annie pointed to the article and then teased, "Want to go?"

"And trade in my Kapp?" Sophia patted her head. "Never."

Annie started the next article about the 54th Massachusetts, a regiment of black men from Boston that would soon be leaving to join the fighting. It was the first such regiment ever, and some of the men, at one time, had been slaves.

"Oh my," Sophia said. "Isn't that something?"

Annie thought of the man she'd met at the Fishers'. Had he been enslaved?

She continued on to the next article. This one was about the 1st Pennsylvania Regiment marching northwest from Virginia.

"Do you think Richert is still with them?" Sophia asked.

"Most likely," Annie answered. It had been months since Sophia or the Fishers had heard from him. And last Annie knew, Harriet's parents hadn't heard from Cecil either.

Fighting, for all Plain people, went against their faith. They were all shocked when Richert and Cecil joined the Union Army, but none of them more than Sophia. Richert hadn't uttered a word of his plan. He'd sent a letter to Sophia once he'd joined, asking her forgiveness, but she'd never fully shared it with anyone in her family, not even Annie. By then she was ill, and Sophia was certainly fighting her own battle, in a way, although she had no hope of winning without a miracle from the Lord.

Sophia began to cough. Annie folded the newspaper and scooted off the bed. "I'll get you more water." She grabbed the pitcher and headed toward the springhouse. They had clean water, clean air, and good food, thankfully.

Some families sent those with consumption off to a dryer climate. Mamm and Dat had proposed the idea to Sophia, but she refused. "What good would it do me to be away from all of you?" she asked. "I want to spend every day I have left in my home, on this farm."

When Annie returned with the water, Sophia had stopped coughing and had her eyes closed.

As she looked down over her sister, she said a prayer for Sophia's healing. Annie couldn't bear to think of life without her sister.

✥

Annie headed out to the garden to weed, starting down the row of corn seedlings first. When a wagon would go by, she'd

86

stand and shield her eyes, hoping it was Samuel returning for some reason or another. Of course it wasn't. He'd probably reached Lancaster by now. Around midmorning, Hiram passed by in his wagon, headed toward town. The bed of the wagon was filled with hay, and no one rode with him.

Annie weeded until dinnertime. Sophia came into the house to eat, along with Josiah. Dat told Josiah the news from the paper.

"Of course, it's over a week old by now," Sophia said. "Anything could have happened."

"We would have heard if there had been a battle," Dat said. "Samuel delivered cheese to Thaddeus Stevens's tavern yesterday. He said there was no more news than in the paper."

"Is Stevens home?" Josiah asked.

Dat shook his head. "No, Congress is still in session."

Stevens had proven, over and over, to be a good friend to the Plain folk in Lancaster County, along with the freed blacks and the slaves in the South too. The Amish and Mennonites would never forget how their ancestors were persecuted in Switzerland and Germany, and how they were welcomed in America. They felt empathy toward the enslaved and oppressed. In Leviticus, God commanded, "If a stranger sojourn with thee in your land, ye shall not vex him. But the stranger that dwelleth with you shall be unto you as one born among you, and thou shalt love him as thyself."

Annie had heard those verses her whole childhood.

"Mamm," Sophia said. "What news did Mammi and Aenti send?"

"The letter was from George."

"Oh?"

"Jah," Mamm said. "He asked for prayer. Harriet has been ill."

"Goodness," Sophia said. "Who is caring for her?"

Mamm pursed her lips together and then said, after hesitating, "George is doing his best."

Sophia let out a gasp. Annie knew if Sophia wasn't ill, she would go to Peach Bottom and nurse Harriet.

After Dat led the family in a closing prayer, he and Josiah headed out to the field, Sophia returned to her bed, and Annie and Mamm cleaned the dishes.

After they finished, Annie headed out to the spring to fill the buckets to refill the stove reservoir.

As she carried the water back to the house, Hiram Fisher turned his wagon into the Bachmanns' driveway. Oddly, he still had his load of hay.

"Weren't you able to make your delivery?" Annie asked as he set the brake.

He gave her a bewildered look.

"The hay," she said. "I saw you leave with it this morning."

"Ach," he said. "I'm afraid there was a miscommunication. But I stopped by the tavern on the highway to check our mail, hoping for a letter from Richert." He sighed and Annie wondered if he checked often. "We didn't have anything, but your mother did. From her sister, I'm guessing."

Annie put one of the buckets down and took the letter from him, slipping it into her apron pocket. Two letters in one day was unusual.

"Tell your parents hello." Hiram released the brake and continued on his way.

Annie picked up the buckets and headed through the back porch into the kitchen. The breeze had stopped and the day had grown even warmer, but it appeared that Sophia slept soundly. Once she put the buckets down in the kitchen, Annie took the

LESLIE GOULD

letter out of her apron pocket and handed it to Mamm. "This
one is from Aenti Elizabeth."

Mamm quickly wiped her hands on her apron and took the
letter and read it while Annie refilled the reservoir.

Mamm's hand went to her throat.

"What is it?" Annie asked, fearing bad news.

"They're finally going to move down here, to live with us."

Annie smiled. Mamm had been hoping for that for years.
They had plenty of room in their big old house for more.

"And soon. We can expect them by next week." Mamm
seemed filled with relief. "They'll help me care for Sophia and
run the house." She met Annie's eyes. "Which means you can
go to Peach Bottom and nurse Harriet."

Annie didn't respond. She didn't want to leave Sophia, but
it wasn't as if Mamm could go.

Mamm lowered her voice. "Harriet's with child. That's why
she's ill."

"Can't her mother go?" Annie asked.

Mamm shook her head. "You know she's not up to that."
The woman had been beside herself since Cecil ran off to war.
"You can cook and clean and care for Noah, and see what you
can do for Harriet too. It won't be long until Harriet's little
one arrives. . . ."

Tears stabbed at Annie's eyes, but she knew Sophia would
want her to go.

"Don't you see?" Mamm put her hand on Annie's shoulder.
"God's sending your grandmother and aunt to make it possible
for you to help Harriet and George. I'm sure of it."

Annie knew it was the right thing to do—even though she
didn't want to go.

—6—

By Sunday, it seemed the news that Annie would soon travel to Peach Bottom had passed through the entire district. That afternoon, Samuel and Annie sat on the front porch of the Bachmann house while Dat rested just inside the house. The front door was open, so they were well chaperoned.

Samuel said he'd miss her while she was gone. "I'll try not to worry," he added. "But Peach Bottom is so close to Maryland. What if the fighting shifts that way?"

Annie had wondered that too and wished Harriet, George, and Noah could come home, but with Harriet's time so close and George farming, it was impossible.

Samuel seemed deep in thought.

"What is it?" she asked.

"I'm just trying to think who else could go."

"I've already thought through all of that," she said, "and haven't come up with anyone. I won't be gone long."

They were silent for another long moment, and then Samuel changed the topic. "Between what I've saved and what my father has pulled together, we've come up with the money to pay for me not to fight. Mr. Stevens is going to see to the documents."

"*Wunderbar*," she said. "Will he be back from Washington soon?"

Samuel took her hand. "Soon enough, anyway." He gazed into her eyes. "Are you sure you won't be gone long?"

She nodded. "Just a few weeks."

"All right, we'll talk more when you return—about our future." His eyes grew soft. "Write to me when you can. You'll be in my prayers."

"And you in mine." Her heart swelled. Jah, Samuel Yoder was a good man. She looked forward to her return. Surely, they'd talk about a time to marry then.

⟡

Dat drove Annie to the train station in Lancaster City before dawn the next day. However, she wouldn't be taking the train. Instead she would ride with a wagoneer by the name of Woody.

The journey to Peach Bottom was just over twenty miles. They'd coordinated her meeting with the driver to fall close to the arrival of her grandmother and aunt. That way, Dat could shuttle Annie to the Lancaster train station and then the other two home all in one trip. Annie would have to wait an hour or so before the wagoneer would pick up his load—and her.

Dat gave her strict instructions to stay in the station. When they arrived, he parked the wagon and sent Annie inside to find her grandmother and aunt while he watered and fed the horses.

The place buzzed with activity as people rushed both toward and away from the tracks. Whistles blew in the distance, and the steam hissed as the trains approached and left the platforms. Vendors sold fruit, bread, and cheeses. Porters pushed carts loaded with luggage and crates. A few soldiers, along with scores of other people, sat on the benches, waiting for their trains.

Annie spotted her grandmother and aunt, waved, and hurried toward them. They had a cart of baggage and boxes. After they all greeted each other, Annie led the way to the wagon as they followed behind her. Once Annie had retrieved her own bag from the wagon and her father loaded her grandmother and aunt's belongings, she told everyone good-bye.

"Do as I instructed," Dat said to Annie.

She nodded, nervous to travel, especially alone. She'd be sure to be prudent every step of the way.

After she returned to the station, she sat down on a bench to wait. Peach Bottom was in York County on the other side of the Susquehanna River. Thankfully the driver would cross it by ferry and then deliver her straight to George's front door.

She ate some of the food she'd packed. One piece of chicken and one biscuit. She'd save the rest for later. She licked her fingers and then wiped them on the cloth she'd packed.

Once she'd finished, she spent her time watching people until the man next to her left his newspaper as he dashed for his train.

She picked it up and began to read, overcome with concern as she did. A battle had taken place at Brandy Station, Virginia, and the South had won. She read on. It seemed the Confederate Army was still on the march. Some were in Virginia's Shenandoah Valley, others still in Maryland. She couldn't find where any had crossed the border into Pennsylvania. It seemed as if they were spread across a large area, ready to congregate in the same location soon. She hoped it wouldn't be near Peach Bottom.

Another man, most likely younger than twenty, sat down next to her and nodded toward the paper in her hand, to the article about Brandy Station.

"Horrid, isn't it?"

She nodded. "Where do you think they'll attack next?"

"Some say they'll head to Philadelphia. Rumor is Lee will swing all of his boys north once he reaches the Shenandoah."

A shiver ran up Annie's spine.

When a family with several children sat down beside her, Annie rose and gave them her spot, moving to a bench at the edge of the waiting area where she could see the loading docks out of the open doors. A freight train, loaded with lumber, came into the station. Three men, one who was black, approached it, checking the strappings that secured the logs on the train car. The group stepped between two cars and disappeared to the other side. After several minutes, the two white men reappeared, but not the black man. She watched, waiting for him to come back too, but after another fifteen minutes the train rolled out of the station.

There weren't many black people in the station, but now and then a black man or woman would walk by. She knew, from Samuel, that the woman who managed Thaddeus Stevens's properties in Lancaster was a black woman who actually owned property of her own too.

Annie continued to watch the tracks as she waited, thinking of the one trip she'd taken to Philadelphia on the train with Mamm, Dat, Sophia, and Josiah three years ago, soon after George had married and before Sophia fell ill. First, they'd visited their grandmother and aunt in Exton and then traveled on to Philadelphia for the day "just to see the sights," as Dat had said.

Along the way, he'd told Annie about a great-great-great-aunt of his who had been a young woman during the Revolutionary War. He kept his voice low, perhaps because he didn't want

Sophia to hear. At that time Mamm and Dat still hoped that she'd shift her affections away from Richert. "This aunt ended up marrying a Scottish man from Philadelphia, but that's another story. The one I'm thinking of now is that, in the dead of winter, she rescued her injured brother from Valley Forge."

Annie had remembered that story when Sophia fell ill and then again when the war started. Other Bachmanns had faced hard times and hard decisions. It wasn't just her family.

Another freight train full of lumber stopped, and this time five men, three white and two black, began checking the straps. Again they stepped between the cars and disappeared on the other side, and, again, one of the men—a black one—didn't return.

Annie thought of Archer at the Fishers'. She'd heard of Englischers smuggling slaves north, all the way to Canada, but had guessed that had stopped once the war started. But maybe not. However, she didn't know of any Plain people, not even Mennonites, who were involved in the practice. And she doubted the Fishers were. She guessed Hiram had simply been looking for a laborer for the day and had hired Archer.

But she couldn't help but wonder about the two black men who had seemed to disappear on the tracks. Was there some hidden compartment where they'd been squirreled away for a ride to Philadelphia and that much closer to freedom?

⁂

In time, Woody stepped into the station and yelled, "Annie Bachmann!" He was tall and stood with his hat in his hands. His head was completely bald, although he was probably a decade younger than Dat.

The man's name was Mr. Woodson, but everyone called him

Woody, and he sometimes hauled hay for her father, so it wasn't that she didn't know him. But she certainly didn't know him well. Dat trusted him though, and so would she.

She quickly gathered her things and followed him out to the street to his wagon. Annie was happy to see that he had another person riding with him, a woman at least Mamm's age. The man gave Annie a hand up into the wagon; then he put her belongings in the back on top of the cabbages he was hauling.

The morning became warmer as they headed out of town and then traveled south. The older woman, a Mrs. Lacey, was heading to her son's place at Peach Bottom. She talked and talked as they passed by pastures, fields, and woods. Thankfully the road was dry, and because six horses pulled the wagon, they made good time. Even though the ride was bumpy, Annie grew sleepy.

She awoke, realizing that she'd rested her head on the woman's shoulder. Startled, she sat up straight.

"Now, now," the woman said. "You rest your head as much as you would like."

Annie appreciated the woman's maternal kindness but stayed awake after that. She'd never been to Peach Bottom before, and she soaked in the countryside. It was hillier the farther south they traveled, but the land was well cared for and the farms appeared to be fertile. The scent of the cabbages in the wagon bed mixed with onions and grain and mowed hay as they traveled along. A horsefly buzzed around her head, and she swatted it away. Then a pheasant flew up out of a field, startling her.

The woman continued talking.

Soon the conversation shifted to the war. Annie asked Woody if he knew anything about the Battle of Brandy Station in Virginia. He said he hadn't heard about it, but the woman had read yesterday's paper too and spouted what Annie already knew.

Then the woman turned around and looked in the back of the wagon. "What's in the boxes underneath the cabbages?" she asked.

Annie turned too. She'd thought the entire load was cabbages, but sure enough the load had shifted and in a few places pine boxes were visible.

The man didn't answer, and Mrs. Lacey put her hand on one hip, bumping her elbow against Annie. "Well?"

"Sorry," Woody said. "My hearing's not so good." With that he urged the horses to go faster.

Finally, in the late afternoon, the road began heading down the steepest grade so far. Soon the wide river came into view and then the ferry.

Woody pulled back on the reins to slow the horses, much to Annie's relief. The grade was steep and the load heavy, she knew. As they neared the river, the watery, organic scent wafted through the breeze. Woody slowed the horses to a slow walk as they neared the ferry, a flat-bottomed boat that already had an empty wagon on board, with three Union soldiers standing beside it.

"My relatives have been using this ferry for over a hundred and fifty years," Mrs. Lacey said. "The road from Peach Bottom goes on up to York. In times like these, I'm guessing there's a lot of extra traffic going back and forth on it."

Woody didn't respond, and Annie didn't say anything either. She simply kept her eyes on the soldiers below, wondering why they were in the area.

When they reached the ferry station, the operator motioned to Woody to stop. He instructed Mrs. Lacey and Annie to get down, and the operator quickly assisted them and then directed the two to board the boat first and sit on the bench near the front, close to the soldiers.

Annie was thankful to be with Mrs. Lacey and follow her lead. As they sat on the bench, the three soldiers tipped their hats. Mrs. Lacey said hello, but Annie ducked her head, knowing her face was hidden under the brim of her bonnet.

Once the wagon was on the ferry, Woody hopped down and struck up a conversation with the soldiers, although Annie couldn't hear the details.

"I really wonder what he's hauling," Mrs. Lacey whispered to her. "Besides the cabbage. And I don't believe for a minute he hadn't heard about that battle yesterday. I think he's working for the Union."

From the tone in the woman's voice, Annie wondered if perhaps she sympathized with the Confederacy.

Annie glanced at the wagon, although at the moment she couldn't see any of the boxes under the cabbages. There was certainly nothing illegal about hauling supplies for the Union Army, and Annie didn't blame Woody for not talking with the woman about his business.

The boat lurched as the operator pushed a pole in the water to get it started, and then lurched again as the current caught it. The rope running through the ferry guided it along as the operator continued using the pole.

The breeze from the river was cool against Annie's face, and she turned toward the water, raising her head. As she did, she caught one of the soldiers staring at her. She quickly turned away from him and gazed back toward the shore.

When they reached the other side, Mrs. Lacey saw her son and waved a big hello. She then quickly told Annie good-bye, grabbed her bag from the back of the wagon, and hurried off the ferry.

Annie waited on the bench as the soldiers first drove the

Army wagon off the ferry and then Woody followed in his. She then walked off, expecting to climb back in the wagon and quickly complete the journey. She was tired, hungry, and dusty from the trip.

"Wait a minute," Woody said to her. "I'm going to drive the wagon over to that lot and then transfer my cargo into the army wagon."

Annie waited for him to pass, turning her body away from the dust. When it had settled, she followed them to the lot.

It was a bit of a process to transfer the cargo to the army wagon. While the men worked, Annie watched the comings and goings around her. Peach Bottom was an interesting crossroads, with a road passing north and south, and one heading west. The river acted as another passageway. Just a few miles south was the Pennsylvania–Maryland border, which was also the Mason–Dixon Line. It separated the South and North. Slave and free.

Jah, Peach Bottom seemed to be a complicated crossroads. Much more so than the straightforward intersections back home that simply separated one community from another.

"Where are you headed?" the youngest of the soldiers asked Woody.

"Over to George Bachmann's place." He nodded toward Annie. "I need to deliver the girl."

"Is that on our way?" one of the other soldiers asked the first one.

"Not really," he answered. And then he hesitated.

"No, it is," Woody answered. "And I'd be much obliged if you could take her with you. I could cross back over the river and get a head start on my trip back to Lancaster." The ferry hadn't left yet.

Annie stepped back. She didn't feel at ease with Woody, but she felt even less comfortable with the soldiers.

The first soldier approached her. His hair was blond and curly underneath his hat. He spoke quietly, "I'm Private Ira King. I promise we'll get you safely to your brother's house."

Annie glanced at Woody, and he nodded in return. "Go on," he said. "Ira can be trusted. I've known him since he was a boy."

She turned toward Ira King and said, "I'm Annie Bachmann, from Lancaster County."

"Are you Plain?" he asked.

She nodded.

"I live here in Peach Bottom with my mother," he said. "Well, I used to. Before I joined the army."

He told one of the other soldiers to ride in the back with the cabbage, and the third soldier climbed up into the driver's seat while Ira helped Annie up onto the bench, putting her in the middle. Her face grew warm. How she wished she were still riding with Woody instead.

The soldier in the back had moved cabbage off one of the boxes and sat behind them. They passed the post office and then a store. The street led them along several houses. Standing on the porch of the last one was Mrs. Lacey, still holding her bag. She shielded her eyes from the lowering sun and shook her head as they passed by, her lips pursed. Clearly she didn't approve of Annie's ride.

As they left the village, climbing up from the river, the wagon rolled along beside fields of alfalfa and grain.

"Hey, what's in these boxes?" the soldier in the back asked.

"What do you think?" the driver asked.

"Boots, I hope," the young man answered and then laughed.

"Ach," Ira said. "Don't expect anything as fine as that."

"Guns." The driver urged the horses to go faster.

Ira rubbed his chin, but the man in the wagon bed said, "It's about time. It won't be long until we'll be getting back at those Rebs."

Annie's stomach tightened. The southern soldiers were God's children too. She hated to think of them being shot with the rifles that had been delivered to Peach Bottom along with her. Then again, she hated to think of the Union soldiers, including Richert and Cecil, being shot at too.

After a few minutes, the driver said, "Tell us about yourself, little lady."

Annie hesitated, not knowing what to say.

"She's from Lancaster County," Ira answered. "And not used to the likes of us."

Annie was grateful for his words but wasn't sure if she could trust any of the men. She sat up straight, trying to leave as much space between her and the three soldiers as she could.

"We could stop for some fun," the soldier in the bed of the wagon said and then laughed.

Annie froze.

"Not if we're going to get back to camp before nightfall." Ira stared straight ahead.

"Ah, you're such a stick in the mud," the driver said.

"Now's not the time for fun," Ira answered. "Now's the time to get our cargo where it belongs." Annie tensed further at his words. Was he insinuating that if they didn't have a job to do, she would be fair game? The thought made her feel ill.

A young buck bounded across the road, and the man in the back yelled for the driver to stop. He pulled out his gun and shot at the animal, but it escaped.

"Keep your eye out for another one," Ira said. "There are plenty in these parts. Fresh venison would be a real treat."

A few minutes later, Ira directed the driver to turn up a lane. Annie practically held her breath, hoping George's farm was at the end of it.

A white house appeared with a wide porch, and she let out the breath she'd been holding. The farm spread out around the two-story home.

When the wagon stopped, Ira quickly jumped down, helped Annie, and then grabbed her bag from the back.

She took it from him and then, empowered that she was so near George, marched off toward the house without saying good-bye or even thank you.

The driver laughed and the soldier in the back joined in. Annie couldn't tell if Ira did or not.

As she reached the porch, Annie could hear wailing. Her nephew, Noah, she guessed. Annie opened the door and called out, "George? Harriet?"

She stepped into a front room with a couple of chairs and a side table. The wood floors were worn and gray.

The wailing grew louder, and Noah stepped out of a room to the right. But when he saw her he turned and ran back into the room. Annie followed him. Harriet lay on a bed in a house-dress, obviously pregnant and near her time, one arm over her forehead. The little boy leaned against the bed and howled.

"Harriet," Annie said. "I'm here. Where's George?"

"Still out in the field." Harriet's voice was so weak that Annie could barely hear her.

Annie got right to work. First she fed Noah a biscuit and a cup of the soup that was simmering on the stove in the small kitchen in the back of the house. Then she got the boy to bed. When George still hadn't come in, she took a bowl of the soup in to Harriet.

Her sister-in-law sat up in bed and took a few bites. She managed to tell Annie that she'd been ill throughout the entire pregnancy. "But it's getting worse again," she said. "I can barely eat or stay on my feet. George has done all he can, but he has to see to the haying or we'll have nothing to feed the livestock. A farmhand is so hard to come by with the war, so he's mostly been working by himself."

"What about help in the house?" Annie asked.

"I had a girl from town come stay, but she got so lonely she went back home. That's when George wrote to your Mamm. Thankfully, another neighbor has brought a pot of soup over every few days or we'd all be starving."

The conversation shifted to Lancaster County. Harriet said that she'd had a letter from her father, and her mother wasn't doing well. The last letter they'd had from Cecil was months ago.

"My father said he's serving with the 1st Pennsylvania Regiment."

Annie nodded. "Jah, that's what we've been told too."

"Have you heard anything about them? Where they're headed?"

Annie shook her head as footsteps fell through the house. Alarmed, Annie stepped to the door. Thankfully, it was George. He must have finished up his chores by lantern.

"Sister," he said. "You can't know our relief to have help."

As he ate, he said he hated to take Annie away from caring for Sophia, but they were at the end of their rope.

"I'm glad I came," she said. And she meant it. And then she explained that their grandmother and aunt had moved to Lancaster County, so there were plenty of people to care for Sophia.

As soon as he finished eating, he joined Harriet. Annie cleaned up the dishes and then carried the bucket of dirty water out into the side yard. Woods bordered it on the side away from the fields, with a full moon rising over the treetops. Annie dumped the water and put down the buckets, stepping toward the trees to admire the moon as she listened to the chirping of the crickets.

She heard a rustling and then a cry. At first she thought it was a feral cat or some other small animal, and she stepped back. But then another cry came. Sure it was a baby, she stepped forward, saying quietly, "Hallo. Is someone there?"

The baby began to howl, but it was cut short as if someone placed a hand over the baby's mouth.

Annie was at the edge of the woods now, peering into the darkness. She couldn't see anything at first, but then a blanket caught her attention. Then the image of a girl with dark skin, curled around a baby.

The girl looked up as Annie fell to her knees. "What are you doing here?"

"We needed a place to hide," the girl whispered. She spoke with a drawl and obviously wasn't from Pennsylvania. "Can you help us?"

"Jah." Annie glanced toward the house. George and Harriet had enough to worry about, but she couldn't ignore someone in need. "Stay here for a minute. I'll be right back."

She hurried to the rear of the house, expecting there to be a door to the cellar. There was. She opened it and peered down the steps, but it was too dark to see. She hurried into the kitchen, grabbed the lamp, and hurried back into the cellar.

It had river rock walls, and bins of potatoes, apples, and onions were stored in the back. It was chilly but clean enough. She left the lamp and hurried back to the girl, scooping up the baby so the girl could stand.

The baby whimpered but did not cry again. The girl limped as she walked, and Annie extended her free arm. The girl, who was a half head shorter than Annie, grabbed her and held on, as if for dear life.

Annie's heart raced. Encountering Archer at the Fishers' had been the closest she'd ever been to a black person. Now, as she slowed her step and helped the girl along, with the weight of the baby against her, she thought of God's love for all of them. Then she thought of her ancestors fleeing Europe after being persecuted, just as this girl was fleeing the South. But other humans hadn't owned her ancestors, not the way this girl and baby had been owned.

Once she had the two in the cellar, she hurried back into the house and found an extra chamber pot. Then she filled a jar with water and collected a few biscuits and wrapped them in a cloth. She also grabbed a couple of rags Harriet used for Noah's diapers and hurried back to the cellar.

She found the girl nursing the baby, who thankfully seemed to be falling asleep. Annie asked the girl where she'd come from and she simply replied, "South of here."

"Where are you headed?"

"I was told folks up north would help me once I reach Pennsylvania."

"You're in Pennsylvania now," Annie said. "Just over the border."

The girl bowed her head. "Thank the Lord—that slave patrol almost caught me last night. Do you think they'll come after me here?"

Annie didn't know for sure, but she suspected they'd cross the state border without hesitation if it meant catching a slave.

"Do you know who can help me?" The girl grimaced as she spoke.

Annie shook her head. Perhaps if she were back home she

could ask the Fishers. She'd have to ask George, even though she hated to bother him when he was worried about the haying and Harriet and the new baby.

⁂

She broached the topic as she served George breakfast. "Do you ever have anyone slip over the border from Maryland in these parts?"

"Anyone?"

Annie inhaled and then whispered, "Any slaves."

George shook his head. "I don't know anything about that." He stood and said, "I need to get out into the field. Hopefully the midwife will come today and check on Harriet—I sent her a message yesterday."

After Annie had cared for Harriet and Noah, feeding both of them, she slipped down into the cellar with gruel and more biscuits. The girl woke, startled, at Annie's footsteps. The baby stayed asleep, however, and by the light coming down the steps, he seemed rather limp.

"Do you know who can help us?" the girl asked.

"Not yet," Annie answered. "I'm praying for a solution."

"So am I," the girl answered.

"Try to get the little one to drink." Annie wondered if the girl had lost her milk.

"I've been trying," the girl responded.

"What is your name?" Annie asked.

The girl hesitated and then said, "I guess it won't matter if you know. Felicity. And this is Mingo."

Annie introduced herself and then said she'd be back as soon as she could. She spent the rest of the morning doing the wash and hanging it on the line. Later, as she fixed the noon

105

meal, Annie heard the baby in the cellar crying and she began to hum loudly and then broke out into song, hoping to mask the sound. Thankfully, Harriet didn't seem to notice.

In the afternoon, after Annie had served George and he'd returned to the field, a buggy rolled up next to the house. Annie stepped onto the porch and a woman jumped down and tied her horse to the hitching post. She wore a bonnet that nearly concealed her face.

She waved. "I'm Kate Baxter," she called out. "The midwife."

"I'm Annie Bachmann. George's sister."

The woman grabbed a bag and started toward the house, her stride long and confident. "How is Harriet today?"

"Weak," Annie answered.

"Hopefully she's close to delivering." Kate reached the steps and bounded up them. Once she was in the house, she took off her bonnet. She wore a head covering that Annie didn't recognize. She wasn't Amish—but perhaps she was from another Anabaptist group. She appeared to be in her forties. Although she was a country midwife, she spoke and carried herself like a city person.

As Kate spent time with Harriet, Annie put Noah down for his nap. When the midwife came out of Harriet's room, she said, "The baby should be here within a few days. Have George send for me as soon as labor starts. Right now the baby is breech, but hopefully it will turn before delivery."

Annie followed Kate out to the porch. "Why is she so sick?"

Kate shook her head. "I'm not sure, exactly. Some women just are—more during the first few months. Very few are ill this late in the pregnancy, but it's not entirely unheard of."

Annie winced, feeling bad for Harriet. "What should I do once she goes into labor?"

"Try to keep her comfortable. Wipe her face. Help her change positions. Keep her calm. Take care of Noah." Kate tied her bonnet and then patted Annie's shoulder. "You'll do fine."

The woman started down the steps, and Annie thought again of the girl and baby in the cellar. Kate seemed kindhearted. Annie felt a nudge to broach the subject.

"I have another question."

Kate had reached the bottom step. "Yes?"

"I'll follow you to your buggy." As they walked, Annie whispered, "What if a person was to find a girl and a baby from south of here hiding in the trees? Is there anyone who could help?"

"Perhaps so." Kate spoke slowly. "Perhaps one might send a driver with a wagon tonight, after dark, after others are asleep."

"If so," Annie replied, "would that someone be able to get the girl and baby to safety?"

Kate nodded. "If anyone could, it would be this one."

Relief swept through Annie. "I would be awake then, waiting."

Kate turned and met her eyes. "So be it."

Annie hesitated a moment longer and then whispered, "What if the baby wasn't well?"

The midwife exhaled. "Harriet was ready to nap—I can take a quick look."

Annie led the way to the cellar and lifted the door. Kate slipped down the steps quickly while Annie busied herself taking the wash off the line.

"Annie!" George approached from the field. "Has the midwife come?"

"Jah," Annie answered loudly. "She's down in the cellar." Frantically, she searched for a reason. "She's getting a bag of potatoes as payment."

George started to the cellar. "Kate," he called out.

"I'll be right there." A moment later she appeared, a burlap bag in her hand. She spoke to Annie. "I don't need all of these— you take out some for your dinner tonight."

Annie took five out as George asked Kate about Harriet.

"I don't think it will be long." She told him what she'd told Annie about the baby being breech and about fetching her as soon as labor started.

"Denki," George said, tugging on his beard. "How's your boy doing? Didn't he join the Union?"

Kate nodded. "The unit he's with is on the move in this area, so he's home for a few days."

George shook his head. "I'm sorry. I know it must pain you. . . ."

Kate shrugged, appearing not to want to talk about it.

George said good-bye, told Annie he'd work as late as the sun would allow, and then headed back to the field.

Annie quickly put the potatoes down next to the basket, closed the door to the cellar, and turned toward the midwife. "You handled that so well."

The midwife gave her a sly smile and then said, "Come with me to my buggy."

As they walked, she said, "Get some cow's milk and a rag down to the girl. I told her to soak the rag in the milk and to try to get the baby to suck it—or to wring it into his mouth."

"I'll do that," Annie said.

As they reached the buggy, Annie asked, "Are you Plain?"

"Jah," she answered. "Church of the Brethren."

Some called them Dunkards. They were Anabaptists too, although the Brethren believed in a baptism of getting dunked instead of having water poured over the head as the Amish did. They'd originated in Europe and had fled to the New World to avoid persecution, just like the Amish.

Kate had a sad look in her eyes, and Annie wondered what

she really thought of her son serving in the Union Army. She admired the woman though for not criticizing him in front of George. "I'll be seeing you soon," Kate said. "I can tell you have a good head on your shoulders. You did the right thing today, and you'll do fine by Harriet too."

Annie watched the woman go, and then she retrieved a jar of milk from the spring. She worked quickly to get a cup of milk and a rag down to the woman. By the time she'd finished, Noah was awake and he played outside while she finished taking the wash off the line. It was hot and muggy, and soon sweat dripped down the back of her legs and the side of her face. She was thankful it was cool in the cellar for Felicity and Mingo.

She continued with her duties throughout the late afternoon, sweeping, mopping, fixing supper, feeding Harriet and Noah, and then putting the boy to bed. George came in and she served him. It seemed he sat at the table forever as she washed the dishes. Finally, he joined his wife.

Annie finished cleaning up and then waited and waited.

Suddenly, she heard a whistle and she slipped out the back door with a lamp. The whistle sounded again, this time from the edge of the woods. A man stepped out of the trees. He wore a Union uniform but that was all she could make out in the dark.

Annie hesitated.

The man nodded at her and then toward the cellar.

"Who are you?" she whispered, stepping forward.

"The less you know the better," the man replied as he lifted the cellar door. Annie couldn't see his face under the shadow of the brim of his hat, but his voice was familiar. "Now hurry. I passed a wagon on the road with two strangers who seemed to be intent on finding something—or someone. The sooner I leave with your cargo, the better."

— 7 —

Marie

When I stepped from my bed the next morning and my feet landed on the floor, the first thing I thought of was Annie. Not because of the cold wood beneath my feet that sent icy stabs up my legs. I knew how hot June in Pennsylvania could be and imagined Annie sweating as she cooked, cleaned, and did the wash, all the while worried about the girl and the baby in the cellar of her brother's house.

No, I thought of Annie because she was away from home. I certainly wasn't facing any hardship, as Annie had, but I did have a trip ahead of me. By tomorrow, I'd be a thousand miles from home. And, unlike Annie, I wasn't the bravest girl in the world. I tried to fight off my rising anxiety.

I fished my slippers out from underneath my bed, slipped them on, and then shuffled to the closet to collect my clothes. How shallow was I that I'd compare my vacation in Florida to Annie's trial in Peach Bottom? She was caring for a sister-in-law who was soon to deliver. And faced with saving the life of a runaway slave. I, on the other hand, had been gifted four weeks in a tropical climate, in close proximity to Elijah Jacobs. I shook my head at myself as I headed down the hall to the shower. Jah, I was nervous about leaving home.

A half hour later, pulling my thick shawl around me, I headed downstairs and found Mamm already in the kitchen.

I stepped to the living room window. More snow had fallen, and in the dim morning light I could make out Milton shoveling the front walk.

Gordon was probably in the barn, helping Arden finish up the milking. I doubted I'd see him before I left, although Aenti Suz and I wouldn't catch the bus for Florida until noon.

Aenti Suz didn't come for breakfast, and I guessed she'd slept in. After we ate and I'd cleaned up, I scrubbed down the cabinets and then began sweeping the floors. Mamm had retreated into her sewing room to quilt. I hoped to have the house in tip-top shape so Mamm would have less to do while I was gone.

When I reached her sewing room, the broom in my hand, she glanced up from her quilt frame. "Mind if I sweep in here?" I asked.

"Not at all." She bent back over the quilt and stabbed her needle into the fabric.

I kept sweeping, and then once I finished, I mopped too. When I was done, I hauled the bucket out through the back porch, thinking of Sophia all those years ago, in her daybed, fighting consumption in the very same place. The rock fireplace from the original cabin was still there, along with the logs, which were still painted white. In fact, I'd applied another coat of paint last year, before Dat fell ill.

As I stepped onto the top stair to the backyard, the bucket

in my hands, I heard a car out front. We certainly didn't expect anyone. I flung the water into the flowerbed. It didn't freeze in midair, as I'd heard of happening before, but by the time it landed on top of the snow it was a sheet of ice.

I put the bucket away in the broom closet in the kitchen and then headed to the living room to see who had arrived. Leisel, Jessica, and Silas were all climbing out of an old sedan. I waited until they were on the front porch to open the door. "What are you doing here?" I asked Leisel, a little miffed. Why had she decided to come when I was leaving?

"I'm so glad you're happy to see me." She grinned. "So nice to have a warm welcome on such an icy day."

I couldn't help but laugh at her sarcasm.

She wore a long down coat, blue jeans, leather boots, and a beanie on her head, with her blond hair sticking out the back in a ponytail. My little sister was certainly no longer Amish. She looked more Englisch than most Englisch girls around here, but perhaps that was from living in the city for the last nine months.

Silas walked beside Jessica, his hand on her elbow as if he was afraid she might fall. Leisel pulled me into a hug.

Mamm called out, "Who's here?"

"Come look," I called back. "And hurry."

As Leisel let me go, I asked, "Why did you come on the day that we're leaving?"

"I finally got a couple days off," she answered. "I left as soon as they let me leave work—around five this morning. I drove straight to Jessica's."

Mamm was in the entryway now. "Leisel, is that you?"

"Jah, Mamm." She let go of me and stepped forward, wrapping her arms around our mother. Perhaps she'd forgotten how resistant Mamm was to affection. Nevertheless, Mamm hugged her back.

Once we were all inside, I stoked the fire again and then said I'd make hot chocolate. "We have to leave in an hour," I said. "We have a driver coming."

"No," Leisel said. "I'll drive you. Silas and Jessica will stay here with Mamm."

"We already arranged for the driver," I said. We had a local man who we used regularly.

"I already called him and canceled." Leisel grinned.

"Will there be enough room?" I asked. "For us and our luggage?"

"Of course," Leisel answered.

Silas headed out the back door and fetched Aenti Suz, bringing her luggage along too. I made the hot chocolate and put out bread, meat, cheese, and leftover apple pie from the day before for a light meal. We all gathered around the table.

Leisel kept us entertained with stories about her work. She worked in a nursing home and seemed to have a true affection for the clients. I couldn't imagine putting a loved one in a home like that, but I knew the Englisch did things differently than we did.

I asked her how her fall semester had gone.

"It was hard," she said. "But I arranged for a tutor to help me with chemistry. This coming semester, I'm taking anatomy, so I've already lined up a tutor for that too."

"How were your grades last term?" I asked.

She blushed.

"What? Straight As?"

She blushed even more. It was nice to know that she wasn't going to brag about it.

I changed the subject. "How long are you staying?"

"Just until tomorrow morning," she answered. "I need to get back. But I couldn't bear going so long without seeing my family." Her eyes teared up. "I've missed all of you."

Jessica stood and wrapped an arm around Leisel. "We've all missed you too."

As Jessica sat back down, I tried to imagine Leisel's life. She lived in a dormitory, went to school, worked, and owned and drove a car. It was a life I would never know—and would never want to know.

When it came time to leave, Silas loaded our luggage into Leisel's car, and then I told Mamm and Jessica and Silas good-bye. I climbed into the back seat and let Aenti Suz have the front. Leisel told Mamm she'd be back soon and then turned the key in the ignition. But nothing happened.

"Uh-oh," Leisel said. "I think I need a jump."

"A j-jump?" I stammered.

"Yeah. It's probably the battery."

"Do we have time for that?"

Leisel didn't respond. She rolled down her window and asked Jessica if there was a portable battery charger around.

Jessica shook her head and then turned to Silas. "Go get Gordon."

⁂

In the end, it was decided Gordon would drive us in case something else was wrong with Leisel's car, besides the battery.

Silas and Gordon transferred the luggage, and then Leisel said she'd ride along so she could see me for a while longer. She climbed into the passenger seat while Aenti Suz and I climbed into the back.

114

I expected Jessica to take a look at Leisel's car to see if she could figure out what was wrong, but she headed into the house, with Silas close behind her. Mamm stayed and waved at us as Gordon headed toward the highway.

His car was as freezing as ever, and Leisel joked that it was even colder than hers. She and Gordon seemed to have an easy rapport, even though it was the first time they'd met, as Gordon came to work for us after Leisel had left.

She yawned a couple of times, and Gordon told her they could stop for a cup of coffee on the way home.

"I'll just wait until I get back to Mamm's," she said. "I can't afford any of that fancy stuff."

He gave her an admiring look, hopefully for her frugality, and then concentrated on passing the truck ahead of us. Gordon asked Leisel about nursing school and then told her about his sister studying political science in Philly. Jah, they all lived in a world I knew nothing about.

The departure destination was the Lancaster Mall, on the Lititz Highway. When we arrived, passengers were already boarding the big, shiny silver bus. Gordon parked in front of a craft store and pulled our luggage from the back. Together, we all carried it to the bus. Aenti Suz pulled our tickets from her purse while I hugged Leisel good-bye. "Come see me in Pittsburgh when you get back," she said. I nearly laughed at her invitation. Both of us knew I'd never do that.

When I told Gordon good-bye, he grinned and replied, "See you soon."

"What?!" Leisel exclaimed.

Still grinning, Gordon told Leisel about his upcoming trip to Florida.

"I want to go," she teased.

I envied how comfortable she seemed with Gordon. But she didn't have to worry about flirting with him the way I did. She could actually date him if she wanted. My stomach fell at the thought, but I chided myself. Gordon would actually be a good match for Leisel.

I followed Aenti Suz onto the bus, surprised at how big and comfortable it appeared, plus the seats were large and plush.

As we made our way toward the back, a man said, "Suzanne Bachmann?"

I hardly ever heard anyone call her more than "Suz."

She stopped and said, "Oh, goodness. David Herschberger. How are you?"

"Just fine." He had a tidy white beard, bright blue eyes, and laugh lines all around his mouth. "It's been a long time."

"It certainly has."

He pointed to the two seats across the aisle. "Why not sit here? We can catch up."

Aenti Suz glanced at me. I nodded in agreement, although I feared David, whoever he was, would keep her from telling me more of Annie's story, which I longed to hear. Who had come to take Felicity and Mingo away?

Once everyone had boarded, the bus driver turned out of the parking lot and headed toward the highway. Soon we were on our way. Snow carpeted the landscape, but the roads were clear.

David turned out to be a real talker, but he also seemed kind and caring. I listened as the two chatted, and what I gathered was that they'd known each other back when they were both Youngie, and I surmised that David had been sweet on Aenti Suz, perhaps, but she hadn't returned his feelings. He lived in Chester County but had cousins who lived not far from us.

In time, he'd married and had six children, all long grown,

and now fourteen grandchildren. Sadly, his wife had died three years before.

"I went to Pinecraft for the first time last year," he said. "I wasn't interested, but my kids paid my way. I was surprised by how much I liked it. So much so that this year I'm paying my own way."

I couldn't see his face, but I knew he was smiling, and I imagined his blue eyes sparkled.

He asked Aenti Suz about herself, and she explained that she'd been living on her family farm all these years.

She patted my knee. "Thankfully I have two nephews, three nieces, and great-nieces and nephews who have made my life full."

He cleared his throat a little before asking, "So you never married then?"

"Jah," she answered. "That's right."

He didn't say anything for a long moment, and I wondered what was behind the long pause, but then he said, "I always liked your brother, Gus. How is he doing?"

As Aenti Suz told him about Dat's death, I closed my eyes and tuned out their conversation, overcome with grief. Perhaps remembering Dat's harmonica playing while at the shelter the other night had stirred up something in me. I didn't want to sing or hum in such close quarters, but music started inside my head anyway. Dat's harmonica music. And a silly song he'd made up. C, *a cat, a curious cat. D, a dog, a doting dog. E, an elephant, who charged into our song! F, a frog, a great green frog. G, a goat, a goofy goat. A, an ant from in the barn. And B, a bull! Run, run, run, run!* Dat started out every music session with the "Cat, Dog, Elephant" song. Next he would have me sing it alone without the music. Then he would ask me to sing

Cat and then *Dog* and then *Elephant*. And then *Frog*, *Goat*, *Ant*, and *Bull* too. Over and over. Sometimes Leisel would join in on the fun, but she seldom replicated the notes. Dat never praised me or criticized Leisel. Sometimes he would smile, but never at me more than her. It was my favorite time of the day and far more enjoyable than school or the wash or cooking or anything else that I did.

Mamm had already forbidden me from singing in the house, so my time in the barn with Dat was my only chance except on Sunday in church. But then the tempo was so slow and many of the voices so off-key that it was a distraction for me and not nearly as enjoyable as the time in the barn.

The last time we sang together, after I'd sung the "Cat, Dog, Elephant" song several times and practiced hitting each note several times, Dat started playing "Amazing Grace." *"Amazing grace, how sweet the sound . . ."* I sang. And danced, just a little. Leisel ran circles around me. I couldn't remember where Jessica was, perhaps cleaning out the milk vat.

We'd been having our music time in the barn probably since I was five. By that time, I was nine, nearly ten.

"That saved a wretch like me. I once was lost, but now am found, Was blind, but now I see."

The music stopped, but I kept singing. "'Twas grace that taught my heart to fear—"

"Gus, what is going on out here?"

I turned slowly. Mamm stood in the doorway of the barn, her arms across her chest and her mouth turned down.

"Now, Bethel," Dat said. "Everything is all right."

"Clearly it's not." She turned toward me. "Marie, you go on into the house and set the table. Leisel, you go with her and help."

118

We did as we were told. After supper, while I did the dishes with Mamm, she told me I'd be doing the cooking the next evening while she sewed. When we went to bed that night, after Leisel had fallen asleep, I asked Jessica what Mamm had said to Dat after she sent me to the house.

"Nothing," Jessica answered. "She just took Dat's harmonica and put it in her apron pocket." Jessica told me not to worry about it. "Nothing will change. He'll get it back."

But as far as I knew, he never did. I never heard him play after that, nor did I ever even see his harmonica again. There were no more sessions in the barn, and I cooked supper every single night after that.

As it turned out, I became Mamm's helper with all of the household chores. A few times, she talked about her childhood and how privileged I was. She was the youngest of seventeen children, and by the time she was grown her mother had died and her father was frail. She and her Dat lived in the Dawdi Haus on one of her brother's farms, and then she took the job at the bakery where she met Dat.

"Your father was more than I ever dreamed of," she said. "I pray God will bless all of you girls with such good husbands."

I knew she loved him, but she never seemed particularly warm to him or cared about his interests. She simply went about her work, not interacting with him much. He was so full of life and interests. I guessed his intellectual needs were met by the work he did researching supplements and recommending them to others, and on the different farming techniques he was always implementing. He traveled too and served, such as in Haiti after the earthquake. I knew he found all of that fulfilling. Not that he didn't love our Mamm—I know he did. What Aenti Suz shared about Mamm changing after Rebecca's death actually made a lot of sense. Fear had changed her after they'd been married for some time.

Jah, I spent most of my time with Mamm, but losing Dat had shaken my world. He was the one who'd truly made music come alive for me. Although, it had only made it harder in the long run.

Still, I missed him every day.

With David across the aisle, Aenti Suz didn't tell me any more of Annie's story. I slept as much as I could, and as we continued through the night, Aenti Suz and David finally slept too.

The next morning, we crossed the border from Georgia to Florida. Pinecraft was located on the western side of the state, on the Gulf of Mexico, midway down. I'd heard that Pinecraft had started out as a tourist camp nearly a hundred years ago, with over four hundred camping sites, a park, and a community building. Starting in the 1940s, the sites were gradually replaced with homes and developed into a residential neighborhood.

Nearly twenty hours after we left Lancaster, we arrived in the parking lot of the Tourist Mennonite Church. It was a plain, one-story white building with an aluminum roof.

I held my coat in my arms as I followed Aenti Suz off the bus. The air was warm and humid and felt wonderful.

Several people on big tricycles, a funny sight because in Lancaster we didn't even ride bicycles, waited to greet us. There were also several golf carts, some of which were quite large. David and Aenti Suz started toward the bags that the driver was pulling out of the luggage compartment of the bus, and I stumbled after them.

"We'll get a cart for the three of us," David said. "I know where your cottage is; it's not far from where I'm staying."

A few minutes later, we were all on a golf cart driven by a

young Mennonite man from Ohio, our luggage stacked behind us. On either side of the street were rows of white bungalows, all quite small. Some had picket fences around them, and all had some sort of front yard that was very tiny. David chatted away with the driver. "Would you tell us what the Youngie do around here?" David asked. "Marie needs to know." He shot me a smile, his eyes dancing. I wondered if he hoped to get rid of me so he could spend more time with Aenti Suz.

"Oh, there's lots to do," the driver said. "Volleyball. Cook-outs. Games in the park. Gospel singings."

"Sounds like back home," David said.

"Jah," the young man said. "But a whole lot warmer. And more fun too."

Everyone laughed, even me. *Gospel singings* sounded especially appealing.

Aenti Suz asked if the young man knew Elijah Jacobs.

"I do," he answered. "I think everyone knows him."

I hoped that was a good thing. We rolled along in the cart, past palm trees and bushes and flowers I couldn't identify. A car passed us, and then a Plain man with three boys, all riding regular bicycles, pedaled by. Then we passed two Englisch girls wearing crop tops and shorts. I had to remind myself it was January. It felt like July.

When we reached our bungalow on Gardenia Street, David helped us carry our luggage to the door and then pointed up the street. "I'm just a few houses from here. I'll come by and check on you tomorrow, after you've had a chance to rest up and settle in."

Aenti Suz thanked him.

Before I could ask her more about David, a Mennonite woman approached with a pie in her hands. "Welcome to Pinecraft," she called out. "I'm your landlady. You're going to love it here!"

– 8 –

The bungalow was about the size of our back porch, but it had everything we needed. Two bedrooms, a living room, a bathroom, and a kitchen—all in miniature. The walls and woodwork were all painted white. Sunlight shone through the windows and onto the wood floors. The living room furniture was beige and the kitchen table and four chairs were all white. The place couldn't have been cheerier, including the itty-bitty backyard with a patio, a table and chairs, a couple of trees, and pots of tropical flowers I'd never seen before.

The next morning, Aenti Suz and I ventured outside to the patio to eat our breakfast. Thankfully, Aenti Suz had sent a shopping list to our landlady, who had stocked the refrigerator—run on electricity, of course. We also had electric lights and air conditioning. Jah, Florida was very different than back home. No wonder Elijah liked it here.

"Hallo!"

I shaded my eyes and looked toward the fence.

David stood on the other side, beaming at Aenti Suz. "Did you get a good rest?"

Aenti Suz nodded. "Why don't you join us?"

David came through the gate. "I already had breakfast, but I'll have a cup of coffee."

I stood as he sat. "I'll get it."

As I returned with the coffee, David was asking Aenti Suz if we would like to go to the beach.

She glanced at me with a questioning look on her face.

"Sure," I answered.

"It's less than two miles," he said. "There's a bus we can take—we'll be there in no time."

After we'd finished our breakfast, David went home to get his things while we cleaned up. Aenti Suz found two folding chairs and two big towels in the closet. "For the beach," she said, holding everything up for me to see. Then she packed a bag with sunscreen, books, water bottles, and snacks.

When David arrived to collect us, Aenti Suz asked him about a nearby bakery.

"There are a couple." After a little bit of discussion, Aenti Suz guessed Elijah worked at one closer to the beach.

"Let's stop by and say hello," she said. That surprised me. Aenti Suz hadn't been very warm to Elijah. Perhaps she'd changed her mind.

We rode the bus for a short ways and then got off near a fancy grocery store.

"The bakery is in here," David said.

We traipsed through the store to the back with all of our stuff. When we reached the bakery, Elijah was working the counter, joking with an Englisch woman. He wore a red apron over what looked like jeans and a button-up white shirt. His hair had grown out since the bowl cut he wore when he was home, and his face lit up when he saw me. After he'd placed the woman's order in a paper bag and thanked her, he said, "Hey, Marie. When did you arrive?"

"Yesterday," I answered.

"And now you're off to the beach?"

I nodded.

"I get off at noon," he said. "How about if I meet you there?"

I turned toward Aenti Suz.

She smiled. "We'd like that." She quickly introduced David to Elijah, and then the two chatted for a moment about which beach we were going to. When they'd finished, I told Elijah good-bye. On our way to the door, I picked up several post-cards, paid for them, and then joined Aenti Suz and David outside.

"We can walk from here," David said. "It's only a couple of blocks."

As we headed toward the beach, I noticed a man, probably about my age, digging in a garbage can. I tried not to stare, but I couldn't help but wonder what his story was. I assumed he was homeless and thought of the shelter back in Lancaster.

But as soon as I saw the Gulf, I forgot the young man. I'd never seen so much water at once, and the sight of it took my breath away. It wasn't as blue as I'd imagined but instead a frothy green. I breathed in the salty air and couldn't help but smile as I gazed over the water. It appeared infinite from where I stood, although there were a couple of islands between the beach and the horizon.

"Those are keys," David explained, pointing. "That's Siesta Key and then Lido Key. They both have incredible beaches."

Considering it was a Wednesday, there were a lot of people at the beach. Some walked along the water's edge. Others sat in chairs. There were volleyball courts, and a young man and a young woman, both in shorts, were bumping a ball back and forth.

I had shorts on underneath my dress, but I didn't plan for anyone else to know that.

We unfolded our chairs, and then David rolled up the legs of his pants. We all kicked off our flip-flops, and I paused for a moment while Aenti Suz headed toward the water with David. The warm sand felt so soothing between my toes that I felt as if I didn't want to move. I dug in deeper, closed my eyes, and tilted my face toward the sun.

"Marie!" Aenti Suz called out. "If you think that feels good, come into the water!"

I opened my eyes.

She gestured for me to join her. I walked slowly, from the loose sand to the hard, cooler sand, and then into the water. The warm waves lapped against my ankles, and I stepped in deeper, joining David and Aenti Suz.

She squealed and grabbed my arm as a higher wave rolled in. "This is wonderful!"

We held up our skirts and walked out farther. David said he should have worn his shorts, and I almost laughed, thinking of a sixty-something-year-old Amish man in shorts. But then I noticed two men with full Amish beards coming out of the water, soaking wet, wearing T-shirts and shorts.

We spent the next couple of hours on the beach, and just when I began to wonder if Elijah would show up at all, he called out my name.

I turned my head toward him. He wore shorts and a T-shirt too, and carried a volleyball under his arm, along with a towel. After greeting Elijah, Aenti Suz and David said they were going for a walk.

Elijah and I bumped the ball back and forth for a while, and then he said he was going for a swim.

Once he was in up to his chest, he yelled, "Come in!"

I waded in to my knees, holding my dress up, but didn't want to go any farther.

"Look at them." He gestured toward a group of girls in the water about fifty yards away. Some wore shorts. Some wore one-piece swimsuits. One wore shorts with a bikini top. One was in a dress but nevertheless in the water. "They're all Plain, either Mennonite or Amish."

I put one hand on my hip, holding my skirt with the other. "You're kidding."

He laughed and pointed to another group of young people. "You can tell the Englisch girls. They're the ones with hardly anything on."

My face grew even warmer than it already was from the heat of the day. I turned away from watching them, but I didn't go in any farther. After a while, Elijah joined me in the shallow water. The warm waves against my legs felt good and being with Elijah felt even better.

When Aenti Suz and David returned from their walk, she said they planned to return to the bungalows. "You can stay here with Elijah," she said. "Although you'll want to get something to eat."

"I need to get lunch too," Elijah said. "We can eat and then come back. Later in the afternoon, a group of friends are coming to play volleyball." He turned to Aenti Suz. "I'll get her home by eight or so. Does that sound all right?"

"Perfect," she said.

I wondered again at Aenti Suz warming toward Elijah. Perhaps she wanted to have more time with David and figured having me spend time with Elijah was her best hope of it.

I'd never known Aenti Suz to return any man's interest though. David seemed like a nice person, but I was still surprised she actually wanted to hang out with him.

❊

Elijah definitely knew his way around the area. We ate at a place not far from the beach, and then headed back to the sand. By then there was a group gathered around one of the volleyball courts. Elijah served the ball he'd been carrying high into the air, landing it in the middle of the group. Another young man, who wore shorts and no shirt, grabbed it and served it back to Elijah, but I stepped forward and bumped it back to the group.

"Who's with you?" one of the girls asked as we approached.

"This is Marie," Elijah answered. "She's from back home."

The guy who had served the ball turned to me and said, "You can be on my team."

I smiled but didn't answer. Elijah quickly introduced me around, first to Billy, who had just subtly complimented my volleyball skills, and then to Paula, who'd asked who I was.

Billy was from Lancaster County, from a district near ours. I hadn't met him before, but we knew many of the same people, besides Elijah. And I remembered Elijah mentioning him when he was home.

Soon we were playing a game, with me on the other side of the net from Elijah, playing next to Paula. She wore shorts, modest by Englisch standards, and a tank top, which I guessed was probably modest to some too.

I asked where she was from.

"Here," she said.

"You live in Pinecraft year round?"

She nodded. "My parents manage several properties. We've lived here since I was eight."

I tried to hide the shock in my voice. "You're Amish?"

She shook her head. "Mennonite."

Most likely from a pretty liberal group.

Elijah had just served a ball. I set it, straight up, and then stepped aside. Paula spiked it over the net. She was nearly as tall as I was and a good athlete.

The other team bungled the play, and it was our serve.

"Where are you from originally?" I asked as we took our positions.

"Ohio. Holmes County."

"Do you get back often?"

Paula laughed as the volleyball sailed over the net. "Not if I can help it. Most of our relatives come down at some point in the winter, thankfully, so we don't have much of a reason to go back."

That sounded sad to me. "You don't want to go back home?"

"It's not home anymore. Pinecraft is." She practically sang the words.

That was hard to imagine.

I enjoyed playing with the others and watching Elijah. He was well liked, that was certain. He and Billy teased each other in a good-natured way.

After several games, Elijah grabbed the ball and held it on his hip. "Anyone hungry? We can cook burgers at our place."

Everyone seemed to think that was a great idea. Elijah turned toward Billy and asked if we could ride with him.

"Sure," he said.

Paula grabbed the volleyball. "Me too!"

After I retrieved my chair and bag, we all headed to the parking lot, to Billy's tiny car with only two doors. After putting our things in the trunk, Paula and I wiggled into the backseat. The floor was covered with fast food bags, and I did my best to find a place for my feet. Paula caught my eyes and rolled hers. We both laughed.

It only took a few minutes to reach Elijah and Billy's house. It was also a bungalow with a patio in the back. The house was a mess—there were dirty plates and glasses in the living room, and the carpet needed to be vacuumed.

"Who all lives here?" I asked.

"Billy and me," Elijah answered. "And two other guys."

"Really?" I glanced down the hall.

"The other two guys share a room," Elijah answered, heading toward the kitchen. "And Billy sleeps on the couch."

I guessed that would make rent a lot cheaper.

"Hey, Billy, turn on the grill!" Elijah called out.

I picked up two dirty plates in the living room.

"You shouldn't bother," Paula said.

"I can't help myself," I replied. "How can they live this way?"

"Oh, this isn't bad." Paula flipped her long hair over her shoulder and rolled her eyes again. "I think they actually cleaned up. You should see it most of the time."

I wondered how often Paula came over. In the kitchen, I helped Elijah slice an onion and tomato.

"We have chips too," he said, holding up an opened bag.

"Great," I answered, wondering what Aenti Suz was having for supper.

Soon the others from the volleyball game arrived, and Elijah put the frozen burgers on the grill while Billy dug a stack of paper plates out of the cupboard.

No one led us in a prayer before we ate, but I paused and

said one anyway. The burgers were overcooked and the chips were a little stale, but it was a fine meal anyway.

After we'd finished eating, Elijah said, "We should take you home."

"I'll clean up first," I said. "It will only take a minute."

"If you insist," Elijah joked, but he ended up helping.

"It's nice to have a woman's sight in here," he said, as I scrubbed the counter. "I know we let things go more than we should."

I bit my tongue from agreeing with him. Instead I simply gave him a sweet smile and batted my eyes, which made him laugh.

We all traipsed out to Billy's car, and Elijah was yawning by the time we reached the bungalow where Aenti Suz and I were staying. "It's time for bed," he said. "I need to get up at 3:30."

Elijah walked me to the door. "I'll see you tomorrow after work."

I juggled my chair and towel. "I'm not sure what we're doing."

"Stop by the bakery and let me know." He grinned. "I'd really like to spend as much time as possible with you while you're here."

He'd said that before, but my heart still fluttered as I told him good-bye.

When I stepped into the living room, I could hear voices in the kitchen.

"Hallo," I called out.

"Marie," Aenti Suz answered. "We're back here."

She and David were washing dishes, and the pie our landlady had delivered the day before sat on the counter.

Aenti Suz asked me how the rest of the day had gone, and I told her what all we had done. I left out how messy Elijah's apartment was and that no one had led us in prayer before the meal.

After David dried the last dish, he said it was time for him to go.

"What about a piece of pie?" Aenti Suz asked.

"Could I take a rain check?" he asked.

"You'll be taking your chances," Aenti Suz teased. "It might all be gone."

He patted his belly, which was pretty small compared with a lot of men his age, and said it was a chance he was willing to take.

As Aenti Suz walked him to the door, he asked, "Is it all right if I come back tomorrow morning?"

"Of course," she said. "In fact, come for breakfast."

As the door closed behind him, Aenti Suz turned toward me. "Isn't it wonderful to be here? In such a beautiful location and in the warmth of God's amazing sun—in January."

I nodded, thinking of my previous self-righteous opinions about Pinecraft. I felt a little guilty at how much I was already enjoying it.

"I'm looking forward to church and the singings for the entire community." I'd heard that musical instruments were used at the singings.

"They definitely do things differently here." Aenti Suz turned her head upward to the overhead light in the kitchen. "We should enjoy the warmth and rest while we can."

That made me think of Dat's cancer and how hard that time had been for our family. Honestly, we were all still grieving him. Jah, I would enjoy this time of rest and relaxation.

That made me think of Annie and her family and all the hardship they faced. They had no hope of rest and relaxation, of escaping to a place like Pinecraft. There was no way for them to avoid the war that was coming their way.

"Could you tell me more of Annie's story tonight?"

"Good idea." She hung up her towel. "Where were we?"

"A man had arrived late at night to take the slave girl and baby. His voice was familiar to Annie, but she didn't know who he was, and she didn't know if she should trust him or not."

"That's right." Aenti Suz turned toward the coffee pot. "Now, you cut the pie while I make a pot of decaf. Then I'll tell you what I can before bedtime."

-9-

Annie

"Who are you?" Annie asked again.

Felicity groaned and tightened her arms around Mingo. "It doesn't matter who he is." She stepped ahead of Annie and to the soldier's side. "Let's get going."

The man tipped his hat at Annie, and she could see it was Ira King, from the day before. "Thank you, ma'am," he whispered to Felicity, but the grin on his face indicated that he recognized Annie too.

"We need to hurry." He put his arm around Felicity and helped her walk faster.

"Wait." Annie hurried after them, remembering the crude talk of the soldiers the day before. "Where are you taking her?"

Ira kept walking, but over his shoulder he whispered, "Trust me, I can't tell you that. I know this area well."

"Maybe you're taking her to the other soldiers. Or . . ." Her voice trailed off.

Ira stopped and Annie bumped into him. "What are you talking about?"

She swallowed nervously. "The soldier in the back of the wagon insinuated . . ."

Ira shook his head. "I won't take this young woman anywhere near him or anyone like him."

Annie's stomach lurched. Ira defused the situation yesterday, but he hadn't stood up for her.

The baby fussed. "Come on." Felicity tugged on Ira's sleeve, and they continued on.

As the trio disappeared into the trees, Annie followed behind, listening. The baby wailed, and then a deep baritone voice, singing a song she'd never heard before, began. She listened carefully and could make out a few words. "Seeing Nellie home, In the sky the bright stars glittered, On the bank the pale moon shone . . ."

But then the voice of another man called out, "Whatcha got, Ira?"

"Shh," Ira said. "Where'd you come from?"

"I've been following you."

"Well," Ira said, "what I've got is none of your business."

"How about the bounty catcher down the road? We could make some money."

"We'll see," Ira said. "Right now I'm going to take them to Peach Bottom. You can ride along, or walk if you can't keep your mouth shut."

Annie's heart sank. She hesitated for a moment and marched through the forest after them, but by the time she reached the road the wagon was on its way.

If she yelled, she might wake up George and Harriet. She didn't care. "Ira King!"

He waved his hand in the air. The other soldier, who also sat on the bench, laughed. Annie sank to her knees in the middle of the road. Had she just endangered Felicity and her baby? Or even sent them back into slavery?

Her heart raced. Finally, she rose and said a prayer and then turned back toward the house. As she climbed the stairs of the porch, the creak of the rocking chair startled her. George wore his dressing gown.

"Is it Harriet?" Annie asked. "Has her time come?"

"No," George said. "Voices woke me."

"Goodness," she said. "I must have heard the same. I went to investigate . . ."

He gave a puzzled look. "Why are you still dressed?"

"Oh, I didn't realize how late it had gotten. I was just getting ready for bed." She yawned and quickly headed into the house.

The next morning, when George came in with the milk, he said, "We'll have an extra person for breakfast."

"Oh?" she asked.

"He's hitching his horses. We're going to talk business."

Annie finished up the corn cakes and sausage and turned to place the food on the table as a soldier came through the back door, taking off his hat. She froze.

"This is Ira King," George said. "Kate's boy."

As the man smiled, his blue eyes twinkled.

"Pleased to meet you." Annie placed the two platters on the table, not bothering to explain to George that she already knew Ira, but she could hardly believe that he was Kate's son. "I'll go look in on Noah and Harriet while you two talk." Why hadn't Kate told her whom she would send?

When she came back with Noah propped on her hip ten

minutes later, the two were negotiating the price of a few loads of hay. She wondered if it was for Kate's horses or for the army.

Annie continued to hold Noah as she ladled porridge into a bowl for him. He reached up and placed his sticky hand against her face as she did. She'd grown quite fond of the boy, and he'd warmed to her too.

"The teamsters will be by," Ira said. "In a day or two."

"I'll have the load ready." George stood and put Noah in his chair. "So, tell me what all you're doing for this army that's headed our way?"

"A variety of things," Ira said. "But because I know farmers in these parts, I'm helping round up supplies at the moment."

"So it's true then? The army is headed this way?"

"I can't really say." Ira's face reddened. "Although I imagine it's pretty clear what's going on."

"I read that Lee is headed north," George said. "I'm guessing Meade is marching toward him."

When Ira didn't answer, George sighed. "It must take a lot to feed an army of men and horses."

"Yes, sir," Ira said.

George leaned forward. "And you don't have any qualms about being a part of all of it?"

Ira countered with, "Do you have any qualms about selling to the army?"

George smiled a little. "That's one way to look at it. But I'd rather sell to you than have the Rebels come through and take it."

Annie shuddered as she put the spoon in Noah's hand. Harriet had told Annie stories of southern soldiers wiping out entire farms in Maryland. Livestock. Food in the cellar. Bags of grain. Coops full of chickens. And leaving families with nothing to get them through another year. But even though they were on the border, Annie still didn't believe the Rebels would cross into Pennsylvania.

"Well, you don't want the Rebs to take it," Ira said, "and I don't want any being to starve, man or horse. So I guess we're in this together." He grinned.

George shook his head. "We still have a fair amount of potatoes—white and sweet—in the cellar, along with onions, turnips, and parsnips. And I have a cow that's gone dry that I can sell too."

"Much obliged," Ira said. He began writing with a pencil on a piece of paper in front of him.

When he stopped, George said, "Is your Mamm doing all right on her own?"

Ira nodded. "She keeps busy with her midwifery."

George stood and said, "Annie, go down to the cellar and fill two burlap bags with potatoes. I'll get the cow." He turned toward Ira. "Come on out with me."

By the time Annie cleaned up Noah and they headed to the cellar, the men were in the pasture.

She quickly bagged the potatoes, with Noah's help. The men returned with the cow and then retrieved the bags from the cellar, carrying them to Ira's wagon. Annie guessed it was the same one he'd been driving the night before.

Noah began to fuss, and she picked him up as the men came up the steps with the last of the potatoes. George led the way, and as Ira passed by, he met her eyes. The deepness of his dark pupils startled her. "Your cargo is safe," he whispered.

She didn't answer. She had no reason to trust Ira King, but she did trust God. And in the moment, she hoped she could trust Ira too. He was either sincere or the biggest fraud she'd ever met.

The day grew hotter and muggier. Annie spent the afternoon mopping Harriet's sweaty body with a cool rag. The woman was miserable from the heat and was hardly eating. Annie forced her to drink water and then some tea.

By the time Annie should have been fixing supper, it seemed Harriet's contractions had started.

"Go get George," Harriet said. "Send him after Miss Kate."

Since Annie didn't want to leave Noah unattended in the house, she hoisted him on her hip and hurried down the back steps. Dark clouds gathered on the horizon. She lowered Noah over the rail fence and then climbed over herself into the pasture. They hurried across to the fields. Along with alfalfa, George grew wheat, barley, and oats. She didn't see how he could keep working so hard, all alone, without ruining his health.

He was on the far end of the field, turning the hay. Annie hoped that the gathering clouds didn't mean a heavy rain was coming that would damage the crop.

She yelled and waved, but he didn't hear her. She picked up Noah and began running through the field, over the cut hay that quickly worked its way into her boots, gouging her skin. She yelled again, and finally he saw her.

"Harriet said to fetch the midwife."

"Is she sure?" he asked.

"Jah," Annie yelled back.

"All right." But he didn't stop turning the hay.

"George," Annie called out. "Kate said to get her right away." Annie didn't want to deliver the baby by herself.

He looked up. "I'll get going in a minute. It took a couple

of days with Noah, and I've delivered enough calves to know this isn't going to happen in an hour."

Annie wanted to remind him that Kate might not be at her house, she might be checking on a patient or at a birth, but she doubted it would do any good. George probably thought he could easily get in another hour or two of work.

By the time they climbed the fence back to the yard, Annie could hear Harriet's screams. She wished she'd left Noah with George, but it was too late to take him back now.

"Ma Ma." The boy pointed to the house.

"Jah, your Mamm will be all right," Annie said. "I'll help her while you eat your supper." Then she would put Noah to bed and hope George returned with the midwife soon.

Harriet writhed on the bed, and Annie remembered what the midwife said about finding a different position. "George is going after Kate. Let's get you up."

Harriet had been in bed so long that she was unstable. Now being in labor added to her weakness.

"No," Harriet moaned. "I feel as if I'm dying. This is so much worse than with Noah."

Annie grabbed the cloth in the basin of water and sponged Harriet's face and then her arms. She hadn't dressed at all that day and still wore her nightgown.

Harriet allowed Annie to help her stand. And she even took a few steps, but then she hung onto the footboard of the bed and wouldn't move.

Annie slipped out and fed Noah a cold supper and then put him to bed, praying as she did that he'd have a baby sister or brother by morning.

When she returned to Harriet and George's room, her sister-in-law was back on the bed with her eyes closed.

Hoping she was asleep, Annie went back to the kitchen and quickly mixed up biscuits. George and Kate would need to eat something when they arrived, but Harriet's screams forced Annie back to the bedroom. She whispered a prayer that George and Kate would return soon. The last thing she wanted was to deliver a baby.

"Help me into a better position," Harriet said.

Annie did as she asked, helping her sister-in-law scoot forward on the bed to her knees, and then Annie climbed onto the bed beside her.

Harriet gasped. "I think the baby is coming."

"No," Annie said. "Not yet . . ." Annie especially didn't want to deliver a baby that was breech. She'd heard whispers of such things between her Mamm and Eva back home. One woman in their district had lost a baby a few years ago who had been breech.

Harriet started to groan. "You'll have to catch it," she gasped.

Annie had seen cows give birth, but never a woman.

Harriet lifted her nightgown to her hips and then groaned again. The baby's foot extended down and Annie grabbed it.

On the next push, Annie pulled. After a few more tense pushes, the rest of the baby slipped out all the way. It was another boy, and at first he didn't make any noise, but as Annie held him, she rubbed his chest. Finally, he sputtered and began to cry. Annie cut the umbilical cord and wrapped him in the bed cover, whispering a praise of thanks. The birth had gone much better than what she'd feared.

Harriet began to shake though, and Annie, with one hand, started to pull the quilt at the bottom of the bed on top of her, but as she did, her sister-in-law began to bleed. It seemed like a lot. Alarmed, Annie tucked the baby beside Harriet and hurried to the chest at the end of the bed for blankets or rags or something to stop the bleeding.

⁂

A half hour later, nothing had changed. Annie remembered that the cows delivered the placenta too and wondered if that was what was causing the bleeding. She regretted not going after Kate and having George attend his wife, but it was too late now.

"What do you remember about the placenta?" Annie asked Harriet.

"It came out quickly last time," she said. "But Kate massaged my belly to help it."

Annie began doing that, keeping an eye on the baby. He was small but alert. His eyes reacted to Harriet's voice, and he seemed to be breathing all right.

Harriet grimaced.

"Does it hurt?" Annie asked.

"Jah, but keep doing it."

Finally, the placenta delivered, and although the bleeding slowed, it didn't stop. Annie got fresh water from the spring and began cleaning Harriet up as best she could, packing a blanket between her legs to hopefully help stop the blood. Harriet closed her eyes, but Annie told her not to sleep. She was afraid she might die if she did.

Night fell, and as Annie lit the lamp, she prayed, asking God to save Harriet.

Annie took the baby and cleaned him up and then put a cloth on his bottom and wrapped him tightly in a blanket she found in the chest. She stood in the lamplight, talking to Harriet as she nursed the baby, when the front door flew open.

141

"Sorry it took so long," George called out as he rushed into the room. He froze and then managed to say, "Oh."

Kate was right behind him. "Is everything all right?" she asked. "The baby? Harriet?"

"I think the baby is fine," Annie answered. "But Harriet is bleeding. It slowed some when she delivered the placenta, but it hasn't stopped. I don't know if it's normal or not."

"George, you take the baby to Harriet. Annie, make a tea . . ." Kate was digging in her bag as she spoke. She handed Annie a jar with dried herbs in it. "A quarter cup in hot water, in a pot. Let it steep for forty minutes." She turned toward Harriet. "You need to stay awake. That's your only job right now."

Annie filled the kettle and then put the herb in the teapot. When the water started to boil, George came out of the bedroom.

After Annie poured the water, she said, "There are biscuits here and leftover stew."

He thanked her as she dished the rest of the stew on the back of the stove into a bowl for him.

As Annie handed him the food, she asked, "Was Kate off on another call?"

George shook his head. "I was delayed by a group of Confederate soldiers."

Annie's heart skipped a beat. "What's going on?"

"They were headed north, it seems to York."

"And then what?"

George shrugged. "Ira was still at Kate's house. I let him know, and he left immediately to warn his commander."

Annie shivered even though it was so hot. Confederates in Pennsylvania. Had the war come this close to home? Did that put Felicity in danger? Annie knew that Confederates would sell any blacks they came across, whether they were free or not. Felicity and Mingo wouldn't have a chance.

When enough time had passed, she poured a cup of the tea and headed into the bedroom.

Kate took it from her. "Thank you—would you pick up the baby?"

Annie took the little one from Harriet's side.

Kate handed the tea to Harriet. "Drink all of it."

Annie stepped back with the baby and asked Kate what the herb was.

"Witch hazel."

Annie made a mental note of what Kate had said. The baby began to fuss, and she started swaying back and forth as she'd seen mothers do.

"Has the bleeding stopped?" she asked Kate.

The midwife shook her head. "But it's slowed."

The baby began to fuss again.

"He needs to nurse," Kate said.

"I can't," Harriet muttered over the rim of the mug.

"Finish the tea," Kate said. "Then you'll be able to."

The little boy fussed more and Annie sat on the edge of the bed and put the tip of her little finger in his mouth. He sucked hungrily.

"He's healthy and alert," Kate said as she felt Harriet's forehead. "Thanks be to God for that."

Annie nodded in agreement.

Harriet took the last sip of tea and then Kate reached for the baby. He wailed as he left Annie's arms. A few minutes later, he was nursing, and although Harriet still seemed miserable and in pain, she stroked the little one's head.

Everyone knew how dangerous childbirth could be and that

many mothers died during childbirth or from bleeding or from childbed fever. So many babies died too.

Annie silently prayed that both Harriet and the baby would survive and that Harriet would regain her strength.

George slept in Noah's room that night, while Kate and Annie continued to care for Harriet and the baby. The bleeding continued, but Harriet slept some while Annie held the baby boy.

"Do you think she has childbed fever?" Annie whispered to Kate.

The woman shook her head. "She isn't running a fever. But she may have torn inside."

Shame rose in Annie. "Was it because of something I did?"

"Oh, goodness, no." Kate put her arm around Annie. "You did a fine job, with this and the other task God gave you too." She gave her a knowing look with her deep blue eyes.

Kate certainly trusted her son. Annie simply nodded, hoping Ira was what he seemed.

– 10 –

George was up early the next morning to finish getting the hay ready for the Union soldiers. Annie feared a battle might take place nearby with both Rebels and Union soldiers in the area, but George reassured her the number of Confederates he'd run into was small. Probably a scouting party.

Annie asked if they'd named the baby.

"No. We will after I'm done with the hay." He grabbed another biscuit and headed out the door.

Annie fed Noah and then took bowls of corn mush to Kate and Harriet. The baby was nursing, and Harriet seemed better. In the morning light, she was pale, but she didn't appear deathly so as she had the night before.

Kate announced that the bleeding had slowed more and Harriet was on her way to recovery. "I'll be back this evening to check on her," she said.

Annie retreated to the end of the bed. "I hope you can get some sleep."

"I will, eventually." Kate grabbed her bag and took out more of the witch hazel. "Give her the tea every four hours."

Annie said she would, suppressing a yawn. She'd dozed some, but she hadn't really slept, although she had slept more than Kate.

"Make sure the baby nurses regularly. Wake him up if you have to. And make Harriet nurse him, no matter how she feels."

Annie assured her she would, but she feared she didn't feel as confident as she sounded.

Late in the afternoon, three unfamiliar Union soldiers driving three large wagons rolled past the house toward the barn.

A few minutes later, one of them knocked on the door asking for George.

"He's out working in the field."

"We need the hay."

"He has it ready, I'm sure." At least Annie hoped he did. She knew the payment would help the family.

She and Noah stood on the side of the porch and watched as George drove another wagon full of hay to the side of the barn. He already had a stack waiting. Annie went back into the house to fix their supper, but every fifteen minutes or so, she and Noah would check on the men's progress. George worked with the soldiers to transfer all of the hay to their wagons and then accepted a stack of bills. He shook the oldest man's hand, and then the soldiers drove off in their wagons.

Annie fed Noah and then Harriet. Her sister-in-law ate more than she had since Annie arrived, and then nursed the baby.

As dusk fell, George came into the house, exhausted. He went straight to Harriet, and Annie couldn't help but overhear him apologize to her.

"No," she said. "You had to do it. It would have been foolish not to fill the order. And you accomplished it. That's what matters."

George thanked her and then said, "The soldiers said they think there's going to be a battle soon."

Harriet's voice was full of alarm. "Near here?"

"No, they said the Confederates are headed for York. But they're not sure that's where the battle will be. Both sides are moving thousands of troops."

"We're lucky the Confederates you saw didn't come here."

"Jah," George said. "I'm afraid they would have cleaned us out."

Annie's heart skipped a beat.

"I'll stay close to the house tomorrow," George said.

Annie knew it wouldn't do any good. He wouldn't use violence against anyone, no matter what they tried to take or do. And it wouldn't matter if he did, not if it was one against many.

Her brother's voice fell as he talked with Harriet, and Annie, embarrassed that she'd been eavesdropping, turned her attention to dishing up the baked sweet potato and ham that she'd made for her brother's supper. When she was done, she walked out to the front porch, hoping for a breath of fresh air.

That's where George found her when he came out carrying the baby.

"Annie," he said. "Meet Nathaniel Bachmann."

She patted the baby's head and cooed. "I'm pleased to meet you, Nathaniel."

George appeared exhausted but happy. "Harriet told me what good care you took of her and the baby. She said you're gifted at caring for others and you could easily be a midwife someday, if you wanted to."

Annie wasn't used to any sort of praise and simply said she was relieved that Harriet and Nathaniel were all right. The truth was, she couldn't imagine being a midwife. Thankfully the delivery had been fairly easy. Even though it had been a breech and Harriet had bled so badly, Annie hadn't had to make any difficult decisions.

Kate arrived as the two talked, and George handed the baby to Annie and went out to feed and water Kate's horse. As Kate reached the porch, she handed Annie a letter that she'd picked up in town.

Annie led the way into the house, the baby in one arm, and sat down at the kitchen table. The letter was from Samuel.

Dear Annie,

Please come home. You need to be with your parents and closer to me at this time, not in the pathway of the Confederates. I've spoken with your father, and he agrees with me.

Samuel

She reread his words and then counted them. Thirty-seven. He'd communicated no concern for Harriet. Or George or Noah. Or the new baby. And no question as to what Annie wanted to do.

On the other hand, she knew his heart was good. He wanted her safe. But could any of them truly be safe in times like these?

She folded the letter and slipped it into her apron pocket, not intending to tell Harriet or George about it. She wouldn't hold the letter against Samuel—she knew his intentions were good—but she wouldn't respond right away either. She couldn't leave Peach Bottom now, not when her sister-in-law still needed her.

Kate came out of Harriet's room and took the baby from Annie. As she examined him, Annie made a cup of tea for the woman and buttered a slice of bread.

As she checked Nathaniel's umbilical cord stump, Kate asked who the letter was from.

"A . . . friend. Back home."

"A young man?"

Annie nodded.

"Was it a good letter?"

Annie shook her head. "He thinks I should go home."

Kate met Annie's eyes. "I take it you don't want to."

"Not yet," Annie answered.

"Perhaps he's used to people doing what he wants."

Annie shook her head. "I think he's just worried, is all."

Kate smiled. "That's good. Some men think a woman should fall in line with their thinking, no matter what. I've been married twice. The first wanted more than anything for me to use the gifts God had given me, which was caring for others. I blossomed, but then he died. The second man I married put me to work behind the counter of his store. I thought I was going to die from boredom." She grimaced. "As much as I hated his store and at times thought I'd made a mistake in marrying him, I didn't want him to die. But he did anyway. I sold the store as soon as I could and began working as a midwife."

Annie gave her a questioning look, not sure what Kate was telling her.

"Being a wife is fine. In fact, I highly recommend it. Just choose carefully. You don't want a husband who doesn't see you for who you are and doesn't acknowledge your gifts and desires."

Kate obviously didn't know Samuel, but before Annie could say anything, the midwife handed the baby back and took a bite of the bread.

Annie decided against saying anything. There wasn't any need to, but Samuel wasn't trying to keep her from doing anything. He was just concerned about her safety. Besides, Annie didn't have any gifts, especially not medical.

Over the next week, Annie cared for Harriet, giving her the tea from Kate and making sure she ate. The baby seemed strong and had a hearty cry. Annie also cooked and cleaned and watched over Noah too. Mamm had trained her well to run a household, and although it wasn't always easy, she was certainly able to do the work. Day by day, Harriet regained her strength until she finally left her bed and said she felt better than she had in months. Kate checked on her one more time, stopping by late in the evening on the last day of June, and declared she was pleased with Harriet's progress.

Annie served Kate a plate of leftovers from dinner, and after the woman said a silent prayer, George asked how Ira was doing.

Kate picked up the piece of bread and said, "He headed west with his regiment."

"Did he have any new information about the Confederates in the area before he left?"

Kate took a bite and then leaned back in her chair, as if deciding what to say. After she swallowed, she spoke. "I've heard from a reliable source that the Confederates have taken York."

Annie gasped.

"And two days ago the Union burned the railroad bridge across the river, from Wrightsville to Columbia, to keep the Confederates from being able to go to Lancaster."

"Oh, thank the Lord," Harriet said.

"How many were injured in York?" George asked.

"Funny thing, the mayor gave up the town to prevent any damage. Instead of putting up a fight, they paid the Confederates not to attack."

Annie stifled another gasp.

"It was a wise thing to do," Kate explained. "They would have taken it anyway—there wasn't enough of a Union presence in the town to make any difference. However, there was a battle, a small one, at Hanover today. The Confederates sacked the train station and destroyed the telegraph wires."

George shook his head. Annie was sure he believed Kate, so she decided he must have been disgusted by what the Confederates had done.

"What now?" Annie managed to ask.

"We wait and see," Kate said. "But most likely the battle will be west of here. There are rumors that it will happen in Gettysburg."

Annie had heard of the town but of course had never been there. She said a silent prayer for the safety of the Union troops and for the civilians in that area.

"Is Ira headed there?" George asked.

Kate shrugged. "He said he didn't know where he was going."

"I wonder where Cecil is." Harriet put her hands to her face, clearly upset.

"We must all be brave," Kate said. "War has come to our land. We must trust the Lord to protect those we love."

Everyone murmured in agreement. Annie thought of Cecil, Richert, and Ira. She felt clammy even though the day was hot and humid.

"Oh," Kate said, reaching into her pocket. "I have another letter for you, Annie."

She handed it across the table. Annie expected another missive from Samuel, but it was from Sophia. She slipped it into her pocket to read later.

It wasn't until after Kate had left and Noah was down for the night that Annie sat on the back steps to read the letter by the light of the fading sun.

Dear Annie,

We were so happy to hear of Nathaniel's birth and that Harriet is recovering.

I have been feeling well and am hoping this is the miracle we've been praying for. Surely God will heal me and bring Richert home too.

I am doing so much better that I believe you shouldn't come home anytime soon (unless you wish to). Please continue to care for Harriet and Noah and the baby. With Mammi and Aenti here, we are all doing fine.

Please do pray for Richert, and if by chance you hear of his unit traveling through the area, would you please let me know?

Your loving sister,
Sophia

Annie couldn't help but guess that Samuel had told Sophia what he'd written in his letter. Sophia instructing Annie to stay was her way of contradicting him in a subtle manner.

Annie stood and went back into the house to clean the dishes. She'd write Sophia back when she could, and of course she'd let her know if she found out anything about Richert's unit. She just couldn't imagine why in the world she would.

It turned out that Kate was right about the site of the battle. The next afternoon, on July 1, a day that was even hotter, a neighbor stopped by to see if they'd heard the news. George was in the field, and Annie and Harriet both assured the neighbor they'd heard nothing since the day before.

"There's a big battle going on at Gettysburg. And the Rebs are winning."

A soft moan escaped from Harriet's lips, and Annie immediately felt ill. What would happen if the Confederacy won a battle in Pennsylvania? Would they take control of the state?

Harriet sat down on the front steps and then said to Annie, "Go tell George. He's in the far field. Ask him to come to the house."

As Harriet continued to speak with the neighbor, Annie hurried out the back door, the hot afternoon sun beating down on her. It took a bit to reach him, and by the time she did, sweat ran down the back of her legs and the sides of her face.

He worked his scythe on the top of the bluff, and in the distance she could see the wide river, making its way toward Maryland.

He glanced up from his work, an expression of fear on his face. "Is Harriet all right?"

"Jah," she answered, "but there's bad news about the war." She told him what the neighbor had said. "Harriet wants you to come to the house."

He shrugged. "There's nothing I can do. Tell her I'll be in for supper soon enough. We'll talk then."

He bent his head down and kept working.

"George," Annie said. "Your wife needs you."

"Jah," he said. "But she's going to need food too. If I don't get this work done, we'll have no feed for the animals. Tell her there's nothing any of us can do. I'll come in when the sun sets." He bent down and started working again.

Annie wasn't sure how he persevered in the heat and humidity, but it took a lot to make a living from the land. Farmers didn't get to take any time off.

Not even when war came close to home.

Annie couldn't hear what Harriet said to George that night, but she knew her sister-in-law was frantic about Cecil. Perhaps those who went off to war never considered what it might mean to actually go into battle—and how those left behind would fret and worry.

The next morning, July 2, dawned humid too. Annie thought of the soldiers on the battlefield, including Ira, and said a prayer for all of them, North and South. As the sun grew higher and hotter through the morning, she prayed over and over.

She thought of her ancestors coming to America, long before it was the United States, for religious freedom. That freedom had always been harder to come by in times of war. The Amish had been left to worship as they pleased during peacetime, but during war they were expected to serve or pay a tax or a fee for someone else to serve for them. But she guessed that some in the past had gone against their faith and chosen to fight, for one reason or another. She couldn't help but wonder if they'd regretted it later.

The day seemed to drag on forever, and no neighbor stopped by with any word. When George was done with his work, Harriet asked him to ride down to the ferry and see what news he could hear.

"It won't matter," he said. "We won't have news about Cecil."

"But it will help me to know if the battle has turned." Harriet held the baby closer. "If the North has the upper hand now."

"Ach, Harriet," George said. "It's war. It's not our business. We must leave it to the Lord."

"Please." Harriet blinked away her tears.

"All right," he finally said.

An hour later he came back and said that from what he'd heard, the South still had the advantage.

Harriet moaned when he told her.

"We'll keep praying," George said. "Now let's get some rest."

They were soon quiet in their room. As Annie finished cleaning, she wondered if George regretted selling the hay to the Union soldiers. As she went to bed and prayed herself to sleep, she begged God to spare Richert, Cecil, and—after a moment of hesitation—Ira, too.

The following day was hot and humid too, and as Annie hung the wash, she stopped every few minutes to wipe the sweat from her forehead with her apron. She thought of Ira in his wool uniform. She'd been critical of his fighting when he was—or had been—a Brethren, but then it dawned on her that perhaps Kate couldn't pay the fee to keep him from fighting. She wouldn't make much as a midwife. Ira's father had died and then so had Kate's second husband. Annie shivered. Perhaps he'd been forced to fight against his will.

Harriet helped get dinner on the table, but after the meal was over and George went back to the fields, she retreated to her room with the baby. Noah played on the floor with his blocks, and then Annie put him down for a nap. Soon after, a neighbor stopped by with a letter for Annie—another one from Samuel. Instead of opening it, she asked the neighbor if there was any news about the battle.

He nodded. "I heard at the post office that the Rebs were still winning last night. It could all be settled today. Maybe even by now."

The next day would be the Fourth of July. The Amish didn't celebrate Independence Day, but the Englisch did. It could be that those who felt sympathetic toward the South, as Mrs. Lacey had seemed to, would have something to celebrate. But there would be many who would mourn.

At least the bridge had been burned across the Susquehanna

and Lee's army couldn't head toward Lancaster. Then again, the Union wouldn't be able to use the railroad to retreat or transport their soldiers either. Annie shivered at the thought of how many wounded there might be on both sides after three days of fighting.

She felt as if she were holding her breath, waiting to know how everything turned out, and not just for the soldiers on the battlefield but for all of them. What would Robert E. Lee command his army to do if they won? Would they head for Washington? Or return to Richmond?

There was nothing she could do but pray.

Finally, she opened the letter from Samuel. It reiterated what he'd said before.

Considering you haven't replied to my first letter, I'm hoping you didn't receive it. I'll repeat what I said. Come home as soon as possible. These are dire times, and you should be back in the safety of your community.

I await your return,

Samuel

She wiped her face with her apron. No doubt she would be home soon, but it wouldn't be because of Samuel's demands. She slipped the letter into her pocket. She wouldn't write him back. They could talk everything through in person.

That evening when George came in from the field, Harriet asked him to go down to the ferry again, but he said he was too tired. Just as Harriet started to protest, they heard a horse and buggy outside.

Harriet moved toward the door. She left it open as she stepped onto the porch. "It's Kate," she called out.

George sighed and followed Harriet out while Annie stayed in the house with the children. After a few moments, all three came up the steps.

"Kate has news," Harriet said as they came through the door.

"I wanted to tell all of you at once." Kate looked as if she hadn't slept in days. "I just came from town. The battle is over, and the Union has won."

Annie's hand went to her chest, and Harriet gasped in relief.

"The losses on both sides are horrendous. Thousands have died and thousands more have been wounded. The North has sent out a request for help—and a messenger from Hanover came with a request, specifically for me. An old friend, a Dr. Carson, has a house in Gettysburg and has asked me to come work with him and bring anyone I can to help."

"Why are you telling us?" George asked. "None of us have that sort of experience."

"Annie does." Kate turned toward her. "You proved that in how well you've cared for Harriet."

Annie took a step backward as her stomach dropped. Why in the world would Kate think she was capable of nursing injured soldiers?

"Taking care of a mother and baby is nothing like nursing those wounded in battle," George said. "Besides, they wouldn't want her. She's just a girl."

"No, they're asking for people with any experience to help. Soldiers will die who could be saved if we don't rally and come to their aid." Kate blew out her breath. "We've been praying. Now we can do something. Please allow Annie to go with me."

"Absolutely not," George said.

Annie remembered her night of prayer for the soldiers. For Richert. And Cecil. And Ira. She turned toward her brother. "I want to go," she said.

He crossed his arms and shook his head. "No. I forbid it."

−11−

Marie

The next morning, as I made my bed, I thought of Annie. At seventeen, she was four years younger than I was now. I'd always considered myself capable, but compared to her, I wasn't. It wasn't that she was fearless, but her actions and convictions both showed a courage I didn't possess. I admired her for not giving in to Samuel, although I understood why he wanted her home.

Thankfully, I'd have no such problems with Elijah. Samuel seemed pretty uptight, while Elijah was as easygoing as could be. *Easy*. I appreciated that about Elijah. It was natural, *easy*, for me to be interested in him. Marrying him and living on a farm not far from the original Bachmann farm the rest of my life would be easy too.

No doubt Annie ended up going back to Lancaster County to marry Samuel. That would make the most sense. But would she go to Gettysburg first, as she hoped? Jah, I admired Annie but was thankful I'd never face the challenges she did.

David came for breakfast, and the three of us ate dippy eggs, bacon, and toast out on the patio. David identified an eastern meadowlark perched in a type of myrtle tree at the edge of the property. Everything was so different from what I was used to.

After we'd cleaned up, the three of us took a walk through the neighborhood. David pointed out the Amish church just down the street from us, a stone building with white trim and wide double doors, flanked by palm trees.

"That's where we'll go on Sunday," Aenti Suz said to me. I'd never, in my entire life, been to a church service that wasn't held in someone's home—or barn or shed. I could see why they needed a church in Pinecraft though. None of the houses were big enough to hold church, and with no outbuildings, there was no other option than a church.

We headed to the park after that. The large oaks, with Spanish moss hanging from their branches, caught my attention, and I couldn't help but think of our oak tree back home, currently covered in ice. A picnic shelter, a playground, and a shuffleboard court also caught my eye. We walked along Phillipi Creek, which bordered the park. It was big enough for canoes, and apparently alligators and sharks at high tide too, according to David. Although he added that he'd only heard that and had never witnessed it himself.

I took a step away from the water, not sure if he was serious or not.

From there, David pointed out Big Olaf's Creamery, which had a huge cone at the entrance. "We'll have to get an ice cream there later," he said. "It's made a couple of miles from here by an Amish man."

"Named Olaf?" I asked.

159

David chuckled and answered no. Aenti Suz and I laughed. None of us had ever heard of anyone Amish named Olaf.

Even though it was only nine in the morning, sweat was running down the back of my legs. But after the icy weather back home, I would rather be too hot than too cold.

After we'd finished our tour of Pinecraft, David and Aenti Suz decided they'd take the bus to Siesta Key for the day and invited me to come along.

"Denki," I said, "but I told Elijah I'd stop by his work and hang out with him."

"Can you get there by yourself, by bus?" Aenti Suz asked.

I nodded. "I paid close attention yesterday."

She turned toward David. "Is it safe?"

"Oh, jah," he said. "She'll have no problems." He turned toward me. "Ask anyone if you need help."

I thought of the homeless man near the beach. Helping people in a shelter in Lancaster was one thing, but encountering them on the streets here seemed unsettling. But I would trust David that I'd be safe.

After Aenti Suz left, I sat at the table on the patio and wrote postcards to Mamm, Jessica, and Leisel. And one to my friend Gail in Ohio too. She and I both used to wonder why people wasted their money coming to Pinecraft, so I downplayed how wonderful it was, simply explaining that Mamm had sent me along with Aenti Suz, implying she needed a companion, which wasn't quite accurate. Especially since she'd run into David.

I introduced the *idea* of Elijah Jacobs, writing that he'd been home around Christmas, that I'd spent some time with him, and that I was enjoying getting to know him as an adult. *He's changed*, I wrote. *He's not the clownish boy he was when we were in school. It seems everyone grows up sooner or later.* I'd never even confessed my crush on Elijah to Gail when we'd been scholars. She would have been mortified. I added, *Interestingly enough, he plans to move home in the spring and eventually take over his father's farm* just for good measure. I didn't want her to be shocked when I wrote to her to say that Elijah and I were courting.

After I finished writing the postcards, I walked down to the post office, bought stamps, and then sent them on their way. After I was done, I read the notices posted on the bulletin board. There was one for a Haiti fundraiser in a couple of weeks. One for a family reunion in the park. Several for properties available to rent in February. And then a notice for an upcoming potluck in the park and then a singing on Thursday of the week after next, also in the park. I'd look forward to that—especially the instruments that I knew would be included. I'd enjoyed singing to Gordon's guitar music so much that I was eager to experience that again.

Back at the cottage, I took out my embroidery, worked on a kitchen towel until lunchtime, and then fixed myself a sandwich. After I ate, I smeared on sunscreen, filled my water bottle, grabbed a blanket and beach bag, and headed to the bus stop. I'd sounded so sure when I told Aenti Suz I wouldn't have a problem taking the bus, but now I felt anxious about it. What if the right bus didn't come? What if it didn't stop where I expected?

Thankfully there were several other people at the stop.

"Marie!"

I squinted and saw Paula. I waved, relieved to see a familiar face. She wore black shorts, a pink T-shirt, a floppy hat, and sunglasses. She looked like one of those movie stars on the front of a magazine at the supermarket.

In no time, she was by my side. "Are you going to the beach?"

"After I meet Elijah. He gets off work soon."

"Fun! Billy will be there too. I'll get off with you at the bakery and then walk with you and Elijah."

"Denki," I answered. "I was a little nervous about taking the bus by myself."

She smiled and patted my shoulder. "I'm glad you came along. My younger sister was going to, but she got grounded for not helping me clean out a bungalow this morning."

"Uh-oh," I said.

"Yeah, well, you know how little sisters can be."

I nodded in agreement, but I really didn't. Leisel was the most responsible person I knew, next to Jessica.

The bus arrived, and I followed Paula onto it. We chatted about our families as the bus made its way down the street. Mine was complicated compared to hers. She had two sisters and a brother. She was the oldest, and her parents were both in their early forties. They ran the property management company together—her mother booked the rentals and cleaned, along with her daughters, while her father did all of the repairs on the properties and accounting for the business. Paula's two youngest siblings attended a high school in the area.

"A public one?" I asked.

She nodded. "My sister, who is just younger than me, and I went there too. It's not too bad."

I doubted that. "Did you wear a cape dress and Kapp?"

She glanced down at her shorts. "No, I wore skirts, mostly. And no Kapp." She smiled at me. "That's what I love about Pinecraft. Anything goes."

"What about your Mamm? What does she wear?"

"A cape dress and Kapp." She laughed. "Although not a heart-shaped one like yours."

"Of course," I said, and then wondered if she was teasing me. My Kapp identified me as being an Amish woman from Lancaster County. Any Anabaptist person in the U.S., maybe even in the world, would be able to identify me. I knew I wasn't supposed to be proud—not about anything. So I wouldn't be. But I was very pleased to wear my Kapp.

I liked the idea of belonging, which made me wonder how Paula tolerated her teenage years. "Didn't you feel like an outsider in public school?"

"Not at all," she answered. "I actually have quite a few friends from high school. People I still keep in touch with"—she held up her phone—"through social media. I hung out with a group of other Christians, some Mennonites. No one harassed us for our beliefs. In fact, there was a group of us in choir who got along really well. We took a trip to Nashville, Tennessee, my senior year. It was amazing."

Of course that piqued my interest.

She held up her phone. "We have a couple of videos online." She pressed a couple of different things and a group of Englisch young people all dressed in black, dresses for the girls and suits for the boys, appeared on the screen. She pressed an arrow and the video clip started.

"Do you know 'Swing Low, Sweet Chariot'?" Paula asked.

I shook my head.

"It's an old African-American spiritual," she explained.

Mesmerized, I watched the choir as they swayed and clapped and sang their hearts out. My heart swelled with emotion. "These are all teenagers?"

She nodded. "It was the pinnacle of my high school experience. It was a festival with students from all over the United States."

I had no idea that sort of thing went on. Without realizing it, I started to hum along to the music. Even though we were on the bus, Paula began to sing. The words were so easy that I joined in. On the last " . . . coming for to carry me home!" I realized that several people were staring at us. Embarrassed, I ducked my head.

"Your voice is beautiful," Paula said.

I shook my head.

"Oh, I know you're supposed to be modest and all of that, and you should be. But it's all right to acknowledge that you can sing."

I didn't answer her, and thankfully the bus slowed.

Paula grabbed her bag and said, "Here's our stop."

She stood and led the way to the door, with me following, thinking about her phone and wondering what other music was on it. I'd never been interested in cell phones before, but now I was. I thought of the songs Dat and I used to sing together, including the silly "Cat, Dog, Elephant" song. What if he hadn't made it up? What if there was some video of someone singing it?

As I stepped off the bus, Elijah greeted me with a grin. "I got off early," he said, "so I decided to wait here."

The three of us started toward the beach. I didn't see the homeless man I'd seen before, but I noticed two girls who looked like they were in their teens sitting on a curb, sharing a bag of chips.

After we'd passed them, I asked if there were a lot of homeless people in Sarasota.

Elijah shrugged. "You see them now and then, but I don't think there are that many."

"Actually, there are," Paula said. "We had a special speaker my senior year who said we have six times the national average."

"Wow." That seemed like a lot.

"Well, all they have to do is find a job." Elijah shrugged. "And maybe three or four roommates." He grinned.

"And even after all of that, a place to live that they can afford." Paula skipped ahead and then turned around to face us as she walked backward. "I had a classmate who was homeless. She had two younger brothers and a mom, who worked two jobs. They stayed with relatives, in cheap motels, and sometimes even camped out. Some days she had no idea where they'd be sleeping that night."

"Things are better now than they were a few years ago," Elijah said, "as far as the economy."

Paula wrinkled her nose. "For some people, but not everyone."

Elijah grinned again. "Jah, especially for the druggies."

I imagined Paula rolling her eyes at Elijah under her sunglasses. "True, some are drug addicts, but not all, including my friend and her family."

"Well, what about the dad? Where was he?"

Paula put her hands on her hips. "Dead."

"I don't believe you. He probably took off for New York or something with some young thing and left his family behind."

I was a little alarmed with Elijah being so cavalier. Paula kept staring at him, her hands still on her hips.

"I know you're trying to trick me," he said. "The guy's probably in prison on drug charges or something."

Paula pulled off her glasses and gave Elijah a dark look.

"I'm just kidding." Elijah reached for my beach bag. "Let me carry that." He took it from me and then started running toward Paula. "And how about if you let me wear that hat and save you from your fancy ways."

The tension of the moment passed as Paula put her sunglasses

back on and then her hand on the top of her head and took off. I
jogged after them, and in no time we'd reached the beach, sweaty
and laughing. Paula seemed as serious as Gordon. Thankfully,
Elijah knew how to lighten the mood.

⁂

We spent an hour playing on the beach. First volleyball. Then
tag. Eventually, Paula started toward the water and called after
me to follow her. "I only have my dress," I said.

"No," she answered. "You have shorts on underneath it."

I laughed. "But no shirt."

She started toward me. "I have one in my bag."

That sounded too immodest.

"Come on." She nodded toward our things on the blanket
and then to the restrooms.

I hesitated.

"Amish girls wear shorts and a shirt down here all the time."
She dropped her voice to a whisper and raised her eyebrows.
"Some even wear swimsuits."

I laughed. I couldn't help but be relaxed with Paula. She was
so easy to be around. "All right," I said. "I'll wear the T-shirt."

I changed in the restroom as Paula confessed to me that she'd
just lied to Elijah. "My friend's father isn't in prison, but he
didn't die. Elijah was right, he did leave the family—not for a
girlfriend, at least I don't think so anyway."

Confused, I asked, "Why would you lie about it?"

"Because Elijah drives me nuts with his self-righteousness."

If Elijah was self-righteous, what was I? He was one of the
most accepting people I knew. "Self-righteousness? Really?"

"Jah." We reached the restroom and Paula pushed the door
open and held it for me as she continued to talk. "He's always

so critical of people who need help. Just because his family has a farm, and he doesn't have anything to worry about, he thinks everyone has the resources he does. And if they don't, it's their fault."

I wasn't so sure his thinking was always wrong. After all, the father in the family Paula talked about did leave. If he hadn't, his family wouldn't have been homeless. But I didn't say that.

Instead, I focused on changing. After I put on Paula's T-shirt, I stared in the mirror. It was baggier than my dress and came down over my shorts. But my legs, past my midthighs, were completely bare.

"You look great," Paula said. "And no one will notice—I mean the Englischers will just think 'why aren't those girls wearing bikinis?' and the Plain folk will just be thankful we're not."

I doubted that would be true of all Plain people. It certainly wouldn't have been true of me, even a week ago. But I wasn't going to say that either.

I followed Paula out the door, and as soon as we reached the sand someone hooted from the volleyball court. *Elijah.*

"Ignore him." Paula took off running.

We dropped our bags back on the blanket, and then I followed her into the water. The warmth welcomed me, wrapping me up in a gentle wave. Dat had taught all of us girls to swim when we were children. I hadn't wanted to learn at the time, but for the first time in my life I was grateful for his instruction. I took several strokes out into the water and then flipped to my back, soaking in the hot sun on my face while the rest of my body relaxed in the rolling waves.

"Don't go out too far," Paula called out.

I flipped over and treaded water. She stood in the waves up to her chest.

"Come on!" I motioned for her to follow me.

She shook her head, and I guessed that she didn't swim. I took a few quick strokes back to where she was.

"I need a flotation device," she joked, and then in a serious voice she asked where I learned to swim.

"My Dat taught me." I stood next to her. "In our pond." I didn't tell her why—that it was because my oldest sister, Rebecca, had drowned the day Jessica had been born.

We spent hours in the water, playing and floating on our backs. Out of the four of us, I was by far the best swimmer, and although I wasn't in very good shape and hadn't swam for a while, it all came back to me. As I floated on my back again, bobbing in the water, I couldn't remember ever being so relaxed. Or so happy. A sense of peace swept over me that I usually only felt when I was singing. There was nothing I felt as if I needed to control. Not myself. Not my sisters. Not anyone in our district. I didn't care about hat brims or dress lengths. Or cell phone use or rules around shunnings. And even though I feared being in Pinecraft was indulgent, I didn't feel guilty about it. It was uncanny for me.

I'd gone from measuring the hems of my sisters' dresses to wearing shorts and a T-shirt and swimming with Elijah Jacobs and people I'd just met. I never wanted to leave the water. I felt a freedom I'd never experienced before.

But eventually we all splashed out to the sand and toweled off, and then Paula and I headed to the restroom to change. After I had my dress back on, I wrung out my hair and then twisted it back into a bun and placed my Kapp on top. Paula changed into a skirt and a dry top. She secured her hair into a bun too, but she didn't place a covering over it. She hadn't had a covering on at all since I'd met her, except her sun hat, which didn't count. I wondered what kind of Mennonite she was, but then she told me she hadn't joined the church yet.

"I'm still trying to figure out what to do." She sighed.

As we left the restroom, I told her I was wondering about a song and if she knew it. I began to sing, "C, a cat, a curious cat . . ."

She began to laugh. "I've never heard those words, but I know the tune." She stopped under a tree. "Tell me about the song."

I explained that Dat had most likely made it up. "It's just a silly song."

"Not really," she said. "You father was teaching you the C major scale."

I shook my head. "I don't understand."

"C, D, E, F, G, A, B. Each of the letters—and the corresponding words—is a note. He most likely got the idea from the 'Do, Re, Mi' song."

"What's that?"

She went on to explain about a movie about a nun and a bunch of kids. She lost me right away. I must have given her a puzzled look because she shook her head. "I thought you'd know all of this. I mean, not the movie but the notes. How can anyone sing the way you do and not?" She exhaled. "Can you sing the words from your Dat's song for me? For example, can you sing 'dog' separate from the song?"

I sang the note.

"Bird?"

I sang that note too.

Once I'd sung all of the words she requested, she asked me to sing a C. I sang "cat." After I'd gone through all of the notes again, but by the letters instead of the words, she said, "You used to sing this with your Dat?"

I nodded.

"He really did teach you the notes without your ever realizing it. Plus, you have perfect pitch."

"Perfect what?"

"Pitch. It's your sound. Your tone. You can hit a note on key without a pitch pipe."

"Is that like a harmonica?"

Paula shook her head. "No, it just has the notes. It provides the sound of a note so those singing can match it."

I shook my head.

She smiled. "Not everyone can hear a note like you can, in your head."

I did understand that because I knew my sisters couldn't and Mamm couldn't either. I believed that Dat could though. He told me one of the hardest things for him about joining the church was giving up music. Although he hadn't entirely, at least not the harmonica, until Mamm forced him to.

Elijah yelled at us from the edge of parking lot. "Hurry!"

We started toward them, but Paula barely strolled along. She certainly wasn't in a hurry.

Elijah yelled again.

"Oh, good grief." Paula increased her stride and I did too. As we reached him, Paula said, "Marie has perfect pitch."

"I don't doubt it," Elijah responded.

Paula stopped. "Do you even know what that is?"

Elijah nodded his head. "I've known all along that she's perfect."

I grimaced.

Paula laughed.

Billy said he was starving, and the discussion about my singing ability ended just as quickly as it started, thankfully.

"Let's go to Yoders," Elijah said.

The restaurant was crowded with Amish, Mennonites, and Englischers, and we had to wait twenty minutes for a table. I was starving, and all the savory smells didn't help. The peanut butter sandwich I'd eaten for lunch wasn't enough, considering all the time I'd spent in the water.

Finally, we were seated. All of us ordered the fried chicken and mashed potatoes. After we finished our meal, we all ordered pie—coconut crème for Paula and Billy, peach for Elijah, and key lime for me.

We talked about our futures as we ate. Paula said she was thinking about enrolling in college the next year. "Cleaning bungalows is fine, but I keep thinking there's something more for me in life."

"What would you study?" I asked.

She gave Elijah a snarky look and answered, "Social work."

He laughed. "That figures. I knew you were a bleeding heart."

She gave Elijah a second snarky look. "Or music."

He groaned. "The world doesn't need another Taylor Swift."

Paula chuckled. "As if."

I'd heard of Taylor Swift but didn't know anything about her. Clearly Paula and Elijah were just having fun though. I asked Billy what he planned to do. He just shrugged and said, "First I need to figure out if I'm going to join the church or not."

Paula kicked Elijah under the table. "What about you?"

He glanced at me. "I'm going home in the spring, probably by May, to farm with my Dat. Then in a year or two, he'll turn the farm over to me."

Paula wrinkled her nose. "I can't imagine."

Elijah seemed hurt. "What do you mean?"

She shrugged. "Oh, you know. The whole thing. Horse and buggy. No electricity. Driving a tractor with metal wheels."

His expression turned into a pout. "What do you have against our tractors?"

Paula rolled her eyes. "Back in Ohio, our tractors have rubber tires."

It was true that the Lancaster County tractors had metal wheels. It seemed perfectly normal to me, but I could see how it would seem odd to others.

"Those silly scooters don't make sense either." Paula's voice was both light and serious at the same time. "We get to ride bicycles."

"Hey," I said, hoping my voice sounded as if I were joking. "Don't make fun of our scooters. We've been riding them our entire lives." The bishops in Lancaster County didn't allow bicycles. Only scooters.

"Yeah." Elijah grinned.

"Sorry to offend you," Paula shot back, but her tone was light. Until it grew more serious. "And farming? Really? Elijah, you are the last man I can imagine dragging a field or pulling a calf."

He shrugged dramatically. "It's my destiny." Then he laughed.

Paula shook her head and then focused on me. "So what do you plan to do, Marie?"

"Well." I drew out the word, trying to stall as my face grew warm. Would she put it together that I hoped Elijah was integral to my future plans? "I'll go back to Lancaster County and help my Mamm run our home and spend time with my nieces and nephews. Take charge of the garden. That sort of thing." I wanted to add, *and wait until Elijah comes home*, but of course I didn't.

I could tell Paula wasn't very impressed with my answer. Instead of commenting, she asked, "Will you come down again next year?"

"No," I answered. "This is a once-in-a-lifetime event, I'm afraid."

Her expression fell into a frown. "Oh, that's too bad." Then her face brightened. "I'll just have to visit you then. If I come in the winter, may I borrow a coat and boots?"

"Of course. I'd really love that," I answered. And it was true—I really would. I liked Paula regardless of her not joining her church. Regardless of her wanting to attend college. And all the nosy questions she was asking. We were absolute opposites, except for our shared love of music, but I found her honesty and genuineness refreshing.

I took the last bite of my pie and then pulled my purse from my bag to pay, but Elijah said he'd get it. Billy did the same for Paula.

When they dropped me off, Elijah walked me to the front door and then kissed the top of my Kapp. "I had a great day," he said.

"Me too." I looked up into his dark brown eyes. I wanted to say more, but feared I might sound too eager.

He leaned down to kiss me, my very first. I closed my eyes and our lips met. Tingles flew up and down my spine. Then he hugged me again, and I hugged him back, feeling as if I were in a dream. Was I really in Florida? My arms wrapped around Elijah Jacobs? In January—but in eighty-degree weather? Jah, it was true. I was.

Long after I'd told Aenti Suz goodnight and went to bed, I relived the kiss. Over and over. Finally, it was my turn to fall in love. Soon it would be my turn to court. And to marry.

As I fell asleep, music played inside my head. It was an old tune, one Dat used to play on his harmonica, something he learned during his running-around years. I hadn't thought of it in years. "Turn, Turn, Turn" was the name of the song. It was about there being a season for everything in life. It wasn't until I was older and someone read the passage in church that I realized it was from Ecclesiastes: *To every thing there is a season, and a time to every purpose under the heaven.*

I was entering the season I'd longed for. Finally, God was rewarding me for my faithfulness.

– 12 –

I spent every minute I could with Elijah through the rest of the week. Aenti Suz continued to be absolutely fine with my hanging out with him, and I guessed that she was spending as much time with David.

On Sunday, Aenti Suz and I met David at the Amish church for the service. A variety of people, Amish and Mennonite, gathered around outside.

Soon we headed into the church, where there were two sides of benches, like in any Amish service. Aenti Suz and I sat on the women's side, while David sat on the men's. I expected Elijah to show up, but he didn't.

I enjoyed the singing, which was very similar to home, but found myself not concentrating on the sermon. I thought of Elijah instead.

When I saw him on Monday, I asked him why he hadn't been at church. A sheepish expression passed over his face. "I slept through my alarm. I promise I'll be there next week."

As Elijah and I got ice cream cones the next day, I asked him if he had any music on his smartphone, curious after seeing the video clips on Paula's phone. He seemed pleased I was interested in his cellular device, as he called it, but said he wasn't that into music.

"Really?"

He shrugged. "I'd rather watch cat videos."

Holding his cone with one hand, he clicked on his screen and then turned it toward me. I licked my ice cream as I watched. A tabby swatted at a banana peel, then a calico stumbled around with a plastic container on her head, and then a gray cat played a keyboard, hitting one key at a time with his paw.

Elijah laughed. "Look, cats and music. The perfect video."

I thought of Dat's silly song. Maybe he would have understood Elijah's bizarre interest. But I was puzzled. "People film their cats and then put it on the Internet for everyone to see?"

"Jah." He kept his eyes on his phone. "And then someone edits all the clips into one long video." Two cats tried to squeeze into the same small box at the exact same time. Elijah laughed. "Aren't these videos hilarious?"

I really couldn't tell if he was serious or not. We'd both grown up with barn cats, but neither of our families actually let cats live in the house, not like the Englischers in the videos. Having cats in the house and filming them, let alone allowing one on a keyboard, all seemed so foreign to me.

I concentrated on my ice cream cone as he continued to laugh at the video.

I didn't see Elijah the following day. And then the day after, Thursday, he ended up working a long shift at the bakery, but he called our landlady and asked her to give me the message.

"How thoughtful of him," Aenti Suz said. "Now you can join David and me for the potluck at the park."

I was disappointed not to spend the day with Elijah, but I was happy to have an event to attend. I helped Aenti Suz make deviled eggs and a potato and ham casserole. David stopped by for us, carrying a box of crackers and a bag of cheese slices. He held both up and joked, "My specialty."

We walked to the park, watching as others whizzed by on bicycles. None of us had ever learned to ride one, and Aenti Suz teased that she was tempted to rent a tricycle. David said he did sometimes, but he didn't mind walking. None of us did. The day was cooler—only in the high seventies—and the afternoon breeze had picked up.

We could hear children playing in the park as we turned the corner. Most were preschoolers who'd come with their parents or grandparents, but there were scholar-aged children too. There was an elementary school in Pinecraft that the area children attended.

Of course there were quite a few teens and lots of young adults too, many who lived and worked in Pinecraft or Sarasota, and others who had come down for the season.

The tables under the picnic shelter were covered with checkered tablecloths and heaped with food. My mouth watered at the sight. Homemade bread. Peanut butter spread. Chow chow. Pickles. Beets. Fried chicken. Ham. Potatoes. Pasta. All sorts of salads. Jah, the food looked and smelled like home.

After we ate, a group of Youngie gathered in a circle on the grass. I almost didn't recognize Paula—she wore a Mennonite dress and Kapp—but she spotted me right away. "Marie! Over here."

"Go ahead," Aenti Suz said. "Just introduce me to your friend later."

"I will." I hurried over to where Paula stood with a group of young people I didn't recognize. She introduced me around, and I quickly gathered that she attended church with most of them. One of the young men had a guitar and started strumming it. He wasn't as good as Gordon, but who was I to judge a musician? Paula began singing, but I didn't recognize the song. I hummed along as best I could.

The young man played another I didn't recognize, but then Paula asked him to play "Just as I Am."

Paula started singing and I joined her. "Just as I am, without one plea, But that Thy blood was shed for me, And that Thou bid'st me come to Thee, O Lamb of God, I come!" We continued on through all six verses, just the two of us singing, and when we stopped, several people who'd gathered around began to clap. I looked away, embarrassed.

Thankfully, Aenti Suz and David approached us and I quickly introduced them to Paula. At the same time, Elijah climbed out of a car and started toward us. "I got off sooner than I thought I would," he called out. "A co-worker gave me a ride."

Aenti Suz shaded her eyes and said, "Grab a plate. There's still lots of food left."

I left the circle of Youngie and joined Elijah as he filled his plate. After he finished eating, we each grabbed a piece of pie and drifted back to the singing. As we did, Aenti Suz said she and David were going for a walk and she'd meet me back at the bungalow.

Elijah and I ate our dessert as we listened. Paula was still singing, this time another praise song that I didn't recognize.

After a few minutes, once Elijah finished his pie, he grew restless. First, he stood. Then he took both of our plates to the garbage. He returned and stood behind me, shifting from foot to foot.

Finally, I stepped beside him and said, "Want to go for a walk?"

"Yah," he said. "That would be great! How about if we head toward your place?"

So off we went as the sun set.

"How are you getting home?" I asked.

He shrugged and grinned. "I'll figure something out."

I guessed that Aenti Suz and David were probably at our bungalow and suggested we go there.

"Good idea." Elijah's hand bumped against mine. He didn't dare take it, even though dusk had fallen. We'd never hear the end of it if anyone saw us holding hands. It was enough to know he was close, to know that he wanted to hold my hand.

We kept on walking. A bat flew overhead. The breeze picked up, and the fronds of the palm trees swayed back and forth above us.

"It's been great spending this time with you," Elijah said. "I'm so glad you came down." He shot me a grin. "I'm feeling much better about going back home now."

He brushed my hand again. "I have to say that I was a little worried when you came in so late with that Mennonite guy though, when I stopped by to see you after Christmas. What's his name?"

"Gordon."

"That's right. Talk about serious—and what a do-gooder. Like Superman without the cape. You were off with him feeding the homeless in the dead of winter, right?"

"We'd been to the shelter in Lancaster. And then at the hospital—"

"Jah. I remember." Elijah's voice grew in volume. "Hey, maybe we could get this Gordon and Paula together. They seem to have the same interests."

"Actually, Gordon will be down here soon." I turned toward Elijah. "Didn't he tell you that?"

He stopped on the sidewalk. "Oh, that's right. I'd forgotten. So he's coming down to see you?"

I quickly assured him that wasn't the case. "He's coming down on a mission trip, remember? To serve—"

Elijah interrupted me. "Let me guess. The homeless?"

"Jah," I said, wondering why Elijah was being so obtuse. "Don't you remember him talking about it?"

He laughed. "I must not have been listening. But I'm glad he's coming. Billy seems to have had enough of Paula—she's even getting on his nerves."

It didn't seem to me as if Billy was annoyed with Paula, and I honestly didn't think it was a good idea to try to fix her up with Gordon, but I didn't say so.

"Enough about Gordon." Elijah turned around and walked backward. Darkness had fallen, but I could see his face under the streetlight. "Let's talk about me again."

I laughed.

He grinned. "No. I'll be serious. Let's talk about you." He cleared his throat, as if he was building up to say something more, but then he tripped.

I reached out my hand, and he grabbed it. He laughed and then said, "You saved me." He let go of my hand, but he didn't say any more. The moment seemed to have been lost. We continued on in silence until we reached the bungalow.

I led him toward the door. The porch light was on, and I expected Aenti Suz and David to be inside. I hoped we could all play a board game together.

The front door was unlocked, and I opened it. A light was on in the kitchen but that was all. "Hello!" I called out.

No one answered.

"Maybe they're out on the patio," I said.

Elijah followed me to the sliding glass door, and I turned on the outside light. No one was out there either. "Want to sit outside or in here?" I asked.

"How about inside?"

"All right." I led the way to the living room and sat down on the couch. Instead of sitting on the other side, Elijah sat in the middle, close to me. Elijah stretched and then put his arm around me. I scooted a little closer, sure we'd hear the door in plenty of time to put a little distance between us when Aenti Suz returned.

Elijah turned toward me, pulling me closer. He kissed the top of my Kapp and then my forehead, like before. Then his lips were on mine again. As I kissed him back, I heard voices out front.

I quickly pulled away.

The door opened, and Aenti Suz said, "It's so good to see you!"

A deep voice replied, "I just thought I'd stop by and say hello. I was hoping to see Marie tonight." I scooted all of the way out of Elijah's embrace.

"The light's on—she must be back." Aenti Suz stepped into the room. "Marie?"

Behind her was Gordon with a smile on his face—until he saw me sitting on the couch with Elijah.

Gordon sputtered, "Hello."

I stood and asked if he remembered Elijah.

"Of course," he answered.

Elijah cleared his throat. "I'd better get going. I'm picking up a shift in the morning."

"Do you have a ride?" Aenti Suz asked.

He shook his head.

"I can take you," Gordon said, still looking at me. I wasn't sure what he'd expected, but obviously he hadn't found it.

"Thanks," Elijah answered. "I appreciate it, but I was going to call my buddy."

"Oh, let Gordon take you," Aenti Suz said. "It won't be out of his way, not much anyway."

Elijah shrugged. "All right." He gave me a wave. "See you tomorrow."

I walked him to the door, and we both followed Aenti Suz and Gordon outside. A big old van was parked along the curb.

"It belongs to our church," Gordon explained. "Everyone else is getting ready to sleep. It was a long drive down."

Aenti Suz stood with her hands clasped together. "And yet you still came here?"

He nodded and then looked at me. "But I shouldn't have. I'm sorry."

Stumped, I wasn't sure what to say in return. Thankfully Aenti Suz came to my rescue. "No, we're so glad you did. What is your schedule like this week?"

"We're working at the shelter through next Thursday, and then we head home Friday."

"Perfect," Aenti Suz said. "There's a singing in the park that Thursday night. Would you join us for that?"

Gordon met my eyes and I nodded in agreement. I doubted Elijah would go—it would be the perfect opportunity to spend some obligatory time with Gordon.

He nodded and then got that serious, intense look on his face. "I was hoping you could join us one of the days we're here. For an outing to the beach or something like that."

Elijah smirked. I wished Gordon hadn't asked in front of him. I managed to mutter, "We'll have to see."

182

Aenti Suz rattled off our landlady's phone number. "Give Marie a call with the details. I'll make sure she gets to the right place." I wasn't sure if I wanted a repeat of the evening at the shelter in Lancaster, not when I had limited time in Pinecraft.

Gordon said that he would as Elijah gave me a grin and raised his eyebrows. Then Elijah said in a singsong voice, "I'll be in touch soon too."

As Aenti Suz and I watched the van drive away, I said, "That was awkward."

"They are certainly very different young men, aren't they?"

I nodded. "A bishop's son and a do-gooder."

Aenti Suz gave me a funny look but didn't say anything more. Instead she turned and headed into the bungalow. "How about some ice cream and more of Annie's story?" As she headed toward the kitchen, she said, "Where was I?"

I followed. "Kate had just asked Annie to go to Gettysburg with her to nurse the wounded."

"That's right." Aenti Suz opened the freezer. "And George said no."

-13-

Annie

Kate stood and thanked Annie, who had retreated to the shadows of the room, swaying the baby. Then she leaned on the table and met George's eyes. "Please discuss this with Annie and listen to her. It would be good for me to have someone to travel with, and her skills would be put to good use. The Lord commanded us to care for the sick and dying. All of us are called to serve, according to our gifts, in a time like this."

George crossed his arms and shook his head. "It's bad enough that men in our communities have been drawn into the fight. My sister won't be supporting this war, not in any way."

Kate stood up straight. "Didn't you sell the Union hay?"

George's face grew red. "That was different—it was better to sell it than risk having the Confederates steal it. I'm responsible for Annie while she's in my home. I won't allow her to go to a battlefield."

Kate smiled at Annie, as if George hadn't just spoken, and

184

then grabbed her bag. "I'll be riding the stagecoach to Hanover Junction tomorrow, and then I'll catch the train to Gettysburg. Come into town in the morning if you want to go with me. I'll have a pass for myself and for you too."

Annie nodded as the baby began to fuss. She moved him to her shoulder and continued bouncing him.

"Do you think the trains are even operating?" George asked. "Don't you think the Confederates probably destroyed what they could?"

Kate shook her head. "I heard the tracks were to be repaired by now."

Annie spoke up. "What about going east, past the river, toward Lancaster?"

"I'm guessing a ferry has been put in place," Kate said. "They'll have to get soldiers from Gettysburg to every hospital in the area, including across the river, as soon as possible. Thousands and thousands are dead and more are injured."

Annie shuddered at the thought again, trying to imagine how horrific some of the injuries might be.

Harriet walked to the door with Kate and thanked her for coming. After she closed the door, she turned toward George. "What about those soldiers? What if Cecil is injured? What if others we know are? What if Ira is?"

George kept his arms crossed.

"And don't tell me they shouldn't have gone off to war. If you were younger and not married, you might have gone."

He shook his head. "Never."

She gave him a pathetic look. "What if it was one of our sons? Wouldn't you want someone like Annie to go care for him?"

George shook his head.

"If you won't let Annie go, then I will," Harriet said.

Annie gasped. A wife was to be submissive to her husband.

Harriet marched toward Annie. "I'll take the baby with me and accompany Kate in the morning."

"Don't be ridiculous," George said. "Both of you are being unreasonable. This is none of our concern."

Harriet, without saying another word to George, headed to the bedroom.

Annie stepped to the table and gathered up the mugs. "I'd like to go," she said to George, speaking as calmly as she could.

He put his head in his hands. "I know you would."

She washed the dishes while he continued to sit in the same position. Finally, he got up and followed his wife into the bedroom. As the door opened, Annie could hear the baby crying.

She wiped the dishes and turned off the lamp, pondering whether she should sneak out in the morning and meet Kate. Harriet would understand, but George would be furious.

She slept fitfully and then rose long before dawn, not sure what she should do. But she couldn't sneak out. If she was going to go, she needed to be honest with George about it. She washed and dressed, careful not to wake Noah.

When she stepped out into the kitchen, ready to revive the fire and collect the water, George sat at the table, already dressed.

As she said, "I've decided—" he said, "I'll give you a ride—"

She stopped and let him continue.

"Into town," he said. "The wagon is ready to go."

She gaped at her brother.

"I'll never be able to answer to Dat and Mamm for this, but if you want to go—which I know you do—I'll get you to Kate."

"Denki." She started back to her room. "Just give me a minute." She quickly packed a bag and grabbed her cloak and bonnet. George wasn't in the kitchen when she returned, so she grabbed biscuits, slices of ham, and a baked sweet potato. As she started out the door, Harriet called her name.

She stood in the doorway to her room in her nightgown, the baby in her arms. Annie hurried toward her and kissed them both.

"My sister," Harriet said. "You are so brave. Please be safe. Find Cecil if you can, and tell him to send word that he's all right."

Annie said she would and then hurried to join George.

They were silent the entire trip, both watching as streaks of orange and pink came over the horizon and then the fiery ball of the sun up over the Susquehanna. As they started the descent into Peach Bottom, Annie asked her brother what made him change his mind.

He grunted but didn't answer.

"George?"

"I didn't change my mind," he said. "And I'll never forgive myself if something happens to you. But I know the Lord cares about those men and that you are capable of helping them."

Annie wasn't sure that she'd be able to. In fact, she feared once she arrived in Gettysburg, she'd want to run the other way. But she at least had to try.

George turned toward her. "So I'm going to do my best to trust the Lord to use you—and keep you safe amidst the carnage."

"Denki," she said, her stomach dropping. *Carnage.* She feared she wouldn't be worthy to do what she believed the Lord was calling her to do.

As Annie and George approached her house, Kate stood on the porch, shading her eyes from the sun peeking over the

Susquehanna hills across the river and through the clouds gathering on the horizon. Around her were baskets of food and stacks of crates.

Puzzled, she wondered how Kate planned to get all of the cargo on the stagecoach.

The woman didn't see them until George stopped in front of her house. Then she dropped her hand from her brow and ran toward them. "George," she called out. "The ferry just arrived, bringing Woody across. Could you wait and help load the supplies into his wagon?"

Of course Kate had a plan. They wouldn't be taking the stagecoach after all.

George jumped down from the wagon and tied the horse to the hitching post, and then all three of them worked together to move the goods down to the street. The clouds grew darker and thicker, and by the time Woody arrived with his wagon already half full, a drizzle had started. As they loaded it, the rain turned into a downpour.

George asked Woody if he'd return to Peach Bottom after taking the load to Hanover Junction.

"I'm taking them all the way to Gettysburg," he said. "I want to make sure they get there safely, along with Miss Kate's supplies and what I've brought too." He took off his hat and ran his hand over his bald head as the rain fell on top of it. "Most likely I'll be going back and forth after that." He put his hat back on. "Hauling supplies there, probably helping to get soldiers out too."

George tugged on his beard. "Would you keep an eye on Annie? And bring her back here if . . ." George's voice trailed off.

The man nodded but didn't say anything.

Annie told her brother good-bye, and then he helped her up

onto the wagon bench, next to Kate. As Woody's team of six horses took off, heading toward Hanover, the rain increased. Kate pulled out an umbrella and held it over the three of them, but the drops still pelted them from both the front and the back.

It turned out that neither Kate nor Woody had gotten much sleep the night before, so when they stopped for their noon meal along a creek, both fell asleep for a short time under the canopy of a tree. Woody woke with a start and called out to Kate. "Let's get going. Others are depending on us."

The rain fell steadily all day and several times turned into downpours, turning the road into a mess. Woody stopped and knocked the mud off the wheels from time to time. Thankfully, he had a team of six horses to pull his wagon or they wouldn't have made it through.

Annie thought of the wounded soldiers. Were they still on the fields, being soaked by the rain? By the time they reached Hanover, darkness was falling and they stayed at the hotel. As they dried out, several men in the dining room talked about the skirmish three miles west of town over a week ago. Others had been to the battlefield around Gettysburg and talked of the devastation there. One of the men nodded toward Kate and Annie after Woody had gone out to sleep in the stable. "Where are you two headed?" he asked.

"Gettysburg." Kate held her head high. "We're nurses."

The man shook his head. "It's no place for women." He shifted his gaze to Annie. "Especially not a young 'un."

Annie ducked her head, staring at the ground.

The man frowned. "Well, Happy Independence Day," he said. "May God save us from ourselves."

The next morning, they were on the road again before dawn. The rain continued, and when they reached Codorus Creek, which was running high, they could see the railroad bridge the Confederates had attempted to burn. The Union had already managed to repair it.

They crossed the creek on the wood-plank bridge and continued on the fifteen miles to Gettysburg. The farmland was as beautiful as back home, but all the livestock was missing. Annie guessed either one army or the other had confiscated the animals to feed their troops.

The rain stopped, and the day became warm and then hot. Woody's horses increased their pace. They were all eager to end their journey.

But in no time, Annie began to change her mind. First, there was a dead horse. Then ten or more soldiers, all Confederates, sprawled out in a field. The wind shifted and she pulled her apron up over her nose. The air had grown foul. And thick.

An abandoned cannon pointed toward them, a dead soldier flung over the top of it. There were more horses, some mangled, and then more dead soldiers. Rifles and ammunition were spread across the field too.

"Last night, in the Hanover Inn," Woody said, "a man told me that many of the rifles abandoned on the battlefield were unfired on both sides."

"Why would that be?" Kate asked.

"Only one reason, Miss Kate—well, two," Woody answered. "First, when it came right down to it, many of the soldiers just couldn't pull their triggers. Killing another person isn't as easy as a lot of people think."

Annie cringed. Who would think taking another life could be easy?

"That, or the soldiers were killed before they had a chance to get a shot off."

Annie swiped at her eyes. She focused on the landscape again. Ahead was a farmhouse that had the east side of it blown away, showing the rooms inside and a staircase that ended midway to the second floor. The fences all around the farm were broken like branches in a storm. And a stand of trees had been mowed down by cannon fire like cornstalks.

They passed a wagon, crushed to smithereens, with no trace of the horses that once pulled it. Bits of clothing, belts, and knapsacks were strewn across another field. A piece of paper blew through the air, and Annie wondered if it was part of a letter that had been written to loved ones back home that would never be delivered.

Her heart ached at the devastation all around them.

In another field, a group of farmers were digging graves for soldiers, stacked like wood, against a fence.

"Oh, Lord, help us," Kate whispered.

Woody exhaled and leaned against Kate for a quick moment.

They passed several tents set up in a field with lots of people milling around and wounded soldiers spread across the ground.

"That must be a field hospital," Woody said. "They'll be getting supplies from the Union. We need to make sure and tell Dr. Carson about it."

The trio passed by a cemetery and then, just before they reached the edge of the town, Kate said, "Turn here."

Up the hill, ahead of them, was a brick house with an orchard to the left of it and several outbuildings around it—a barn, stable, and washhouse were visible. Scattered across the front lawn, under two trees, were wounded soldiers.

Annie gawked at the house. "This is where Dr. Carson lives?"

Kate nodded. "I worked with him in Philadelphia before Ira and I moved to Peach Bottom. Soon after that he bought this house, but he's served with Ira's unit over the last year and that's how we got back in touch."

Woody drove the wagon to the back of the house, parking it by the porch. A soldier hobbled up to the wagon. "Do you have supplies?"

"Yep," Woody answered. "And two nurses."

"Good. We need both." The soldier limped around to the back.

"And we're looking for Ira King," Kate added. "Is he nearby?"

"He went to procure supplies," the soldier said, "from the U.S. Christian Commission that set up in a store in town. It's not far from here. He should be back soon."

The soldier with the limp was called Howdy. He was in charge of documenting all of the donations. As Woody and another soldier unloaded the crates, he recorded the items.

With teary eyes, he thanked Kate as he counted twenty basins. Annie didn't know how Kate did it, but she must have gone from house to house in Peach Bottom, persuading each family to give as much as they could.

Kate went into the house to find the doctor, but Annie stayed outside and helped Howdy record the rest of the goods. Loaves of bread, vegetables, and even berries—although very ripe— filled the baskets, along with stewed fruit and canned beans and tomatoes. Toward the end, several hams and slabs of bacon were pulled from the wagon. Woody had brought more food, all the way from Lancaster County. Sacks of flour, beans, and tea. And more vegetables and hams.

He looked at me and said, "These are from your people."

Annie shook her head.

"Yep," he said. "Your father collected them."

That warmed her heart. Perhaps Annie's parents wouldn't be as angry with her as she feared.

As soldiers hauled the food off to a makeshift kitchen in a tent close to the orchard, the soldier went through the crates. They were packed with linens, blankets, towels, and fabric for bandages. Annie wondered if there was a bed left in Peach Bottom that was made. It seemed Kate had stripped every single one.

As they finished going through the supplies, Kate came out the back door, followed by a doctor who wore a bloody apron. She introduced him to Woody and then to Annie as Dr. Carson.

The doctor welcomed them both. "You and the supplies you brought could make all the difference," he said. "We have a long, long road ahead of us, and the more help we have, the greater the distance we'll be able to cover."

He gave Kate and Annie a quick tour, pointing out the tent to the side of the stable. "That's where the amputations are done." He turned to Kate. "I'll need you to assist me."

Annie felt her knees grow weak, but she did her best not to show her alarm. Then he pointed to the door to the house. "Kate, you saw inside, but I'll show you around more. And Annie too."

Before they headed up the steps, the doctor pointed out the bullet holes in the brick on the side of the house. "At one time," he said, "the battle came to us. Thankfully, it moved on quickly."

Annie shivered as she followed him and Kate up the steps and onto the back porch. Ten soldiers were spread out on cots. Annie thought of Sophia back home, and her heart swelled. Several of the soldiers were asleep, but three were awake and watched as they walked through. One was missing an arm. Another a leg. All were wrapped in bloody rags. Again her knees weakened.

Inside, distracted by the iron smell of blood and the scores of wounded soldiers, Annie did her best to listen to the doctor. They'd been doing triage since the battle. Those with wounds to their extremities had a chance of survival. Stomach, chest, and head wounds were another matter, however.

Each room of the house was filled with the wounded, even the kitchen. By the time they ended their tour, Annie felt light-headed. Perhaps the doctor guessed so because he instructed her to go to the kitchen and get a bite to eat. "A cup of tea is a good idea too," he said.

Kate joined her. As they neared the tent, Ira stepped out, holding a cup in one hand and his hat in the other. His blond hair curled even tighter in the heat and humidity.

He greeted his mother warmly, but he didn't seem happy to see Annie.

First, he introduced them to Dr. Carson's cook, an older woman named Meg. She seemed harried and was on her way to the storeroom to fetch her assistant, whom she'd sent to retrieve a bag of potatoes.

Ira handed his mother his cup of tea and whispered, "You shouldn't have brought her."

Kate shook her head and passed the cup to Annie.

Even in the heat of the day, an icy tingle ran down Annie's spine, causing the cup to shake. George was right. So was the man at the hotel last night. And so was Ira. She'd been fooling herself. Gettysburg was no place for her. She'd thought she could do the work, but she'd been prideful. It was all much worse than she'd ever imagined.

❧◦❧

Kate and Annie slept on cots in the attic with three other nurses. All were older than Kate and from York. One commented on Annie's age, saying she didn't fit the description required by Dorothea Dix.

"Who's Dorothea Dix?" Annie asked.

"Goodness, girl," the oldest of the group said. "She's the Superintendent of Army Nurses."

"Oh." Annie had never heard of her before, but it sounded like she had an important job.

"She says female nurses should be matrons, not pretty young things like you."

The attic was stifling, but Annie's face grew even warmer.

"Annie's here to assist me," Kate said. "That's all. I don't think even Dorothea would mind."

The woman snorted. "Well, you're not exactly matronly either."

"Oh, I am," Kate said. "Old enough to be a mother to a soldier. Ira King is my boy."

"Ira?" One of the other women perked up. "You must be proud of such a fine young man."

"Well," Kate said, "I am grateful for his compassion and care for others."

"Some of the wounded have told stories about his bravery. How he rushed out onto the battlefield over and over to carry off the wounded."

Annie couldn't figure Ira out. He'd been part of the Brethren church, but he didn't have a problem fighting.

When Kate didn't reply, the other older woman said, "Perhaps that's not what a mother wants to hear."

In the dim light, Annie could see Kate shake her head. "No, it's fine. I'm just so grateful the battle is over and he's still with us. I know lots of mothers are mourning today. More will be in the months to come. I know we all mourn with them as we tend those who are still battling to survive."

"On that note," the oldest of the nurses said, "we'd better

get to sleep. Those working the night shift will need some relief soon enough."

Annie tossed and turned in the heat of the attic. Finally, she called out to God, struggling against her fear. *Give me strength*, she begged. *And wisdom. Strength enough to do your will. Wisdom to know whom to trust. That's all I ask.*

– 14 –

The first morning, Annie worked with Kate, feeding the soldiers toast and soft-boiled eggs, and giving a thin gruel to the ones who could barely swallow. Then Kate taught her how to change the dressings. As they worked, Kate chatted with the soldiers, but Annie kept quiet. Most of them were boys. Some were weepy. Others still seemed scared to death. None were profane or rude in any way.

As Kate showed Annie how to dress the stump of a leg taken at just above the knee, Annie asked how she learned about medicine.

"In Philadelphia," she said. "My first husband worked in the same hospital as Dr. Carson."

"Was your husband a doctor too?"

"Yes," she answered. "I worked alongside him until Ira was born. And then I turned my attention to midwifery." She paused for a moment. "Ira was three when his father died. We got by, but then I met and married a merchant from Peach Bottom. But then, like I said before, he died too. I guess you could say I don't have much luck with husbands."

197

"Did your second husband belong to the Brethren church?" Annie asked.

Kate shook her head. "No, he was a Presbyterian. I was raised in the Brethren faith. I left when I married my first husband—and returned after the death of my second."

"What about Ira?" Annie asked.

A sad expression fell over Kate's face. "He's finding his way." She met Annie's gaze. "Which all of us have to do, correct?"

She nodded. After they'd served the soldiers a dinner of mutton, vegetable soup, and bread, Dr. Carson asked Kate to help him in the tent out back.

Annie spent some time writing letters for the soldiers and then reading out of the scriptures to the group on the back porch.

She had a view of the amputation tent. Ira and another soldier carried a man through the back porch on a litter and headed that way. Annie said a prayer for the soldier—and for Kate. She was amazed at what the woman could do. The other litter bearer came back, but not Ira. She guessed he was helping with the amputation, and she wondered if he planned to become a doctor like his father had been.

The day progressed. They fed the wounded bread and stewed fruit for supper with slices of cheese and another cup of tea. Kate told Annie to go to bed, that she'd stay up for a few more hours and then join her.

"I'm going to get some fresh air first," Annie said. She'd survived, but inside she felt raw and unsettled and wondered if she'd be able to keep up with the work day after day. Her knees continually felt weak, and several times she wondered why she hadn't obeyed Samuel and returned home.

Kate nodded. "You're doing a good job. I don't know what I was thinking to bring you here—but thank you for coming."

Annie nodded and said, "I'll be all right." She slipped down the hall, by Dr. Carson's office door. Through the open door she saw him checking on one of the three patients on cots in the room. Then he stepped to his desk, picked something up, and took a drink. She hurried on, not wanting him to see her. Perhaps it was a flask of whiskey in his hands, something to get him through the end of the day. She never thought she'd be sympathetic toward someone taking a drink, until now.

She slipped out the back door, past the soldiers on the porch, and headed toward the orchard. First she heard whistling and then a song she didn't recognize. "Where the blossoms smell the sweetest, come rove along with me. It's ev'ry Sunday morning when I am by your side. We'll jump into the wagon, and all take a ride. . . ." She did recognize the voice, however. It was Ira's. The song sounded so happy, so contradictory to the devastation around them.

The light was fading, and she could see Ira in the trees but didn't want to venture that far. Kate had warned her not to leave the grounds alone. She stopped near the kitchen tent.

"Annie?"

She glanced over her shoulder as Ira stepped out of the orchard.

"Wait," he said. "I've been meaning to speak with you."

Annie remembered what he'd whispered to his mother the day before. Perhaps he wanted to chastise her too. She squared her shoulders. "What is it?"

"I'm sorry my mother brought you here. She means well, but I don't think she realized how . . . ghastly it would all be."

He was right. It was ghastly.

"You have no obligation"—he gestured up toward the cemetery—"to be part of this mess. Woody will be back tomorrow, and then he'll either be heading back to Peach Bottom or perhaps Lancaster. He can take you away from here."

By the light of the fire coming from the kitchen tent, Annie met his eyes. "Do you want me to leave?"

His blue eyes narrowed. "As a matter of fact, I do. This is no place for you."

"You don't think I can tend to the sick? Dress wounds? Feed the infirmed?" Annie put a hand on her hip as a determination to succeed rose inside of her. For the first time all day, her knees felt steady. She would prove Ira King wrong. Before he could answer, she said, "I won't be taking you up on your offer to ship me home with Woody."

She turned toward the house, surprised by her own outburst.

"Annie." He reached for her arm.

She jerked it away.

"I'm only thinking about your well-being."

She faced him again. "And why would you bother yourself with that?"

She expected him to be defensive, but his blue eyes were full of compassion. "Why wouldn't I?"

Tears threatened to escape her eyes. "You didn't stand up for me the day you met me. And then you joked with the other soldiers about Felicity."

"That's right," he said. "It's the way soldiers talk. I was only playing along, to protect you both."

"What do you mean?"

"I had to tread carefully. If I'd offended the soldiers who were with me, I'd have a hard time getting them to cooperate. I had to play my hand carefully." He sighed. "I'm sorry. It's hard to explain."

Annie knew she didn't understand, but Ira seemed earnest about what he felt he had to do.

"Hopefully Felicity and her baby are in Philadelphia by now. I know she made it across the river by train before the Union had to burn the bridge at Columbia."

Annie thought of the train station at Lancaster and the black men who seemed to disappear.

"I've told you too much." Ira sighed again, and Annie thought of how exhausted he must be. "Hopefully the Rebs are on the run and this whole nightmare will soon be over. And God's children will all be free."

She didn't respond, but already she regretted doubting him.

"I know you're nonresistant," he said. "It must be hard to be here."

"It certainly strengthens my beliefs. War—or at least the aftermath—is more horrific than I ever imagined. No wonder Christ wants us to live in peace."

"I agree," he said.

She motioned toward his uniform. "Then why would you fight?"

"I don't fight. I joined up to help others. That's why I'm here."

"You don't fight?"

"No," he said. "I'm a medic. And now Doc is teaching me all he can."

"Do you hope to become a doctor?"

He shrugged. "We'll see. . . ."

"Did you ever join the Brethren?"

He nodded. "When my mother did. As you can imagine, they weren't happy about me joining the army." He glanced down at his uniform. "As long as I'm wearing this, I'm not in communion with them."

"But you'll go back?" Annie asked.

He nodded. "God willing." Then he pointed to the house. "I'll walk with you. You shouldn't be out here after dark."

As they walked, Annie thought of Felicity. "I'm sorry I was rude to you that night you came to get the girl and baby."

"No offense taken," Ira answered. "I admired you from the beginning for being so willing to defend her."

They'd reached the back porch. Annie thanked Ira and started up the steps. She turned and watched him walk toward the stable, where he and the other men slept in the loft.

He started to sing again. "Where the blossoms smell the sweetest, come rove along with me. . . ." If only the smell of honeysuckles filled the air instead of blood and rot.

***

Several days passed by, each one filled with tasks of feeding, bathing, and dressing wounds. Annie continued to read and write letters for the soldiers. Gradually, she grew used to the smells and sights of the hospital, and each day she grew more comfortable with her tasks.

A week after the battle, as Annie finished serving breakfast, Kate asked her to accompany Ira to the Christian Commission at the Schick Store to gather more supplies while the other nurses bathed the patients. Annie thought it odd she'd send them unchaperoned, but it dawned on her that the rules were much different during a time of war. Obviously they were, or she wouldn't be in Gettysburg at all.

Ira hitched a horse to a cart, and they headed down to the main street, turning right toward the town square. Again, Annie held her apron up to her nose. The stench of death was thick in town too. It seemed nearly every house along the street had been riddled with bullets during the battle. Broken glass, doors, and splintered furniture littered the yards. It appeared most of the houses had been turned into hospitals, all much smaller than Dr. Carson's home. Doors on sawhorses were being used as beds, and even front porches served as spaces for soldiers.

The store was just before the town square, and beyond that was the train station. Annie could see them both as Ira stopped the wagon in front of the store.

"They've repaired the railroad tracks to York," Ira said. "I heard they expect to start shipping the wounded out this morning."

"Where all to?" Annie asked.

"York first. There's a hospital there. They'll try to send others home if they can."

Annie mentioned Cecil, Harriet's brother, and Richert.

"Do you know what regiment each one is in?"

"They joined up together. The 1st Pennsylvania Regiment, Company F."

"That helps," Ira said. "Let's ask at the Commission and see if they know where the injured from that company might be."

Annie thought Ira might forget to ask as they carried out boxes of gauze, bandages, morphine, chloroform, and ether, but as he signed for all of the supplies, he asked about Company F.

"Check at the white house with the cots on the porch, on your way back. They might know."

Ira stopped at the house, and Annie waited while he stepped inside. When he came back he said, "The doctor in charge said to go out to the field hospital, just outside of town. He heard they have quite a few Pennsylvanian soldiers there."

"Can we go now?" Annie asked.

"Let's drop off these things and then go." The cart rolled forward. "I'll try to get some more supplies at the hospital and maybe some food too."

Thirty minutes later, they were back on the road headed toward the field hospital. In the six days since they'd passed by before, many more Confederate soldiers had been buried. This time Annie noticed crops that had been damaged. Trampled grain. Destroyed vegetables. Demolished orchards. She couldn't imagine the horror of a battle taking place on her family farm. Lives had been lost on this land. Forever gone from this world. She shivered even in the heat, and offered up a prayer for both the families of the dead and for the farmers and their families who'd been witnesses to the devastation all around them. Heaven was the hope they all had in common.

When they reached the field hospital, Annie stayed in the wagon again while Ira approached another soldier. There was lots of activity around her. Orderlies moving patients. Soldiers moving supplies. Nurses hurrying from one tent to another. A soldier carrying a crate marched by, singing, "I have seen Him in the watch-fires of a hundred circling camps. . . ." Annie hadn't heard the song before but listened intently. "His day is marching on." And then the man sang, as he hurried along, "Glory, glory, hallelujah, glory, glory, hallelujah . . ."

Ira disappeared into a tent, and then returned a few minutes later to her side of the wagon.

He reached out a hand to help Annie down. "A fellow said there are several wounded soldiers from Company F three tents down. Do you mind coming with me?"

She agreed and followed him once she was on the ground. The field, which had probably been a muddy mess a few days before, was pockmarked with ruts. They ducked into the third tent, where the canvas walls were covered with splotches of mildew and flies buzzed around.

Cots packed the tent, spaced just inches from each other. The stench was much worse than at Dr. Carson's hospital. It was nearly unbearable, but Annie didn't pull her apron to her nose. If the soldiers could endure their surroundings, she could too.

When Ira asked an orderly about men from Company F, he pointed toward the end of the tent. Annie followed Ira, side-stepping between the cots. One of the soldiers was leaning on his elbow, staring at the soldier across from him.

"We're looking for boys from Company F," Ira said.

"Richert Fisher and Cecil Troyer in particular," Annie said.

The man propped up on his elbow glanced up, his eyes glassy. "Cecil headed off with the unit to chase Lee south." Then he nodded toward a soldier a couple of cots from him. "That's Richert over there."

Annie stepped closer. The soldier's head was wrapped in a bandage that covered his eyes.

"He has a bad leg injury too," the man said. "He talks some and has eaten a little, but he's not doing well."

Ira thanked the man and bent down beside Richert. "Can you hear me? We've come to check on you. Annie Bachmann is here with me."

Richert reached out his hand and Annie took it. "Jah, it's me. I'm here." She knelt down beside him.

"Take me home," he whispered.

Annie looked up at Ira.

He shook his head but said, "We'll see what we can do. Eat what you can. Try to gain your strength back. We'll return tomorrow."

They told Richert good-bye, and then while Annie stood by

the wagon, Ira spent some time talking to one officer and then another. When he returned, he carried a crate of supplies and three soldiers followed him, carrying crates too.

Once they were both back up on the bench of the cart, Ira said he'd managed to procure flour and canned goods, plus more medical supplies.

"Did you talk to anyone about Richert?"

"I did. They said he'll be transported to the hospital in York, probably by early next week."

"Do you think we could get him home instead? Would Woody take him?"

Ira wrinkled his nose as the wagon bounced over the ruts. "I'm not sure he'd make it." He glanced at Annie, a concerned look on his face. "Honestly, I'm not sure he'll make it to York."

Annie's stomach roiled. She exhaled and then asked Ira, "Do you think he'd get better care under Dr. Carson?"

"Perhaps, but I'm not sure that would matter either. I'm so sorry." He glanced at her again. "But let's ask Doc." He kept his eyes on her. "I think that would be best. Don't you?"

She nodded.

They rode in silence for a few minutes, and then Annie thanked Ira for his help.

"I can tell Richert means a lot to you."

"Jah," she answered. "He's my sister's beau. She's ill—"

"Pardon?"

"Sophia has consumption."

"No, what did you say before? Richert is your sister's beau?"

"Jah," she said.

He chuckled.

"What's funny?"

"Nothing," he said. "Absolutely nothing." His face grew

serious. "I shouldn't have laughed. It's just that I thought that Richert was your beau, not your sister's."

Annie wasn't sure how to answer.

"Then again, you probably have a beau back home, right?"

She wasn't sure how to answer that either. Finally, she said, "Time will tell."

Ira snapped the reins as they reached the road. His tone was light, but his words were serious. "I suppose it will."

❦

Annie never knew exactly how Ira managed it, but the next morning he left in the wagon and then returned with Richert in the back. He and an orderly carried him up the stairs and placed him on the back porch on the cot of a soldier who'd died during the night.

Both Kate and Dr. Carson examined him as Annie fed an egg to a soldier who had broken one arm and lost the other.

Richert was alert and answered the doctor's questions as he removed the bandage over his eyes. The cannon he was loading had exploded.

"I can't see anything, sir, except a bit of light." He reached up to his face, but Kate caught his hand. "Will my sight come back?"

Dr. Carson said he didn't know, that time would tell.

Annie thought of her exchange with Ira two nights before. Even though he'd wanted her to go home, he hadn't been as bossy about it as Samuel. Then again, Samuel had only been able to communicate through a letter. He probably wouldn't have sounded that way in person. A wave of homesickness came over her, for her family and for Samuel.

"Right now," Dr. Carson said to Richert, "I'm more concerned

207

about your arm." He unwrapped the bandage as he talked. "What did the doctor at the field hospital say about it?"

"That time would tell. . . ."

The doctor smiled, although Richert couldn't see his expression of course. Annie couldn't help but smile too. They were all waiting on time.

"I have a wound in my thigh too." Richert reached down below the sheet.

"I'll look at it next," Doc Carson said and then asked Kate to move the basin closer. "They missed some shrapnel in the muscle of your arm."

Annie turned her attention back to the soldier she was feeding.

That afternoon, she took some time and wrote a letter to Sophia, telling her how thrilled she was to read that she was feeling better. Then she wrote about finding Richert in the field hospital and Ira bringing him to Dr. Carson's house. *I believe he is getting the best care possible. We will do what we can to get him home as soon as we can.* She listed his injuries, hoping that Sophia would surmise how serious they were. Then Annie added a note to her parents, assuring them that George had not wanted her to go to Gettysburg, but she couldn't stay away when she knew she could help. It was her doing, not her brother's, and she asked them not to be angry with him.

Next, she wrote a quick note to Harriet and George, letting them know she'd found Richert and passing on the news she'd heard about Cecil, that he had survived the battle without any injuries and was now traveling with his unit.

Finally, she wrote Samuel, wishing she'd done so earlier. She said she didn't plan to come home anytime soon, that she was in fact presently in Gettysburg helping to take care of soldiers and perhaps, God willing, she'd see him soon, which she longed for. She assured him she was well and thanked him for his concern.

Each day, another soldier would die, while another grew stronger. Often, Annie was surprised by who passed and who survived. Sometimes it seemed as if there was no rhyme or reason to any of it.

Annie grew more and more confident in nursing the soldiers, and Kate said, several times, that Annie had a gift for medicine. She also began helping in the kitchen tent some, assisting Meg with the meal preparation when she was short-staffed. It was a nice break from the sadness in the house. Meg was kind and good-spirited, never sinking into despair despite the hardships all around them. One afternoon, Annie was helping Meg make tea for the staff when Kate headed for the tent, followed by Dr. Carson.

"Kate," he called out. "Wait!"

She marched ahead. Annie couldn't imagine why she was ignoring the man.

When she reached the tent, Kate spoke quietly to Meg. "He needs a cup of coffee. And keep him away from the house." With that, Kate spun around, without even acknowledging Annie, and headed back to the house, walking brusquely by the doctor.

He stopped and looked after her until Meg yelled, "Come on, Doc. We have a cup of coffee for you. And a piece of cobbler."

He turned toward her, his eyes red.

Meg stepped toward him. "Come along." Then she turned back to Annie and said, "Go ask Kate how you can help."

Annie did as Meg instructed. Dr. Carson didn't acknowledge her as she passed by him, and she didn't say anything either. She caught a whiff of alcohol though. It seemed he didn't just drink at night. At least not today. She turned and watched as Meg removed something from the pocket of the doctor's work apron and then took his hand and led him into the tent. Meg gestured for Annie to keep moving. Embarrassed, Annie did, hurrying to the house.

The next day Dr. Carson seemed fine and no one mentioned his indiscretion from the day before. He, Kate, and Ira performed more amputations. Annie's heart would have broken for the soldiers, except that, surprisingly, the majority of them survived their operations, although she knew they had a hard recovery ahead. Annie never assisted during an amputation. There was no need for her to, thankfully. But she prayed each time the orderlies carried another soldier to the tent.

Richert grew a little stronger, although his vision didn't improve and the wound to his thigh continued to fester. Several patients had been transported to York by train, while others were still being brought to Dr. Carson's from the field hospitals, including several soldiers who hailed from Lancaster County. After a visit from Dr. Letterman, the surgeon general of the Union, Dr. Carson stood in the hallway of the house, outside his office door, and told Kate it would be good to transport the Lancaster County soldiers home so their families could care for them and free up hospital beds for soldiers from Maine, New York, Massachusetts, and other faraway places. Annie, tending a soldier in the dining room, could hear the conversation.

"Ira, Annie, and I can take the wounded by train," Kate said.

"No," Dr. Carson said. "We need you here. We'll send someone else."

Kate said she'd stayed as long as she intended to. "We've been here three weeks."

Dr. Carson guffawed. "It's not that simple."

Annie strained to hear if Kate responded. If she did, it must have been very quietly.

"I need to speak to you in private," the doctor said to her. Footsteps fell in the hall and then his office door slammed.

Annie kept tending the soldiers, but Dr. Carson's voice rose a couple times. "I already apologized for that," he yelled at one point. And then he said, "I beg you to stay."

After that, Kate marched out the door with him calling after her. She stood in the hall where Annie could see her, and in a calm voice said to him, "Ira will return. But I need to get back to my midwifery business. I've neglected my duties long enough."

Before the doctor responded, Kate walked through the dining room, her head high, on her way to the back porch. Dr. Carson spent the rest of the day in his office. Later, Annie asked Kate if she was all right, and she simply nodded but didn't say a word.

The next morning, Woody arrived with another load of supplies. After everything was unloaded and recorded, Woody ate breakfast while Ira and the other orderlies loaded soldiers into his wagon and Dr. Carson's wagon too. Ira and another soldier drove the wagons to the station, unloaded them, and then returned.

Annie packed her few things and Kate's too, while the older woman redressed wounds.

When she reached the back porch, Ira and Woody were loading Richert, the last of the wounded to leave the hospital that day, into Woody's wagon. They would be traveling with twelve patients in all. Four could walk, but the rest were immobile.

Kate followed Annie out of the house and down the stairs, taking off her bloody apron. Annie put their bags in the back of the wagon as Woody greeted Kate by taking his hat off and saying, "Hello, Miss Kate."

But then before he could say anything more, Dr. Carson approached and again asked Kate to stay.

She shook her head. "As I already told you, it's time for me to go home."

"Then please return."

She shook her head but didn't say anything more. Instead she handed her apron to Annie, who took off hers too.

"Then leave Annie here," Dr. Carson said. "She's done a good job, much better than I expected. . . ."

Annie headed to the washhouse with both aprons and couldn't hear the rest of the conversation, but she wouldn't stay without Kate. She took a quick detour to the kitchen tent and told Meg good-bye. The woman gave her a warm hug and said, "I'm going to miss your help and smile. I hope I'll see you again someday."

Annie couldn't imagine when she would, but she hugged the woman back and then returned to the wagon. Kate sat on the bench by Woody, and Ira sat in the back. Dr. Carson had already returned to the house. Annie climbed up onto the bench beside Kate, and Woody snapped the reins. As they passed by the side of the house, Annie saw a figure in the office window. She was certain it was the doctor.

Kate, Woody, and Ira all seemed tense and remained silent. Annie didn't say anything either.

The depot platform was covered with wounded soldiers. Kate told her the area had operated as a hospital before the train tracks had been repaired. Now it was in transition—half hospital and half station—as train after train of wounded soldiers left Gettysburg for York.

Ira and Woody carried the immobile soldiers to the platform while the ones who could walk shuffled along. One had his arm amputated and the other had taken a bullet in the neck. Somehow it had missed his artery, and he'd survived.

After he and Ira lowered the last patient, Woody and Kate spoke at the end of the platform. From what Annie could hear, he was going to take several soldiers from Hanover to Peach Bottom. Then he planned to drive to Lancaster for another load of supplies.

"Hopefully I'll see you there, Miss Kate," he said.

She gave him an idea of their itinerary, as best she could.

"Will Annie be going home?"

"Yes," Kate said. "I believe that's her plan, although I would love to have her assist me in Peach Bottom if she ever wanted to."

Annie's face grew warm with the words. She felt it would be best to remain on the farm, with her family, but she would do as the Lord led.

When the train they were waiting for finally arrived, some people got off. Annie guessed a few were searching for a son, brother, or husband because many of the fallen were still unaccounted for. Other passengers carried bags of supplies. As they passed by the soldiers, they searched their faces.

Once the train was vacated, Ira and other able-bodied soldiers carried the wounded aboard. Soon the train was full and took off, lurching forward.

Annie and Kate walked up and down the aisle, checking on each soldier. Richert slept most of the way, but when he woke he seemed disoriented. Annie explained their plan to him again. The train would stop in York, and then they would go on to Columbia, where all of the soldiers would be taken off the train, loaded onto a boat, and taken across the Susquehanna River. Once they were on the other side, they'd board another train and continue on to Lancaster.

Annie had sent letters to both Richert's parents and to Sophia, letting them know they would be heading home soon. Ira said they'd need to hire a wagon at the station in Lancaster to get Richert to Leacock. Annie wished Woody would be able to transport him, but he wouldn't be back from Peach Bottom by then.

When they reached York, Annie and Ira stepped off the train, weaving their way between the soldiers covering the platform, to buy bread for those in their care. As they stepped into the station, looking for vendors, a man called out Annie's name.

She turned. Samuel hurried toward her.

"What are you doing here?" she sputtered.

"I was headed to Gettysburg to bring you back."

"There's no need for that," she said. "I'm headed home now."

"Why didn't you write that you were leaving Gettysburg?"

She wiped the palms of her hands on her apron. "I didn't have time." Although she'd taken the time to write to the Fishers and to Sophia. The truth was, she hadn't thought to write Samuel. And she'd never expected that he'd come after her, but she was touched that he had.

Ira had gone on to buy loaves of bread and then rejoined them. Annie introduced him to Samuel, and the two men shook hands.

"I'll go change my ticket," Samuel said, "and travel back with you."

"Great," Ira answered. "We need an extra set of hands to help carry the stretchers."

Once they were back on the train, Ira kept Samuel busy, directing him to help feed the soldiers. Richert recognized Samuel's voice immediately and the two chatted for a couple of minutes, but Samuel appeared uncomfortable with Richert's injuries—

or perhaps that he'd been fighting—and quickly moved on to feed another patient. When the train reached Columbia and it was time to disembark, it seemed providential that Samuel was available to help. Men from the town assisted too, and soon all of the soldiers were safely transported to the boat. Annie knelt beside Richert as they crossed, the breeze from the river helping to cool them from the midday sun.

When she looked up at the Susquehanna hills in the distance, she noted that Samuel was watching her. Kate wanted Annie to return with her to Peach Bottom, but Annie wanted nothing more than to stay in Lancaster. To court Samuel. To tend the garden. To care for Sophia.

There was nowhere safer for her than the Bachmann farm in Lancaster County.

But, still, there was so much healing that needed to happen. If God had given her a gift, as Kate claimed, then He wanted her to use it to serve others. Yes, she didn't believe in violence, but that didn't mean that God didn't want her to care for those who'd chosen it or were forced to participate. All had suffered because of it.

By the time the group had reached the other side of the river and boarded the next train, Annie was exhausted and could only imagine how the patients felt. And Ira and Samuel. They were the ones doing the hard work. She only carried supplies.

The closer they drew to the city of Lancaster, the more she longed for home. The weeks she'd spent away felt like a year.

It was dark by the time they arrived. Five of the wounded soldiers had parents or brothers meet them at the station. Annie had written letters for them too, and their loved ones had been coming to the station day after day. Finally their hopes had been realized.

One of the soldiers who could walk lived not far from the train station. Ira escorted him to his parents' house. Kate sent messages to the other two soldiers' families, but they lived farther away. It was too late and too dark for them to come tonight, and too late for Annie to start home with Richert too.

Ira returned and they all, including Samuel, found a place to rest in the station. Annie felt ill with fatigue and wondered if the stress of the last couple of weeks had caught up with her. During the night, Richert took a turn for the worse, and Kate tended to him. Annie woke a few times, aware of the situation, but she was unable to rouse herself to help. Early in the morning before the sun had risen, she stumbled over to where Richert was on the floor. Ira had taken over for his mother.

"He's running a fever," Ira said, "and he's been restless all night."

"I'll take a turn," Annie said.

"I'll go find a wagon," Ira said. "The sooner we get him home, the better."

By the time the sun rose, a father and an uncle of the other two soldiers arrived. Kate explained the care the soldiers needed and told the families to fetch their own doctor that day.

After they left, Kate told Annie that the local doctors had probably never treated a bullet wound, let alone an amputation. "They'll do the best they can, however." Kate yawned. "We'll get you, Richert, and Samuel on your way, and then Ira and I will find a ride to Peach Bottom."

"Come to my family's farm and rest," Annie said. "Perhaps Woody will be back by morning and can give you a ride."

Kate shook her head. "We don't want to impose."

"You have to be exhausted." Annie felt bad that she hadn't been able to stay awake and help.

Ira returned, saying he'd secured a wagon. As Kate stood, she wobbled a little, and Annie grabbed her arm. Ira helped steady his mother too.

"Please come with us," Annie said. "Get some sleep and good food. Then start home tomorrow."

Ira gave his mother a questioning look.

She nodded. "I'm tired, is all. But I think a day of rest could make a big difference."

Annie held on to Kate as Samuel and Ira carried Richert out to the wagon. Annie assumed they'd drop Samuel off at his home, but he chose to ride on with them.

They dropped off Richert at the Fishers' first, to his relieved and grateful parents. Kate instructed them to send for a doctor immediately, explaining that his leg was infected and that he was running a fever.

Eva assured her they would and then gave Annie a hug. "It was the Lord who led you to Richert."

Annie hugged her back, praying Richert would survive.

They traveled the short distance to the Bachmann farm. Again, Annie assumed Samuel would go back with the driver, but instead he jumped down, lifting his hand to help Annie. "Josiah will give me a ride later," he said. "I need to speak with you, in private."

Mamm, who was weeding in the garden, shaded her eyes and then shouted in joy, calling out Annie's name.

Annie started toward her mother, but then another yell, this time from the back door, caught her attention. Sophia stood tall, wearing a dress and apron. Mamm and Annie both headed toward her, and all three fell into each other's arms.

When Annie pulled away, she said, "We have visitors who need a place to stay for the night, Kate Baxter and her son, Ira King." She nodded toward the group. "And Samuel is here too."

Mamm hurried down the steps to greet the visitors.

"How is Richert?" Sophia asked.

"He's not well, but he's home. They'll have the doctor tend to him today."

"I want to go see him," Sophia said.

Not sure that was a good idea, Annie said, "Perhaps you should let him rest today and go see him tomorrow."

Tears welled in her eyes. "Do you think that's what he wants?"

Annie's heart swelled, and she shook her head. "No, of course not. He wants you to be with him as soon as possible."

Her eyes brightened through her tears. "Then I should go."

Annie nodded in agreement, touched once again by their love for each other.

–15–

Marie

Aenti Suz leaned back against the couch and yawned, quickly covering her mouth. Then she said, "I'm exhausted. It's been a long day."

I reached for her bowl. "How about some more ice cream? It'll keep you awake."

She shook her head. "I'm off to bed."

"But what about the story?"

Aenti Suz stood. "It will have to wait."

I tried not to let my disappointment show too much as I told her good-night and then washed our bowls. After all, Aenti Suz needed her rest. But I wished she'd tell me how the story ended. Had Sophia recovered? Would Annie stay in Lancaster and marry Samuel?

A wave of homesickness came over me. Annie had loved our farmhouse as much as I did, yet she'd left it—and Lancaster County—to serve others. She reminded me of Jessica and Leisel.

As I dried the bowls and put them away, I thought about the

desires of my heart—to marry a farmer in our district and stay close to Mamm and our farm. Annie seemed to have the same desires, and yet she was willing to leave the safety of home to care for others. It was hard for me to admit, but I only wanted to care for myself and my family.

I tossed and turned through the night. The first time I awoke, my thoughts were on Annie and the past. The second time, my thoughts were on the present. First on Elijah's kisses. Then on Gordon. Was he a do-gooder, only seeking attention, as Elijah had implied?

I'd certainly never been much of a do-gooder. Sure, I'd make a pie or even help sew a quilt for an auction, but I too believed people needed to take responsibility for their own lives. As Amish, we certainly did. But Paula was right. Not everyone had the resources we did or the community support we offered one another. Eventually, I drifted off to sleep.

When we first arrived in Pinecraft, Aenti Suz had stated that she was hoping for a mix of outings and down days during our vacation. She deemed Saturday a down day. I spent the morning with Aenti Suz, sitting out on the patio. As she read, I wrote letters to Mamm, Jessica, and Leisel.

A cool ocean breeze blew through the treetops, enough that I put on a sweater. I prayed for my Mamm and sisters as I wrote to each of them, fighting off another pang of homesickness. Of course, I'd been missing Leisel for nearly the last year, but now I was farther away from her than ever.

Halfway through the morning, our landlady dropped off a letter for me. It was from Gail. I opened it quickly, scanning her news about how cold and snowy it was in Ohio and how she'd just started courting a man who worked in his father's buggy-making business. Then she responded to my comments about Elijah. *Reading between the lines, I'm guessing you're interested in Elijah. I hope your affection for his parents and your desire to stay in the district aren't clouding your judgment. As we both know, you and Elijah are as different as can be. They say opposites attract, but two people must have something in common to forge a relationship. If you start spending more time with him, please enlighten me and let me know in which ways he truly has changed.*

I folded the letter. Talk about self-righteous. I was so glad that I'd been maturing and becoming less judgmental, even if Gail hadn't. I wouldn't bother to write her back. Not yet, anyway. She had no idea what she was talking about. I had more in common with Elijah than any other man I knew.

On Sunday, David joined us for breakfast and then we walked to the Amish church for services again. I was surprised to see Elijah and Billy leaning against the railing of the ramp, along with Paula. All were dressed appropriately, at least by Florida standards. Paula had on a print dress and Mennonite Kapp. Billy and Elijah both wore slacks, white button-up shirts, and suspenders. They weren't dressed for Lancaster, but they fit in fine for down here.

Paula waved and grinned. "Mind if I join you today?"

"I'd love that," I answered.

We traipsed into the church. Billy and Elijah went to the men's side, while Paula, Aenti Suz, and I sat with the other women.

As we sang "Das Loblied," I imagined Mamm singing the same hymn back in Lancaster County. Again, I longed for home. Soon enough, I'd be there. In the meantime, I'd enjoy every moment I could here.

I sang louder. " . . . word through grace to understand, What Thou would have us to do . . ." I'd known the words by heart from the time I could talk.

My mind wandered to Gordon. He would be worshipping at the Mennonite church close to the shelter today. Perhaps he was leading singing. Or playing his guitar for the children. Whatever he was doing, I was sure he was serving others and doing the Lord's work.

After several songs, the bishop read from Psalm 37. I lifted my head after the first couple of verses, as I heard *my* verse being read. How apropos that here I was in Florida, with Elijah across the aisle, and this very passage was part of the service. "'Delight thyself also in the Lord: and he shall give thee the desires of thine heart.'"

The minister continued on to the end of the chapter. "'But the salvation of the righteous is of the Lord: he is their strength in the time of trouble . . . because they trust in him.'"

I had trusted and delighted in the Lord my entire life. I had no doubt He was my strength. I had no doubt that now He would give me the desires of my heart.

After the scripture reading, another minister stood and began to preach from the third verse of the chapter, "'Trust in the Lord, and do good; so shalt thou dwell in the land, and verily thou shalt be fed.'"

He talked about serving others and then about how blessed we were, as a group of people, to have property and plenty of resources. He preached that we needed to look for ways to share those blessings with others. He then started talking about our ancestors in Switzerland and Germany and how persecuted they were. . . . My mind began to wander . . . to Elijah's family's farmhouse back home. Perhaps his parents would live with us or build a Dawdi Haus out back. Our children would benefit from having their grandparents close by.

Of course, I'd have Mamm come over on a regular basis to

help me with the children, the laundry, the baking, and also the quilting.

I continued daydreaming, thinking about how our home would be a center for both of our families, until the minister said, "Blessed be the name of the Lord."

Paula nodded in agreement.

After another scripture reading and a final prayer, the service was over.

Paula stood. "What a great sermon."

I nodded in agreement.

"It was much more proactive than I anticipated."

"Oh?"

"That story about the minister's work in Haiti. Wow."

Dat had gone to Haiti after the 2010 earthquake. Perhaps I should have listened instead of imagining my future life.

"There's so much work that must be done," Paula said. "So many people in need."

I nodded. "We can't do it all."

"Jah, that's right. But how about that verse out of James? The one about if we know the good we ought to do and don't do it, it's a sin?"

I didn't remember that reference.

Thankfully, Elijah called out my name from across the aisle and I could escape Paula's intensity. As I stepped away from her, she turned to Aenti Suz and continued her train of thought.

"What's with Paula?" Elijah asked.

"She's reflecting on the sermon."

Elijah yawned, hooked his thumbs in his suspenders, and then whispered, "I couldn't help but reflect during the sermon on how much I needed a nap."

I smiled. I wouldn't tell him what I was reflecting on.

Paula stepped across the aisle and elbowed Elijah in the side. "When are you going to grow up?"

He grinned. "Probably later rather than sooner."

❧❦❧

On Monday, Aenti Suz and I picked up a few more groceries and then spent a quiet day at the bungalow. I embroidered while Aenti Suz read. Of course I wanted her to tell me more of Annie's story, but I didn't push her. She was on vacation. She deserved to rest.

Elijah stopped by Monday afternoon and again on Tuesday. On Wednesday, David joined us at noon for sandwiches. Just as we finished and started cleaning up the kitchen, there was a knock on the front door. As I walked toward it, I feared Gordon might be on the other side. To my relief, he hadn't called during the week with any information about an outing for me to join in on. But perhaps he decided to deliver the details in person.

Thankfully, it was Paula, a little out of breath.

I sighed in relief and gave her a hug.

She nodded out toward the street. "Billy and I are going to go pick up Elijah from work and go to Coquina Beach. He asked us to stop by and get you."

I glanced toward Aenti Suz, who could hear us from the kitchen. "Go on," she said. "Have a good time."

Paula followed me into my room while I threw a towel, shorts and T-shirt, and sunscreen into my bag, guessing that Gordon had changed his mind about contacting me at all. Perhaps he realized that Elijah and I were, essentially, courting. I was relieved at not being contacted by Gordon but also weirdly disappointed. I did enjoy spending time with him, even if we didn't have that much in common.

Ten minutes later, we picked up Elijah and headed for the beach, a long stretch on the southern end of Anna Maria Island. The beach had picnic tables and grills. Preschool-aged children swarmed over the playground and several volleyball games took place on the courts. Lots of people swam and others snorkeled.

Elijah headed toward a picnic table, and as he did someone from a distance away waved. A man. When he stood and waved directly at me, I realized it was Gordon. Around him were a mix of Plain folk and Englisch youth. Their grill was fired up, and from the smell of it, they were roasting sausages. Gordon waved us over. "Would you like to join us? We have plenty of food."

Elijah turned around and rolled his eyes, but Paula called out, "We'd love to!"

She turned toward me, whispering, "Is that Gordon?"

"Jah," I answered. "That's him." I'd told her a friend from back home was in the area for the week. I hadn't told her Elijah wanted to fix her up with him. And why would I? She and Billy seemed to be doing fine.

Paula grinned and marched forward. When she reached Gordon, she extended her hand. Elijah groaned. Billy didn't react, but he didn't exactly look pleased. I followed and quickly introduced Paula to Gordon—and then Billy to Gordon. Then Paula introduced herself to everyone else in the group. There was an older couple from Gordon's church, and a woman, a little younger than me, wearing a head covering, and eight youth who appeared to be between seventeen and twenty-two or so.

Paula boldly asked all of them where they were from. Two were siblings from Sarasota who lived with their family on the streets. One claimed New York City as home, but it seemed she was from somewhere else originally and didn't want to say where. One was from Delaware, and the rest were from Pennsylvania. One of them—Shayla—laughed and said she'd never expected to see Amish in Florida but she'd seen them "everywhere!"

We chuckled with her, and then Paula asked what made her leave home.

She quickly responded, "Addiction, abuse, and misuse. The big three. For some there's no place like home—for me, home was no place to be."

"I'm sorry," Paula said.

She shrugged.

The girl from New York said that her mother was mentally ill and kicked her out when she was fifteen.

"You're mentally ill too," replied Shayla.

The girl slugged her, and not in a playful way. I stepped back.

"Hey," Gordon said. "Remember what we talked about. No sharing someone else's story. It's not ours to tell." He glanced over to where the Mennonite women were pulling the sausages off the grill and then said, "Looks like it's time to eat."

I gathered that the younger woman was the couple's daughter. Her name was Abigail and her mother was Miriam. The man, Howard, led us all in prayer, and then Gordon told the guys to let the girls go first. There was a lot of jostling around and teasing and then a few angry words between Shayla and one of the other girls from Pennsylvania.

Gordon was talking with two of the boys, and the woman stepped between the girls just as Paula said, "Hey, Shayla. How about if you sit over here with me?"

Shayla sat on one side of Paula, while Billy sat on the other.

Elijah didn't say anything or really do anything either. None of his usual smiles or grins. But after he'd filled his plate, Howard struck up a conversation with him. They were soon exchanging names of people they both knew, starting with Elijah's Dat. Before long, they figured out they were distantly related.

"How long are you down here for?" Howard asked.

"Just until May," Elijah answered. "I'll go home and farm with my Dat after that. He plans to retire in a year or so."

The boy from Delaware muttered, "That must be nice."

Elijah stared at him for a moment but didn't reply. He turned back to Howard. "I'll join the church as soon as possible after I return."

The boy from Delaware, whose name was Josh, left his plate and walked toward the water. A few minutes later, Gordon followed him and then they returned together.

After we'd finished eating, Elijah nodded toward the volleyball court, but just as he did, Paula pointed toward Gordon's guitar case. "Who does that belong to?"

Abigail flipped the ties of her Kapp over her shoulder and answered, "Gordon."

"Were you all going to sing?" Paula asked.

Gordon smiled at her. "That's the plan." As he spoke, Abigail nodded her head. She seemed quite enamored with Gordon.

Elijah looked at me and rolled his eyes again and pointed toward the courts. I smiled back at him, but the truth was—no surprise—I'd rather sing than play volleyball. Howard nodded. "Let's sing and then play."

I sat at the table with Elijah while the others, including Paula and Billy, gathered around Gordon while he tuned his guitar.

"Do you know the 'In the Beginning' song?" Paula asked.

Gordon nodded and began playing a tune. Once he'd played it through once, Paula began singing and then the others joined in.

Miriam put the rest of the food in a cold box and then sat

down beside me. "He does such a good job with the music—and the kids too. He's really an incredible young man." She smiled. "I keep hoping he and Abigail will start courting, but so far . . . Well, I can keep praying."

"Jah," I said. "You never know. . . ."

Elijah bumped against me.

I didn't blame Miriam for wanting Abigail to court Gordon. If I were a Mennonite mother with a daughter, I'd want the same thing. I just thought it odd that she'd say something about it to me.

"Gordon said he works for your family. That you're old friends."

I nodded. Perhaps that was why she confided in me about her wishes—maybe she thought I could influence Gordon in some way.

"How has your week been?" I asked as quietly as I could.

"Honestly?" She lowered her voice. "Hard. This is our third year in a row serving at the shelter down here, and this has been the most difficult yet. So many wounds and needs. So many injustices." She sighed. "We have to trust the Lord Jesus that our work will minister to these souls in some way."

"So will this be your last year?"

She shook her head as a smile crept across her face. "Oh no," she said. "We'll be back. With some different ideas, perhaps. And a year full of prayers. You know, God doesn't call us to do what's easy—He calls us to do what is necessary. And everyone needs to be loved and cared for, regardless of how difficult their lives are."

"How come you brought them to the beach today?" I asked.

She folded her hands on the tabletop. "We planned it early in the week, for this group of eight. We wanted to have a special outing. After working with them, I wasn't sure if it was a good idea. Thankfully, they do seem to like the music though. That seems to be a unifying factor."

Not all of them were singing, but all of them were at least listening. I longed to be singing, but it would have been rude not to talk with Miriam.

"Do they all live at the shelter?" I asked.

She shook her head and lowered her voice to a whisper. "Shayla does. And so do two of the boys. But the others are on the street and just come to the shelter to eat and for events."

"How about the ones from Pennsylvania? Have any of them been at the Lancaster shelter?"

She nodded. "Shayla has been, on and off."

"Wow," I said.

"How do they get all the way down here?"

"Hitchhike. Generally speaking, some are trafficked—by relatives and acquaintances and strangers."

I swallowed hard. I'd heard of that. I looked at the group again and felt sick to my stomach, noting the similarities between their lives and Felicity's in Annie's story. They were dependent on the help of kind strangers, just as Felicity had been. I didn't want to hear any more about trafficking, so I asked, "Is it normal to, you know, bring them on an outing like this?"

"We've never done it before but decided to give it a try. It was really a blessing that all of you showed up. It's nice for them to be around—" she hesitated—"other young people."

Elijah yawned.

Billy glanced back at him, and Elijah nodded toward the volleyball courts. Billy grinned and slipped out of the group. Elijah grabbed the ball that we'd brought and gave me a questioning look. I didn't want to go with him, but it felt disloyal not to.

"Go ahead," Miriam said. "Perhaps we'll venture over that way soon."

They didn't. I couldn't tell what happened, but Josh shouted something and then took off toward the waves again. Gordon followed him, once again, and brought him back. But then Shayla yelled about something.

I couldn't tell what happened after that, as I did my best to keep playing, but Gordon put his guitar away, and Paula helped Miriam and Abigail pack everything up. Soon, everyone grabbed something and marched toward the parking lot while Paula headed toward us.

When she reached the court, I asked, "What happened?"

"Josh had a meltdown and Shayla started berating him. Then the girl from New York said she was going to hitchhike back downtown. So Howard said they'd all leave."

"What did I tell you?" Elijah spiked the ball over the net as he spoke. "Manufactured drama."

Paula ignored him.

I wanted to point out that he hadn't actually told us anything, but perhaps he'd said something to Paula earlier.

Billy sent the ball back over the net, and Paula bumped it, hard, sending it way outside the court. Billy went running after it.

"Gordon, Howard, Abigail, and Miriam all have tomorrow off before they leave the next day for Lancaster." As she spoke, she stared straight at Elijah. "So I invited them all to the singing."

Elijah made a face.

Then she turned toward me. "Gordon said your aunt already invited him."

I nodded.

"Well, he plans on coming although he was a little worried about how you would react."

"No, it's fine," I answered.

Elijah rolled his eyes at Paula and then asked, "Did you invite all the homeless kids too?"

"No," she said. "But I'm going to check into volunteering down there on Friday. And I hope I'll see them—every one of them—again." She gave Elijah a sassy look and then slipped under the net, ready to play on Billy's side, against us.

As we sent the ball back and forth across the net, I kept thinking about what Miriam had said as far as serving the homeless. That it had been hard. But, still, they planned to come back next year. And that God didn't call us to do what was easy—but to do what was necessary. And that everyone deserved to be loved.

My stomach clenched with the realization that the only difference between me and those kids was the family I'd been born into. I'd done nothing to deserve the life I led.

− 16 −

I spent most of the next day out on the patio finishing embroidering my tea towels while Aenti Suz read another book. I kept hoping she'd tell me more of Annie's story, and she said she would, but by the time she got to a place in her book where she wanted to stop, it was time to start preparing our early supper so we'd be ready for the singing.

David arrived at six, and we walked to the park. Elijah had said the day before that he might come with Billy, but he wasn't sure. I hadn't expected him to because I knew he wasn't crazy about singing. It was obvious—and not just the day before at the beach.

I decided that even if Gordon did come to the singing, I hoped Elijah would come too. I believed the more time Elijah and I spent together in Pinecraft, the sooner we'd be seriously courting when he returned to Lancaster.

As we approached the park, the first thing that came into view was the number of bikes, trikes, and golf carts parked along the perimeter. Families eating their supper filled the picnic tables. And several men played bocce, which David described as a ball game brought to the U.S. by immigrants, on the grass.

The music had already started inside the shelter. As we approached, I wasn't surprised to find Paula, wearing a dress and Kapp but no apron, up on a little stage. I was surprised that she was holding a microphone though.

As we stepped into the back of the shelter, I saw that Gordon was sitting on the right side of the stage, playing his guitar. Sitting beside him was Josh, from the day before, playing a tambourine. I wondered if the boy really played it or if Gordon had simply brought him along and wanted to give him something to do so he could keep track of him. I didn't see Miriam, Abigail, or Howard. Or any of the rest of the youth.

"Look!" Aenti Suz pointed toward the stage. "Gordon came! I'm so glad we'll get to see him before he heads home."

I nodded.

She motioned for David and me to follow her and then led us toward a row of empty chairs that was pretty close to the front.

As we sat, she whispered, "Isn't that your friend Paula?"

I nodded.

Paula gave us a smile as the musicians—there was a keyboardist besides Gordon and Josh—started playing, "When the Roll Is Called Up Yonder." Paula started the singing without missing a beat.

I joined in, joy rising in my soul. I'd never sung to keyboard music, but I liked it. Aenti Suz must have been smiling at Gordon, because he spotted us and smiled back.

"Is Elijah coming?" Aenti Suz whispered.

"Hopefully." I patted the chair beside me. I'd saved him a place.

The woman playing the keyboard sang along into a microphone. She was an alto too, like Paula, and possibly Mennonite. It was hard to tell, as she wore a scarf instead of a Kapp. Both blended in with Gordon's baritone. We sang and sang, a mix of hymns and praise songs, some that I'd never heard, until Paula announced that the group would take a fifteen-minute break. "Because we want to get some pie," she said, "before it's all gone."

I looked behind me, and sure enough single pieces of pie were spread across a table on paper plates, served by a crew of women.

Aenti Suz, David, and I stood and made our way to the back. That was when I noticed Elijah playing basketball over on the court.

"Looks like he made it," Aenti Suz said.

"Jah." I tried to hide the hurt in my voice that he hadn't come to sit by me.

Aenti Suz put her arm around me. "He probably peeked in and didn't want to interrupt the singing."

"You're probably right."

"Why don't you take him a piece of pie?" It was cherry and looked delicious.

"Good idea," I answered. When we reached the table, I took two and headed toward the basketball court.

Elijah didn't acknowledge me until I called out his name and held up one of the plates.

"Not now." He grabbed the ball. "We're playing to twenty-one, then best of three." He dribbled down the court.

I stepped away.

Elijah made the basket and one of the players called out, "Six to two!"

I figured he might not be done any time soon.

As I turned back toward the shelter, I noticed Gordon standing off by himself under one of the oak trees with a water bottle in his hand. He smiled, and I started toward him. "Want some pie?"

He nodded as he took a drink of water and then put the bottle down, taking the plate. "Denki."

I took a bite of my pie and then said, "The music was beautiful."

He nodded. "It's not what you're used to, is it?"

I smiled. "Jah, I was surprised by the keyboard, stage, and microphones."

"You should sing with us," he said.

I shook my head. "I've never done anything like that. Besides, I'm not good enough to be up on stage." Whether or not I had perfect pitch.

He met my eyes. "That's not true." His expression was so kind that my throat grew tight. So I took another bite and swallowed, but the pie caught and I began to cough.

"How about a drink?" Gordon reached down for his water bottle.

I quickly took it and sipped a little water. The pie went down. "Denki," I said, handing it back to him. "Where's Josh?"

He pointed over by the swings. "Paula is introducing him around."

"That's nice." I took another bite and concentrated on chewing.

"Yeah, she's great. She has a real knack for connecting with other people."

I nodded. She'd certainly connected with me.

As we both finished our pie, Paula and Josh headed our way. As they neared, Gordon called out to Paula, "Don't you think Marie should sing with us?"

"Definitely! We could use a soprano up there."

I shook my head. "Ach, you don't want me on stage."

Paula grabbed my arm. "Just stand beside me and sing. You don't have to say anything or even use a microphone."

"It's good to try things that scare us," Josh said.

"Jah, this does scare me. But it seems so—" I stopped. I didn't want to accuse Gordon and Paula of being . . .

"Prideful?" Paula asked and chuckled. "It depends on if you're thinking about yourself or about God and others. If you're all nervous, you'll be thinking about yourself. . . ."

"Just give it a try," Josh said. "I'm doing the tambourine— kind of. Honestly, I don't even know a lot of the words, but I'm listening, and that makes me think of God, which Gordon told me is what worship is. "

"I don't even know all the songs," I said. "I've never heard some of the praise songs."

"We're going to do all hymns now," Paula said. "I promise you'll know them."

The keyboardist started to play, and Paula grabbed my hand and yanked on it.

"Here," Gordon said, "I'll take your plate."

I handed it to him and followed Paula down the center aisle of the shelter. A minute later, Josh and Gordon joined us and the other musicians.

The first song was "When I Survey the Wondrous Cross." I stood by Paula and sang, hoping the mic didn't pick up my voice.

Both Aenti Suz and David smiled at me, and I smiled back, hoping I didn't look prideful. Then I remembered what Josh had said and concentrated on the words. "Forbid it, Lord, that I should boast, Save in the death of Christ my God! All the vain things that charm me most, I sacrifice them to His blood. . . ." I thought of the things that charmed me most. The thought of marrying Elijah. And living in our district, on a farm, close to my Mamm. The truth was, I wanted my life to be charmed.

Honestly, I hadn't done much in my life that was hard. I'd basically loved those who were easy to love and avoided those who weren't. Even when Jessica left the church, I avoided thinking about her or praying for her or writing her more than the one letter where I scolded her for leaving. When she returned, still Englisch, I did everything I could to make her want to leave again.

My stomach twisted at the thought of it.

The musicians began playing "Blessed Assurance," and Paula and I sang the first line of the chorus. "Jesus is mine; Oh, what a foretaste of glory divine! Heir of salvation, purchase of God, Born of His Spirit, washed in His blood."

We didn't talk much about being assured of our salvation, even though we sometimes sang the song. But I did believe I was washed in Christ's blood. Didn't that mean that I should be able to love others, including the ones who weren't easy to love? To serve others, including the ones who weren't easy to serve? My eyes teared up at the thought, and I swallowed hard before Paula started the next verse.

We continued on, song after song. With each one, my own self-awareness lessened as my focus on the Lord increased. Soon the words were welling out of me. I experienced affection toward the Lord that I'd never felt during any service, singing, or personal prayer. Emotion swelled inside of me as the music filled my soul.

The words and music burrowed deep in my heart, and I longed to continue on forever. But of course I couldn't. The singing had to come to an end, and it did, with "Wonderful Love."

By now I was singing as loud as I could, not caring whether

the mic picked up my voice or not. The musicians stopped playing for the last stanza, and Paula stepped closer to me as we sang, "Come, let us sing of a wonderful love, Tender and true, tender and true, Out of the heart of the Father above, Streaming to me and to you . . ." *Out of the heart of the Father above, Streaming to me and to you.* Worshipping the Lord made me want to serve Him, to share His love with others. I thought of Josh and the growth in his life because of Gordon. Paula understood the value of helping others. Maybe I was beginning to also.

"Come to my heart, O Thou wonderful love! Come and abide, come and abide, Lifting my life till it rises above, Envy and falsehood and pride: Seeking to be, seeking to be, Lowly and humble, a learner of Thee." Tears filled my eyes as we came to the end of the song.

Paula put her arm around me and whispered, "That was beautiful."

I swiped at an escaping tear and hugged her back. "I'd like to volunteer with you at the shelter, if that's all right, even once before I leave."

"I'd love that," she answered.

Gordon was still sitting on his chair as Aenti Suz approached him and told him how much she appreciated his music. He introduced her to Josh, and Aenti Suz and David spent the next few minutes talking with him.

I stepped to the keyboard, and Paula followed me. The woman who'd been playing it had left. Paula hit a note. "This is C," she said.

I sang, "C, a cat."

She laughed and then showed me the other notes.

I placed my index finger on C. "May I?"

She nodded and I hit the note. Then I continued on, repeating what she had just played. Then I picked around and soon had the entire song figured out.

Paula shook her head. "You're playing by ear."

"What's that?"

"You don't have to read music to play it—you can re-create a song simply by having heard it."

I had no idea—this was the first time I'd ever touched a keyboard. I glanced over at Gordon, who still held his guitar. I knew from watching him that the way he pressed the strings determined the notes. I wondered how hard it would be to learn to play it.

Two men stepped up on stage and said they needed to pack up the keyboard, so we stepped away from it and drifted over to Gordon.

"You did great," Gordon said to me. "You seemed completely at ease."

I smiled. "Josh's advice helped."

Gordon smiled back. "So what's been your favorite thing while you've been down here?"

"Oh," I answered, "I've loved it all. The people. The weather. The water. The beach yesterday—and getting a glimpse of the work you've done down here was good too."

He nodded. "But what's been the best?"

"Honestly?"

He nodded.

"A story Aenti Suz has been telling me about Annie Bachmann, a great-great-great-aunt who grew up on our farm." I mentioned that she'd worked as a nurse after the Battle of Gettysburg. "She reminds me of Leisel," I said. "But of you too. Ready to jump in and make a difference."

"That's fascinating," he said. "I'd love to hear it."

"I'll tell you sometime, after Aenti Suz finishes it." My words startled me as soon as I said them.

"Great." Gordon placed his guitar into his case. "Well, I guess I'll see you back home. On the Bachmann farm."

"Wait," Paula said. "I thought you were going to start working at the shelter in Lancaster."

Gordon's face turned pink. "I'm thinking about it, that's true."

I took me a moment to find my voice. "What?"

Gordon shrugged. "Tony offered me a job. I haven't decided—and haven't talked with Arden about it yet either."

"I see," I said, even though I was stunned. And then I felt surprised at my shock, at the loss I felt at the thought of him leaving. But of course Gordon wouldn't work for us forever.

"Well." I tried my hardest not to sound off kilter. "Hopefully you won't be gone before I'm home."

"I won't be." Again his eyes were kind and caring, but then they moved past me, to the back of the park shelter. I turned and saw Elijah, holding a basketball against his hip.

Gordon looked at me. "Are you two courting?"

I inhaled.

"I'm sorry," he said. "It's none of my business."

I shrugged. "He hasn't joined the church yet." Then I pivoted toward Elijah and headed up the aisle. My heart raced. Why would Gordon ask me that?

"How was your game?" I asked when I reached Elijah.

"Great." He nodded toward the stage. "I saw you up there."

"I was just helping Paula out," I said.

"But you like singing, right? I could tell by how into it you were."

My face grew warm.

"It's okay if you like it," he teased. "I'm not saying it's a bad thing. But you won't ever be able to do that again, not in Lancaster."

"I know," I said. "I don't need to do it again." But that wasn't how I felt. I longed to sing that way again. And not because I was up in front of everyone, but because I'd worshipped God in a way I never had before.

On Friday, I thought of Gordon driving home in the church van, taking turns driving with Howard, figuring they'd get home sometime late Saturday. Most likely he'd be back at work on our farm by Monday morning. It would be cold and probably still icy. What a shock for him.

Saturday afternoon, Elijah and I went to the beach, but the wind was cold and we didn't stay long. As we rode the bus home, he took my hand and said, "You should just stay down here until I go back. I bet you could live with Paula."

"That would be great," I answered, not really thinking about what I was saying.

Elijah squeezed my hand. "I'm serious. Ask Paula."

As much as I liked Paula, I couldn't imagine staying with a family I didn't know. And besides, I was missing home enough to figure that after another week I'd be ready to leave. But I didn't say that to Elijah. Instead I snuggled against him. He smelled of spicy aftershave and the cinnamon gum he chewed.

"Are you looking forward to farming?" I asked.

He laughed. "Honestly, it's not my favorite thing."

I sat up straight. "What?!"

"Don't act so surprised," he said. "I've already told you I'm not crazy about it. I'm going to do it, don't worry. It's by far my best option."

I leaned back against him. I guess I hadn't listened very carefully before. "What would you rather do?"

"That's a good question." He was silent for a long moment. "I'm not sure."

I'd always wanted to be a farmer's wife, and I was shocked that Elijah hadn't always wanted to be a farmer. Then again, he had said he didn't know anything about cows. And he never talked about farming.

We were silent after that. My mind was racing. Surely he could be happy doing something he didn't enjoy. I thought of Gordon. He did such a good job on our farm, tending the animals, plowing, planting, and harvesting. And yet he was considering working at the shelter. Just because Elijah didn't enjoy farming didn't mean he couldn't be successful at it.

Aenti Suz was at the bungalow when we returned, and I could tell that Elijah wasn't happy to see her. Perhaps he hoped we'd have time alone like we did the night Gordon came to town.

My heart beat rapidly at the memory. Elijah stayed around for a while, hanging out with me on the patio, but then he said he had an early morning the next day and needed to get home.

Monday, Elijah and I ate at Yoders, and then Tuesday, Paula and I watched him and Billy play basketball at the park. She'd stopped by the shelter and planned to volunteer the upcoming Friday. I planned to talk with her about going too, when Elijah wasn't around. After a while, Paula yawned and said she was bored and was going home. "Want to go with me?" she asked.

I hadn't visited her home yet and would have liked to, but I didn't want to leave Elijah, so I stayed. After they were done with their game, Elijah said he needed to get home and get to bed. He and Billy dropped me off, and Elijah walked me to the door.

"It's supposed to be eighty-five tomorrow," he said. "Let's go to the beach. We'll take the bus again—just the two of us."

"Sounds great," I answered.

I went to bed, wondering if I should talk to Paula about living with her family until May.

Wednesday morning, as Aenti Suz and I sat on the patio sipping our coffee, I looked forward to the day ahead with Elijah.

As I took another drink of coffee, our landlady called out from the gate, "Are you two back here?"

"Jah." Aenti Suz stood.

"You have a phone call."

I guessed it was David hoping to make plans for the day, and Aenti Suz must have too because she hurried toward the gate. I took another sip of coffee.

Aenti Suz returned in less time than I expected. "It was Gordon," she said. "Jessica is in the hospital."

"What's wrong?"

"Ectopic pregnancy. She's in emergency surgery. She's lost a lot of blood."

I had no idea what all of that meant, and the expression on my face must have given away my confusion.

"She was pregnant, but the embryo attached in the fallopian tube, which made it burst."

I put my hand over my face. "Oh no."

"We need to go home." Aenti Suz grabbed her coffee cup and headed toward the kitchen.

Go home? I was going to the beach with Elijah. And I wanted to volunteer at the shelter with Paula on Friday. We still had over a week left in Florida before going back to the cold and snow in Lancaster County.

Aenti Suz stood on the other side of the open sliding glass door. "Marie." Her voice was firm, as if she could read my mind. "This can be a very dangerous situation. We're needed. Your Mamm won't be up to caring for Jessica alone."

"Maybe Leisel will be able to." She was the one training to be a nurse.

Aenti Suz gave me a wilting look. "She's in college, remember? Do you want her to fail?"

I exhaled. I hadn't thought about that.

Aenti Suz continued. "Gordon said Jessica didn't want us to come home early, so she asked that we not be told. But Silas asked Gordon to call us anyway. Frankly, they're all very worried about her. She's already lost a lot of blood." She put one hand on her hip. "We're going to pack and get to the parking lot at the Tourist Church as soon as possible. The bus leaves at eleven—if there aren't two seats available on it, we'll need to find another way home, immediately."

I clutched my coffee cup.

"I already called David. He's arranging for a cart to be here within the half hour. And he'll let Elijah know why you had to leave without talking to him."

I felt sick at not telling him good-bye, and Paula too.

"Marie." Aenti Suz was staring me down. "You have the chance to put your sister before yourself. Perhaps you don't think you have the gift of caring for a person's physical health, but at least acknowledge that perhaps you can help care for her spirit."

I stood, mulling over her words as I followed her into the bungalow.

There were spots left on the bus, and David found a Mennonite couple with a cell phone and asked if he could pass their number on to Gordon so he could call with an update on Jessica. They agreed.

Soon we were on the bus, driving over the Phillipi Creek Bridge, past the park, and out of Pinecraft. Aenti Suz sat by the window, but as I clutched my winter coat in my arms, I stared past her at the scenes slowly rolling along. Silently, I said good-bye to the community I'd enjoyed being a part of for far too short of a time.

The palm trees swayed, as if waving good-bye.

Once we were out of town, Aenti Suz said she understood it was hard to leave. "But it's the right thing to do."

I nodded in agreement, embarrassed that I'd been reluctant. Would I ever learn to put others before myself? I said all the right things, but my actions lacked conviction.

Aenti Suz sighed. "How about if I tell you more of Annie's story?"

"I'd like that," I answered, thinking about Annie arriving home. And now I would be soon too.

-17-

Annie

After Kate and Ira ate, served by Aenti Elizabeth, Mamm showed them to Annie and Josiah's rooms to sleep. Annie's grandmother sat in the rocking chair and clucked her tongue until the two strangers, to her, had left.

"Aren't they the ones who forced you to go care for those soldiers?"

"They didn't force me, Mammi," Annie answered. "I chose to go."

Her grandmother clucked her tongue again. "You're just a child."

Annie ignored her grandmother and slipped out to the back porch to sit with Sophia while Samuel stayed at the kitchen table and had a second helping of Aenti Elizabeth's hotcakes.

Sophia definitely had more color in her cheeks. Also, her breathing wasn't as labored.

Sophia clasped her hands together. "Dat said he would take me to see Richert."

246

Annie put her arm around her sister. "You need to know that he's been running a fever and his leg is infected."

"Has his sight returned?"

Annie shook her head.

Sophia exhaled. "It doesn't matter. I'm getting stronger, and I'll be able to help care for him."

Annie pulled her sister close. "I'm praying that will be the case."

Dat arrived in the buggy as they talked.

"I know you're exhausted," Sophia said. "But will you come with me?"

"Jah." Annie scooted off the bed. "I'll let Samuel know."

He was still eating as she told him she wouldn't be gone long.

"All right," he said. "I'll wait."

When they arrived at the Fishers' house, the doctor was examining Richert, and Eva was in the room too. When the doctor and Eva came out to the sitting room to talk with Hiram, Sophia led the way into Richert's room with Annie a step behind.

"Richert?" Sophia said, her voice soft. "It's me."

He turned his head toward her and reached out his hand. She took it and sat on the chair beside the bed. His body began to shake and he cried.

Annie stopped a few feet away. Sophia put her head on Richert's chest and began to cry too.

Not used to witnessing such a mix of affection and grief, Annie felt uncomfortable. She stepped back to the door but stayed in the room, mesmerized by the love between her sister and her beau.

Her heart contracted. Would she ever know such love? Such commitment?

Richert's hands went to Sophia's back and then her head.

Then they moved around to her face. "I wish I could see you," he said.

"It doesn't matter." She kissed his finger. "All that's important is that you're here. I'm so sorry for what you've gone through."

"I suppose most will think I got what I deserved."

"No one's going to say that," she said.

Tears filled Annie's eyes. It was true that many would think it though. And some would say it—just hopefully not to Richert or his parents. Or to Sophia.

"I shouldn't have joined," Richert said. "And not because of my injuries. When all was said and done, I couldn't shoot another person. I thought I'd be able to—but I couldn't."

Annie thought of all of the unfired rifles on the battlefield. He wasn't alone. There were Englisch soldiers who couldn't do it either.

Eva opened the door and motioned for Annie. As she left, Sophia was still by Richert's side.

Annie joined the doctor and the Fishers.

"Richert is under his mother's care, where he belongs." The doctor frowned. "I can't guess what the end result will be. He's badly injured, as you all know."

Annie's stomach fell, but she knew the doctor spoke the truth.

"I'll get a poultice made for his leg," Eva said, "and give him a tincture to help him sleep. Rest and good food is what he needs."

"And we'll all keep praying." Dat patted Hiram on the shoulder. Annie thought of how opposed Dat was to Sophia's relationship with Richert, and then how mortified he'd been when Richert joined the Union Army. But now he simply shared in his neighbor's grief—and hope.

After the doctor left, Annie fetched Sophia. She didn't want her sister to tire herself or Richert. Both of them needed their rest.

When they returned to the house, Samuel sat on the front porch, chatting with Mamm. Annie walked with Sophia up the back steps and waited as she reclined on her bed. "I believe everything will be all right," Sophia said. "It won't be what we expected, but God will see us through."

Annie sighed and then answered, "I believe so too."

"What does Samuel want to speak with you about?" Sophia asked.

Annie didn't answer.

"Do you know your heart for him?"

Annie nodded. "He's a good man."

Sophia pursed her lips.

"What is it?" Annie asked.

"Jah, he's a good man. But when you were gone, he spoke as if he owned you."

"He was worried about me, is all. Besides, isn't a woman supposed to submit to a man?"

"A wife and husband are to submit to each other," Sophia said. "That's what the scriptures say. You were only courting him. He shouldn't have been so presumptuous."

Sophia had always had strong opinions. Perhaps Samuel wasn't as gentle as Richert, but he did have Annie's best interests at heart. Annie simply told Sophia that she appreciated her concern and then walked through the quiet house—her grandmother was now napping in the rocking chair—to the front porch.

Her mother stood as she stepped through the door. "I need to get dinner started shortly," she said, "after I gather the beans from the garden."

Annie sat next to Samuel. His eyes were tired, and she felt a rush of appreciation for him. He'd been willing to go all the way to Gettysburg to find her.

"Denki for waiting for me," Annie said. "I know you're tired."

He nodded.

"What did you want to tell me?"

"Well, my message has changed now that you're home. I was going to tell you that you had no business traipsing all over the state, caring for soldiers. But now that you're home, I'll spare you the lecture."

He smiled as she bristled. "I imagine you've been doing much the same, traipsing all over, doing deliveries and helping Mr. Stevens."

"That's different."

"God doesn't call us to be safe," she said. "He calls us to serve others. Correct?"

"Jah," Samuel answered. "But let me serve. And you stay safe."

Annie crossed her arms. "But He showed me a way to help—I had to obey His calling."

Samuel shook his head. "It wasn't your responsibility to be a nurse on a battlefield. It was enough that you left to go to Peach Bottom."

She inhaled sharply. "I was caring for my sister-in-law."

"Jah, that was all fine and good for a short time . . . but going on to Gettysburg? What was George thinking, letting you do something so foolish?"

Annie stood. "I found Richert. I brought him home."

"But it wasn't your responsibility. He reaped the consequences of his actions. His fate was up to God—not to you."

She paced to the far end of the porch. Jah, she knew people

would think that. She just didn't expect it to come from the man she thought she'd marry. Ira hadn't wanted her to serve in Gettysburg after the battle either, but then he respected her decision to stay.

Samuel followed Annie, and she spun around, saying, "I need to go rest before I say something I might regret."

"Annie . . ." His tone betrayed his frustration.

She stepped toward the door. "We'll see each other soon enough. We'll talk more then."

He reached out his hand, but she didn't take it. Instead she told him farewell and entered the house, overcome with fatigue. She made it out to the porch and crawled up on the bed next to Sophia. A few minutes later, she heard Josiah say he would take Samuel home. After that, she fell fast asleep.

⊱❦⊰

Annie awoke to voices in the kitchen. Kate's and Ira's. And Woody's. She sat up. Sophia wasn't beside her.

She took a moment to gather her senses, and then stood, smoothing her skirt and apron. Then she stepped into the kitchen. Sophia and their grandmother sat at the table, while Ira and Kate stood in a huddle with Woody, Mamm, and Dat.

The talking stopped.

"What happened?" Annie asked.

It was Mamm who finally spoke. "Woody found Cecil along the road, ill."

"I delivered him to Peach Bottom. As you can imagine, Harriet was frantic—but also relieved—to see him."

"So she's caring for him now?" Annie asked.

"That's right, along with a group of other injured and sick soldiers," Kate explained. "Woody is going to take Ira and me

251

back to Peach Bottom now." She stepped toward Annie. "Can you come back with us? To help? You're a well-trained nurse now."

Annie didn't feel as if she were a well-trained nurse, but she knew she could be of use. But then she thought of Samuel. What would he think if she went? And what about Sophia? She was doing better, but with Richert injured she would need Annie too.

Ira cleared his throat. "Mother, don't pressure Annie to go with you. She should stay here. She's served well, but it's time for her to be with her family."

Kate gave Annie a pleading look.

Ira shook his head. "Annie, with God's guidance, must make the decision." He turned toward her. "Ma will accept whatever you decide."

Woody stepped forward. "Miss Kate, Ira's right. God will provide the help needed in Peach Bottom. And I'll certainly assist as I can."

Mamm put her arm around Annie but didn't say anything, which Annie appreciated. Annie was exhausted and had longed to recover in the safety of her family. But Kate, Ira, Woody, and now Harriet didn't have that choice.

Did the Lord want her to go? She said a quick silent prayer, asking for guidance. Her throat felt dry, and she couldn't seem to find her voice. Ira gave her a sympathetic look, and she managed to mutter, "I think it's best if I stay."

Her heart broke saying it. She respected Kate more than anyone, but Annie didn't have the fortitude the other woman did.

Sophia stood and stepped to Annie's side. "Are you sure, sister? I don't want you staying if you feel you should go."

Annie nodded. She'd never felt so conflicted about anything

in her life, but she couldn't see going back to Peach Bottom. Not now.

After Mamm fed Ira, Kate, and Woody again, they gathered their things. Annie didn't have a chance to speak to Ira in person before they all climbed into Woody's wagon, but she hoped he knew that she was grateful for his intervention. She appreciated both Kate and Ira, but sometimes the son seemed more observant and sensitive than the mother.

The weather stayed hot and muggy as the days passed by. Even though she was back in the safety of her home, Annie slept fitfully and often awoke with a nightmare. Dead soldiers, cows, and horses. Richert in the field hospital tent. Screams from the patients. She could smell the scent of blood in her dreams. Often, she was in Dr. Carson's hospital by herself, searching for Kate. Then Ira.

Soldiers were dying. She didn't know what to do. She'd wake up, sometimes crying. Sometimes sitting up in bed, with her feet on the floor. Sometimes in a cold sweat.

One time she must have cried out, because when she awoke Mamm sat next to her, rubbing her back. Annie wondered if the dreams would ever stop. She felt ashamed by them. She hadn't gone through what the soldiers had. No one had shot at her, and she hadn't had to shoot at anyone either. She hadn't been injured, lost a leg or arm, or lost her eyesight. She didn't have a gaping wound in her thigh or stomach or back, like so many.

But still the nightmares continued, much to Annie's chagrin. The second week she was home, Mamm asked if Annie was sleeping better. She simply nodded in response. She must not have been yelling in her sleep, so that was good.

Sophia, with Annie tagging along, visited Richert a few times. Each time it was obvious that he was failing more and more.

Even Sophia admitted it—and as soon as she did, her own rally began to fade. Her cough grew worse, and she spent more and more time in bed.

Samuel visited often, and as far as Annie knew, no one had told him that she'd been asked to return to Peach Bottom. Never once did he ask her about what she'd experienced in Gettysburg. Of course, she didn't say a word about her nightmares or about all the horrors she'd seen. It would only give Samuel more reason to think it had been a mistake for her to go. A couple of times, he tried to bring up their future, but each time she asked to postpone the conversation.

When they sat on the porch together, she felt restless and bored with their interactions. If Samuel had any news, he didn't share it with her. Perhaps he thought it would inspire her to leave on another adventure.

However, late in August, he did bring an old newspaper from July. Annie read it to Sophia, including an article that the 54th Massachusetts Colored Infantry led a fight in South Carolina. Sadly their commander, Colonel Robert Gould Shaw, was killed along with many others. The article said he was buried with the other dead from his regiment.

Annie shook her head in sorrow. The killing continued.

"That's so sad," Sophia said. "When will this dreadful war ever end?" Annie feared the bad news would wear Sophia out even more and wished she hadn't read the paper to her. Sophia's cough had grown even worse, and Richert's infection continued to spread.

The next time Samuel visited, he brought two letters for her. One was from Harriet and the other was from Ira. Samuel frowned as he handed her the second one, postmarked from Gettysburg.

Annie ignored him and slipped the letters into the pocket of her apron.

After Samuel left, she opened the one from Harriet first. Cecil was on the mend, but Kate had diagnosed his illness as typhoid, and several of the other soldiers had come down with it. Annie knew the only thing to do was treat the symptoms and hope the patient recovered. Harriet wrote that their home was essentially a hospital, and they were all doing their best to care for the ill and the wounded. *Of course George never would have chosen such circumstances, but he has resigned himself to serving as the Lord has led. We are shorthanded, as you can imagine, and could not carry on without the help George can give, although he is as busy as ever tending to the farm. We all miss you,* Harriet concluded, *and hope you can come visit when Sophia's health allows.*

Annie hadn't made the wrong decision to stay home, especially with Sophia's health failing again, but she also longed to be in Peach Bottom, helping to care for the soldiers. Obviously Harriet had regained strength to be able to do what she was doing, but Annie knew her sister-in-law still wasn't strong, not after the hard pregnancy she'd endured.

Next, Annie opened the letter from Ira. He was back in Gettysburg, working with Dr. Carson. He said that many of the wounded had been shipped out, but that Dr. Carson's hospital had nearly as many as when Annie had left, due to more being transferred from the field hospitals. Ira added that he continued to learn new things from Dr. Carson. *I think of you often and your time here,* Ira wrote. *I know it was trying for you, but your help was invaluable.* He went on to write that he hoped she was doing well and that Richert, along with Sophia, continued to heal. *I know you're courting Samuel, so please don't be offended by this letter. I just wanted you to know that I appreciated your help during a trying time and pray that the Lord will bless you for your service.* He signed his name as, simply, *Ira*.

Annie slipped the letter back into the envelope as a wave of sadness washed over her. She missed Ira. And as hard as her time in Gettysburg was, it had changed her. She wouldn't be the person she'd become without that experience.

It was in the middle of September that Richert passed away. Sophia collapsed in Annie's arms when Dat told her. The night after they buried him, as Annie mopped her sister's forehead with a cool rag, Sophia said she hoped Annie would find a man as loving as Richert.

"Jah," Annie had answered. "I think Samuel is that man."

Sophia shook her head. "Samuel is a good man, but he's not right for you."

Alarmed, Annie asked Sophia what she meant.

"You've changed since you were in Gettysburg, but Samuel wants you to be who you were. Not who you are."

Annie swiped at her eyes. Sophia was right. She truly was a different person than she'd been before she'd gone to Gettysburg.

The next week, in desperation, Mamm suggested sending Sophia west where the air would be drier, in hopes it would slow the consumption, but Sophia insisted she didn't want to leave the farm.

Annie doubted the change in climate would make a difference, not when Sophia's health had failed so quickly. In the wee hours one morning, as Annie sat beside her sister and mopped Sophia's forehead with a damp cloth, her sister opened her eyes and reached for Annie's free hand and squeezed it. "I've been dreaming about Richert. He can see again, and he has no pain. He's at peace. . . ." She struggled for a breath and then managed to say, "I'm so happy for him. . . ."

Annie knew Sophia would die soon too, but she didn't cry in front of her. She simply willed herself to do all she could to make her passing as comfortable as possible.

And she did. She slept on a cot on the porch beside her sister's bed, and when Sophia coughed up blood, Annie cleaned her. When Sophia grew too weak to feed herself, Annie spoon-fed her soup and then wiped her mouth. She bathed her and changed her clothes, soaked from the sweat of her fever. Each day, her sister grew weaker until she stopped eating altogether. Except for coughing, she only slept.

Sophia passed away during the night toward the end of September, just as the leaves on the old oak tree began to turn copper. Annie pulled the covers up to her sister's chin and then tiptoed into the house and woke her parents.

Sophia's suffering was over.

They buried her in the cemetery at the edge of the farm where their ancestors had been laid to rest too. Richert's grave was only a row away. Annie's heart swelled at the sight. No other Mennonites were buried in the cemetery. Dat had allowed it as a good-will gesture to the Fishers—and to comfort Sophia.

Samuel and his family joined them for the service and the burial. He shared kind words with Annie about his sorrow for her, but she felt hollow as he spoke.

Later, after they'd all shared a meal, he asked if he could speak with her in private. She followed him outside.

"I've waited a long time to talk about our future," he said. "I can't wait any longer."

Annie shook her head. "I can't think of that now." She turned toward the cemetery on the corner of the property. Maybe she had only been using Sophia's illness as an excuse—and now her death.

His face fell, as if he'd realized how he'd sounded. Behind him the leaves of the oak tree shimmered in the sunlight.

He took a step toward her. "I shouldn't have brought this up—not when you're in mourning. We can talk about it later, but please, let that be soon."

She shook her head. "I'm glad you did. I'm not sure—"

His tone was patient now. "Wait. We can work all of this out," he said. "Don't say anything you'll regret."

She nodded and headed back to the house, leaving him by the garden. Perhaps she was feeling unreasonable and did need more time. She hurried up the steps to the back porch and sat on the edge of Sophia's bed, fighting back tears.

When someone called out a hello, she stood and peered out the screen. A wagon had turned into the lane. It was Woody, with Cecil beside him. Annie hurried back down the steps, stopping at the bottom.

As Woody pulled the wagon to a stop, Dat walked toward him.

"What's happened?" Woody asked, glancing back to the horses in the field and the buggies by the barn.

Dat explained that Sophia had passed and the service and burial had just been held. The man dipped his head and expressed his sorrow.

Cecil jumped down from the wagon. "Harriet is ill now, with typhoid. And Kate is exhausted." He handed Dat a letter. "George wants Annie to return. Woody can transport her—I'm going to see my folks and then join my unit in West Virginia."

Dat turned toward Annie. She nodded in agreement. Of course she would return.

Samuel, who still stood where Annie had left him, didn't say a word, but marched off toward the barn. Woody caught her eye, his expression full of concern.

"I'll pack my bag," she said to Woody. She would go, and work things out with Samuel later. "You get something to eat. Josiah can water and feed your team, and then we can be on our way." She glanced toward the porch but Mamm had already gone inside, most likely to pack a basket of food for their trip. Relief filled Annie that her parents agreed she should go nurse Harriet. God willing, she could help enough to make a difference.

–18–

Marie

The young Mennonite man stood next to us on the bus, tapping my shoulder, holding up his cell phone. "It's for you."

As I thanked him, I took it and handed it to Aenti Suz.

I listened closely as Aenti Suz held the phone to her ear, trying to figure out who was on the other end of the call. It was Gordon. My heart raced. While I was dragging my feet returning home, he was most likely at the hospital, supporting Silas.

My thoughts went to Sophia and her tragic death. Annie had lost her sister, unable to do anything to save her. My palms grew sweaty and my heart began to race.

"I see," Aenti Suz said, her face pale.

There was more talking on the other end of the call. Then Aenti Suz said, "Thank you so much for letting us know."

I expected her to hang up, but Gordon said something more. Aenti Suz responded with, "We have our coats on our laps—and our boots on our feet. We'll take a taxi to the hospital as soon as we arrive."

I guessed the weather was even worse than when we left.

Aenti Suz handed the phone back to the young man. "Thank you. You've helped us rest easier."

I exhaled. The news couldn't be all bad.

As the man walked away, Aenti Suz told me, "Jessica's out of surgery. She needed several transfusions. Of course, the fallopian tube was already damaged beyond repair and there's a lot of scarring."

My eyes widened at the thought of Gordon relaying that news to Aenti Suz. "He told you all of that?"

She raised her eyebrows. "You know, the issue here is Jessica's well-being—her very life. Not what offends you." She shuddered a little. "Do you ever think of others before yourself?"

Before I could stammer out an answer, she leaned her head against the seat, closed her eyes, and pulled her coat up to her chin.

I stared straight ahead, dumbfounded. She'd never been cross with me before. Well, she had been firm, just that morning.

Did I ever think of others before myself? I told myself that writing Jessica the letter when she left the Amish was for her own good, but honestly I did it because it was required of me to keep in the good favor of Bishop Jacobs. And when Leisel left, because she hadn't joined the church, I didn't write her at all. Not even to tell her that I loved her and missed her, even though I did.

I did care about Elijah, didn't I? I took out my embroidery. I was sure I could be a good wife to him, whether he ended up enjoying being a farmer or not. I knew I'd think of him before myself—hadn't I in Pinecraft? He didn't like music so I'd spent time playing volleyball and watching him play basketball when I could have been singing instead.

I wouldn't resent him for that because I believed he'd grow into a good man like his father. Strong. Wise. A leader. I knew Elijah could be all of those things too.

My palms still felt clammy. Was I coming down with the flu? I took a sip from my water bottle, wiped my hands on my apron, and then resumed my embroidery. Why did I feel so unsettled?

Deciding whom to marry was a big decision that would determine the course of my entire life.

My thoughts fell to Annie and Samuel. Annie had unselfishly helped others. I couldn't imagine ever doing such a thing. Traipsing off to care for wounded soldiers at the scene of such a horrible battle.

Leisel had nursed our Dat when he was dying, caring for him day after day. Sleeping on the floor by his bed. Giving him his medicine, feeding him what she could get him to swallow, making sure he was comfortable. Honestly, I couldn't have done that either.

Jessica was always quick to serve others too. She'd been like a daughter to Mildred Stoltz, caring for her as she fought cancer. And she was tender with animals too, and with the land.

Caring didn't come naturally to me, but my own selfish desires did. I cringed again at my gut reaction that morning. It was all about what I was going to miss, not about Jessica or that she'd lost a baby or that her life was literally in danger. Tears filled my eyes, and I put my embroidery away. Was it too late for me to change?

I looked beyond Aenti Suz and out the window into the pitch

dark. I put on my coat, zipped it, wrapped my scarf around my neck, and pulled my hood over my Kapp, ready to reach Lancaster in a few hours. Then I put my head back against the seat, determined to get what sleep I could.

I awoke to a scream from a woman a few seats ahead of us. Then the awareness that the bus seemed to be sliding. The snowy world outside the window began to tilt, and a bank of snow came straight toward the window.

Aenti Suz had just opened her eyes, and I grabbed her around the shoulders and pulled her toward me, covering her body with mine, yanking her down into my lap, my head facing the window. Time slowed as the bus spun around.

The screech of metal and the shatter of glass jarred me, but I held on tight to my aunt, even as cold air rushed through the broken window and my body was flung forward, pulling Aenti Suz with me. But as the bus collided with the snow bank, the force yanked Aenti Suz out of my arms. Time sped back up as I scrambled to reclaim her. But the bus came to a crashing stop, and her head slammed against the jagged frame of the window.

"Aenti!" I yelled, grabbing at her, pulling her body back toward me. There were more screams, and then someone calling out, "Are you all right?"

Someone else shouted, "Call 9-1-1!"

Then the bus lurched again and then righted, with a bounce. The snow bank had kept it from rolling.

I wrapped my arm around Aenti Suz again, feeling the sticky blood immediately. "You're bleeding."

She reached up to the side of her head and turned toward the broken glass and twisted metal. I unbuckled and unwrapped my scarf from my neck. Kneeling on the seat, I pressed my scarf against the side of her head where the blood was soaking through her Kapp.

"You know head wounds," she said. "They bleed like crazy. It's probably nothing."

I knew it wasn't "nothing." I just hoped it wasn't as bad as it seemed.

"Are you all right?" she asked.

"Jah," I answered. "I'm fine."

She pointed to the blood on my hands.

I was bleeding too, cut by the glass when I still had hold of Aenti Suz, but they were just nicks.

The bus driver, clearly shaken, walked down the aisle and checked on all of us. I told him Aenti Suz was injured, and we needed an ambulance.

"Oh, I don't think I—" Aenti started to say.

"*Jah*, she does," I said, firmly. "She's bleeding."

He nodded. "It's better to be safe than sorry."

Several people were bruised. A couple of passengers had fallen to the floor, but most had been wearing their seatbelts. Both Aenti Suz and I felt tender where our belts crossed our laps, and I imagined others were too.

A few people on our side of the bus who were sitting nearest the windows were also bleeding. And an elderly man seemed badly injured. It appeared he'd hit his head rather hard and was confused and dizzy, possibly suffering a brain injury. Aenti Suz squeezed my hand. I was sure she was praying for him. I joined in, and then prayed for her too. A Good Samaritan stopped and brought a blanket onto the bus. A man quickly took it and put it over the elderly man. The bus was freezing now from the broken windows and the lack of heat, and I zipped Aenti Suz's coat up to her chin.

Soon a police officer arrived. I continued to apply pressure to Aenti Suz's head, but the blood had soaked through my scarf. I repositioned it with my bloody hand. A person across the aisle asked if anyone had a towel. From the back of the bus, obviously from a family with children, came a baby towel. I hated to ruin it, but the terrycloth did absorb the blood better.

It seemed to take forever, but finally the ambulances arrived— four of them—as the gray light of dawn filled the bus. All of the passengers who were able to disembark did, but I was told to stay on, of course, and continue to apply pressure to Aenti Suz's wound. The EMTs came on and took the man with the possible head injury off first. Next they checked on Aenti Suz. She convinced them she could walk off, holding the towel against her head. I wiped my hands as best I could on the part of my scarf that wasn't already covered with blood, and then followed with our purses.

The bus driver assured me that our suitcases would be transported to their office in Lancaster. Then he gave me a card with their phone number. The EMTs helped Aenti Suz into the ambulance, and I climbed in after her. We were headed to Lancaster General—where Jessica was.

Once we reached the emergency department, after I washed my hands, I dialed Gordon's cell phone from the nurse's station. He didn't pick up, so I left a message, telling him what happened and that I'd try to get up to see Jessica once I knew Aenti Suz was all right. The nurse put a compress bandage on Aenti Suz, and then the doctor did a neurological check. The two discussed whether they needed to do a CT scan, with Aenti Suz saying that wasn't necessary. The doctor said that because it had been over an hour since the accident and because she wasn't exhibiting any signs of a concussion or brain injury, that she didn't need one. She did need stitches, however, which we both already knew.

The doctor said he'd be back in a few minutes, just as a nurse poked her head around the curtain and told me there was a young man out in the hall, hoping to see me.

It had to be Gordon or Silas.

I told Aenti Suz I'd be right back and followed the nurse.

Gordon stood with his winter coat on, holding his hat.

"How is Jessica?" I asked before either could speak.

"A little better," Gordon said. "She's out of recovery and in a room." Gordon's face was pale and his eyes grew huge. "I got your message, but what exactly happened?"

I explained again about the bus wreck. "Aenti Suz has a gash on the side of her head and needs stitches."

"What about you?" Gordon's expression was full of concern, and he pointed toward me.

I looked down at my open coat. Blood covered my apron. I quickly zipped my coat. "It's from Aenti Suz."

"What about your hands?"

I glanced at them. I thought they'd stopped bleeding by the time I washed up, but there was fresh blood coming from the cuts. "I just need some bandages," I said. "It's nothing."

I nodded back toward the emergency department. "I'll go sit with Aenti Suz until she gets her stitches. I'll need to get her home, but maybe we can stop and see Jessica—and Silas—first."

His eyes were full of concern. "Silas has the flu—respiratory with a fever, aches and pains, cough, and sore throat. He can't be around Jessica."

My stomach fell.

Gordon continued. "I'll take Suzanne home as soon as she's ready to go."

"Denki," I said.

"And you too."

"What about Jessica? Is Mamm with her?"

Gordon shook his head.

"Maybe you could take Aenti Suz home and Mamm can tend to her while I stay here with Jessica." I glanced down at my coat, imagining my bloody apron. I could take it off, but the blood had probably soaked through to my dress.

"Do you have your suitcase?"

I shook my head. "The bus was going to be towed to the company warehouse." I pulled the card from my pocket.

"I'll go get it," he said. "Why don't you write a note giving me permission? I'll get both yours and Suzanne's."

I pulled a pen from my purse and wrote on the back of the card. "They have identification tags on them, so they should be easy for you to find."

He nodded. "I'll come straight back here." Then he gave me Jessica's room number and told me to call her and let her know what had happened.

I called from the nurse's desk so Aenti Suz didn't have to listen to me describe what happened again. When Jessica answered, her voice was so weak I could hardly hear her.

"It's me," I said.

"Marie?"

I began to shake as I spoke and then, to my embarrassment, I began to cry. "Are you all right?"

"I'm fine," she said. "Sad but fine. Where are you?"

Ashamed that I was crying when she was the one who just

lost a baby, I told her about the bus wreck. "I tried to protect Aenti Suz, but she still got a gash on her head. A bad one."

"No wonder you're so upset," Jessica said. "Thank the Lord that Aenti Suz isn't any worse and that you're okay."

I told her I'd be up as soon as I could.

"You should go home with Aenti Suz," she said.

"No," I answered. "Gordon will take her home to Mamm. I'll stay with you."

Jessica didn't protest again. Instead she said, "It will be good to see you."

I returned to my aunt's room, asking the nurse if I could clean up my hands. After I washed them, she put bandages on the cuts. Then I held Aenti Suz's hand while the nurse shaved the side of her head.

As the doctor started to stitch, even though I was on the other side and couldn't see, I began to feel queasy. Partly from the movement of the doctor. Partly from the smell of the disinfectant.

As if sensing my discomfort, Aenti Suz said, "You don't have to stay."

"I'm fine." Silently I recited the Lord's Prayer, determined to stay strong. I thought of Annie and wished I were as brave as she had been. Finally, I asked Aenti Suz what her favorite thing about Pinecraft had been. "The community," she answered. "Wasn't it wonderful to get to know so many people from so many different Amish and Mennonite groups?"

I agreed.

"What about you?" she asked.

"How relaxed I felt," I answered. But I wasn't being entirely truthful. Along with hearing Annie's story, in retrospect, my favorite thing had been singing with Paula and Gordon in the park. Well, it wasn't even that, exactly. It was what I'd experienced during it—that I'd truly worshipped God. Then, as a result, I felt compelled to volunteer at the homeless shelter.

As I held my aunt's hand, I wondered if worshipping God could give me strength to do other things too.

– 19 –

The doctor gave her fifteen stitches across the bald swath where her salt-and-pepper hair had been.

Gordon returned just after the doctor finished his work, and I met him in the hall again. Thankfully, both of our suitcases were in his hands.

I took mine, and he headed in to sit with Aenti Suz. I wheeled my suitcase into the women's restroom and retrieved a wrinkled apron and dress, but at least neither was covered with blood. I changed, rinsed my bloody clothes out in cold water, and then slipped them into an extra plastic bag I'd packed.

As I returned to Aenti Suz's room, I saw the woman from the bus whose husband had been taken off first. She told me he was getting a CT scan and would then get stitched up, and it seemed the older man did have a brain injury, but hopefully a mild one. "Ach," she said. "It could have been so much worse. I'm glad your aunt will be all right."

Just before noon, Aenti Suz was released. As the nurse pushed her down the hall in a wheelchair, Gordon and I walked on either side of her. I'd grabbed my toiletries bag so I could spend the night with Jessica, but he towed both of our suitcases behind him.

"You must be exhausted," Aenti Suz said to me.

"I'm fine." I looked over her head at Gordon. "Tell Mamm to read the discharge paperwork and keep a close watch on her. The doctor said Aenti Suz probably doesn't have a concussion, but Mamm should be extra attentive, nevertheless."

"Don't worry about me," Aenti Suz said. "Give Jessica a big hug and tell her I'm sorry. And you try to get some rest."

When we reached the exit, Gordon told me he'd come back after the milking to check on Jessica and me.

I thanked him, hugged Aenti Suz, and then thanked Gordon again. "What would we do without you?" I asked.

"You'd get by just fine," he answered.

I knew we wouldn't. But we'd have to figure out how to if he took the job with the shelter.

I stopped by the cafeteria and ordered a bowl of soup, a half sandwich, and a large coffee. I ate the food and then took the coffee with me. When I reached Jessica's room and stepped inside, she had her eyes closed but then opened them slowly. "Hallo." Her voice was as soft as it had been on the phone, and her face was as white as the sheet pulled up to her chin.

"How are you feeling?" I asked.

"Better."

I shivered. If she was better now, Aenti Suz was right about how ill she'd been. She had a bag of fluid hanging on a pole with a tube going into her arm. And there was also a bag of what looked like blood. Again, I felt weak-kneed. I sat down beside her and sipped on my coffee as we talked. "Have you talked to Leisel?" I asked.

She shook her head. "Silas did. I don't want her to come. The roads are bad, but I think she may try anyway on Saturday.

Hopefully I'll be home by then." She shifted a little in the bed. "Silas is sick with this flu that's been going around."

"That's what Gordon said."

She nodded. "He feels horrible to not be here, but of course he can't."

I agreed and then thought of how reluctant I was to celebrate their marriage the day of their wedding. And why? Because I'd been critical of Jessica for the last four years, even after she returned to the Amish. Because I felt as if I deserved what she had—more than she did.

And now she'd nearly died.

My face grew warm in shame.

Jessica didn't notice. "I think it's harder on Silas than on me right now."

I didn't know about that, but I wondered if perhaps she'd rather not have my company and would like to rest instead. I asked her what she needed most. "Stay and talk," she said. "I'll let you know when I'm tired."

She asked me more about the wreck and Aenti Suz and then about Florida. In a lighter voice, she asked, "How is Elijah?"

"*Gut*," I answered.

"Did you see him much?"

"Jah," I answered. "Nearly every day."

"When is he coming home?"

"In the spring, probably May."

I told her about the beaches we went to, the volleyball and basketball games, and the community of people in Pinecraft. Then I told her about the singing.

"Sounds amazing," she said. "I know how much you love music." She reached for my hand and squeezed it.

"I think you and Silas would really like Pinecraft."

She smiled a little. "Maybe when we're retired. I don't see how we could go before then." She came back to the topic of Elijah. "So he's going to farm, right?"

I paused a moment. "Jah . . ."

"What's with the hesitation?"

I shrugged. "He said he's not thrilled about it, but he'll do it anyway."

"Oh, that's too bad." Jessica grimaced. "It's a lot of work no matter what, but even more so for someone who doesn't enjoy it."

When I didn't respond, she sat up a little in bed. "Gordon told us some about his week there. He was happy to see you."

"It was good to see him too."

"I'm sorry you had to come home early. And now, with all of this that happened with Aenti Suz, you shouldn't have. I feel horrible."

"Don't be ridiculous. We're so sad about you losing the baby and so glad Gordon called us." Again, I felt embarrassed by my initial reaction. Sitting beside her, I *was* relieved Gordon had called. How could I have been so selfish when I first heard the news?

She told me that Arden's family had the flu too. "Gordon did the milking by himself yesterday."

That must have taken him hours. Hopefully there was a neighbor boy who could help today.

Soon, her eyes drifted closed. There was a recliner in the room, and I curled up in it and slept too. When I awoke around supper time, Gordon was back in the room, and a doctor was talking with him and Jessica. I pushed the recliner down and stood.

"You can go home tomorrow as long as you stay away from anyone who is running a fever. You're susceptible to illness and infection, not to mention pneumonia."

"You can come to Mamm's," I said. "Or, better yet, Aenti Suz's. I can care for you there until Silas is well."

"Poor Silas," Jessica said. "He doesn't have anyone to take care of him."

I asked, "Can't his Mamm?" But as I spoke, I realized how hard it would be for Edith to travel back and forth to the farm where Jessica and Silas lived. She had a few calves to take care of at her place.

"I'll check on him tonight," Gordon said. "And then I'll be back in the morning. If all goes well, I can give you both a ride home, hopefully before noon."

The doctor nodded. "That sounds like a good plan."

As the doctor left, a nurse came in with supper. Jessica raised the bed and said, "I'm going to try to eat as much as I can. You two should go down to the cafeteria and do the same."

I covered my mouth as I yawned. "Don't you want some company?"

She smiled and shook her head. "Just come back when you're done."

I wasn't sure I wanted to go eat with Gordon, and he appeared uncomfortable too. But I didn't want to make a big deal about it in front of Jessica.

Once we reached the main floor, Gordon pointed toward the exit. "There's a little café around the corner. Want to go there?"

"All right," I answered, although I still felt groggy and uncomfortable. But I figured the fresh air might do me good.

Gordon ordered a hamburger, and I ordered a bowl of minestrone soup. Being awake for so long and the trauma of the day was catching up with me, and I thought the soup was all I'd be able to get down. I felt shaky again, and it must have shown.

"Are you all right?" Gordon asked. "Do you want me to take you home?"

I shook my head. "No. I mean, I'm not feeling horrible. Just out of sorts. And, no, I don't want to go home."

He looked at me appraisingly for a moment, and then must have decided to try to take my mind off of the day, because he switched from being so serious to being chatty. After the waitress delivered our food, we shifted to talking about Florida. I told him how powerful the singing had been for me.

"In what way?" Gordon asked and then took a bite of his burger.

"There are a couple of ways. I shouldn't admit this, but I really enjoyed singing with the instruments. I also felt as if I were worshipping the Lord in a way I'd never experienced before. I felt a new freedom, a harmony different from what I've felt before."

"That's wonderful," Gordon said.

I nodded, taking a bite of my soup, and then saying, "It felt transformative. I just hope it will last."

He smiled gently. "I know the feeling."

I asked if he'd heard from Josh since coming home.

He nodded. "From what he told me, the singing at the Pinecraft Park was the highlight of the week for a lot of us. But that's not all he said. The director of the shelter has a contact who may give Josh a job, and another who might be able to help him find housing."

"That's great," I said.

Then he shared his thoughts for the next year in Pinecraft when his team would return for another week of ministry. My heart contracted. I wouldn't be there. Most likely, Elijah and I would be married by then.

As he finished his burger, I asked if he'd decided about the job at the shelter, and he shook his head, his face reddening.

"I haven't said anything to anyone," I assured him. "And I promise I won't." I hoped he knew that I would be a good friend to him.

Changing the subject, I hesitantly said, "I have a question about playing the guitar. Was it hard to learn?"

He shook his head. "I started when I was eight."

"How about the harmonica? Is that hard to learn?"

He shook his head again and then said, "For you, any instrument would be easy to learn." Then his face reddened again and he said, "I'm sorry, I keep sticking my foot in my mouth."

I laughed. "I'm the one asking the questions."

He leaned across the table. "But why? It's not as if you can play any of them."

"My Dat played the harmonica," I said.

Now he leaned back in his chair. "You're kidding."

"No. I remember it from when I was a child. I'd sing along. Sometimes he'd let me try."

"I'm so surprised," he said. "I really wish I could have met your Dat."

I nodded. He had died right before Gordon started working for us. "Dat was very gifted—and sneaky. He made up this silly 'Cat, Dog, Elephant' song when I was little, and Paula said that in doing so, he taught me notes."

Gordon raised his eyebrows.

"Jah. The other 'notes' were frog, goat, ant, and bull."

Gordon laughed. "Paula was right. He did teach you the notes." He leaned forward. "She told me that you have perfect pitch."

My face warmed, and then I shrugged. He was right, but it

wasn't as if any of this would make a difference in my life. "Do you know a song called 'Turn, Turn, Turn'?"

He smiled. "My mom used to sing that when I was little."

"My Dat played it on the harmonica," I said. "Sometimes he'd sing it too."

Gordon began humming the tune, and I joined in. Then we both smiled. "To everything there is a season," Gordon said.

I added, "And a time to every purpose under the heaven." My eyes filled with tears as I spoke.

"It's from a passage in Ecclesiastes."

I nodded. "Chapter 3."

"Maybe that's why your father sang it," Gordon said.

I swiped at my eyes, thinking about Dat choosing that particular song. Another tear escaped.

Gordon placed his hand on the table, as if reaching out to me. "You okay?"

I nodded, swallowed hard, and pushed my half-eaten bowl of soup forward. "We should get going." Why did it hurt to share a sweet moment with Gordon?

He stood to pay at the counter, even though I insisted I could pay for my own. Once we bundled up, we headed out into the cold. As we walked, he asked when Elijah was coming home.

"May," I answered.

He didn't say anything more until we reached the front doors of the hospital. "I'll leave you here." He opened the door for me. "And see you in the morning."

I stood at the door and watched him through the glass as he headed to the parking lot. He walked briskly into the wind, his head up.

How would I feel about Gordon Martin if he were Amish?

And owned a farm? I shivered, even though the lobby was warm. I was pathetic.

When I arrived back in Jessica's room, she was sitting up and reading a copy of *The Budget* that I guessed Gordon had brought her. She said she was feeling a little better. "How was your supper with Gordon?"

"*Gut*," I answered.

"I don't know what we would have done without him the last couple of days."

I nodded. If nothing else, Gordon was dependable. But the truth was, he was much more than that.

"Have you ever asked if he'd join the Amish?" She smiled for the first time all day. And then winked at me.

I just shook my head, not bothering to answer. We all knew he wouldn't.

"I know this sounds like a ludicrous question, but have you ever thought of becoming Mennonite?"

I gave her one of my looks.

"Jah," she responded. "I didn't think so."

The next morning when the doctor arrived, he spoke with Jessica for several minutes. When they finished the conversation, he told her again how sorry he was that she'd lost the baby. "Your chances of conceiving are lower now, of course, but there's no reason to think you won't go on to have a normal pregnancy. Most likely, many more."

She thanked him, and then he typed some notes into the computer, saying he was writing up the discharge order. "The nurse will be in soon to help you get ready."

I called Gordon to tell him Jessica was being discharged.

By the time he arrived, Jessica was dressed and had signed

all of the paperwork. Gordon went to get his car and met us at the hospital exit. Once we reached the first floor, there was a woman ahead of us in a wheelchair, a baby in her arms. My heart ached for Jessica.

Thankfully, Gordon's car was waiting, and the nurse and I quickly got Jessica into the back seat. Gordon handed me a quilt to put over her. I'd forgotten how cold his car could be. Thankfully, it wouldn't take us long to get home.

When we reached the house, I hurried up the steps first so I could talk with Mamm about if we should have both Jessica and Aenti Suz out in the Dawdi Haus. When I stepped inside, Aenti Suz was standing at the kitchen sink, the stitched side of her head toward me.

"What are you doing?" I asked.

"Your mother came down with the flu. I'm fixing her some tea."

"Oh no," I moaned. "I'll be right back." I headed up the stairs to Mamm's room. The door was opened, and I stopped there. I told her I was sorry she was ill, and then presented my proposal. Gordon would bring Silas to our house and then ask Edith to come care for both Silas and Mamm, while I cared for Aenti Suz and Jessica in the Dawdi Haus. A neighbor would have to take care of Edith's calves.

"Good idea," Mamm answered. "I was careful to stay clear of Suz this morning because I felt feverish. She's making me tea, but she was going to leave it in the doorway."

"*Gut*," I answered. "Hopefully she hasn't been exposed." The truth was, Silas had probably already exposed Jessica, but I believed we should still do our best to keep her from being exposed again. I told Mamm I'd come see her soon, and then hurried back downstairs.

Gordon and Jessica were in the living room, but I told them to keep on going, straight out to the Dawdi Haus. And then I asked Gordon if he could go get Edith and Silas and bring them both to the farmhouse. It meant John Stoltz would have to do his chores by himself until Silas recovered, but at least John didn't have a dairy herd, so there was no milking to do.

My plan worked. I took care of Jessica and Aenti Suz while Edith nursed Mamm and Silas. Gordon did find a neighbor boy to help with the milking, and it turned out that Vi had fallen ill first in their family and was now on the mend enough to care for Arden and their children.

There were several times when I saw Jessica with tears in her eyes, and the rush of emotion I felt for her surprised me. Both for my sister and for the baby that had been lost. On Saturday, around noon, Leisel arrived. Unannounced.

I gasped in delight when she walked through the door, bringing a burst of freezing wind with her, although my next reaction was worry. "How were the roads?"

"Fine," she answered. "How is everyone here?"

Jessica was on the couch and gave her a little wave. Leisel sat down beside her and gave her a hug and then whispered, "I'm so sorry."

Aenti Suz came out of her bedroom and Leisel sprang to her feet, rushing toward her. "Oh, you poor thing!"

After she gave her a hug, she examined her stitches. "Your scar won't be bad, and your hair will cover it up anyway." She stepped back. "The doctor did a good job with the sutures."

I put the kettle on, and then we all gathered around Jessica in the living room and drank tea and ate sticky buns I'd made the evening before.

After a while, Leisel yawned. Finding out that she'd worked the night before, we sent her to bed.

Jessica soon fell asleep too, and as I washed our dishes, Aenti Suz came in to dry them. "Want me to tell you the rest of Annie's story?"

"Jah," I answered. "But pull up a chair. There are so few of these dishes, I'll have them done in no time."

I reminded her where we'd left off. Annie was returning to Peach Bottom with Woody while Cecil went on to join his regiment in West Virginia.

–20–

Annie

For the next two weeks, Annie nursed Harriet night and day. The baby had been sent to a wet nurse in Peach Bottom, and then neighbors took Noah in so that he didn't have to see his mother suffering. Kate helped care for Harriet as she could, but Cecil had been right. She was exhausted too. So much so that Woody stayed to help take care of her.

Only five soldiers were still at the house. Two had typhoid, one was still recovering from an amputated leg, one was recovering from a chest wound, and the last from a neck wound.

Woody helped with the cooking and also with feeding and bathing the soldiers. He helped George in the fields some, although he didn't stay away from the house for long. In fact, he hovered over Kate until she convinced him she was all right. "I just overdid it."

She did ask Woody if he would drive her to check in on her patients, and one night when she attended a birth, he stayed with her the entire time.

Annie was afraid Kate would come down with typhoid too, but thankfully she didn't. Typhoid ran a course of about three weeks, and Harriet was in the second when Annie arrived. As Annie took care of her sister-in-law—forcing her to drink, cleaning her up and changing her clothes and feeding her soup and anything else she could keep down—she prayed, asking God to spare Harriet. For George. For the boys. For herself too. She couldn't bear the thought of losing another sister.

Several times, usually in the middle of night, Harriet would hallucinate. A couple of times, she thought Cecil had died. One time she thought she'd literally lost the baby and couldn't find him. Another time she thought Noah was off at war.

She rapidly lost weight, and her fever raged. Annie continued caring for her, fighting her own fatigue and despair. By the end of the third week, the two soldiers turned a corner, and a few days later, Harriet did too.

Annie kept diligent, fearful her sister-in-law might relapse. Harriet began asking for the boys, begging George to bring them home. He said he would, as soon as she was stronger.

Ira wrote his mother, asking if Woody could take the remaining soldiers who were staying at George and Harriet's to Hanover Junction to catch trains back to their homes or to meet their units, if they were healthy enough. He added that he was doing well and told his mother that Dr. Carson hoped she'd return to Gettysburg. Kate paused as she read the letter aloud.

"Are you thinking about going?" Woody asked.

She shook her head.

"Not even for Ira?"

She smiled a little. "He doesn't need me. And I have plenty to do here."

Woody took the soldiers west to the train and then returned.

Kate moved back to her house and Woody to his shack, but he came back to help George with the harvest. Annie asked him if he planned to return to Lancaster any time soon.

"No," he answered. "I've decided to take a break from hauling cargo. I've done well over the last few months and saved everything I could. Besides, the need isn't what it used to be."

He certainly didn't have cargo to haul for the Union anymore. Annie wondered if, since the Confederates retreated back to Virginia, not as many slaves were coming over the border from Maryland. Perhaps they hoped the war would end soon and they'd be liberated without risking their lives to gain freedom. She guessed that Woody was helping with that cause. She didn't know for sure.

Many were disappointed that General Meade hadn't attacked Lee's army again before it reached Virginia. "Perhaps the war would be over if he had," Woody said one night as he and George talked after supper.

George said he didn't know anything about that, and the conversation turned back to the crops.

Harriet grew strong enough for the boys to come home, and gradually things returned to normal.

Annie received a letter from her mother, saying she'd seen Samuel recently and he'd asked after her. *Daughter, don't hold his concerns for you against him. He has a good heart and cares for you deeply. I hope when you return, you'll be ready to move on with your life. He seems to regret words he shared with you in his worry—perhaps he, like so many of us, has changed through these difficult times.* Annie folded the letter and slipped it into her pocket. She knew it was her duty to forgive Samuel, just as God forgave her. Surely his behavior was due to the stress they were all under. Her mother was right. War had affected them all.

It was now late October, and she felt she should go home. Jah, her mother had her sister and mother's company, but perhaps she'd prefer to have her only living daughter home too. It was time to return to the life God had for her.

The first of November, after the leaves on the trees along the river had turned yellow, orange, and a brilliant red, she pulled her shawl tighter and broached the topic with Harriet. Her sister-in-law begged her to stay. "Just for a couple more weeks."

George, with Woody's help, finished the harvest, and they all relaxed a little. The Rebels were long gone. Harriet was gaining her health back. Cecil, as far as they knew, was well. Nathaniel was a healthy baby. The corncrib was full, and the calves were growing. The cellar was stocked with squash, turnips, cabbage, and onions. George and his little family had survived.

Tears welled in Annie's eyes. She missed Sophia, and going home would be hard, but she needed to honor her parents. They'd honored her, allowing her to do what she believed God had called her to do.

Both Woody and Kate visited often. It was as if they'd all gone through a fire together and survived. They'd all been bonded.

One day, Woody stopped by, saying he'd heard at the Peach Bottom store that the National Cemetery would be dedicated in two weeks. "November 19," he said. "There are rumors that the president will be there."

Annie thought of Ira and hoped he'd still be in Gettysburg for the ceremony. He'd be honored to see President Lincoln. If anyone deserved to, it was Ira.

The next week, Annie began to prepare to go home. She helped George dig the last of the potatoes in the garden and added them to the stores already in the cellar. She cleaned the house from top to bottom and washed all the bedding. She dried the rest of the apples and made kraut from the last of the cabbage. She started cheese and stored it in the cellar to finish.

On November 17, as she dumped the dishwater out in the backyard, a wagon turned into the driveway, coming from the west. She shaded her eyes from the setting sun, realizing it was Woody. Someone was with him, and it wasn't Kate.

She squinted. It was Ira. He waved.

"What are you doing here?" She started toward him, the basin in her hands.

"I have a proposition for you." He sat tall on the bench. "There's a dedication for the National Cemetery in two days. Ma is considering going, but she suggested I ask you too."

⁂

Annie lit the lamp, and George and Harriet joined Woody and Ira at the table. Next, she poured tea for all of them and served the apple pie she'd made for the next day—the day she'd planned, God willing, to leave. She'd hoped to find a ride at the store in Peach Bottom to Lancaster. Or that perhaps Woody could take her, but she doubted that now.

Ira explained that those at Gettysburg planning the dedication of the National Cemetery were inviting all sorts of people to the event: soldiers who survived, but also nurses who'd come from all over the state and pitched in to care for the wounded after the battle. "Ma is hesitant about going," he said. "But she said she would if you'd be willing." He looked kindly at Annie, his blue eyes sparkling. "I wanted to extend the invitation, if going wouldn't bring too much heartache for you."

Her nightmares had subsided, although they weren't entirely gone. But the truth was, she wanted to see Gettysburg again

286

without blood in the streets and the stench of death in the air. Without mangled horses and decaying soldiers.

Annie believed that it might bring healing to herself to go, and she wondered if Kate felt the same. She'd been so adamant about not going back to Dr. Carson's, but this would be different.

George rubbed his brow. "Do we need to go through more of this? I thought you were heading home—not traipsing west again."

"I could escort her home after the dedication," Ira said. "I'm going to ride the train to Philadelphia right after the ceremony and will be going through Lancaster on the way."

"Why Philadelphia?" Annie asked.

"I'm going to work in an army hospital there, to be trained as a surgeon. Doc arranged it for me."

Annie sensed Woody bristle, but he didn't say anything. She turned her attention to George. "I'd like to go back to Gettysburg."

"Will your mother go for sure?" George asked Ira. "I need to know Annie will be well chaperoned."

"I'm sure she will go if Annie does."

Woody shifted in his chair.

Ira seemed oblivious to Woody's anxiety. "We'll need to leave tomorrow. We can stay at Doc's house while we're in Gettysburg and then head to Lancaster on the twentieth."

"Is your mother all right with that?" Annie asked.

"I think so," Ira said. "Doc sent a letter apologizing for his behavior last summer." He lowered his voice. "He hasn't had a drink since Ma left."

Annie glanced at George, but he didn't protest again.

Ira turned to Woody. "Could you take us to Hanover Junction in the morning? And then pick Ma up in York on the twentieth?"

Woody crossed his arms but agreed. He didn't look happy. Perhaps he worried about Kate seeing Dr. Carson again too. Annie wasn't sure about the relationship between Woody and Kate, but they seemed to care for each other.

"It's settled then," Ira said.

"Go with them tonight," Harriet said to Annie. "You'll need an early start tomorrow."

Annie wondered for a moment if she had the clothes she needed, and then realized it didn't matter. She was who she was. A simple Amish girl. No one would expect anything more. She had her cloak to keep her warm. That was what mattered most.

She rose and excused herself to go finish packing her bag, and prepared herself to tell George, Harriet, and the boys good-bye. Life was about to shift again, but first she had an excursion to take, thanks to Ira. One she'd never expected.

A half hour later, Kate welcomed Annie into her home. It was the first time Annie had been inside. Kate took her bag and cloak and then led her to the fireplace in the parlor. Annie had never seen so many fine things. A velvet settee and two chairs. A cabinet filled with china and glass. A large mirror over the mantel. Thick rugs. It was nothing like the plain parlor back home.

Ira disappeared upstairs, and after Annie had warmed up, Kate called her down the hall. "You can sleep in here," she said.

The room had a four-poster bed, a china pitcher and basin, and a maple wardrobe. On the bed was a woven indigo coverlet.

"It's all so fancy," Annie said.

"It's our guest room," Kate said. "The things on the first floor are from my past that I haven't given away yet. My room is upstairs. So is Ira's."

The woman put her arm around Annie. "I'm so glad you're

here and that we're going back to Gettysburg. I think it will be good for all of us."

Annie nodded. "Thank you for inviting me."

❧

The next morning, Woody picked them up at Kate's in a buggy with two benches, pulled by four horses. "I borrowed the team and buggy," he said. "We'll make better time, and hopefully you'll all keep warmer."

The day wasn't freezing, but it was still cold. Kate had warmed bricks in the stove to put at their feet, and had packed wool blankets too.

She gave Annie a second cloak to wear and a pair of thick wool socks that made Annie's boots too tight, but she wore them anyway. The two women sat on the second bench while Ira sat up front with Woody.

The teamster didn't speak much as he drove.

Dr. Carson had finally succeeded in getting Kate to return to Gettysburg. Ira must have been right about the man changing, because otherwise Annie was sure Kate wouldn't have agreed to go back.

The wind whipped the buggy as they traveled north. Woody stopped several times to feed and water the horses. Kate had brought along food, and they stopped to eat too. After they started on the journey again, Ira started singing. "Steal away, steal away, steal away to Jesus! Steal away, steal away home, I hain't got long to stay here. . . ." The words and tune were simple. The others joined in. When they finished, Annie asked where he'd learned it.

He shrugged but Woody answered, saying, "It's a Negro spiritual."

"Oh," Annie said.

She turned toward Ira. "Who taught it to you?"

"Felicity," he answered, glancing at Annie. "I thought you'd enjoy learning it."

"Denki," she answered, thinking of the girl and her baby. Hopefully they were in Canada by now.

They reached Hanover Junction with just fifteen minutes to spare to catch the train. Woody assured them he'd be in York by the next day. Kate thanked him and told him they'd be there as soon as they could. The man seemed concerned, which wasn't like him. Kate thanked him for the ride. He jumped to the ground and helped her down while Ira helped Annie.

The train was packed, but Annie still managed to sleep all the way to Gettysburg. When they arrived, night had fallen. The town was already crowded, and Ira asked the women if they minded walking, as he couldn't find a driver to take them.

Both agreed they could walk. Ira grabbed both of their bags and set a fast pace, which warmed Annie but pinched her toes in her tight boots.

When they reached Dr. Carson's, he greeted them all warmly, but he seemed especially pleased to see Kate. Meg had soup and warm bread waiting for them. After all those months of having her kitchen in a tent out back, she was happy to be back in the house. The rest of the interior was different than it had been in the summer too. Meg said the last soldier had left just two days ago for his home in New York. The house was spotless, and all of the cots had been moved out and the furniture—Victorian style, Annie believed—was back in place.

The dining room table, made from cherrywood, had ornate legs and a large, oval top. There were several others joining in for the meal because Dr. Carson had invited friends from Philadelphia to also stay in his house for the festivities. Although the supper was simple, Meg served it in the dining room.

"We heard every room in town is taken," one of the men said. "Is that true?"

Dr. Carson nodded. "We've been planning for weeks for the dedication. Over ten thousand people are expected."

Annie couldn't imagine that number of people.

Dr. Carson seemed eager for his friends to get to know Kate. All were doctors in various Philadelphia hospitals, and a couple of them remembered Ira's father.

Soon the conversation turned to Ira's upcoming training. Kate seemed pleased that he was making connections with the men, and Annie wondered if that was part of Kate's motivation for coming—to support Ira and see him off to the next stage of his life. After Meg cleared all of the dishes, she called Annie and Kate away from the table and showed them a room on the first floor. "Ira will sleep across the hall from the two of you in the room he's been using the last couple of weeks," she said. "And the others will sleep upstairs."

Annie said she thought she'd go ahead and go to bed.

"I'll be in soon." Kate glanced toward the door. "I'm tired, but I should go back out with the others."

Annie could still hear all of the men, including Ira, talking. Then there was laughter. She didn't fit in, not at all. But this would soon be Ira's life. She had far more in common with Samuel than she did with Ira.

She changed into her nightgown and crawled into the high bed. Everything was much fancier than she was used to, even more so than at Kate's, but it didn't take her long to drift off to sleep.

She awoke to shouting. It was Dr. Carson. "You misled me! All these months I expected you to come back."

Kate's voice wasn't as loud as Dr. Carson's, but it was definitely raised. "I never told you I would. In fact, I clearly said I had no plans to."

"It's that teamster, isn't it? That uneducated, common man. What do you see in him?"

A crash launched Annie to her feet, even in her half-awake state. She grabbed her cloak and hurried out of the room and down the hall. She reached the dining room to find a mirror broken on the floor and Dr. Carson gripping Kate by the arm. He dropped it as soon as he saw Annie.

No one else seemed to be around. The others must have all gone to bed. Annie stood paralyzed for a moment but then found her voice. "Come with me." She reached out her hand to Kate.

Dr. Carson stepped backward, and Kate grabbed hold of Annie. As they stumbled down the hall, Kate said, "Doc had too much to drink. We'll leave first thing in the morning."

As Annie drifted off to sleep, she wondered why Ira hadn't come out to protect his mother. Was he that heavy of a sleeper? Or was he out, perhaps visiting a sweetheart he'd found in Gettysburg?

⁂

Before dawn, Annie awoke, washed with the cold water in the basin from the night before, and dressed quickly as Kate continued to sleep. She tiptoed into the icy-cold dining room to find Meg picking up the glass on the floor by lamplight. Annie bent down and helped her as the woman said, "I'll get breakfast going and feed you folks as soon as this is cleaned up."

"We should be on our way before then." Annie intended to rouse Kate soon. "I just wanted to see if the doctor was in his room or down here."

"Oh, you have time. From the looks of all this, he won't be up for a while. And you're not going to find anywhere else to eat around here, not with half the state in town." The woman put another piece of glass in the bin. "I need to make breakfast for the others anyway." Meg smiled at Annie, her face kind. "Besides, you'll need someplace to stay tonight."

Annie shuddered. "It shouldn't be here."

"I'll handle Doc," Meg said. "You enjoy your day and come back after the dedication."

Annie didn't know how they could after last night. It wouldn't be easy to forget what he'd said about Woody, his harsh words toward Kate, and the force of his hand on her wrist.

Once Meg and Annie picked up all the glass, Annie carried it out to the trash heap by the washhouse, and Meg started fixing breakfast. Then Annie checked on Kate. She was awake and dressed, sitting on the end of the bed. "Is he out there?"

Annie shook her head. "Meg cleaned up the mirror and is cooking breakfast. She said he won't be up for hours, and we should go ahead and eat."

"All right," Kate said.

"Where was Ira last night?" Annie asked.

"Out," Kate answered. "He said he had gone for a walk to clear his head and pray about some things. But I told him just now what happened, and he agreed we should be on our way after the ceremony."

Ira joined them in the kitchen, and they gathered around the fireplace while Meg finished baking biscuits in the oven.

"Eat in here," she said. "When the others get up, I'll feed them in the dining room." She directed Annie to get plates out of the cupboard and Kate to pour them all a cup of coffee from the kettle on the back of the stove. Ira took the plates from Annie

293

and set them around the table while Annie collected the cutlery from the chest on the bench under the window.

A breeze blew through the bare branches of the trees in the orchard, and she was thankful for the warmth of the kitchen.

They ate quickly and then thanked Meg. "We should be on our way," Ira said.

"Leave your things," Meg said. "And stay again tonight, like I said. I'll have supper waiting for you."

Annie bristled, wanting to leave and never come back.

Kate glanced at Ira and he frowned.

"Thank you," Kate said. "As long as you think it's safe."

Meg nodded. "I'm sure it is. Doc will have an outburst and then feel bad about it. I suspect it will be weeks until he has another one."

Annie packed her bag, left it in the bedroom, and then put on her cloak and joined Ira in the foyer. Meg handed them a bag of sausage, cheese, and leftover biscuits for their lunch, along with a jar of tea for them to share.

"Denki," Annie said. "You've been so good to us."

Footsteps fell on the stairs, and Dr. Carson said, "Don't you mean 'Doc has been so good to us'?"

Ira winced.

Kate hurried from the bedroom to the front door and silently stepped onto the porch.

"Good morning," Ira called out, his voice calm.

Dr. Carson came around from the staircase. "You're all bundled up early."

Ira nodded.

"Where's your mother?"

"She already left. We're going to meet her."

Dr. Carson rested his hand on the newel post. "A little early, don't you think?"

"There's going to be a crowd," Ira said. "She wants to secure a place."

"Tell her I need to speak with her. I'll join all of you there." He glanced upstairs. "After my other guests are fed."

Ira didn't respond one way or the other. He simply said, "We'll be on our way then." He opened the door for Annie, and she led the way onto the porch and down the steps.

Ira caught up with her, and they hurried down the walkway to the street where Kate waited for them. It was hours before the dedication would start, but they headed toward the cemetery anyway.

"What did he say?" Kate asked Ira.

"That he wants to speak with you." Ira took his mother's arm. "I'm sorry I trusted him."

Kate shook her head. "I trusted him too. Trusted he would take my word about how I felt back in August. And then last night he was so charming with the others around that I trusted him again." She exhaled as she wrinkled her nose. "I never should have returned."

"I'm afraid I didn't understand your hesitation." Ira slowed his pace and put his arm around his mother.

"I didn't tell you everything because I didn't want to harm your chances of a post in Philadelphia. I knew you needed Dr. Carson's help—I believed if I just stayed out of the way, everything would be all right." She leaned her head against Ira's shoulder. "And then I believed that enough time had passed that Dr. Carson would have moved past his feelings from this summer."

Annie felt awkward overhearing their conversation and fell

behind them on the sidewalk. She'd read Dr. Carson completely wrong. She'd been sure Kate would be interested in him. He was smart and successful. He owned a beautiful home. He was respected and admired. But he wasn't the man that she'd thought, even though she'd had clues about his character. Obviously, Kate had realized that months before.

Ira and Kate stopped and glanced back at her. "Come on," Ira said, extending his free arm.

Annie caught up with them and hooked her arm through Ira's. The three continued on up the hill, linked together, the cemetery ahead of them.

– 21 –

A platform had been built in the open field at the crest of the hill, away from the fresh graves, and a crowd was already gathering. Kate chose a place to stand several rows back from the stage and to the left, farthest from the street.

And then they waited as more and more people gathered. Annie couldn't imagine ten thousand people, but after a few short hours, she believed she had a glimpse of what that many would look like. A sea of people stood behind them and spread off to each side too. In the distance, Annie could hear music, growing closer. She remembered the tune from the summer at the field hospital. Several people around began to sing along. "Mine eyes have seen the glory of the coming of the Lord . . ." Annie closed her eyes. Thankfully, the coming of the Lord would mean no more violence. The others kept singing, belting out, "His truth is marching on."

His truth *was* what mattered. The Lord wasn't a soldier, ready to kill. The Lord was a savior, ready to heal. Ready to bring peace. And reconciliation for all men. To bring oneness for all—slave or free, male or female, Greek or Jew—in Christ.

Oh, how He must grieve for all who fell in the town and fields of Gettysburg and throughout the horrid war. It was against everything He wanted for His children. Annie crossed her arms against her sadness, against the cold, against all that was lost to the battle that had raged all around and still marched into her dreams.

The band reached the platform and continued to play song after song as dignitaries arrived. Annie didn't recognize any of them, but Ira whispered that one man was Governor Curtin.

After a while, as the music continued, Ira said, "I'm guessing they're waiting for the main speaker, Dr. Everett."

"Where's President Lincoln?" Annie asked.

"I don't see him yet."

A man with snowy white hair arrived. Then a minister prayed, and the band played another song. Finally, the man with the white hair was introduced as the Honorable Edward Everett. He had an extensive list of credentials over a lengthy career, including U.S. representative, governor of Massachusetts, and president of Harvard University.

He began to give a speech entitled "The Battle of Gettysburg," practically shouting so as many as possible could hear. His speech went on and on, starting with ancient Greece and continuing through time. After about an hour, at one in the afternoon, Kate took the basket of food from Ira, opened it, and passed the food around the three of them and then the jar of tea. The beverage was cold but still welcomed. Others in the crowd began to wander around, most likely stretching their legs. Annie stomped her feet, trying to warm them up even though she wore the wool socks. She feared she'd be limping by the time the ceremony was over.

The Honorable Everett continued to speak. An hour later,

he concluded, "But they . . . will join us in saying, as we bid farewell to the dust of these martyr-heroes, that wheresoever throughout the civilized world the accounts of this great warfare are read . . . in the glorious annals of our common country, there will be no brighter page than that which relates the Battle of Gettysburg."

Brighter page seemed an odd reference to all the loss of life and limb, but Annie feared she might have missed something in the man's speech. Or perhaps he hadn't any idea of what Gettysburg actually looked like during and after the battle.

The band began to play another hymn, and Annie wondered if perhaps President Lincoln hadn't come after all. She asked Ira.

"He's there, on the platform." Ira motioned for her to step in front of him.

There he was, sitting tall and still as the band continued to play. He had a beard similar to her Dat's, except shorter and with less gray.

The band stopped and President Lincoln was introduced. He took two pieces of folded paper from his coat pocket and faced the crowd. Annie clasped her hands together, mesmerized as he shouted, "Four score and seven years ago our fathers brought forth on this continent, a new nation, conceived in Liberty, and dedicated to the proposition that all men are created equal."

Annie hung on every word, and on the applause that interrupted his words over and over again.

"We have come to dedicate a portion of that field, as a final resting place for those who here gave their lives that this nation might live. It is altogether fitting and proper that we should do this." As he scanned the crowd, his eyes landed on Annie for a brief moment before falling back down to his notes. A shiver ran down her spine.

Tears rushed into her eyes as he continued. "It is for us the living, rather, to be dedicated here to the unfinished work which they who fought here have thus far so nobly advanced." *The living*. She'd cared for the living and had helped save some so they could go on in this life.

But she'd also seen the dead.

The president continued, "It is rather for us to be here dedicated to the great task remaining before us . . . that we here highly resolve that these dead shall not have died in vain—that this nation, under God, shall have a new birth of freedom—and that government of the people, by the people, for the people, shall not perish from the earth."

A new birth of freedom. That was what Annie prayed for. That some good would come from the devastation of Gettysburg and the entire war.

President Lincoln understood the losses. It seemed as if all the hurts of Gettysburg—of the entire nation—were on his empathetic shoulders. She felt drawn to him. He seemed to be intelligent and caring, much like Ira.

Lost in her thoughts, she expected more of a speech from the president, but then she realized he was done. Applause erupted all around, and she joined in as a tear rolled down her cheek. She doubted if President Lincoln's speech lasted more than a few minutes, but it had been powerful and moving. Her soul had expanded with his words.

As the president stepped backward, a choir assembled on the platform and sang a song that Annie didn't recognize. Then another minister said a closing prayer. After that, a group of military personnel escorted President Lincoln off the platform and toward town.

As the crowd began to disperse, the mood was upbeat, al-

LESLIE GOULD

though the three of them weren't. Perhaps those celebrating, like Edward Everett, hadn't been around for the battle or the weeks afterward. Annie thought of all of the soldiers they'd cared for and wondered how many had died between then and now, as Richert had. Others were back with their families and some with their units. Perhaps they'd soon be fighting in another battle. But all of them had been changed forever.

A wave of weariness came over her.

Undaunted, Ira forged a way, with Annie and Kate following, through the thickest part of the crowd, but instead of heading back to the street, Ira led them through the cemetery to the ornate Italianate gate and then back to the street, toward Dr. Carson's.

Thankfully, the doctor hadn't joined them as he said he would.

"How about we collect our things and go to the train depot?" Ira proposed. "Perhaps we'll beat the crowd trying to leave."

"Good idea." Annie looped her arm through Kate's. "Woody said he'd be in York, at the station, tonight."

Kate nodded. "Let's give it a try. The sooner we leave the better."

Thankfully, Dr. Carson wasn't at his house, and Annie guessed he hadn't returned from the cemetery with his other guests yet. They grabbed their bags and told Meg thank you and farewell. By the time they reached the depot, the platform was packed, but Ira was able to secure tickets. Additional trains had been added to the schedule to accommodate the masses of people, and thankfully it seemed the majority of them weren't as eager to leave Gettysburg as Kate, Ira, and Annie.

301

Before the train stopped at York, Kate had her bag in her lap and was telling Ira good-bye. "Write to me and let me know when you've settled in Philadelphia."

He nodded. "I will." He took her hand as the train came to a stop. "What are your plans?"

On the platform stood Woody, appearing to search the windows of the car.

He broke out in a grin when he saw the trio and called out, "Miss Kate!"

She pulled away from Ira and stood quickly. "Once I have your address, I'll write and let you know." She gave Annie a hug. "Come back and help me if you can," she said. "I'll always have a place for you."

Annie hugged her back, and then both she and Ira watched as Kate hurried down the aisle and then disappeared. They turned their attention to the platform, but Woody was walking away from them, toward the door. Ira stood and opened the window, letting in a rush of icy air. He stuck his head out.

Annie nudged him to make room for her, and he did.

Kate hurried down the steps of the train to the platform and rushed toward Woody. He swept her up in a hug. Ira jerked back into the car, bumping Annie's head.

"Ouch." Her hand went to her bonnet.

As she rubbed her skull, he muttered, "Sorry."

They both sat down, facing each other.

"I totally misread that," he said. "I thought, I guess because my father was a doctor, that Ma and Doc would make a good couple. I couldn't have been more wrong."

"Me too," Annie said.

"Do you think she and Woody, you know . . ." Ira met Annie's eyes.

302

"Care for each other?"

He nodded.

Annie thought of Sophia and Richert and their devotion to each other. She saw that in Woody and Kate too. "I believe so."

"Do you think they have for a while?"

It was Annie's turn to nod.

Ira continued to stare into her eyes until she looked away, back to the platform. Woody and Kate were now in view. He carried her bag, and they strolled along, arm in arm. Annie imagined them traveling back to Peach Bottom together, talking or not talking. It wouldn't matter. She'd seen them be perfectly comfortable in their silence before. That was something she'd never experienced with Samuel, but she had with Ira.

"What are you thinking?" he asked.

She met his eyes again, her face growing warm. "Nothing."

He smiled. "I don't believe you."

She laughed. "No, I don't expect you would."

"Annie . . ."

Her heart lurched.

"Could we talk?"

She shook her head. "No."

He opened his mouth.

She shook her head again. "Stop."

They rode in silence, both staring out the window as the afternoon light faded. After a while, Annie asked where he'd be living in Philadelphia, and he began talking again, telling her first about the barracks he'd stay in and then about the hospital. "Training to be a surgeon has been a dream for me since I was a boy."

As Annie listened, bittersweetness filled her heart. She was thrilled for Ira and the opportunities ahead of him. But she'd no longer have any sort of relationship with him.

"After the war, I'll open a practice," he said.

"Where?" she asked.

He leaned forward. "That depends."

"On?"

He shook his head. "You told me to stop, so I can't say anything more. Is that correct?"

She nodded as the whistle blew and the train began to slow. They'd reached the river, and it was time to disembark and take the ferry. Then it wouldn't be long until they reached Lancaster. She had only a few hours left until her time with Ira would be over—forever.

❧❧❧

Sunset fell as they crossed the river, and an icy wind blew over the water. "May I put my arm around you?" Ira asked. "To shield the wind?"

She agreed. He gripped her shoulder and pulled her close, tucking her head under his chin. As the sun disappeared beyond the western hills, Annie leaned against him. She'd never been so close to a man, not even Samuel. It wasn't proper, not at all, but at the moment she didn't care.

She breathed the cold, mixed with his spicy scent, savoring his closeness. Both longing and loss welled up in her. She closed her eyes, no longer able to deny the affection she felt for him, until the ferry bumped against the dock, landing them back in Lancaster County.

By the time they boarded the next train, it was completely dark. Once they'd settled in their seats, Annie longed for Ira to put his arm around her again, but of course he didn't.

They traveled on. Annie tried not to count down the time, but she couldn't help herself. Anxiety filled her more and more with each passing minute. Ira sat with his hands clasped together, a pained expression on his face.

When the train pulled into the station, she told Ira good-bye.

"I'm not leaving you here," he said. "I'll get off and find a reliable driver to take you the rest of the way home."

"But that will delay your arrival in Philadelphia."

He shrugged. "A few hours won't make a difference."

Relieved, she followed Ira off the train. As they entered the station, someone called out her name.

Samuel.

"George sent a message to your parents that you were headed home. I told them I'd look for you here." He crossed his arms. "But he didn't say Ira would be with you."

Ira quickly explained that he was headed to Philadelphia.

"And Kate just left us at York." Annie did her best to keep her voice calm. "Ira was a gentleman to see me off the train."

Samuel seemed to calm down some. "Well, thank you, Ira. You can get back on the train now." He held up the box in his hands. "I just need to deliver this to Mr. Stevens. Stay here," he said to Annie. "I'll be back to take you home shortly."

Annie shook her head.

Samuel's face grew red, and she realized she'd humiliated him. But she didn't want him to take her home. "I'll find a ride," she said. She couldn't ride home with him. She couldn't court him. And she certainly couldn't marry him. She felt so small around him. So unseen. Sophia had been right—he wasn't the right man for her.

He clenched his fists. "Annie."

His behavior wasn't the result of too much alcohol, but still he scared her. She thought of the broken mirror in Gettysburg. Samuel might not be violent, but she feared he would break her just the same. No doubt he did well in his work for Representative Stevens, but he did no good when it came to his interactions with her. He didn't want to know about her life, about both her hurts and accomplishments. And he didn't want her to care for others. He only wanted her for himself.

But God had called her to serve others.

Samuel didn't share that vision.

Ira stepped closer to her.

"I'm staying here with Ira for the time being," Annie said. She could send a message to her father to fetch her, if needed. If Ira had to leave before Dat arrived, she'd be safe at the station.

Samuel frowned and grabbed her arm.

She jerked it away, and Ira quickly stepped in front of her.

Samuel shook his head, a disgusted look on his face.

"I'm not going with you. Ever," Annie said.

His face reddened. "Then I'll leave it to God to deal with you." He marched away without looking back.

Annie put her hand over her mouth.

Ira exhaled and then asked, "Are you all right?"

She nodded. "Denki."

This time he did put his arm around her and led her to a bench. "Can we talk now?"

As they sat, she put her head against his shoulder for a moment and whispered, "Jah."

"What's to become of us, Annie Bachmann?" he asked.

She sat up straight. It wouldn't do for anyone to see an Amish girl propped up against a soldier. "I don't know, Ira King."

"Am I wrong in caring for you?" he asked.

"No," she whispered, but she wasn't ready to both admit that Samuel was the wrong man for her and that Ira was the right one. "Though I need some time."

As they sat on the bench, Annie did her best to collect herself as Ira said he'd ride with her to the farm. "I'll come back and catch the train to Philly in the morning," he said.

She didn't want him to have to do that, but he insisted. However, he had a hard time finding a driver. Once he located a man with a cart who said he'd rent it to Ira for the night, they stashed their bags in the back, and after lighting the lantern the man provided, climbed up onto the bench of the cart.

They traveled on in silence as they headed east and out of town. Finally Ira asked, "May I write to you once I'm in Philadelphia?"

"Of course."

"Your parents won't care?"

She pulled her cloak tighter. "Jah, they will," she answered. "But write anyway."

He was silent again.

Then, at a crossroads, he pulled the horse to a stop and turned toward her. "Annie, I must bring this up because we don't have much time." He hurried on with his words. "Once I've set up a practice of my own, hopefully near here, will you consider me? Once this war is over?" Ira's voice caught for a moment. Then he added, "Will you consider me as your husband?"

She didn't answer for a long moment. She was at a crossroads too, but she was realizing it wasn't as complicated as she'd feared. In fact, the direction she needed to take was becoming quite clear. *It is for us the living . . .*

He repeated, "When the war is over—"

"No," Annie answered.

"I was afraid so." His face fell in the shadow cast by the lantern. "Is it me? Or the differences in our churches?"

She shook her head. "Neither. I've already considered you,

Ira King. And I said I needed time, but I've already changed my mind. Jah, if you'll have me as your wife, I'll have you as my husband." There was no reason to put off telling him—not when she knew for certain.

Their hands met and Ira pulled her close, kissing the top of her bonnet. Then the horse lurched forward and the cart rolled through the crossroads as they continued their journey on to the Bachmann farm.

—22—

Marie

I sat on the edge of my chair. "Why did you stop?"

"That's the end of the story," Aenti Suz answered.

"It can't be. What did Annie's parents say? How long until the war ended? Did she leave the Amish and join the Brethren Church? When did they marry? What about George and Harriet and their boys? And what about Kate and Woody?"

"Oh my, what a lot of questions." Aenti Suz rubbed the back of her neck. "Let's see, Kate continued on with her midwifery business."

"She and Woody didn't marry?"

Aenti Suz smiled. "No, they did. In fact, by Christmastime of 1863 they were wed. They stayed in Peach Bottom and bought a little farm."

She went on to say that Ira finished his training in Philadelphia and was back on the front line by the end of the war, saving the lives of soldiers. "Altogether, around 620,000 soldiers died from disease, wounds, and accidents during the Civil War.

At Gettysburg alone, 51,000 soldiers were killed, wounded, or captured. It was the largest and bloodiest battle ever fought on U.S. soil."

I paused for a moment, trying to comprehend such massive numbers. I couldn't, so I changed the subject. "When did Ira and Annie marry?"

"The summer after the war ended, June of 1865. There was so much to mourn—all who died, the death of Sophia, the assassination of President Lincoln, the deep wounds in the nation. But there was also much to celebrate for the young couple."

I jumped to my next question. "How about the Underground Railroad? Who all was helping with that?"

"Well, that's hard to know because no one talked about it much. After the war some groups did, such as the Quakers, but the Anabaptists were silent about their part in it for years. Surely, Samuel was involved. There's now evidence that makes it seem probable that Thaddeus Stevens had a hiding place in the back of his pub that was a stop on the Underground Railroad. It's also likely that the Fishers were active, and we know that there were several stops around Peach Bottom too. Many Union soldiers, including Ira, did everything they could to protect runaway slaves once they reached the Union Army. And Woody also helped transport fleeing slaves."

"They were all heroes, weren't they?"

Aenti Suz nodded. "But they would have hated to be seen as heroes. They were simply doing what was right, what God compelled them to do."

I nodded. I saw that in Gordon. He didn't think the volunteer work he did was anything special, even though it changed lives—Josh's, for example. It was simply what Gordon felt led to do. I thought of the verse in James that Paula had quoted back in Florida. I'd looked it up since then. It was James 4:17 and read, *Therefore to him that knoweth to do good, and doeth it not, to him it is sin.* The Fishers, Woody, Kate, Ira, and Annie all did the good that God required of them.

I jumped ahead in time. "So did Josiah end up with the Bachmann farm?"

Aenti Suz shook her head.

"What? How was it passed on down to Dat then?"

"George and Harriet returned to Leacock. Noah ended up with the farm. He was your great-great-grandfather."

"Wow," I said, taking it all in. Immediately, however, my thoughts returned to Annie.

"How did Annie's parents react to her leaving the church?"

"They were disturbed, as you can imagine. They begged her to stay and then tried to guilt her into staying, but ultimately they resigned themselves to her marrying Ira. He did set up a practice in Lancaster, and Annie helped him, learning more about medicine than she ever thought possible. Ira and Annie both became active members of the Brethren Church, but they still visited her parents from time to time. Annie and Ira had seven children, and they all grew to know their Bachmann grandparents, uncles, aunts, and cousins."

"But surely it wasn't that easy for Annie to leave the Amish, even for the Brethren Church. Even though she lived in Lancaster, close to her parents and the Bachmann farm, she was actually a world away."

"She wasn't exactly a world away."

"But she left the Amish. Wasn't she horribly lonely?"

"She had Ira. And, like I said, she still saw her family some."

"But weren't they terribly disappointed in her? Didn't she feel guilty for what she did to them? She could have married

Samuel and lived near her mother. Sure, Samuel was controlling, but he most likely would have changed."

Aenti Suz looked at me questioningly, but I ignored it, continuing on with my rant. "Her poor Mamm had already lost Sophia. How tragic for her to lose Annie too."

Now Aenti Suz gave me a sad look. "Marie, parents can't control their children forever. Jah, I'm sure it was hard on Annie's parents to have her leave the Amish, but they survived. Each person must make decisions about his or her own future."

I shook my head. "No, we're part of a family. Each of our decisions affects everyone—our parents, our siblings, future generations." I crossed my arms. "You should have told Leisel this story, not me. She's the one who left—the one who is never coming back, the one going into medicine. I've always known I'd stay, that I would never leave."

Aenti Suz just shrugged, stood, and took her teacup to the sink. As I was still mulling over the story, Leisel came out of Aenti Suz's bedroom, yawning and stretching. She said she'd get a shower and then rejoin the living. Then Jessica stirred on the couch.

Jah, my sisters had both left the Amish. Jessica had come to her senses and returned, but still, at one time she abandoned her church and family. Everyone knew I would never do such a thing. So much so that I thought it time I write a letter to Elijah.

I told Jessica and Aenti Suz that I would be right back, that I was just going to check in with Edith to see how Mamm and Silas were doing.

Edith was in the kitchen, and she reported that Silas hadn't had a fever since the morning before. "If it doesn't start up again by this evening, I think he could see Jessica. That would do them both good."

I agreed.

She said Mamm was still running a fever. "So don't go up there."

I promised her I wouldn't, saying I just needed to get something from Dat's study. I slipped into the room. I walked around Mamm's quilting frame to Dat's desk and found paper, a pen, an envelope, and a stamp. I sat down in Dat's old chair and twirled the pen.

After I wrote that I was sorry I didn't have a chance to say good-bye, the details about the bus accident, and how Jessica was doing, not much more came to mind. I thought about writing to him about Annie and Ira, but quashed that idea right away. First of all, the story would bore him. And second of all, it would be odd to tell him, considering Annie had left the Amish and married a Brethren, when she had the chance to marry Samuel, the eligible Amish bachelor.

I twirled the pen some more and then finally wrote how much I missed him. Then I bundled up and headed out to our mailbox, even though the mailman wouldn't pick it up until Monday.

I considered going out to the barn and calling Elijah, but he'd still be at the bakery. And besides, if Gordon was on our property—say, in the barn—I didn't want him to overhear our conversation.

But as I reached the mailbox, Gordon drove up in his car. He waved and rolled down the window.

I asked where he'd been. "Over at the Stoltz farm. John came down with the flu and Mildred is in no shape to do any chores, so I fed the animals and made sure they have enough wood on their porch to stay warm."

"Do they need any food?" I asked. "I'm going to make beef and barley soup for supper. And bread." I needed to get started on that. "It will be a big batch. You could take some over for them."

Gordon smiled. "That would be great. Thank you."

For a moment I considered asking Gordon to stay for supper, but I felt awkward about that. The truth was, he'd been interested in Annie's story and I really wanted to tell it to someone. Who was I kidding? I wanted to tell it to Gordon. For some reason I believed he would appreciate it the most. But on the other hand, why would I tell him about my ancestor's leaving the church and marrying a man from another one? I didn't invite him for supper.

Aenti Suz did though, when he brought a load of wood to the door for her woodstove. He thanked her and then ate quickly so he could deliver the soup and bread over to the Stoltzes.

Aenti Suz said he should rest after that, but he confessed that he was volunteering at the shelter that night. "It's been so cold that they've been overwhelmed again," he said. "And, at the moment, they're understaffed." His cheeks grew red, most likely remembering what he'd told me about Tony asking him to work at the shelter. But then he said to me, "Oh, I almost forgot. I saw Chrissie and Rory last week. And the baby."

"Oh no," I answered. "Are they back on the street?"

He shook his head. "She's worked things out with her mother and is attending vocational training. She had some baby clothes the little one had outgrown that she brought by."

"That's great," I said.

Gordon nodded. "She said to tell you hello and to thank you for your help that night."

I gave him a small smile, unsure how to respond.

"She said Rory still talks about you and your 'costume.'"

I laughed. "If you see them again, please say hello. And tell Rory that I think of him often too."

314

After he'd left, we all continued to sit at the table, including Jessica. Leisel sighed and said, "Gordon is going to make some lucky girl a great husband."

Jessica smiled and said, "That lucky girl could be you."

"Nah," she answered. "He's a little too serious for me." She glanced at me. "But he'd be perfect for Marie."

No one said anything for a moment.

I rolled my eyes and said, "You're joking, right? He'd never become Amish, and I'm never going to—"

"—jah, jah, jah," Leisel said. "You're like a broken record. Forget I said anything, because I'm certainly not thinking you would leave. That would be crazy talk."

As Leisel and I started to clear the table, a knock fell on the door. Aenti Suz opened it, and Silas stepped inside. I hadn't told Jessica he was better, so she was surprised to see him—and so relieved. They sat down on the couch, huddled together in their grief. Silas swiped his index finger across Jessica's face, and then pulled her into an embrace. Showing public displays of affection was something Amish couples didn't do, but the two seemed completely oblivious to the rest of us.

A lump formed in my throat, and I tried to swallow it down. I was unsuccessful. Instead, I turned toward the dirty dishes as I swiped away a tear of my own.

A couple of minutes later, Leisel's cell phone rang.

"Oh, it's Nick." She stepped out of the kitchen. "I'm just going to take this in the bedroom."

"Looks like it's just you and me." Aenti Suz flashed me a grin.

"Jah." I plunged my hands into the hot, soapy water. Two old maids, but hopefully not for long. For both of us. I imagined that once David returned to Chester County, he'd be down visiting Aenti Suz as soon as he could.

315

Aenti Suz and I went to church Sunday morning, while Leisel and Silas—and Nick—stayed with Jessica. He'd shown up just before we left. Leisel always claimed they were "just friends," but I had my doubts. I was surprised Silas and Jessica weren't going to church but then chastised myself. Both were recovering. Empathy was the correct reaction—not judgment.

As I sat through the service, I thought of the church in Pinecraft and missed it in some ways. We were all so different there, but still the same. And meeting in a building instead of on a farm hadn't been as odd as I'd anticipated.

After the service, Bishop Jacobs sought us out and asked how Jessica was doing. We filled him in, and then he asked about Elijah, a hopeful look on his face. I wasn't going to give too much away, but I told him how much I'd enjoyed spending time with his youngest son. Bishop Jacobs beamed and then said he spoke with Elijah the night before, and he was coming home sooner than May—perhaps as early as March. The bishop gave me a grateful smile. "Denki," he said. "We attribute all of this to your good influence on him."

I returned the smile, pleased I'd made a difference in Elijah's life.

By the time we returned home, the day was warming up, the temperature climbing above freezing for the first time in weeks. The ice hanging on the lines and trees started to drip, and the snow on the side of the road grew slushy.

When we reached the farm, Leisel and Nick both had their coats and boots on and were having a snowball fight out in the backyard. They'd also built a snowman. As soon as Aenti Suz had parked the buggy, Leisel and Nick ran up to the horse and started to unhitch him. By the time we'd climbed down, they were unharnessing him too.

"Go in," Leisel said. "We'll take care of him."

"Denki," Aenti Suz said.

When Nick and Leisel returned to the Dawdi Haus, it was time for Nick to leave. He'd been visiting his parents, who also lived in Lancaster County, but needed to head back to Pittsburgh for work. We all told him good-bye and then Leisel walked him to his car.

After they left, I asked Jessica if the two were serious.

She shrugged. "They're definitely good friends."

"What do we know about him?" I asked. "I mean, we know he's not Plain, but does he even go to church?"

Jessica assured me that he did. "I think he grew up Baptist or something like that."

Soon after that, Gordon arrived to take Jessica and Silas home, and he asked me if I wanted to ride along. Aenti Suz told me to go ahead, that she would enjoy spending time with Leisel. I took that as a sign that she wanted me to go. Perhaps she wanted to quiz Leisel about Nick.

Jessica and I sat in the back, while Silas sat up front with Gordon. The snow continued to melt, although there was enough of it that it wouldn't be gone in a day, even if the temperature stayed above freezing.

As we drove along, the men chatted away about farming. In a low voice, I asked Jessica if she remembered Dat's harmonica.

After a long moment, she said, "Wow, I hadn't thought about that in years. But, jah, I do remember."

"Any idea if it's still around?"

She tilted her head. "I have no idea. I know Mamm wasn't happy about it. . . ."

I couldn't think of where Dat would have put it, and I couldn't imagine him hiding it somewhere. Perhaps Mamm had never given it back to him, but I was hesitant to bring it up with her.

After we dropped Silas and Jessica off at their house, Gordon said we weren't far from his home. "Would you like to stop and meet my mother?"

That seemed a little odd to me, but I was curious about his home, and his Mamm too. "Sure," I said.

Their house was in a group of modest homes, a small subdivision off the main road. He pulled into a driveway, behind another black car. The house was painted sage with forest-green trim, and a welcome sign hung on the front door. Gordon opened my car door, and then stepped ahead of me to open the door to his house.

As we walked inside, he called out, "Mom! Marie is here with me."

I could hear music from down the hall, but then it stopped.

"Oh, how nice," a voice called out. "I'll be right there."

The living room, to the left, had a brown leather couch and a platform rocking chair. There were also shelves flanking a brick fireplace, filled with books. There were no pictures on the wall, and overall the décor was very plain.

Gordon took my cape and then asked, "Would you like a cup of coffee? Or hot chocolate?"

"Coffee would be great." I was chilled from riding in his car, even though the weather was warmer than it had been.

He stepped into the kitchen, and I followed. It was small but efficient, with a small island in the middle.

As he poured the coffee, which was already made, a woman stepped into the kitchen. She wore a blue print dress and black sweater, and had her brown hair pulled back in a bun at the nape of her neck.

She extended her hand to me. "Hello," she said. "I'm Randi, Gordon's mom."

I shook her hand. "I'm Marie."

"I've heard so much about you." She smiled warmly. "All good, of course."

Not sure how to respond to that, I said, "I'm pleased to meet you."

Gordon handed me a cup of coffee, and I took a sip. He turned toward his mom. "I thought I'd show Marie our music room. Is that all right?"

Randi nodded, grabbing a mug out of the cupboard. "Go on down. I'll be there in a minute."

"This way." Gordon nodded his head toward the hallway. We passed three doors that were closed. But the fourth one, at the end of the hall, was open. He motioned for me to enter first.

There was a large piano, which I guessed his mother had been playing. There were also two different guitars, propped up in holders, and several music stands. There was also a case shaped like a guitar but smaller, sitting on a table. I guessed it was a violin.

"That belongs to my sister," Gordon said, following my gaze. "She left it when she went to college." He smiled. "She was kind of forced to play an instrument but never really took to it."

That surprised me. I couldn't imagine passing up the opportunity to play an instrument. I stepped to the piano, wanting desperately to touch the keys. I hadn't given it a second thought in Florida when I played the keyboard, but here it seemed I shouldn't. *What happens in Pinecraft, stays in Pinecraft* floated in my mind. Even though the saying bugged me, I'd followed it. I hadn't once felt guilty about singing down there or playing the few notes.

But here, it all felt different. Still, I held my hands over the keys. "May I?"

He nodded.

I took another sip of coffee, put the cup on the table, and then sat on the bench and placed my fingers on the piano keys. They felt different from the keyboard in Pinecraft. I plunked C. The weight was definitely different. I liked it. I picked out "Cat, Dog, Elephant" and thought of Dat. I played the C scale several times. Then I began picking out "How Great Thou Art," which had been Dat's favorite hymn. Halfway through I remembered, "Turn, Turn, Turn" and began playing that. Gordon and I sang the words, "To everything, there is a season . . ."

Randi stepped into the room as we finished it. "I haven't thought of that song in over a decade, I'm sure."

I rose from the bench.

"No," she said. "Go on."

I shook my head. I'd done more than I should have. "Would you play?"

She put her coffee cup down on the little table. "If Gordon will too." She sat down.

He nodded. I'd guessed he was going to play one of his guitars, but instead he sat down on the piano bench next to his mother.

I picked up my coffee cup and took another drink as they started to play "Oh, Wondrous Name."

Randi began to sing along as they played, and then Gordon did too. He glanced up at me and nodded, so I joined in too. "Oh, glorious Name, the angels praise, And ransomed saints adore . . ." and then sang the rest of the song with them.

When they'd finished, I asked Randi about the music classes she taught at the high school Gordon had attended.

"I teach choir, piano, and handbells," she said. "We don't have a band or anything like that."

"Did you play the guitar too?"

She shook her head. "His father taught him when Gordon was little."

"One chord at a time," Gordon added.

I remembered Gordon told me his father had taught him to play the guitar, but it meant more to me now.

Gordon explained, "I was ten when Dad left." He didn't seem bothered to talk about his father, but then he changed the topic and asked if he could show me some chords on his guitar.

I was a member of the Amish church—I shouldn't be playing musical instruments. But at the moment I didn't care. I certainly didn't feel as if this was taking me away from the Lord—in fact, like before, I felt a harmony in my soul.

I'd confess to Bishop Jacobs later, if necessary.

I smiled at Gordon. "Sure, I'd love to learn a couple of chords."

He spent the next hour giving me a lesson while his mother played quietly on the piano. At first, I had a hard time stretching my hand, and the strings cut into my finger pads, but I soon got the hang of it and was able to pick out a few songs.

Finally, I thanked Gordon, and Randi too, and said I should get back home.

"How about if we warm up our coffee?" Gordon asked. "Would that be all right?"

I nodded. "I'd like that."

We sat in the living room and finished our coffee while his mother continued to play the piano down the hall.

"I can't imagine what it must have been like to grow up in a house full of music," I said.

"But a cappella singing is so beautiful," Gordon said. I was pretty sure he was just trying to make me feel better. "And your voice is such a gift."

I hesitated for a moment, but then explained that Mamm had forbidden me from singing in the house.

With a shocked expression, Gordon asked, "Why would she do that?"

"She was afraid singing would make me prideful." Guilt was now setting in about playing the piano and guitar. Confessing to Bishop Jacobs was one thing, but telling Mamm would be even harder.

"I can't imagine you being prideful."

I shook my head. "Then I've fooled you all these months. There have been all sorts of things I've been prideful about. Me staying in the Amish church when Jessica left, to start. Mamm favoring me over my sisters. How 'good' I've always been."

He rubbed his chin and then smiled. "None of that has to do with your singing."

I shrugged. "It has to do with me." Maybe the afternoon of music had made me more open, more honest. "Sorry." I took a drink of the coffee.

"There's no reason to be sorry. Self-reflection is good. We all need that. And we all have things that we need the Lord to transform." He leaned closer. "But don't sell yourself short. You have a lot of good qualities too."

I didn't want to ask him to elaborate, just in case that would put him on the spot and he wouldn't have an answer. He was probably, like always, just being nice.

When we finished our coffee, we traipsed back down the hall and I told Randi good-bye. As Gordon retrieved my cape and his coat, I told her quietly what a good son she raised. "I don't know what my family would do without him."

She reached out and squeezed my hand. "He feels the same way about all of you."

Gordon and I didn't speak much on the way back to the farm. He walked me to the door of Aenti Suz's Dawdi Haus, stopping before we got to her little porch.

"See you tomorrow?" he asked.

I nodded. I hoped so.

When I stepped into the Dawdi Haus, Aenti Suz greeted me with a smile. "My," she said. "That certainly took a while." Both she and Leisel sat on the couch.

Leisel nodded and then looked at her watch. "Hours." She raised her eyebrows at me.

My face grew warm as I took off my cape. "We stopped by Gordon's house, and I met his mother."

Leisel blinked several times. "Sounds serious."

I rolled my eyes. "It's not." I turned toward the spare bedroom where my things were. "I'm going to pack up and stay with Mamm tonight." I wouldn't ask her about the harmonica, not until she was feeling better. Edith planned to stay until the morning, but I could take over caring for Mamm tonight.

As I headed back to the living room, Leisel said she'd walk over with me and tell Mamm hello but not get too close to her. "I really can't afford to get ill," she said. She would leave early the next morning to get back in time for her swing shift at work.

Before we left, I thanked Aenti Suz for everything. Then I hesitated for a moment.

"What is it?" she asked.

"Do you remember Dat's harmonica?"

She nodded.

"Was he allowed to play it, by the bishop at the time?"

Aenti Suz nodded again. "Jah, it wasn't unheard of for Amish men to play a harmonica."

"Do you know what happened to it?"

She shook her head. "I have no idea. Your mother might."

-23-

I quickly took over Mamm's care while checking in on Aenti Suz several times a day. The snow continued to melt until the brown grass actually showed and there were only patches of snow left in the field. I did see Gordon a few times that week, mostly at a distance. Each time he saw me, he'd smile and wave, and I'd wave back. But that was all.

The flu had weakened Mamm, but she grew a little stronger each day. All week, I longed to ask about the harmonica, but I waited until Friday as we ate chicken noodle soup for our supper. Aenti Suz didn't join us, giving me the perfect opportunity.

Mamm was still pale, but she was dressed and had her hair pulled back in a bun. She wore a heavy sweater and her slippers.

As soon as I broached the subject, I knew she didn't want to talk about it because she pursed her lips.

"Do you know where the harmonica is?"

"I have no idea," Mamm said. "I gave it back to him."

It was my turn to purse my lips.

She crossed her arms. "I just know he never played it after that."

"Because you wouldn't let him."

325

"Marie," Mamm said. "Don't get snippy with me. I had your best interests in mind. Your Dat had no business doing what he did."

"But Aenti Suz said the bishop at the time was fine with harmonicas."

Mamm exhaled. "No bishop would be all right with a little girl becoming prideful about her voice, being encouraged by her own father. After I lost Rebecca . . . I could not risk losing another daughter."

"Mamm," I said. "Did you think God would punish you for my singing?"

"No, but He might for your pride. It was my responsibility to keep you from it."

"By doing away with any temptation? Wouldn't it be better to teach me how to sing without being prideful?"

"No. At the time, the best thing to do was to remove the temptation. You were too young. And—" She paused.

"And what?"

"Too gifted. Much too gifted for your own good. I had no choice but to discourage you. It's not as if you couldn't still sing at church—where you were singing with our community, not on your own. I didn't think there was the same danger of you becoming prideful there."

She wouldn't talk about it anymore that evening, but I brought the topic up the next day, as I folded towels while she sat at the table with a cup of chamomile tea.

"Do you think Dat got rid of the harmonica?"

"Marie," she snapped. "I have no idea."

"Where would he have put it? In your room? In his study? In the office in the barn?"

Mamm pursed her lips.

"Do you mind if I look?"

"What will you do if you find it? You can't play it without talking to Bishop Jacobs first."

"Mamm," I responded. "I just want to find it. That's all." That's what I told myself too, but I couldn't imagine if I did find it that I wouldn't play it. My stomach fell. I hadn't yet confessed to playing the instruments to Bishop Jacobs. Would I? And if I found the harmonica, would I speak with him about it too? Or hide the instrument from everyone, especially Mamm?

I deep-cleaned the entire house, humming loudly as I did. As I worked, I searched for the harmonica. In Dat's study. In Mamm's bedroom. Behind the books in the shelves in the living room. Everywhere I could think of, but I didn't find it anywhere. I continued cleaning.

After the house was back in order, I decided to look in the barn for the harmonica. Perhaps Dat had left it there that very night that Mamm forbade us all from making music.

One morning, after I finished hanging the wash, I continued on toward the barn. Gordon, who was in the field, called out my name. He stood on a ladder up against our old oak tree, cutting a broken branch. I waved and hurried on. At least he wasn't in the barn. Hopefully Arden and my nephews weren't either.

I pushed open the door slowly and called out, "Hallo!" No one answered and I continued on in, heading to the office first, where Arden kept all of the paperwork for the dairy farm business. There was a desk, a file cabinet, and cupboards along the wall. I started looking in the cupboards first. There were stacks of papers and some boxes. I knelt to the floor and felt along each shelf, finding a few pens and paper clips but nothing else. Next I checked the desk drawers. There was a stapler, a three-hole punch, and more pens and paper clips, plus a notebook

of paper. But no harmonica. The file cabinet was locked, but
I doubted it was in there either. I stepped out of the office, my
arms crossed. Where would Dat have put it?

The barn door creaked, and I froze. If it was Arden, what
would I say to him? I knew as soon as I heard the singing that
it wasn't.

"Hey," Gordon said. "What are you doing in here?"

"Looking . . ." I uncrossed my arms. I could tell Gordon.
"For Dat's harmonica."

"I'm guessing it wasn't in the office."

"That's right."

Gordon leaned the ladder up against the wall and put the
saw down. "There's the storage room. There's some old furniture back there. Maybe he stashed it in a bureau drawer or
something."

"Good idea." I turned and marched toward the room. We'd
left a few pieces that we'd moved out of the house for Jessica's
wedding in the storage room, thinking we didn't need them in
the house.

There were a couple of old bedsteads, tables, chairs, a couple
of benches, and a few sets of bureaus. I thought of Annie and
her family and wondered if any of the pieces dated back to
them. Gordon opened the top drawer of a bureau and worked
his way down. I squinted in the dim light coming through a
high window. Up against a couple of bedsteads was a bedside
table. Dat's. It was from his and Mamm's room. I made my way
around a table and several chairs and a bench. I opened the bottom drawer first—it was completely empty. So was the middle
drawer. There was no way the harmonica would be in the top
drawer, but of course I opened it anyway . . . and there it was.

I snatched it and held it up. "Here it is." I turned around and showed it to Gordon. The weight felt so good in my hand, as did the cold metal. I ran my fingers along the comb as I made my way to Gordon, but before I reached him, he met me in the middle of the room.

I handed it to him, and he examined it carefully. "It's a Seydel," he said. "An old German company. It's really good quality." He extended it back to me.

I shook my head. "Play it."

"No, you play it," he said.

I shook my head, tears stinging my eyes.

"Marie," he said. "What's wrong?"

I wanted to sob—but not in front of Gordon. I just shook my head and pushed the harmonica back toward him. He put it to his mouth and played a scale. He stopped.

"More. Please?"

He began to play again, this time "Amazing Grace."

It was beautiful. I closed my eyes and felt the music deep within me, remembering Dat. Remembering myself as a girl. Remembering my sisters. I began to sing as Gordon played to the end of the song. When the last note stopped, I opened my eyes.

He handed me the harmonica. "Your turn."

I shook my head, but I took the instrument and slipped it under my cape into the pocket of my apron.

"Why won't you play it?" Gordon asked.

"I'm not supposed to."

"Oh." His eyes grew soft. "The Ordnung?"

I nodded. "I shouldn't have played the piano or guitar at your house. I was wrong." But I still hadn't confessed. "It's just that the music makes me feel so . . . at peace."

Gordon nodded.

"I don't know what to do."

"Pray about it," Gordon advised. "And I'll pray for you too."

I thanked him and then turned to leave, but then I faced him again. "Have you decided about the job at the shelter?"

"I didn't take it," he said.

"But it was perfect for you."

He shrugged. "I didn't feel as if the timing was right, is all."

I thought he was foolish not to take it when it suited him so well, but I was relieved and then concerned all at once. I greatly valued Gordon's friendship—who else would do what he just did for me? And yet, there was no place for him in my life. At least not in my future. The sooner I truly accepted that the better.

That night, I stuffed the harmonica into the bottom of my hope chest, wedging it into a stack of dishtowels. Every night I took it out and held it, but I never played it.

Over the next couple of weeks, I spent my time keeping house, cooking, and sewing. I prayed as I worked, asking for God's guidance. Several times I asked that He'd take away my desire for music, but I still thought about the harmonica with an intense longing.

Finally, Elijah left a message on the phone for me, but when I called him back he didn't answer, even though it was in the evening. I guessed he was playing basketball.

I started trying to avoid Gordon. Just being around him made me long to talk about music, which made me long to sing, which made me remember that evening in Pinecraft and the adoration I felt for the Lord.

Oddly, when I thought of Pinecraft, I thought of that first. Not of Elijah. I told myself that was because I hadn't seen him for weeks. Once he was back in Lancaster County, I'd feel differently.

David Herschberger did come down to see Aenti Suz. He joined me, Mamm, and, of course, Aenti Suz for dinner. He was as attentive as ever, and at first, quite emotional seeing her for the first time since the bus accident. Her hair was just starting to grow back, and her Kapp mostly covered the scars, but her injury was still evident.

However, Aenti Suz seemed distant. Not the warm and personable soul she'd been in Florida.

I asked her about it the next day as we visited in her living room, saying that she and David were the perfect match, and I hated to see them at odds.

"Time will tell," she said. "I don't want to rush anything."

I decided to mind my own business rather than press her. Instead, I asked why she'd been favorable of me spending so much time with Elijah when we were in Pinecraft, even though she didn't seem to care much for him before that.

She shrugged. "Your mother and the bishop hoped the two of you would have a chance to get to know each other. Who was I to get in their way?"

"So what did you think of Elijah by the time we left?"

"I think he's a very personable young man," she said. "Very likable."

"And a match for me?"

She jutted out her chin.

"Aenti Suz?"

"Goodness, child, don't put me on the spot like that. It doesn't matter what I think." As she spoke, Gordon walked past her window, probably on the way to the house with a question. But Mamm was resting.

"Quick," Aenti Suz said. "See what he wants."

I stepped onto the porch, calling his name. He turned around before he reached the house.

"What do you need?"

"Bandages," he answered. "Milton cut his finger and the first-aid kit needs to be restocked."

"I'll get them," I said.

After I did, I told him I'd walk back with him to the barn and take a look at Milton's finger.

We walked along in silence. I wondered if Gordon was thinking about our time in the storage room, when he'd played the harmonica for me. Just as we reached the barn, he cleared his throat as if he might say something. But then he didn't. Instead, he stepped ahead of me and opened the door.

Milton had cut his finger on a piece of wire, but it wasn't bad. I sprayed antiseptic on it and then wrapped a bandage around his finger and left the rest of them in the first-aid kit.

The next day, I had another message from Elijah on the answering machine in the barn, thanking me for my letter. He was sorry about the wreck and hoped that everyone was well and that Aenti Suz had recovered. He kept thinking he'd write to me, but that took too much of an effort. Then he quickly said, "Call me back as soon as possible! Bye!"

This time, he answered. "Hey," he said, "I'm coming home next week. Dat wants me to start helping him right away."

My heart raced. Finally, Elijah would be back in Lancaster County, and I could get on with my life. With Elijah here, I wouldn't be consumed with thinking about Dat's harmonica and music. And, honestly, Gordon. I could get back to planning my future.

"And I'll be taking the classes." He paused and then continued, with a hint of teasing. "You know, the ones to join the church."

I knew exactly which ones. Everything was going according to plan, according to the desires of my heart.

His voice softened. "The class starts next Sunday. That's one of the reasons I'm coming home early. . . ."

"Denki," I whispered.

"You're welcome," he answered.

We chatted for a while. Billy and Paula weren't seeing each other anymore. "Paula said to tell you hello. I helped her with the homeless youth she's been working with the other day."

"You?"

He laughed. "Jah, surprising, isn't it? She put me in my place a couple of weeks ago and told me my 'privilege' was showing. She's a bossy one, that's for sure."

That surprised me to no end. I was glad Elijah had changed his thinking about the people who were served by the shelter.

"Well," he said. "I'll be home next Thursday morning. Billy's coming too. We're catching a ride with a Mennonite family he knows. Pray we make it."

I assured him I would.

"Is there a singing Sunday night?"

"As a matter of fact there is," I said. "At our place."

He groaned, and then said, "Just kidding. I can't wait to see you, even if it means going to a singing."

⋘⋙

I spent the next few days scrubbing the house from top to bottom to get ready for church at our house. Wednesday dawned bright and warm for March. Milton and Luke were tasked with cleaning out the shop for the service. When I headed out that way, I could hear them singing. Gordon's deep baritone and my nephews' higher pitches harmonized as they sang "Rock of Ages." I stood on the other side of the door listening as they sang, "Rock of ages, cleft for me, Let me hide myself in

Thee . . ." I thought of Dat and my grandparents and great-grandparents and Sophia, of Annie and Ira too, as Gordon and the boys continued to sing.

As their voices faded away, Gordon said, "Good work, guys. Now let's go pick up limbs in the woods next."

Suddenly, being out in the trees sounded wonderful. I remembered playing tag with Jessica, Leisel, and Dat when we were little, but I hadn't been out to the woods in years. I pushed open the door. "Need help?"

Gordon smiled. "I'm sure you have plenty to do to get ready for Sunday."

"Actually," I said, "I could use a break." Elijah would be home soon. I didn't need to be as cautious around Gordon as a month ago—as even a week ago.

"Do you have boots? It's going to be muddy."

"I'll get a pair," I answered and then hurried to the house. I reached the back porch, grabbed an old pair of rubber boots, put them on, and then traded my cape for Jessica's old coat. When I reached the shed, the boys had finished sweeping and were chasing each other around. Gordon was closing the door.

"Ready?"

I nodded.

"Grab the wheelbarrow!" he called out to my nephews. A few minutes later, the boys came around the corner with Luke in the wheelbarrow and Milton pushing it, dipping it from side to side. Gordon came behind them, carrying the ladder and the saw. I hurried to his side and took the saw.

The boys and I spent the next two hours collecting branches that had been torn from the trees by the ice and wind during the winter, while Gordon sawed off broken limbs. The fresh air filled my lungs, and I breathed deeply as I worked. The boys teased each other, and then, probably to distract them, Gordon started singing. Milton and Luke joined in, and so did I, of course.

Just as we were finishing, Arden stepped into the woods. He was clearly surprised to see me. "Marie," he said. "Why are you helping with this?"

"It's so nice out." I'd taken off the coat and hung it on a branch. "I couldn't bear to spend another day inside."

"Is everything ready for the services on Sunday?"

"Not quite," I answered. "But it will be."

He nodded toward Gordon. "Go ahead and stop with this for the day. Let's get started on the milking."

I stepped to the ladder to take the saw from Gordon. He handed it to me, and then climbed down.

"Don't you need to go start supper or something?" Arden asked me.

"I've got it covered," I said. "But, jah, I'm headed back to the house if that's what you're getting at."

He nodded.

Arden and I were the most alike out of all of our siblings. No nonsense. Pragmatic. Strict. At least, I'd always thought we were. But the truth was, I'd had more fun in the woods than I had since my time in Florida. Life didn't have to be all work and no play. Sometimes it could be work and play combined.

Although I'd been quilting some with Mamm and spending time with Aenti Suz, I was lonely. And I wasn't even sure exactly what I was missing. But I hadn't felt that way in the woods with Gordon and the boys.

I told Arden good-bye and then waved to the boys and to Gordon. Milton and Luke barely acknowledged me, but Gordon waved back.

Elijah would be home the next day though, and the empty

feeling that had stalked me since I got home from Florida would be gone.

The next day, I thought of Elijah and Billy driving home as Mamm, Aenti Suz, and I washed the windows and scrubbed the woodwork. When I didn't hear from Elijah by late Thursday, I thought perhaps he'd changed his plans, but then I had a message from him on Friday. He said he'd do his best to stop by the next day and tell me hello.

On Saturday afternoon, Bishop Jacobs drove the church wagon up our driveway as I took towels off the line. I dropped the towel into the basket and waved. He waved back and smiled. I felt a twinge of guilt for never confessing my instrument playing to him, but then I pushed the thought aside. It would be hard to explain to him why I'd gone to Gordon's house that day.

The wagon disappeared on the other side of the house, and I headed across the backyard to meet him by the shed. By the time I got there, he'd jumped down from the wagon.

"Marie," he said. "It's so good to see you." Before I could answer, he continued on. "I don't know what you did, but Elijah truly is a different man. I'm so thankful you went to Florida." His gray eyes grew misty. "God has answered our prayers."

I smiled, not sure what to say, and stumbled over my words. "I-I didn't do anything. And I think he'd already made up his mind to come back. "

"Well, whatever the reason—if God worked directly in Elijah's heart or worked through you—we're very grateful."

The sound of a horse and buggy coming up the drive caught my attention.

Bishop Jacobs took his hat off and ran his hand through his hair. "Speaking of . . ."

It was Elijah. He sat tall on the buggy bench, his straw hat perched atop his head. His jacket was open, showing his white shirt and suspenders. My heart swelled at the sight of him.

He smiled and took off his hat and waved. I waved back and started toward him, stretching my stride as long as I could make it. He jumped down and tied the horse to the hitching post close to the house and then ambled toward me. When we reached each other, he lifted me up and spun me around, which was quite a display of affection, considering his father was a few yards away.

As he put me down, he said, "I've missed you."

"Jah," I said. "I've missed you too." I smiled up at him. "You're here—ready for the rest of your life."

"Our life," he answered, and then tugged at the collar of his shirt.

I knew the transition would be a challenge for Elijah—he would have to adjust to so many changes—but my heartbeat quickened nonetheless. He was home. Ready to start his new life, with me.

Arden came out from the barn to greet Bishop Jacobs and Elijah. Gordon stood in the doorway, but he didn't venture our way.

I hoped I'd have some time with Elijah, but he and his Dat were soon on their way home. No matter. I'd see him the next day. I headed back to the house as Arden, Gordon, and the boys started setting up the benches in the shop.

– 24 –

The next morning, Elijah arrived late to the service, Billy at his side. They snuck in the back and down the side aisle on the men's side during the singing. Billy was dressed Amish too, which made me smile. I hardly recognized him not wearing shorts and a T-shirt.

When I turned my head back to the front, Bishop Jacobs was staring at his son. He had a stoic look on his face, and I couldn't tell if he was pleased he'd arrived or annoyed he was late.

The service continued with another song, then a scripture reading, and then a sermon from Bishop Jacobs from Proverbs 22:6. *Train up a child in the way he should go: and when he is old, he will not depart from it.* It wasn't as if he were preaching on the prodigal son, but still it seemed to be inspired by Elijah's homecoming. For a moment, I feared Elijah might disappoint his Dat again. If he did, he'd disappoint me too.

Surely he wouldn't. Both the bishop and I had invested our trust in him. He knew how much we cared for him.

I snuck out just before the service ended and headed to the house to join Mamm and Aenti Suz in the kitchen. We put out the dishes from the church wagon, arranged the bread and

338

peanut butter spread, and stirred the soup one more time. Soon the men were setting up the tables. Finally, Elijah and Billy came into the house, each carrying a bench.

After the first group was seated to eat, I found Elijah and Billy huddled by the front door as if they were ready to dash.

I asked Billy what he did with his car. He frowned. "I left it with Paula. She's decided to go to college. She can use it to get back and forth."

"But she doesn't have her license."

"She'll get it soon." He appeared grim. "I taught her how to drive last month. She's the only one out of all of us who is going to stay Englisch."

I gave him a sympathetic look, guessing he missed her, even though Elijah had told me the two weren't going out anymore and even though Paula had said they never really were.

Elijah, seemingly oblivious to Billy's mood, grinned. "Everyone who's overzealous needs a car."

I didn't react. I knew he was joking, but I wasn't sure if Billy did. He looked so sad.

"So are you coming to the singing with Elijah tonight?" I asked Billy.

He gave Elijah a questioning look.

"Jah, he is." Elijah fixed his gaze on me. "He needs to get over Paula as soon as possible."

Something was up, but I couldn't figure out what.

The rest of the day went without incident. Elijah left soon after he and Billy ate. By the time we'd cleaned up from the noon meal, we had a couple of hours to rest until it was time for the singing. Vi was doing the snacks because it was going to be Milton's first singing, so at least I didn't have to worry about that.

Surprisingly, Elijah and Billy were among the first to arrive. I took that as a good sign. We all chatted outside of the shed, and then just before it was time to go in, Billy wandered off to chat with some other girls.

"So," Elijah said. "Want to go to a party with us tonight?"

"When?"

"After the singing," he said.

"Where's the party?"

"Down by Strasburg. At a friend of Billy's."

"Why?"

He shrugged. "Why not?"

I did my best to keep my voice calm. "I thought you came home to join the church."

"That's exactly why I'm going to the party. I have two weeks until I start the class. I don't have much time left."

"But I already joined the church."

"You didn't act like it when you were in Florida."

My face warmed. "I didn't go to any parties. Not where there was drinking or anything."

He shrugged. "I asked my buddies not to drink around you, is all." He poked me in the side. "There you go getting all uptight. I thought you'd changed."

I took a step away from him. "I thought you'd changed."

He laughed. "What do you mean? I've always been honest with you about who I am. What you see is what you get."

From looking at the Amish clothes he wore, I had believed that he had changed. But he was right. He had been honest with me. He didn't want to be a farmer. He was joining the church because it was time, because he couldn't think of anything else to do. He thought I'd make a good Amish wife.

What had I been thinking?

Elijah and I sat at tables on opposite sides of the room. Me with the other young women, and Elijah and Billy with the young men, including Milton and a group of his friends.

In a few years, my nephew would marry. Eventually, he would take over the farm from Arden. Would I end up living in the Dawdi Haus as Aenti Suz had all these years? As the old maid, living off the kindness of my relatives? Jah, it was the Amish way, but I found no comfort in the idea. It wasn't what I'd ever planned for.

I also found no peace in the singing.

I'd come up with a plan that had Elijah as the hub, but what was I willing to sacrifice? Would he ever truly settle down—or only pretend to? As his Dat had once said, Elijah Jacobs was definitely a free spirit. If I married him, what would my role be? Would I always be trying to get him to change? Never accept him as he was?

Arden was leading the singing and started with "Trusting Jesus, That Is All." Had I put my trust in Elijah instead of God? Had I, all along, loved the idea of him instead of actually loving him?

Across the aisle, Elijah elbowed Billy, and they both stifled laughs. Elijah had a lot of good qualities, but we had little in common. Jah, he was Bishop Jacobs's son. And he'd inherit a farm. Jah, I'd had a lot of fun with him in Pinecraft, and I had to admit he was a good kisser, not that I had anything to compare it with. I was definitely attracted to him—but did that mean I should marry him?

We finished "Trusting Jesus," and I mouthed the words to the next one, "Steal Away to Jesus." *Steal away, steal away home,*

I hain't got long to stay here. Where was home for me? What did Jesus have for me, if not to be an Amish wife, homemaker, and mother?

The truth was, I'd been much more focused on *home*, my idea of home, than I had been on Jesus. On hem lengths and hat widths. On my own desires, not God's.

I thought of Ira singing "Steal Away to Jesus" and remembered that it was a Negro spiritual from so long ago. Enslaved people sang the words and meant them. People whose very lives were owned by others. People who had absolutely no choice where they lived or often even with whom they lived. Who had no control over their *homes*.

I had those choices. Was I going to court and perhaps marry a man just because I, and others, expected it? Because it was the easy thing to do?

The weight of Annie's story fell on me again. Not only had she not married the man everyone thought she would, she'd also been willing to do everything she could to care for others, to put them first. Could I put others before myself?

I shuddered. The question wasn't whether I could, but if I was willing. Was I willing to trust God and make His desires my own? In doing that, I'd truly learn to put others before myself.

⚜

I knew the singing would soon be over. Arden had just started "How Great Thou Art," but I couldn't sit still a minute longer, and slipped out the back of the shed. I couldn't go to the house and face Mamm, so I decided to go to the barn, past all of the buggies and the few cars belonging to those on their *Rumschpringe*. The weather had stayed warm. I turned and looked at the field where a breeze blew through the top branches of

342

the oak tree. Then my eyes fell on the house, on the back porch where Sophia had died over a century and a half ago.

The daffodils in the beds along the back of the house were just starting to bloom. Dat had told me once that the bulbs had been planted in the mid-1940s by his Mamm, soon after she married my grandfather and moved onto the Bachmann farm.

My life was rooted on this property, in this community. Of course I wanted to marry and stay close. I turned back and continued on to the barn. As I pushed open the door, singing greeted me. I groaned. What was Gordon doing in the barn on a Sunday evening?

As I stepped back, he called out, "Hello?"

"Ach," I said, stepping forward. "It's just me. Marie."

He stepped out from a stall.

"What are you doing here?" I asked.

"A heifer's in labor and having a hard time. Arden called and asked if I'd check on her."

I closed the barn door behind me and started toward him. "How she's doing?"

"Mostly she's scared." He shrugged. "Which is pretty normal."

I stopped at the stall and watched the heifer for a moment. Her tail twitched, and her eyes were big and wild.

Gordon rubbed his chin. "How come you're not at the singing?"

I shrugged. He was the last person I wanted to talk to about my reason. Instead, I still had a burning question for him. "How come you're still working here? Why didn't you take the shelter job Tony offered you?"

He stepped back and leaned against the rail. "That was unexpected."

"Why? That job is perfect for you."

"And this job isn't?" He smiled. "I don't know. I feel at a crossroads."

I gave him a puzzled look.

"It wasn't the desire of my heart, not at the moment." He shrugged again. "Perhaps another job will come open at the shelter and the timing will be right, but in the meantime I can still volunteer there and do my job here."

I frowned. He hadn't really answered my question.

"How about you?" he asked. "I saw Elijah is back. It looks like what you've wanted all along is happening."

I flinched. "Actually, it's not."

"What does that mean?"

"That I've been more focused on my own desires than God's. And, it seems, more focused on my desires than trusting Him." I tried to smile, but I'm afraid it came out as a grimace.

Before Gordon could respond, I told him I needed to get back to the singing.

"Wait," he said. "Could we talk? I've wanted to—needed to—for quite some time."

My heart raced. I wanted nothing more than to talk with Gordon, but I needed to sort things through with Elijah first. And I wasn't sure how long that would take. "Soon," I said to Gordon. "I promise."

I slipped out of the barn, thinking that my friendship with Gordon had made me more empathetic, more aware of the suffering of others—and more aware of my own shortcomings too. But being around him also made me hopeful that I could become a better person—and friend.

I stepped back into the shed. "How Great Thou Art" hadn't been the last song. "Amazing Grace" was. As I sang "how sweet the sound that saved a wretch like me" it was as if I were singing the words for the very first time.

I thought about how determined I'd been to follow all the rules and not sin, but in doing so I'd separated myself from God. I'd been all about following the law and not living by grace—and not showing grace to others.

I had no idea what God had for me, what He truly wanted my desires to be, but I needed to be willing to do whatever He asked of me. My eyes filled with tears as I sang, but my voice was strong: "I once was lost but now am found, was blind but now I see."

I was just beginning to see clearly. The question was, what would I do with my growing vision?

Elijah must have sensed my discontent, because he and Billy stayed on the edge of the group during the refreshments. Once they started inching toward the door, I walked over and told Elijah I needed to speak with him.

"Ach," Elijah said, "Can't it wait?"

I shook my head.

"All right then," he said. "But make it fast. Billy and I need to get going."

I led the way out the door toward the fence line, where, in the background, our old oak tree was a silhouette against the setting sun. I smiled at Elijah as kindly as I could. "This isn't what you want, is it?"

"This?"

I inhaled, trying to build up my courage. "Your Dat's farm. Courting me. Marriage."

He ducked his head. "It's not just you. I don't think I can adjust back to this." He raised his head and gestured his arm wide.

"Elijah! Come on!" Billy stood, dangling a set of keys. Either he'd bought another car already or had borrowed one.

"I'm sorry," Elijah said.

"So am I." And I meant it. I'd been pursuing him under false pretenses too. We'd both hoped the other was a ticket to the future expected of us.

On Monday and Tuesday, I only saw Gordon at a distance. And that was fine. I still needed time to sort through what had happened.

On Wednesday afternoon, Bishop Jacobs showed up at our house, asking to talk with me. His expression was grim, and I feared something had happened to Elijah.

I invited him into the house and offered him a cup of coffee. "No." He held up his hand.

"Please sit." I gestured toward the couch.

"This won't take long." He sat down anyway. "I wanted you to know that Elijah headed back to Florida this morning."

"Oh?"

"I don't know what happened between the two of you, but I have to say I'm disappointed. Everything seemed so promising. Why wouldn't you court him?"

"Is that what he said? That I wouldn't court him?"

The bishop tugged on his beard. "Basically."

"It was more complicated than that," I answered.

"Does this have anything to do with Gordon Martin?"

I shook my head. It did and it didn't. I knew from the way I felt around Gordon that things weren't right between Elijah and me. That I couldn't court and marry someone with whom I didn't share a spiritual connection. And, honestly, the musical connection didn't hurt. But it wasn't as if I'd planned to court Gordon instead.

Bishop Jacobs crossed his arms. "I knew I should have insisted Arden let him go before Elijah returned."

"Pardon?"

"Jah. Arden and I talked about it, but he was convinced that Gordon wasn't a problem." I thought of that day in the woods when Arden seemed concerned about me helping Gordon and the boys. Was that what that was all about?

"I'm sorry Elijah left," I said. "There was a time I thought he and I could court, could . . ." My voice trailed off. "But I think there's a chance that even if we had started courting he may have returned to Florida anyway."

Bishop Jacobs shook his head. "You were the stabilizing force we'd been hoping for, praying for."

"I couldn't control Elijah. You know that." I sighed. "The fact is, through the years, there were a whole lot of people I thought I should have been able to control. Jessica. Leisel. Even my Dat at times. But I was wrong to try. I should have left the rules I wanted them to follow up to them and God." I wanted to tell him that the Lord Jesus had been showing me quite a bit about myself as of late, but I feared I'd sound prideful.

But what was more important? To fear pride or to speak in truth?

I shared with him that I'd been so set on my desires for my future that I hadn't even asked God what His desires might be for me. I did tell Bishop Jacobs that I'd been praying about what God would have for me, and that I'd be willing to accept whatever that might be, even if it meant I'd never marry and have a family.

Then I confessed to playing the instruments at Gordon's

house. It was the first time I'd ever made a confession, and I found it ironic it was about music—and not my self-righteousness, something I should have confessed years ago.

His eyes narrowed, and after he stated I'd need to confess before the congregation, which I'd expected, he shook his head. "I thought you were more mature than that. This is how people stray from our church and community. I believe you've entered dangerous territory. Next thing we know, you'll be headed back to Pinecraft too."

I assured him I wouldn't.

He stood. "You'll be in my prayers, Marie. You've always been so level-headed. Don't be misled by your own fancy thoughts about God's will and Bible verses taken out of context. Remember our traditions. That's where your guidance will come from."

I walked Bishop Jacobs to the front door and then watched as he lumbered down the steps and to his buggy. I was sorry for the pain Elijah had caused him. And sad that I'd disappointed him too. But, honestly, for the first time, I understood the struggles Jessica had with him. At the time, I thought his responses to her were totally justified. In fact, it was my reporting of her behavior that led him to discipline her. I felt ill at the thought of what I'd done.

As I headed out to the clothesline to take down the sheets I'd washed that morning, Aenti Suz stepped out onto the porch of her house and then started toward me. "I'll help you fold," she said.

"Denki," I answered.

I expected her to ask me what Bishop Jacobs wanted, but we worked in silence until I said, "Jessica told me once that you were in love with a Mennonite boy. That you would have married him if he hadn't died in Vietnam."

She nodded, but then said, "I think I would have married him. I guess I don't know that for sure."

"And left the church?"

"Jah," she answered. "I would have left the church. I do know that."

I walked toward her with my end of the sheet. "Did you consider leaving anyway, after he died?"

She smiled. "Jah, I did. More at first, and then less as I grew older."

"Do you ever regret *not* leaving?"

She shook her head. "But I'm guessing if my sweetheart hadn't died, I wouldn't have regretted *not* staying either."

"But doesn't it seem disingenuous to leave or stay based on a relationship with a man? Shouldn't we leave or stay based on our relationship with God?"

"Many people do decide to leave or stay based on their relationship with God. But don't judge the ones who decide based on a relationship with someone else. Who you marry has a big effect on your relationship with God. Don't minimize that. I heard an Amish woman say once she could marry *any* Amish man and make it work. I don't believe that for a second. Each couple finds their own way as far as roles in the relationship, but if a man doesn't encourage you to have a closer relationship with the Lord, then you have no business marrying him."

I wrinkled my nose. Elijah hadn't encouraged me to do anything except have fun.

As we folded the last sheet, Gordon yelled my name from the barn door. "You have a phone call."

I dropped the sheet into the basket.

"I'll take these in," Aenti Suz said.

I wondered if the call could be from Elijah as I headed toward the barn. My heart grew cold at the thought.

It wasn't. It was Paula.

After greeting each other and catching up, she said, "Hey, I have a question for you."

"What's that?"

"Did you hear Elijah is headed back down here?"

"Jah," I answered. "His Dat stopped by today and told me."

She groaned. "You two didn't break up, did you?"

"Jah . . ."

"Well, the reason I called is . . . because he left me a message, and said he was coming back, and that he hoped to see me, a lot."

"Paula," I said. "It's okay. Elijah and I weren't really even courting. I'm fine if you go out with him."

She groaned. "But I don't want to. I like him as a friend and someone to tease, but he's not the kind of guy I want to date."

I smiled. I knew opposites attracted, but I really couldn't see them together either. After she gave her reasons—he was untrustworthy, too clownish, and too quick to dismiss the needs of others—I brought up what Billy said about her not joining the church.

"What?"

"Jah, he said you're going to college."

"That's right, but I'm going to join the Mennonites. Probably by next year. I can go to college and drive. Why would he say that?"

I didn't know. Maybe it was to make himself feel better about her breaking up with him. I twirled the phone cord. "So do you think Elijah will stick around Sarasota?"

"No," Paula answered. "In fact, he said if I wouldn't go out with him he thought he'd go to Orlando and find a job up there."

"Wow." That would take Elijah even farther away from an Amish community.

"Hey," Paula said, "I still want to come up and see you sometime. Seriously."

"Anytime," I answered.

"How about this summer? After I'm done with classes."

"Perfect!"

She told me more about her courses, and then I found myself telling her about my conversation with Gordon and what I learned about myself.

"I love that," she said. "And you know what? I'm really looking forward to seeing you this summer. I promise I'll make it happen."

After we said good-bye, I thought about Paula being so bold with Elijah while I'd been so careful with him. I didn't feel that way with Gordon though. I could say what was on my mind without being afraid of being teased or not taken seriously. The truth was, Elijah and I never really talked about anything important. And I'd never inspired him in any way, not the way Gordon inspired me.

I stepped out of the office into the barn, sure I'd never inspired Gordon in that way either.

Lost in my thoughts, I finally realized that Gordon was waving at me from the milk vat. I approached him. "That was Paula."

He nodded. "We chatted for a few minutes. She asked me how my volunteer work at the shelter was going and told me some about what she's been up to."

"She knew you didn't take the job?"

He nodded. "We've talked a few times since I got back home."

My face warmed even in the cold air. "Oh" was all I could manage to say.

Elijah had been right. Gordon and Paula did make a good couple.

"It's not like we're interested in each other or anything," he said quickly. "She got my number from the director at the shelter in Florida. She had some questions about different Mennonite missions."

"Oh." My heart raced. I'd been jealous. Out and out jealous.

He smiled down at me, his deep brown eyes as kind and caring as always.

"When do you volunteer at the shelter again?" I managed to ask.

"Tonight," he answered.

"Would you like to join us for supper before you go?" I knew it would save him time.

He nodded. "Very much. Thank you." His eyes met mine. "Would you like to go with me to the shelter tonight?"

I paused for a long moment, sensing that my answer might determine my destiny—or the realizations of the desires of my heart. Then I nodded. "I would like to go with you tonight. Absolutely. Maybe we can . . . talk . . . on the way there."

He nodded. "I'd like that."

⁂

We did talk that evening, about us. We both decided to spend time together, to get to know each other better, to pray and ask for God's guidance. We both made it clear that we cared for each other, but I was Amish and he was Mennonite. There was no easy solution.

More important, I began working to change more on the inside, in ways that were the opposite of measuring hem lengths and hat brim widths. I'd felt so insecure that I'd looked at the

supposed faults of others to make myself feel better. By pointing out their failures, I hoped to increase my own worth, in
some twisted way.

Now I knew it had never worked. My judging others had
only made me feel worse about myself.

And I began to understand why Dat served others. Why he'd
gone to Vietnam as a Youngie. Why he went to Haiti to serve
after the earthquake. It was *Gottes-deenst*—service to God. It
was part of our faith. For so long, I thought it could be done
through baking pies and making quilts. Which was all beneficial
and very important, but apparently God calls some people to
more than that.

In mid-April, I hired a driver to take me to Jessica's for the
day. She'd recovered from her surgery and had mostly gained
her strength back. We sat at her kitchen table, and over coffee
and muffins I apologized to her for how critical I'd been of
her through the years and confessed that I'd pulled the bishop
into a dispute that was entirely between her and Arden, that
Dat was fully capable of moderating. "I was so focused on the
behavior of others, including you," I said, "that I failed to see
the work of the Spirit."

She said she'd forgiven me long ago. "But thank you," she
said. "I want nothing more, after my marriage, than to have a
good relationship with you. And with Leisel."

I nodded. That was my hope too. Then I went on to confess
that I never felt as if I'd measured up to her or Leisel. "You
were so capable and strong. Leisel was so smart and caring.
I felt invisible. I wasn't conscious of what I was doing, but
now I see that by being critical, I was trying to make myself
look better. By being self-righteous, I was trying to make you
look bad."

"Wow," Jessica said. "You've been doing some soul-searching."
I nodded.

"I'm impressed." She reached over and took my hand. "Denki
for telling me," she said. "But now put it behind you." Then she
wrinkled her nose. "I know I wasn't always kind to you either."

"No," I said. "You were frustrated with me before you left
and then again when you came back for Dat's service. But I
deserved it. Besides those two times, you were always kind to
me. You were the best big sister, honestly."

Her eyes filled with tears, which made me cry too.

"I'm praying you'll get pregnant again soon. And that you'll
be blessed with many children."

She squeezed my hand but didn't say anything more about
that. Instead, she told me Mildred Stoltz was doing a little better,
and that it was so good for Silas to work with John. "They're
like father and son," she said. "God has been so good to us."

I nodded in agreement. If Jessica could recognize God's goodness after losing her baby, I could too. No matter what He had
for my future.

Before I left, she said, "Marie, you really are gifted musically.
I think your lack of opportunity to practice your gift, because
of Mamm's rules, probably made you more self-righteous. You
were frustrated. Maybe that's something to consider."

I assured her I would.

I wrote to Gail right after Elijah left and explained to her
everything that had happened. Then I asked her to forgive me
for how I'd drawn her into my world of judgment and shame.

She wrote back right away and said that of course she forgave
me. Then she included, *God has been working in my heart too
and convicting me of my own shortcomings. I'm praying for
both of us as we grow in our relationships with the Lord.* Her

words only confirmed that everyone was capable of changing, including me.

I started volunteering every Monday night at the shelter with Gordon. Then I began attending his church with him on our off Sundays. Each time I attended, my soul expanded more and more. It was through serving that I understood Christ's gift to me. It was through giving that I truly comprehended grace.

Mamm and Arden turned a blind eye to what I was doing. I think they thought I, of all people, would come to my senses. But it wasn't long until Bishop Jacobs expressed his alarm. He insisted that I stop attending the Mennonite services.

I was at an intersection as complicated as the crossroads at Peach Bottom.

But finally I had to admit that I couldn't continue living the way I was and not be shunned. Again I thought of Annie and the crossroads in her life.

On a warm June evening, after Paula had visited and then returned to Pinecraft, I asked Gordon for a favor. Would he drive me to Peach Bottom? I knew the farm that George and Harriet had owned was now underwater due to the Conowingo Dam, along with the entire original town. It had been moved to the east side of the Susquehanna River, to Lancaster County. But I wanted to see the area. I wanted to see if I could gain clarity in my own life from seeing where Annie had spent a pivotal part of hers.

It didn't take long to reach Peach Bottom from our farm, not more than half an hour. I told Gordon the short version of Annie's story as he drove.

I lowered my window as we began the descent down to the Susquehanna. I could smell the river as it came into view, and in no time, we were parked alongside it, near the train tracks, gazing toward the western side.

It was impossible for me to imagine how the river and the land had appeared to Annie. But I could imagine Felicity in the woods, trying to save her baby. And Annie hearing Ira's song. And the courage it took for her to travel to Gettysburg with Kate and care for the wounded soldiers.

Aenti Suz had made Annie's decision to leave the Amish and marry Ira sound so easy. But I doubted it was. I imagined she struggled with leaving her church and her family.

Gordon stepped closer to me. I remembered Miriam's words on the beach in Florida back in January. *God doesn't call us to do what is easy.*

But maybe I thought it harder than it actually was. Leaving the Amish wouldn't be easy—but if I took it a step at a time, it would be manageable. Maybe it was just step by step, day by day, following His calling. There was one thing I did know for sure: loving Gordon was easy. That didn't mean our relationship always would be, but the love and commitment I felt toward him couldn't be stopped.

Miriam had also said everyone deserved to be loved. I felt with all my heart that God wanted Gordon and me to love each other.

He reached for my hand.

It was the first time he'd done that, and I couldn't believe how natural it felt. "What are you thinking?" he asked.

"That God's ways aren't my ways."

He didn't say anything for a long while until I leaned against him.

He pulled me close. "Care to give me an explanation?"

"I've decided to leave the Amish," I said. "And I'm going to go live with Leisel for a while, in her apartment." My family would be required to shun me, and I couldn't bear to be in Lancaster County while it happened. Arden and Vi would write me letters. And Mamm. "I'll find a job and a Mennonite church."

His hold tightened. "And then what?"

"I'll trust God as I wait and see what's next for me."

I enjoyed living with Leisel in Pittsburgh. It was a good transition into the Englisch lifestyle, and I enjoyed getting to know Nick too. She continued to claim they were just friends—but I wasn't so sure. They reminded me of Annie and Ira in their dedication to learning medicine and in the way they supported each other. They didn't show any affection, at least not in front of me, but I could tell there was a commitment between them and guessed they may have a future together, perhaps after Leisel graduated.

After I'd been in Pittsburgh just a few weeks, I came to the realization that Gordon was my spiritual anchor. Because of him, I'd finally learned to love others as myself. Being shunned wasn't the worst thing in the world, as I'd feared. Being away from Gordon was.

I moved back to Lancaster after that, rented a room from a couple who attended the Mennonite church downtown, and took a job at the shelter, where Gordon was working now too. Bishop Jacobs had convinced Arden to fire him after I left home.

Working at the shelter taught me to trust God in a deeper way, and to live out my singing in a way I first learned in Pinecraft. I sang to the babies I had the privilege of helping with, taught the children songs after school, sang with the cooking crew, and led the singing after supper sometimes too. With each song, my faith grew deeper, as did my determination to serve. Aenti Suz had been right. God had given me the chance to minister to the souls of others.

I also played an old piano, tucked away in a room upstairs, during every break I had. Soon Tony, Gordon, and some other men moved it into the dining hall, where I played it for the singings, accompanying Gordon on his guitar.

The first time Gordon kissed me was on the sidewalk outside of the shelter. It was spontaneous, on both of our parts. It was late August and ninety-five degrees. Tony was on vacation, and we'd had one emergency after another, but we'd made it through and cared for those who needed it. As we told each other good-bye, Gordon leaned down as I turned my face toward him and our lips met.

Here I was, the girl who wanted nothing more than to be an Amish farmer's wife, kissing a poor Mennonite boy. I'd never dreamt I could be so happy.

Here I was, living in the city and loving it. Just like Annie, I'd found my place in Lancaster, away from the Bachmann farm. And just like Annie, I had a new life ahead of me.

Gordon and I married in early November. My wedding was in Gordon's Mennonite church instead of on the Bachmann farm with the backdrop of the old barn and the changing leaves in the woods, as I'd dreamt for so many years.

Leisel and Nick came to the wedding and so did Aenti Suz, Silas, and Jessica, who was six months pregnant at the time. However, Mamm and Arden and his family chose to stay away. I expected as much and didn't let it affect my day. I was shocked, however, when Amos and Becca traipsed in just as I was about to walk down the aisle. Jah, I'd invited them, but I hadn't expected them to come.

Leisel and Paula, who'd turned out to be just the friend I needed once I joined the Mennonites, stood up with me, and several times during the service, I caught Jessica, who sat in the front row with Silas, Amos, and Becca, wiping her eyes.

After Gordon and I pledged our lives to each other, we had an old-fashioned singing with our guests. And through a couple of our favorite hymns, Gordon played Dat's harmonica. My eyes filled with tears as I led those songs, with those we loved joining in.

My heart soared in gratitude. God had given me the desires of my heart—what *He* desired for me. Gordon took my hand and we sang from the depths of our hearts, as a sense of harmony deeper and wider than I'd ever experienced before filled me completely.

Acknowledgments

I'm grateful to my husband, Peter, for his medical expertise, Civil War knowledge, and love of adventure. Traveling with you and learning about the history of our world is one of my favorite things to do.

I'm also grateful to our four children—Kaleb, Taylor, Hana, and Lily Thao—who put up with my deadlines and constantly help me see the world in new ways.

I'm deeply appreciative of my dear friend Marietta Couch, who shares her knowledge of the Amish with me and helps me brainstorm my stories.

I'm also grateful to Deidre Moss for her insights into music, singing, and perfect pitch.

A big bouquet of thanks to Elaine Shorb and Tina and Joe Loveless for a wonderful evening spent in Gettysburg and for the information they shared about both the Amish and the Civil War.

I'm also indebted to: the staff at the National Civil War Museum in Harrisburg, Pennsylvania, and the National Military Park in Gettysburg, Pennsylvania, for answering my questions; Randolph Harrison, consulting historian, for his Underground Railroad tour in Lancaster, Pennsylvania; and the Lancaster County Mennonite Historical Society for information on Anabaptists before and during the Civil War. (Any mistakes in the story are mine and mine alone.)

I'm also very thankful for Chip MacGregor, my agent, and for the crew at Bethany House Publishers, including my talented editors, Jennifer Veilleux and Dave Long.

Most important, as I wrote this story, I was grateful for the Lord's timeless teachings to care for those who are suffering, and to love with actions and truth.

Leslie Gould is the #1 bestselling and award-winning author of twenty-eight novels, including the COURTSHIPS OF LANCASTER COUNTY and NEIGHBORS OF LANCASTER COUNTY series. She holds an MFA in creative writing and enjoys research trips, church history, and hiking, especially in the beautiful state of Oregon, where she lives. She and her husband, Peter, are the parents of four grown children.

Sign Up for Leslie's Newsletter!

Keep up to date with Leslie's news, book releases, and events by signing up for her email list at lesliegould.com.

More from Leslie Gould

Returning home for her father's funeral, Jessica faces the Amish life—and love—she left behind. As she struggles with regrets, she learns about a Revolutionary War–era ancestor who confronted similar choices. Will she find peace along with the resolution she hopes for?

A Plain Leaving
THE SISTERS OF LANCASTER COUNTY #1

You May Also Like . . .

Willow Bradford is content taking a break from modeling to run her family's inn until she comes face-to-face with NFL quarterback Corbin Stewart, the man who broke her heart—and wants to win her back. When a decades-old family mystery brings them together, they're forced to decide whether they can risk falling for one another all over again.

Falling for You by Becky Wade
A BRADFORD SISTERS ROMANCE
beckywade.com

Nurse practitioner Mia Robinson is done with dating. Instead, she's focused on caring for her teenage sister, Lucy—who, it turns out, is pregnant and plans to marry her boyfriend. Mia is determined to stop the wedding, but she's in for a surprise when she meets the best man.

The Two of Us by Victoria Bylin
victoriabylin.com

After a tragic mine accident in 1954, Judd Markley thought he had abandoned his Appalachian roots forever by moving to Myrtle Beach. Then he meets the privileged Larkin Heyward, who dreams of moving to Kentucky to help the poor of Appalachia. Drawn together amid a hurricane and swept away by their feelings, are their divergent dreams too great an obstacle to overcome?

The Sound of Rain by Sarah Loudin Thomas
sarahloudinthomas.com

BETHANYHOUSE